The Magnolia Dilemma

The Magnolia Dilemma

A LILY LIST MYSTERY

C.L. BAUER

Book design - Myra Miller, PhD

Cover illustration - Ellyce Prendergast

For information contact: www.clbauer.com

ISBN: 978-0-9987318-9-6

First Edition: November 2021

10 9 8 7 6 5 4 3 2

The Lily List
Mystery Series

The Poppy Drop
The Hibiscus Heist
The Tulip Terror
The Sweet Pea Secret
The Magnolia Dilemma

Lily List Mystery Exclusive

Stilettos Can Be Murder

Dedication

Years ago, I was introduced to a little island in Florida. I fell in love, not because it was paradise, but because I met friends who became family. Thanks to that special family for sharing their home and providing wonderful memories.

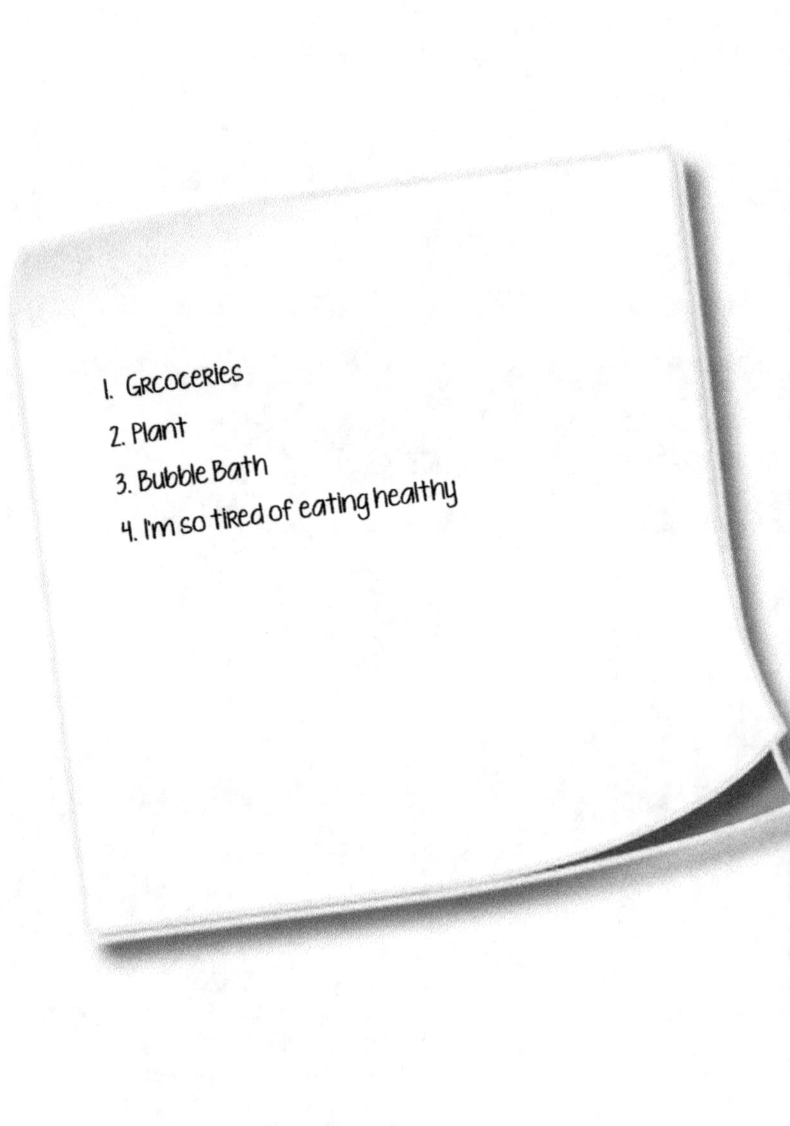

1. Grcoceries
2. Plant
3. Bubble Bath
4. I'm so tired of eating healthy

Chapter One

Lily Pierce wiped her brow as she knelt in the dirt. She wanted a little color in front of the porch, and this was her first opportunity to get out into the yard since winter had finally decided to take a hike. In just a few months she'd have a son entering the terrible twos. When Andrew was born in August, fall hit Virginia early that year. There just wasn't any time for yard work. Everything was **baby**. She absolutely adored her son, but he was a handful. Having a baby in your thirties was highly overrated. There were days when Lily would have rather been designing a funeral flower display while prepping for a wedding. Truthfully, there were those days when she missed running her flower shop back in Kansas City.

But she was happy, until her husband was called out of town. He didn't want to go, but when you were on assignment with the DEA, you went when and where they told you. He was gone for weeks on end, and another spring and summer passed.

Life is passing me by! I think too much when I plant, and that's good and bad. I feel alone. Even my supposed bestie Gretchen has been investigating on her own, and she finally has a man--not men--in her life. That's an oddity for her!

Lily took a drink from her water bottle and looked toward the street. Her husband, Devlin Pierce, came running toward her. He waved as he pushed the stroller.

She could hear Andrew's laughter as his father sped up for the homestretch.

"Thank God for those runs," Lily said out loud. Dev's at-home workout was her break from a sometimes cranky son. Andrew was her first born and a blessing, but even Lily Schmidt Pierce could grow tired of a good thing. Besides, she figured her son needed a break from her too. Lily brushed her hair out of her eyes and looked up at their house. "I love this place."

They acquired the home from Dev's Aunt Maggie. She had moved to her vineyard and didn't need a six-bedroom home. For Lily, it was a daunting effort to keep it clean, but a couple of the bedrooms remained empty. A shut door solved any problem. It was a fine old Southern home with a lovely front porch and massive backyard. Thankfully, her husband liked to mow, and she enjoyed watching him.

Lily's thoughts turned to a time when Dev mowed her small yard in Kansas City. It had been so hot that day he'd removed his shirt. She didn't swoon, but she sure looked and took in the view. She gazed upon a broad muscled chest with a light covering of fine hair. He was nice looking. She was in lust; soon she would be in love.

Dev certainly wasn't perfect. He growled, he spurted toothpaste from the top of the tube, and he missed the hamper when he attempted a rim shot. But he was pretty near perfect in her eyes. *But who does that with the toothpaste? Doesn't everyone know you push it from the bottom like I do?*

Dev stopped in the driveway and removed his shirt to wipe his face. He looked down into the stroller to see a child who had suddenly fallen asleep. "You fall asleep faster than I do, little guy," he said out loud. Dev still marveled that Lily and he had created this perfect little being.

Lily's hand shielded her eyes as she admired her husband's chest. She fell asleep on that part of his anatomy every night. He didn't seem to mind. "Thank you, God," she muttered. *But, Lord, he sometimes looks like the hot guy in the soap commercials. He's too good to be true, sometimes.*

"Did you say something, honey?" Dev yelled. "I couldn't hear you."

You weren't supposed to hear me. God and I are talking. "I was just wondering again how our child ended up with red curly hair."

Dev pushed the stroller closer to her as she stood up. "I told you before, recessive genes. My mom had curly red hair. You have curly hair. Ta da, you get this kiddo." He kissed her on the top of her head before she looked inside to discover a sleeping son.

"I know, but I just never expected it. You should've warned me. Look at him. He looks like the grandson in that vampire cartoon."

"I was stopped at the intersection up at the boulevard, and two lady walkers said he was the cutest boy they'd ever seen," Dev said proudly as he wiped his forehead. "I need a shower. Are you done out here?"

"Not yet. Go on in. Andrew can stay here with me. By the way, thanks." *A good run or a ride in the car always puts the little guy to sleep. She'd driven around nearly all of northern Virginia anytime Dev had been away on assignment.*

As Dev headed toward the front door, he turned around and winked. "Of course. You need your time. But later, you owe me."

Lily stuck her arm out straight and motioned to the door. "Go. Now." He blew her a kiss and vanished quickly within the house.

She looked down at their child. "Daddy should know that I'm a given by now, shouldn't he? He's been away way too many times in the last year. Besides, we can't have you growing up by yourself without some nagging little sister or brother. If you were alone, who would you visit with at the family reunions?" She laughed at her joke and moved the stroller closer to where she needed to plant the azalea bush. "I should get your daddy back out here to dig this hole."

Again, Lord, thanks for having him fall in love with me. I'm still not sure how or why. Lily regarded herself as a regular woman. She was intelligent, skilled, friendly, but she'd never been the tall, pretty model type. She was short. Her hair became one big frizzy mess in humidity, and before Andrew's birth she always hated those charts that insisted she be a certain weight. She had curves. She had dimples. She had never worn a size eight. *Well, there was that one time when I was actually eight years old! But Dev saw me. He has his dangerous DEA world of drugs and cartels, and I have ice cream. Works for me!* But running after Andrew as a woman in her mid-thirties, the weight began to drop. It was exciting, yet Lily knew it was a fleeting experience. *Again, I like my ice cream.*

Lily reviewed the three bright reddish-pink azalea bushes she had selected to plant across the front of the house. Next week, she'd have Dev pick up the magnolia she ordered from the nursery. That would go right at the corner of the porch where an old-fashioned white swing hung. She'd never had time to plant anything in her Kansas City yard. She had been much too busy running her flower shop. After she met Dev, fell in love, married him in a surprise wedding she knew nothing about, moved twice, and had a baby, she was more than ready to really nest. She'd also helped thwart a drug dealer twice and assisted in the apprehension of a terrorist. But now it was time to just settle in and plant. At least that's what she kept telling herself.

Lily knelt down on the ground and began to dig more of the hole she began earlier. She heard Andrew stir. She stood up and checked.

"Come on, Andrew. Work with me. I just need to get this bush into the ground." She touched his cheek and lightly stroked. His blue eyes closed. His sigh was a sign that he was asleep again. "Thank you, baby."

Once more, she knelt down and began to dig deeper. The hole wasn't wide enough, so she continued to extend the perimeter. She needed a larger shovel, and she needed to get off her knees to do it, but she hit something. She dug down again and pulled up a clump of dirt and sifted through it. Lily pulled away the soil and plucked away until she was face to face with an item that seemed to be older than her.

"What the heck is this?" Lily looked at the piece of muddied metal and wondered out loud. She studied her find.

Dev appeared on the porch, his hair still wet and his feet bare. Years in the Army programmed him for quick showers. He dressed in shorts and an Army tee shirt and held a bottle of his favorite beer.

"I've been wondering why a florist wants to be around plants. Aren't you sick of flowers after all of these years?"

Lily laughed. "You would think that, wouldn't you?" She focused on her hidden gem. She cleaned off enough dirt to reveal a bullet, a very old bullet.

"Honey, could you take a look at this? I think I found something." Lily lifted the bullet up into the air. Dev's shadow covered her as he took it in his hand.

"It's a Minié ball, named after the man who invented it," he answered calmly.

Lily shielded her eyes. "Okay. Exactly, what is that?"

You've found one of the many relics of the Civil War, or the War Between the States, depending on how you were brought up. The state of Virginia had so many soldiers travel though for so many battles you never know what will turn up, even after all these years. This is in fantastic shape. Good job." He handed her treasure back to her.

"So, do we take it somewhere?"

"No, we can keep it. I'll put it in the office. Or I can turn it into a national park battlefield. It's up to you." Dev took his perch on the steps and took a sip of cold beer. "Do you want me to grill steak tonight?"

Lily studied her find, turning the bullet over and over. "Sure, that sounds good." She had never found anything of significance in her own yard. In Kansas City, she found candy wrappers, an occasional chip bag, and a broken DVD. She moves to Virginia, and she finds a civil war bullet. "This is really something."

Dev watched her intense fascination. He didn't want to rain on her parade, but thousands of artifacts from the war appeared over the years. He had found an arrowhead while digging in a creek bed by a campsite near Williamsburg. He and his brother had fought over it. His mom had confiscated the treasure. Upon his high school graduation, she had presented a small box with the arrowhead displayed nicely. He still kept it on his desk, along with other Civil War bullets, another arrowhead, and a Senate credential from his first testimony before a committee on drugs.

"Well, honey, I better get moving or we'll have no dinner. Do you want me to grill anything else?"

"What?" Lily's distraction was broken by his voice. "I'm sorry. This is just so cool. Which army do you think this was from?"

Dev laughed. "Well, one of two. Around here, it could be north or south. I could go online and do some research for you."

"No," Lily answered quickly. "I don't need to know." She finally stuck the bullet in her pocket and took off her gloves. "I'm done for today, and yes, I have some vegetables for you to grill. It is just the two of us tonight, right?"

Dev finished off his beer. "As far as I know. Dad is dining out tonight with his neighbor Arlene. Danny and JT are busy."

"And your brother? Is he even in town?" Andrew was awake. Lily picked him up out of the stroller, and Dev quickly moved it into the garage until tomorrow's run.

As he returned, he grabbed his son. "I think he's in Europe. He's got something going on, but that's not unusual for him."

As Lily followed Dev into the house, she laughed. "Yes, but is he working for the FBI, or is he up to some other business with a certain international super-agent?"

"With Jackson, you never know. If he is with your friend Ari then it can't be good," Dev muttered. Andrew smelled, and not in a good way. He handed his son back to Lily. "I think he needs a diaper change."

Lily became nauseous quickly. "You think? You can take care of him." Dev was already in the kitchen. "I have to cook. Besides, you're so good at diaper duty."

"If your father wasn't fixing me food, or wasn't so cute, he'd be fixing your stinky diaper." She rubbed her son's nose with her own, and he giggled. "I'll potty train you as soon as I can." Andrew wiggled out of her arms and began to crawl up the stairs. Lily scooped him up. "We need to work on stairs, don't we? Come on, little man. You need a bath too. Let's get you clean."

Lily bathed her son, took a shower, and had dressed them both by the time she joined her husband on the back deck. Andrew squirmed out of her arms and ran out into the yard. Lily's daily life was changed forever when her little guy had taken his first tentative steps and never looked back. Now, he seldom walked slowly, but with speed came occasional crashes. She closed her eyes briefly and breathed in slowly. Sitting in her favorite chair, she watched her husband, the master griller. Her life was a whirlwind, but she always seemed to thrive in an organized chaotic world. If she had her lists and her post-it notes, she could survive any amount of chaos. That's how she used to do it when she managed her flower business. Saturdays were always busy back then, but this was a different kind of Saturday.

I need to remember to call Abby. Even though Lily remained the shop's owner, it was her former assistant's now. Abby was doing a great job as the manager. Lily's Saturdays used to revolve around weddings and events, but now planting, taking care of her son, and sitting on the deck drinking iced tea was her new normal, a much-loved new life.

"Are you planting the other flowers tomorrow?" Dev asked as he arranged the steaks and vegetables on two plates.

"Yes, I've run out of steam for today, and you're going to have to dig large holes for those azaleas. The tree goes into the ground next week. You'll need to pick it up from the nursery."

Dev brought the food to the table. "Just tell me when. I wonder what else you'll find in this old yard."

Lily's Zen state was broken with that statement. Her face lit up. "Are you telling me I could find more artifacts? Oh, honey, would you get the salad in the refrigerator, and I'd like a glass of that pinot please."

Dev bowed. "Yes, your highness. And yes, you could find more items, maybe a few more bullets." Dev headed into the house, returning with the salad, two glasses of wine, and Andrew's food.

They said a prayer of thanks and began to have a quiet meal together.

Dev," Lily said softly. "This is so nice. I love you."

"I love you too. I feel like I can finally breathe after the last few years. I thought I'd be around for Andrew's first year, but I missed so much. But now, there's absolutely nothing we need to do, and nowhere to go."

Lily laughed. "As soon as you say that out loud you know that's bound to change, right?"

Dev's one brow rose suspiciously. "With you around, it always does. I'm getting used to that. Let's just take the down time while we can enjoy it. Something is bound to be just around the bend."

Lily smiled, but she felt that something would happen. She felt their next adventure was just around the corner, actually at the corner of their own front porch.

Chapter Two

"Do you two need help with the tree?" The very next weekend, Lily watched as Dev and Father Dan dropped the magnolia from Dan's truck bed onto the driveway. She shielded her eyes with her hand and laughed. "You two seem to be a little out of shape."

Dan bent over, his hands on his legs. "Says the woman who has lost all her baby weight and a little more in the last year." He looked up at his friend and saw Dev sitting on the side of the back of the truck. "Really, agent man? You are supposed to be in top form."

"I am. I'm just preserving my strength. We have to move this thing up there. Besides, this thing is awkward." Dev pointed to the corner of the house.

"You would lose weight if you were taking care of Andrew. Now that he's walking, I'm running faster, and I'm using muscles I never knew I had. Besides, I eat like a squirrel. While Dev was gone, I would get a bite here and there. I never sat down and enjoyed a meal." She leaned down to hear the rhythmic breathing of her son through the baby monitor. He was napping in the pack 'n play she placed just inside the doorway. Lily placed her foot on the shovel and sunk it into the ground. Now that she saw the tree, she knew she needed to make the hole a few inches larger and much deeper. As she dug, she hit a rock. "You two take a break. I've hit something."

Kneeling down, she dug with her hands to remove the rock, but this was smaller than a rock. *Maybe it's another civil war bullet?* She began to tear the soil away. It was a bullet, but it didn't look like the one she retrieved last week.

"Honey, could you look at this?" Lily shouted.

"Oh, geez, what did she find this time?" Dev asked as he began to walk up the driveway.

Dan followed behind. "Knowing your wife, she probably found a dead body! The DEA should hire her."

Dev turned and scowled at his attempt at humor. "Not funny. She found a bullet the other day, circa civil war."

"I don't think this is from the 1800s." Lily held up the bullet between her thumb and finger.

Dev took it from her and showed Dan. "9 mm?"

Dan examined it closely. "It looks like it."

Lily stood up straight and removed her gloves. "And that means what?"

You're right. It isn't from the 1800s. I'll take it into work and have them look it over."

Lily sighed. *Now what?* She was sorry she wished to find more buried treasure. "May I still plant my tree?"

Dev looked up at her. "Yes, of course. Are you sure you want it right by the garage? Maybe we plant it over there." He pointed on the other side of the driveway.

That would destroy her design plan. She placed her hands on her hips and stared at her husband. He didn't flinch. He smiled. *Since when did he care where I plant anything? And the bigger question, why?* She decided to stand her ground. "No, I need it here. I've already dug the hole. I'm not giving up my design because of that bullet." She turned her back and picked up her shovel. "I just need a little deeper." She shoved the shovel into the ground and pulled up a large clump of dirt, with a shoulder strap of a purse. Half of the purse dangling in the air.

"Whoa, flower girl," Dan yelled. "Stop Lily, just stop."

Dan pulled Lily back by her shoulders, slowly removing the shovel's handle from her hand, and Dev crouched down in the dirt. He put on a gardening glove and gingerly began to remove the purse from the dirt. A brown leather bag was revealed. The contents began to spill out, including a Virginia driver's license for a woman.

"Danny, take a photo of this. I need to go get some plastic bags to put the bullet and all this stuff in. Don't touch anything." He looked up and directed the last sentence to his wife. Her mouth gaped open.

Dev ran into the house to retrieve the supplies. He picked up a pair of needle nose pliers, and briefly stopped to check on a sleeping Andrew.

"Your mommy is creating chaos again," he muttered before seeing the baby monitor on the nearby table. "Well crap. You heard that."

He walked outside, his head hanging low. Dan was bent over laughing. Lily's eyes spit fire. Dev didn't realize she had that special talent. *Note to self, just spy for the baby monitor before speaking.*

"Yes, I did. Chaos, huh? All I was doing was trying to make our house beautiful. This could happen to anyone."

Dan laughed harder as he stood up. Tears were coming to his eyes, and his face was reddening. "Oh, it could, but it doesn't. It happens to you!"

"I suppose so." Lily's answer was followed by her tongue stuck out in his direction. She and God had decided there were times when she could be disrespectful to a priest, and this was definitely one of those times. It did seem like in the last few years she had been around sociopathic drug dealers, seen a couple of shootings, and been the target of a terrorist kidnapping. But she had never dug up a dead body. *What if there's a body buried in our yard? I really don't want to move again.*

Dev did his agent thing while Lily went into the house to check on their son. She'd heard him stirring. *Dev shouldn't have talked to him!* Andrew was laying there, his bright blue eyes looking up at his frazzled mother. He smiled. He smiled just like his father, and both males could melt her heart with just that flash of happiness. "DaDa."

"Hello, little man. And it's Mama. Can you say Mama? Let's get you changed while Daddy collects his evidence." She turned off the monitor before she said anything stupid. *Perhaps I'm a little smarter than my husband in some things? And why doesn't my son ever say Mama? Has Dev inserted some chip in the poor little guy, so he only says DaDa, but he isn't programmed to call out for his mother?*

Danny joined Dev on the ground. "So, a spent bullet and a buried woman's purse tells you what? Your aunt doesn't have any secrets, does she?"

Dev slid some soil into one of the bags with the bullet. "No, well I hope not. Her husband had this house. There was a family before them and probably many more. This house was built in the late 1800s. Lily loves a historical home, but frankly, I wouldn't have moved here had it not been completely restored by my aunt five years ago. This house may have a host of secrets."

Dan shook his head. "Lucky you! Your wife will find them, you know. It's what she does. She digs, and this time she literally did dig. And, if you try to stop her, I might as well give you the last rights now, because she will kill you. I'm just happy you're home to deal with it."

Dev growled. "Don't worry about me. But you aren't helping. Don't you encourage her one bit. And tell our friend JT, not to encourage her behavior either. She needs to stop this amateur sleuthing stuff."

Dan stood up. His knees were sore. Age was grasping onto every body part and holding on for dear life. He hated getting old. It didn't help that the Army always had them running, crawling, and carrying equipment on their backs.

"Have you met your wife? She notices everything, every little detail. Have you gone grocery shopping with her? I have. She can tell you what the woman on aisle six was purchasing. She can tell you every store manager's name, and they know her! I needed milk the other night, and they asked me where Lily was. Not to mention, I bought rocky road ice cream, and they informed me that Lily prefers peanut butter and chocolate. You'd think they thought she was my wife the way they were going on about how nice she was. Oh, and they know about her obsession with mint cookies."

Dev stood up slowly with several bags of evidence. "Just don't encourage her. I'll tell JT myself. I don't want the two of them having little playdates where they find out who this woman was, and why this bullet has any significance."

"You know, some law enforcement group may want to dig up the rest of this ground to see if there's anything else," Dan suggested.

Dev cursed under his breath. "She's going to be mad when they destroy her design and turn her yard into an apartment complex for gophers. Let's just hope this has nothing to do with anything. I'll call this in, but let's hope."

As they headed into the house, Dan patted his friend's back. "You can hope, but you know this is something. And it isn't good."

"I know. They'll be out here with metal detectors, ground penetrating radar, thermal imaging, people analyzing air and soil chemicals, cadaver dogs…"

Dev's voice trailed off. Danny smiled. *Lily is absolutely going to love this!*

Chapter Three

It was almost three in the morning when Lily walked slowly downstairs for a glass of milk. A cold glass of milk would put her back to sleep. Dev hadn't heard her when she left the bed to check on Andrew. Thankfully, he was sound asleep. One advantage of a child growing older was that he slept the entire night, but Lily was the one who had to wake to check on him. But the milk helped.

Her feet shuffled along the floor from the kitchen, with milk in hand, toward Dev's office. Something was bothering her, and when it woke her up in the middle of the night, she knew she needed to sort it out. She wasn't sure her husband would appreciate her curiosity, but it never had stopped her before.

As she flipped the office light on, she saw the bags on his desk. Lily moved the specimens around, surveying the evidence before her. She didn't know anything about bullets, so she moved onto the contents of the purse. *I know purses!* She snorted out loud in amusement.

She saw a couple of prescription bottles one for Margot Flanders and another for Margot Fleischman. Those names could offer more information. One drug was for depression and the other was codeine. *Yikes, that'll take you to lala land.* Usually, Lily only carried a generic painkiller or the liquid prescription to rub on Andrew's incoming teeth. She shifted one bag to reveal lipstick, mascara, and a small comb. *I bet there's DNA on that.*

She flipped over another bag so she could see the Virginia driver's license. The photo showed a beautiful woman, probably in her early thirties. *It's my address so she did live here.* When Lily did the math, yes, the woman was only thirty-one. She was five feet six inches tall, and her weight was one hundred and twenty-five pounds. *I wish I was that weight and height.* The woman's name was Margot Fleischman. The expiration date on the license was nearly twenty years ago.

Lily felt something. Another energy was with her. *Oh, come on, we don't need a ghost now. But somebody's watching me.* The hair on the back of her neck rose. She looked up quickly and gasped from fear and delight. Her husband was leaning against the door frame, his arms crossed in front of his naked chest. There was a scowl on his handsome face. She had been caught, but despite her infraction she enjoyed seeing him look at her like that. She was a pushover for that chest and that scowl. But he was mildly irritated at her. *Crap!*

"Lily, what are you doing?" His voice was flat and devoid of any emotion. She knew he was more than upset, possibly verging on mad at her, or even disappointed in her actions.

"I couldn't sleep." *If I just pretend, I'm not doing anything, perhaps he'll just ignore my snooping? Not a chance.*

"So, you thought you'd come down here and look over your treasure?"

She raised her glass of milk. "That and get a glass of cold milk. Do you want some?"

Dev sighed. It was futile to discourage her. He knew she was already hooked.

He walked over to her, removing the glass of milk from her hand, and setting it on the desk.

"Honey, you can take photos or jot down whatever information you want, tomorrow. Now, let's go back to bed and not think about all of this." By now, he knew to give up, to surrender, which he never did in any other situation. But he always raised a white flag to Lily.

"You promise?" Lily looked up at his twinkling eyes. She couldn't read him right now. He was doing that government agent thing where he acted dispassionately, and his eyes became slits of steel and resolve. "You really are going to let me copy this information?"

"Yes."

Lily knew he was up to something. Was he going to rush to work with all the evidence before she woke up?

"Dev, you can't take this stuff to work before I can get a good look at it."

Dev's head bowed in despair. She caught him. She was becoming very good at being one step ahead of him. He didn't like it one bit.

"Fine, yes, now, can we just go back to bed?" Dev softly grabbed her hand and her glass of milk. "Come with me."

Lily followed slowly as they headed back up the stairs. "I know you're up to something, but I'm not sure just what yet. But I'll figure it out, you know I will."

Dev handed the glass back to her as they stood next to the bed. "Drink your milk."

She squinted her eyes at him. She grabbed the glass and finished the liquid off. "So, now what?"

"This," he whispered. He took the glass and set it on the nightstand. His left arm reached around her and pulled her close to him. "And now this."

The passionate kiss that followed left her breathless. Having a child was exhausting, but what was more taxing was that sometimes you lost yourself. You were a mom now, not a wife, or a lover. But Dev had the knack of reminding her she was all three. He positioned her to the edge of the bed and slowly placed her down on it as if she were a China doll.

"You don't want me to think about all that stuff on your desk, do you?" Lily whispered in his ear as his lips lowered to her neck.

"No." Dev moved lower, unbuttoning the front of her nightgown, and laying light kisses to the exposed skin.

"You want me to stop--"

"Talking," he added. "Andrew is asleep, and I'm willing to go into work tired. Let's just enjoy this."

She ran her hands in through his hair. "You're distracting me."

Dev looked up to her face. "Is it working?" His smile was intoxicating.

"Oh, it's working, Mr. Delicious," she murmured and grabbed his face. "I surrender." *And I'm thinking about food, but I won't tell you that. My one aunt used to say that a man could melt butter with a smile like Dev's. Oh, melted butter on crab legs sounds amazing.*

Dev's smile vanished. *Lily never surrenders. But I'm taking the win right now.*

Just three hours later, Dev kissed her goodbye. Lily turned over to enjoy a few more minutes of sleep before Andrew woke up and the day began. She had almost faded into slumber when she sat up quickly.

"I bet he took that stuff! I didn't get my photos." She jumped from the bed and began her morning mad. That very rarely made the rest of the day go smoothly. Lily grabbed her phone and saw a text from her husband.

There were no words, instead there were multiple photos of every piece of evidence. She sat back on the edge of the bed and smiled.

"That man!" Her heartbeat slowed. She heard Andrew's laughter. She'd look these over later, but she had a dirty diaper to change and a son to feed.

"Wow, how the mighty have fallen!" Taking a look at herself in the mirror, she shrugged her shoulders. Her hair was flat on one side and curly on the other. It would be another no makeup day, and a shower would have to wait. "It is what it is." Her life had changed so much in just a few years, but she wouldn't change one thing about it. Her life was filled with so many different distractions, and now she had another adventure.

Chapter Four

That afternoon, Lily and Andrew took a trip to the next door neighbor's house. Mrs. Parrot had lived in the neighborhood longer than anyone else. She was the grand dame. As a former high school history teacher, she knew most of the adults in the area. So many of them had been her students. The Pierces didn't have much interaction with her, but Dev had offered to mow her lawn a couple of times, and during the winter storm he brought her groceries. That's when he discovered she loved history as much as he did. Her family had lived it. Dev came back home after two hours of talk and coffee raving about Mrs. Parrot. Her ancestors had been slaves on one of the founding father's estates, more had been enslaved in the Charleston area around the time of the Civil War.

With Andrew's birth came a learning curve for Lily. Getting used to being a mother took over a year. She'd look out the window on most days to see her neighbor unloading groceries or greeting the postal worker. Lily had yelled the occasional salutation, but today would be the best time to become a friendly neighbor. Besides, the woman was doing her own planting and knew the soil like the back of her hand. Maybe she knew other secrets about the neighborhood too.

"Hi Mrs. Parrot." Lily smiled, halfway laughing about the name. It just made her laugh. She could only imagine what the students had done to the poor woman.

The neighbor looked up from the ground where she was kneeling and waved. "Are you two out for a walk?"

"I needed to get out of the house. He's napping so it was a perfect time to come visit." Lily's admission made the woman smile. "I've realized I haven't ever been over to visit. I'm sorry about that."

Mrs. Parrot shielded her eyes from the sun. She pointed with one hand to Andrew. "You've been busy, honey. You've shared your husband, and I've really appreciated what you two have done for me."

"And he enjoys discussing history with you. You know, the man could talk for hours about the American Revolution or the Civil War, especially with you."

"That's kind of you to say. Why don't you two come on up here? I need a break, and I brewed tea this morning. How about a cold drink on my porch?"

Lily looked down at a sleeping Andrew. "That sounds great." She pushed the baby stroller up the drive. "I may just sit down on the steps. I don't want to wake him."

"Oh, I remember those days. If it had been legal, I would've drugged my boys." Yvonne Parrot slowly stood up. She brushed away an errant strand of salt and pepper hair. She dabbed at her slender, long neck with a small towel. Her almond colored eyes were bright, and Lily noticed the woman had no frown lines. The history teacher could've been a Hollywood siren in the golden age. "I'll go in and get us the tea, and I'll get you a cushion for your bottom."

Lily settled herself in and positioned the stroller so the sun wasn't warming the baby too much. It was becoming a warm spring, but there was still a cool breeze, and no humidity. She looked around at her neighbor's perfect yard. Every plant was there with a purpose, every tree offered just the right amount of shade in the afternoon sun. And Mrs. Parrot had a porch swing just like Lily's.

Mrs. Parrot dropped two pillows down onto the concrete. "Sit yourself on one of these. Here you go, Lily," the neighbor said as she passed down a large glass of iced tea with a slice of orange laying on top of the liquid. "I like to punch it up a bit with the orange. Lemon seems so, well, normal."

Lily smiled. She wasn't interested in normal either. She pinched the slice and the juice ran into the liquid. After she submerged the rind, she took a drink and relished in the refreshing taste.

"Well? What do you think?" The former school teacher waited for an answer.

Lily's eyes closed. When she opened them, she smiled. "It's perfectly abnormal. Love it."

"I knew I'd like you," Mrs. Parrot patted her shoulder. "So what's up with your planting?"

"I was attempting to have a yard like yours. I thought we needed some color, but," Lily said, closing her mouth suddenly. *I shouldn't say anything about what we found. Surely, she wouldn't be involved, but I can't be sure.*

Mrs. Parrot leaned in. "You stopped?"

"Dev is worried about the water line. I have to call the utility company before I plant the magnolia." Soon she would be a professional liar. *Perhaps there's a circuit out there where I could become king of the liars and win tons of money if people believe my tall tales?*

"That husband is not only pretty, he's smart too."

Lily giggled. "Well, yes he is, on both counts. So, I was wondering about our neighborhood. I know Dev's aunt and her husband had the house before us, but who was before them?"

Yvonne Parrot wasn't born yesterday, besides her years of teaching had fine tuned her radar. "Ah, so you've heard about the doctor's wife? How she disappeared years ago?"

Lily gulped, sputtering a cough. "What? No, I haven't heard anything about a missing woman."

"Your husband's aunt's husband, now that's a mouthful, got that house for a steal! He swooped in and bought it. I think he knew Dr. Fleischman. His wife is the one who went missing."

Andrew began to stir. *Not now, little man! I need to hear more about this.* She rubbed his stomach, his small hand reaching up to wrap around one of her fingers. She sighed. This was the baby she loved, not the poopy one. The baby's breathing was even and deep once more. *Just like your father!*

"Tell me about it. Was the wife nice? Was the doctor a little loony? What happened?"

Yvonne took a drink. "Well, no one really knows what happened, but it was all over the news. Our little paper covered it all, and I think *The Post* even did a few stories on it. I'm pretty sure it was televised too. I just didn't watch much television back then. I was too busy grading my students' papers."

Lily shook her head knowingly. "I remember those days. I wasn't a teacher, but I was a florist. There were days when I'd sit down and watch some mystery on TV. My favorite character was Jessica Fletcher."

"I do love a good mystery, and I did watch that one because she was my favorite actress. Her style in that mystery show was impeccable, and those clothes were timeless. I tried to follow her fashion sense. I'm not sure I succeeded. Well, back to the Fleischmans. They seemed to be a normal couple. My husband Edward, God rest his soul, and the doctor would talk. That man loved his wife, but he confided in my love that his wife was distant. They had only been married five years. The doctor wasn't having an affair, and the police didn't find any indication that she was. She was a stunning woman. I wanted to fatten her up. She was so skinny she could've been one of those runway models. We had them over for dinner a couple of times, and she couldn't wait to get out of here. But the doctor was lovely."

Lily was anxious. Something didn't sound right. "So, what happened?"

"Doctor Fleischman was at a conference. I think it was somewhere in Europe. Margot, his wife, received her usual flower delivery that summer, so that would've been a Thursday."

Lily touched Yvonne's arm. "Wait, what flower delivery?"

The woman's smile widened. "I assumed it was from her husband, but now, looking back, maybe it wasn't, but every Thursday, just like clockwork, the Popping Petal Flower Shop delivered a beautiful bouquet to her. I waved over to her, and she waved back. That was the last time I ever saw her."

"The flower deliveries were every Thursday? It was just during the summer?" Lily asked. She now had more than just a passing interest. *My mouth is watering! I thought it just did that when I saw a piece of lemon meringue pie.*

"Well, I was off during the summer. She may have been getting them weekly all year. I don't know. They were only in that house two years when it all happened."

"Mrs. Parrot, was there anything else about the delivery? Did the flower person go into the house, or just hand her the flowers? Did she give them a tip? Were they a certain flower or color?"

"Slow down, Lily." Yvonne Parrot looked into her neighbor's eyes and saw pupils enlarged with excitement. "I'm not used to being interrogated."

Lily hung her head down. "I'm so sorry. I guess I need to get out of the house more often. A good mystery always intrigues me."

"Well, alright then. The truck would pull up into the drive. There's more to the house now. Dev's aunt remodeled and restored and added that attached garage with the master suite above. But, it was always the same delivery man, young, nice looking. The flowers varied from week-to-week, so there wasn't a pattern or a favorite color or flower. Oh, and the driver always brought them into the house."

Lily's eyes narrowed in suspicion. *That didn't sound right.* "Really? Did he stay long?"

"No." Mrs. Parrot stopped. She was in deep thought. "Now, that was unusual, wasn't it? He was there for about five minutes or so, and then he left. She always walked him out to the truck. Five minutes doesn't seem like enough time to do anything, if you know what I mean."

The two women shared a giggle, but Lily knew what her husband could do within a brief interlude. "That seems very weird."

"Lily, you're right. Now that I think about it, the whole thing was a little off. You know, my husband talked to Dr. Fleischman about how he spoiled his wife with those flowers. The man acted like he didn't know anything about it. That was about a week before she went missing."

Lily sipped her tea quietly. Andrew was beginning to stir again. He'd be awake in minutes, and he'd be hungry. She needed to cut to the chase.

"Mrs. Parrot, do you think the doctor killed her?"

Yvonne Parrot closed her eyes to think. "You know, the police asked us that same question all those years ago. My husband told them no, but I'm not sure. If he was angry about whatever his wife was doing, I believe anyone is capable of anything, if they are desperate enough. He could've been hurt like a wild animal and just lashed out, but he was at that conference. There was no way he could've done it."

"Paying someone to do it would have been possible," Lily interrupted. She needed more details about the doctor and his wife. *Where did she need to begin? She needed to call a friend. Oh sure, her husband had contacts, but he wouldn't approve of her project. Danny was busy. Her father-in-law didn't need to know. Paul didn't like participating in crazy investigations. Jackson and Ari were away. JT, my buddy in crime, would tell Dev. He's just too protective now that Andrew is here. I'll need a glass of wine when I call her.*

As if on cue, Andrew opened his big eyes and smiled at the neighbor.

"Where did he get that red hair?"

Lily sighed. "Recessive genes. Apparently, from Dev's mom. I need to get the little man home for a snack. Thanks for the tea and the much needed conversation."

She handed her glass to her neighbor and stood up.

"Lily, let's do this again, real soon. You have my juices going. I used to journal. I'll check and see if I had anything in there about all of that."

Lily turned the stroller and smiled back at Mrs. Parrot. "I would love that. Thank you. You saved my sanity today." As she hurried back to her home, Lily had more than one thing to think about. She needed to make a list!

Chapter Five

Lily's days passed by very quickly with a baby in tow. After she fed Andrew, and placed him in the living room surrounded by his favorite toys, she headed to the kitchen to begin something, anything for dinner. She looked in the refrigerator as if she was watching a television program, a very dull, boring one.

"Dev grilled last night. I still have leftover meatloaf, but that doesn't sound appetizing. Besides, I need to call Gretchen before Dev gets home." She shut the door quickly and headed to her laptop near Andrew.

She hit the number on her cell phone and waited for the voice on the other side, over a thousand miles away in her hometown of Kansas City, Missouri.

"Come on, Gretchen. Answer the phone." Lily looked up at the wall clock. Dev could be home in less than thirty minutes if the traffic wasn't too bad, or he didn't have a last minute meeting.

"Bestie," Gretchen said in her very unique style. "How are you, dear? And how is Mr. Delicious, and my little Andy?"

Lily rolled her eyes. Gretchen had nicknamed Dev Mr. Delicious the very first time she met him. Now, Lily used that term when she wanted to irritate her husband in a good way, or in a bad way. And she hated it when anyone called the baby Andy, but this was Gretchen. She had to ignore or absolve. Primarily because Gretchen wouldn't ever stop labeling either of the main men in Lily's life.

"Mr. Delicious is still delicious, and Andrew is really good. He's growing like a weed, and his favorite food is cheese pizza.

"Well, of course he is. He's my adorable little boy." Gretchen's voice seemed to be oozing with more than her usual saccharin sarcasm.

"Gretchen, I need a little input from you. Put on your detective hat." As soon as Lily's words flew from her mouth she was regretting her decision.

"Oh my. Are we resurrecting the Malloy and Pierce Detective Agency? We are, aren't we? This is magnificent. What or who are we after this time? A drug shipment? A philandering husband? A murder victim--"

"Gretchen, stop. Just stop. Actually, it may be a combination of all of those. I know I can look up everything on the internet, but if I want to talk directly to people who might have been involved, where would I go? I need some information about a missing woman."

"I would hit up the local newspaper if you all have one. Reporters will talk to anyone about their writing. I work with one here. Their egos are huge. Maybe there was some television coverage? Yes, you can find it all on the internet, but speaking to a human, seeing how they react is priceless in an investigation, or as you remember from your wedding flower days, in a consultation. You just have to see a bride's eyes and mouth to discover if she likes you, remember?"

"I remember. Anyone can do wedding flowers, but you have to trust and like the florist. You know, that's with any job," Lily admitted.

"But weddings and events are the most important jobs in the world!" Gretchen's laughter filled the living room. Andrew smiled up at his mother.

"Okay, I'll research online, then if any of the reporters are still around, I'll go talk to them. Got it. I just needed your confirmation."

Gretchen said nothing and then asked, "You need me to give you permission? What's going on with you?" Lily didn't usually want her approval with anything, much less some murder, drug, cheating husband matter. *Oh my Lord! It can't be about Dev!*

"Lily, Dev would never cheat on you. I know I'd take him on in a New York minute, but he'd never betray you. Maybe he's being forced by some cartel sorceress who has threatened your life."

"Wait, what? What are you talking about?"

"This investigation. It's all about your life, you poor dear. Here you've just had his first child, that we know of, and he's cheating on you. There has to be a reason, Lily. I know he loves you."

Andrew squealed with delight, but that was because a toddler didn't understand Gretchen. *Heck, did anyone?*

"Gretchen, this has nothing to do with Dev, in fact, he knows nothing about it." Lily's annoyance was thick in her tone.

"Oh, okay, then it's you! Oh my, it's with that very attractive gentleman with the accent. Ari, right? My, and they think I'm a cougar. It's because I am. I'll admit it, and never ask forgiveness for it. I'm not faulting you. He is very delicious, not like Dev, but in that Cary Grant kind of delicious, or Bond way. But why? You love Dev."

Lily held the phone away from her face. She wanted to scream. *Why did I think this was a good idea?*

Finally, Gretchen took a breath, and Lily was able to answer. "I love Dev. I am not cheating on him with Ari, or anyone else. I found the driver's license of a woman who has been missing for close to twenty years. I dug it up in our yard. I'm curious, and I want to do a little looking."

"Oh, well, why didn't you just say so. You're bored, and this will keep your mind working. Good idea. Idle minds, you know."

Lily shook her head and made a face that made her son laugh. *What in the world is Gretchen talking about?*

"Gretchen, I need to let you go. Dev will be home soon."

"Yes, good decision to keep him in the dark. You know the man gets a little cranky when you use your investigation skills. One thing before you go. I can count on you to do the flowers for Abby's wedding, right?"

What in the world? "Gretchen, what in the blue blazes are you talking about?"

"Abby and Jeremy are getting married. Didn't you know?"

"No," Lily whispered, her voice catching with emotion. "Gretchen, I have to let you go. The baby needs me. I'll call you soon." Before Gretchen could say goodbye, Lily ended the call. Tears fell slowly down her face. She hadn't cried in awhile. *Why don't I know? Why didn't Abby tell me?*

Andrew sensed her distress and began to cry too. Lily gathered her son up in her arms and the two wailed away. She'd given up everything, but she never thought her assistant, her friend would forget her. For Abby not to tell Lily that she was marrying the little nitwit, seemed like an end to their connection. Lily heard the front door open and close. Her husband was home.

"How are my two favorite people?" Dev's smile vanished as he looked in at the site. He quickly threw his jacket and bag down on the couch and ran to hold his wife and son. "What's happened? Who died?"

Lily laid her head on his shoulder. Andrew held his arms out for his father to embrace him.

"I've got you little guy," Dev murmured. "Honey, please tell me what is going on."

Lily backed away and wiped her nose with her sleeve. "My friendship with Abby is dead."

Dev let out a sigh of relief as he stood up with Andrew in his arms. "Why? Is that what all these tears are about?"

"Yes," Lily screamed out. "I don't understand why she wouldn't tell me about them getting married."

"The wedding is in August."

The tears stopped. Lily blinked, looking up at her husband in disbelief. "You know about it? Why didn't I know about it?"

"I left the mail over there the other day. I saw the address and opened it. Abby had a note in there that she was going to call you. I told you about it, but you were busy wondering about the bullets and that missing woman." He began to walk into the kitchen to grab a beer.

"But you didn't say anything to me," Lily yelled. "How could you do that? Besides, she should've called me first. I shouldn't get an announcement like everyone else."

Dev continued to hold a now happy little boy while he expertly opened his beer bottle on the side of the counter.

"And don't do that," Lily yelled again. "That's quartz. I don't need you ruining it because you want to open a beer like a college student."

"Mommy has had a bad day," Dev murmured to his son. "Did you do it? No, you don't make mommy unhappy."

Lily stood in the middle of the kitchen with hands on her hips, and a reddening face. Her glare was directed at the man she loved, but disliked immensely right now. Her heart raced, but all she could do was remain speechless. She stamped her foot, but Dev just took another drink from his bottle and peeked a glance at her.

Dev looked down into Andrew's mouth. "I think he's getting his bottom molars. Have you seen this?" Diversion was his best line of attack to distract her fury.

His question didn't receive an answer. He finished the remainder of his beer quickly then walked a few feet to stand in front of his wife.

"Honey, I told you. I can't help it if you don't listen to me. You were too busy thinking about other things, perhaps?"

Lily bit her lip. He seemed to hover over her like a vulture. *Did I hear him? I didn't listen. It was too exciting to think that there might be something more interesting than just taking care of the baby. But Abby should've called me! Dev should've made sure I knew.*

Lily removed her hands from her hips and turned away. "I'm going upstairs to take a nice long bath. Make yourself dinner. Andrew has eaten, but if he wants to eat again he can eat with you."

Before Dev could disagree with any of the directions, Lily vanished upstairs.

"Andrew, what shall we have for dinner while mommy is going nuts upstairs? Maybe you have the gourmet jar of peaches, and I have leftovers?" The baby cooed with approval. "But first, we'll give her a few minutes and then take up a glass of wine."

When Dev heard the water stop running upstairs, and after Andrew had enjoyed his favorite peaches by applying them as a face mask, the two males headed upstairs with a rather large glass of moscato. He found Lily soaking in bubbles, her eyes closed, and her head leaning back against the side of the tub.

He cleared his throat and her eyes opened immediately. Handing her the glass of wine slowly as if he was reaching into the cage of a man-eating animal, Dev smiled. "Now, take a drink and tell me what this is really all about."

"Honestly, I'm not sure. I think I'm looking at my life in the rear view mirror. It's like my prior life, before you, didn't ever exist. It didn't help that it seemed like a longer than usual winter with the baby. Maybe it's hormones. Who knows?" Lily took a sip of her wine and let it linger in her mouth. "Thanks for this. Sorry about earlier. I didn't listen to you."

"No apology needed. You know, you are right. Abby should've told you first. I talked to Tom back in Kansas City the other day, and he speculated that Jeremy and Abby were planning to get married. I bet Abby has a very good reason."

Lily managed a half-smile. "Yes. She's forgotten about me. I'm not relevant. She pays me rent. I'm her landlord. I'm the person she pays rent to, and she shares the shop's profits with me. That's all I am now."

Dev swept a little water onto Andrew's feet to the baby's delight. "Come on. You know that's not true, but we all get busy. We all have our own lives."

"Smaller lives sometimes," Lily murmured. She didn't really mean that statement. She really did have everything, and a life most people would barter with the devil to live. But her mind seemed to need more, more lists, more to-do's, just more.

Dev's left brow arched as he studied his wife. She'd

been the commander of her own ship until he walked into her life. He knew she didn't need him. He had walked away then, leaving her with the thought that he didn't need her. He was wrong. He definitely did.

"Honey, you aren't pregnant, are you? I mean, the tears, the lack of confidence, the focus on the missing woman?"

Lily shook her head quickly. "Oh, heaven's no. I mean, we should have another baby, and you know we owe Gretchen a little girl to spoil, but I'm not pregnant right now."

"So, let's get this straightened out."

She playfully sprinkled her son with a little water, and Andrew squealed. "Dev, you always want to fix things."

"And you don't, Jessica Fletcher?"

He had her there. "Fine. I'm just upset about the whole Abby thing. I haven't worked on a wedding in months, and I miss it, but just a little bit. Your aunt doesn't need me out at the vineyard for a wedding until June."

Dev placed his finger in Andrew's mouth to run it over his teeth. "You could ask Dan if he needs any help at the church."

"He has a coordinator he likes now. Besides, I don't need to be up there all the time. People talk about a priest having a female friend."

Dev's tone changed with his inquiry. "What do they know? Is there anything I should know about the priest and you?"

Lily laughed and took a drink of wine to finish the glass. "With as much time as we spend together, the grocery clerks are beginning to talk."

Dev shared the laugh. "He told me. So, what do you need?"

Lily thought. She already knew the answer, but she didn't know how to convey it to her husband without creating a disagreement. But he was in a good mood.

"Honey, I need to do research on that missing woman, and what happened in this house. This is our house now, and we need to know."

Her words were quiet and deliberate. She could tell Dev was thinking, probably wrestling with his answer.

Dev sighed. "You know I'm out of town next week. You do your research to your heart's content, but I don't want to hear that you've been kidnapped by some elfin tribe and taken to the island of cookies. I'll worry about you being in danger, so please don't get yourself into any. When I get home, we can go over any evidence you gather, but tell me everything. Secrets get both of us in trouble.

Lily's mouth gaped open. *He's agreeing?* She smiled coyly and managed a salute in agreement.

"Yes, sir. One week with no danger and no secrets, only researching would be perfect, and I'll fill you in when you get home."

Dev touched his finger to Andrew's belly. "And you, little man, have to keep your mother busy so she can't do too much research."

Lily stuck her tongue out and handed her glass to Dev. "You two, out. I'm turning into a prune."

"I'll get him ready for bed and a little down time." Dev headed out of the bathroom as Lily closed her eyes for just a minute.

"I would be kidnapped by a revengeful terrorist, not an elfin tribe," she murmured. She snorted in laughter at another thought. *But the island of cookies sounds pretty good!*

Chapter Six

1. Meet reporter
2. Talk to Mrs. Parrot
3. Draw up timeline
4. Find the doctor
5. FBI coming

Lily heard him. She opened her eyes slowly in the darkness of her bedroom. The only light came from the bathroom. It illuminated the white gold band on the side table, along with Dev's West Point ring. Even his St. Christopher's medal his mother had given him on his graduation day would be left behind with his wife. *I should be used to him leaving by now, shouldn't I? But I am never comfortable with it. It's only a week this time. How could a spouse send a loved one off to war? I wouldn't have made it.*

Lily slid over to his side and grabbed his wedding band. She slipped it onto her thumb. A light switch was touched and the room was bathed in darkness. She heard his steps even on the carpet. He leaned down and kissed her cheek. Lily reached up and held him around the neck.

"Please be careful," she whispered. "Come back to me."

"What if I'm just going to a meeting in Miami of regional DEA officers?"

"But you aren't. I know things, remember? So be careful, Boy Scout. I love you."

Dev pulled her up into his arms. "I promise I'll be careful. I love you, honey. Now, go back to sleep before the little guy wakes up. I'll call when I can."

Lily finally opened her eyes as he removed his arms from around her. He turned to pick up his bag and didn't turn around to catch one more look at her. He couldn't. She leaned over to see him walk down the hallway. He stepped into Andrew's room for a few minutes. Then he disappeared down the stairs and into the early morning darkness. Lily turned over and cried.

She was able to sleep another hour and take a quick shower before Andrew stirred. As she threw a light sweater over her jeans she heard him. He was laughing and talking, playing in his crib.

As she entered her son's room, he popped his head up over the railing. Andrew was holding the pink camel that Gretchen had purchased for the "other" baby's room. The woman had insisted that Andrew would be a girl. Lily told her no, she resorted to showing the woman the sonogram, but it did no good.

"Well, that could be a shadow," Gretchen had insisted.

"It's not a shadow, for heaven's sake, and don't say it's a foot! Look," Lily had commanded. "There's two feet and two arms with two little hands, one head, and one, well it's not a shadow."

But Gretchen had grumbled and mumbled and made them promise that the next child, if there was one, would be a girl. She also decided she would get him little sailor outfits. JT, the only Navy member of the group, was thrilled. Dev uttered a few obscenities that his son wouldn't be wearing anything of the kind. *That was a fun night!*

"Good morning, little man," Lily cooed as she picked him up. He immediately hugged her around the neck. Usually, Andrew was the best in the morning. He was loving and happy. "Let's get you fed, and then we will get you dressed, and we're going to go see your grandpa today so mommy can meet up with a reporter."

A couple of hours later, Lily was with her only and favorite father-in-law. Andrew immediately climbed into his grandfather's arms.

"So, where are you off to? Are you going to get your nails done, maybe take some time for yourself?"

"Nope, I'm going to interview a reporter about a cold case, a missing woman. We found her identification buried in our yard."

Jack was in shock. "You mean he's letting you do a little detective work? My, he is maturing."

Lily narrowed her eyes. "Are you being vague on purpose? Are you talking about your son, or your grandson?"

Jack nuzzled Andrew's head. "This little guy is perfect, so I must be speaking about my son."

They shared a laugh at Dev's expense. "He agreed that as long as I didn't get into any trouble, I could do a little snooping. I have to give the boss a report when he gets home next week."

"Do humor him, and don't get yourself into any trouble, please," Jack pleaded. Before Andrew was born, Dev's nemesis actually attempted to kidnap Lily. He knew his son couldn't live without the woman, even if she didn't realize it. "Make sure you have your cell phone on and with you at all times."

"I'm going to visit with an elderly reporter, Lawrence T. Livingood. He covered the story of the missing woman."

Jack's smile faded quickly. "You aren't talking about Dr. Fleischman's wife, are you?"

"Yes," Lily answered slowly. "Do you remember the woman?"

"I remember all of the coverage. People were searching for her everywhere. Someone thought they saw her driving on I-95 around Savannah, Georgia the day after she disappeared. They tried to pin it on the doctor, but he was at some conference, in London, I think. He was a good man, well at least he did good things. You know, I've seen him out at the vineyard. He stays in touch with Maggie and Maureen. He loves wine."

Lily would've jumped for joy, but she didn't dare. Jack might actually rat her out to Dev, and she couldn't take that chance. She had some ideas already formulated. First, she would interview the reporter, and then, yes, she would interview the doctor himself. Instead of sharing her glee, Lily looked down at her watch.

"I need to go. I don't want to be late. Everything you need is in the diaper bag."

She was almost out the door when she turned around to kiss her son. She hugged the baby and her father-in-law.

"Thank you for taking care of him."

"Just be careful. I'll see you in a couple of hours, right?" Jack's question received a nod as an answer as Lily quickly headed to her car. He looked at Andrew and smiled.

"Why can't your mommy have a safe hobby like jewelry making? Or maybe even an unsafe one like skydiving? At least we would know what she was getting herself into! Heck, your daddy might join her. He's jumped out of a few perfectly good planes in his life."

As Lily checked the addresses on the street, she really didn't know what she was getting herself into, or why it was so important to discover the truth of a cold case. She pulled in front of a small brick house with an immaculately manicured yard. There was one car in the driveway, a rather old Dodge Neon with a few dents in the body.

She pulled out her bag, notepad in hand, and headed toward the front door. Before she reached the stoop, a tall thin man greeted her. His straw hat shielded his eyes.

"Are you Mrs. Pierce?"

"Yes, sir. Thanks for seeing me today."

He shrugged. "What else am I doing? Come on in. We're going to sit on my back porch."

He led her through a very organized living room, and a kitchen that was so neat she probably could've eaten off the floor. As they stepped into the screened porch, she was greeted by a small terrier sniffing at the hem of her jeans.

"Ernest, stop that."

"It's fine. I love dogs." Lily saw a lovely table set with a large pitcher of lemonade and several plates of cookies and fruit. "You didn't need to go through any trouble, Mr. Livingood."

"I like to entertain. Have a seat, and let's get these questions out of the way so we can visit."

Mr. Livingood poured a glass for her and one for himself. "Now, how did you get involved with this case? You didn't say who you were with?"

Lily placed her pad and pen on the table. "Frankly, I am curious. You see, I found some things in my yard that I believe belonged to Mrs. Fleischman. We, my husband and I, have contacted the FBI, but I wanted to talk to you. You did the most comprehensive job on the story. I read all your articles."

"Ah, you found some things? Interesting. Where did you read my columns?" He removed his hat and placed it on the table. His dog jumped up into his lap and settled in.

"Online."

He smiled. "That's not all of them. They didn't download everything. I'll let you have a look at them if you tell me what you found."

He reminded her of a father attempting to negotiate the price of wedding flowers. "I found her purse, well what I think was her purse," Lily answered coyly. She wasn't about to tell him all the details. "And it's been sent to the FBI for testing."

"Hmm, that's more than what the FBI found when they were looking. They won't do anything with it, not after all these years. They've given up." He looked right in her eyes and sat quietly just staring at her. "What are you, some bored housewife?"

Lily smiled. "I'm not just some bored housewife. When I find something in my yard, I want to know more. I talked to the next door neighbor."

"Mrs. Parrot," he said as he smiled. "I always remembered that name. Did she tell you about the weekly flower delivery?"

"Yes, she did, and the same young man who went into the house. I used to have my own flower shop, and I hardly ever went into the home, unless I knew the client very well, or if there was some reason to go in." She thought back to the time that she did her own "wellness check" on Mrs. Notte, one of the shop's longtime customers.

"That shop was closed a few months after Margot Fleischman went missing. I always thought that was a bit unusual and perhaps connected. I never could find out how. The building is still there at the corner of the parkway on this side of Lake Ridge."

Lily wrote a few notes. That bit of information about the shop would go in her timeline. Maybe she could determine if it went out of business, had a fire, or closed for some other reason.

"Mr. Livingood, do you think the doctor killed his wife?"

The retired reporter took a sip of lemonade. He nervously tapped his hand lightly on the table. "I suppose he could've, but he didn't. He adored that woman, and she didn't deserve it. I met her a couple of times. She did a few things with the Chamber of Commerce. I believe she had a friend with the Chamber and just showed up at a few of the luncheons. She was haughty and distant. If you could do something for her then she talked to you. She only wanted to be involved in big money projects."

"So, she had a job?" Lily scribbled down a few notes to think about later.

"Oh, heaven's no! That woman was a trophy. She worked on a couple of charity events, but only if they involved a lot of money and all of the right people. One time, I told her about a library project that involved young children pulling in a couple hundred dollars for books to go to underprivileged kids. She scoffed at the idea. She informed me she didn't waste her time on nickel and dime money-makers. Yes, she was something else." Livingood shook his head in disgust.

"I'm assuming the couple didn't have any children?" Lily asked quickly. She wanted to distract the elderly man. His face was contorted by the memory.

Livingood smiled. "No. The doc was a widower when Margot met him. I believe he had a daughter. Yes, that's right, he did. I met her once. She came into the newspaper once, frantic with fear. She was afraid her dad was going to jail, and that her stepmother was going to kill her. I think the girl received threats."

Lily wrote down "daughter" in her notes. She was about to ask another question when Livingood pounded the table.

"That woman is out there somewhere. I just know it. She put that man through hell, and messed up that girl. His daughter swore that some of those threats were from Margot. And she was stalked. There's probably a few police reports somewhere, but I'm getting into the weeds now."

"You know you can grow flowers among the weeds," Lily quietly commented and smiled. The reporter's anger vanished. He grinned as he passed a plate of lemon bars.

"Yes, but weeds can choke flowers. I make these lemon bars. They've won blue ribbons at the county fair before. Have one."

Lemon. I love lemon. Lily grasped the bar in her hand and held it up to her nose. The fragrance of lemon was better than any flower, except the scent of lilacs and magnolias. She needed to ask the manager at the nursery if lilacs would grow in Virginia. She had the perfect place right under the kitchen window. If she had her favorite flower there, in the spring she could open the window and enjoy her work in the kitchen while relishing in that amazing scent.

Lily took a bite and closed her eyes. "Oh my." She caught the powdered sugar from falling onto her sweater. "This is so good. I've been trying to lose weight recently, and this is the best thing I've eaten in months."

"They were my wife's favorites, in fact, it's her recipe. After she died, I found her hand-written notes, and now I make a batch every week. Mrs. Pierce, give me a day or two to get my notes together, and those columns for you. I'll call you when I have them ready. Find something, if you can."

Lily's mouth was full with another bite of lemon bar. She swallowed and wiped her mouth with a napkin. "Thank you. Will you have it all ready before Friday?"

Livingood eyed her suspiciously. "You don't have a deadline, do you?"

Lily cocked her head to the side. "Actually, I do. My husband's given me the week. He should be home Friday night."

"Huh. He sounds like a bear."

Lily laughed. "No, it's not like that. He's afraid I'll get hurt." *He does growl like a bear though.*

"For just researching?" Livingood shook his head in displeasure.

Lily smiled meekly, her shoulders rising in embarrassment. "The last time I did research I ended up kidnapped by a terrorist."

The seasoned retired reporter shook his head. "You just might break this mystery open. I'll get that stuff together by Thursday, how's that?"

Lily eyed the plate of lemon bars. "That would be fantastic. Do you mind if I have another? I really have been starving myself lately."

Livingood pushed the plate closer to her. "Your husband, the non-bear, wants you to lose weight, right?"

Lily was enjoying another lemon bar. "No, he doesn't care. I just haven't had time to eat. Taking care of my son keeps me busy, and now my curiosity is going to keep me up at night."

Livingood examined his guest. He didn't understand what her angle or interest was in the Fleischman case, but he was sure happy that someone had picked up the cold case. His hope that some government entity or a professional detective agency would open up the investigation had long been lost. But Mrs. Pierce would do. She just needed some encouragement to send her in the right direction. He could do that.

"What if I pack a few bars to go?"

Lily was surprised but thrilled. "Would you? They are so good."

"Drop by Thursday afternoon, and I'll have a box of research for you, and another batch of lemon bars."

Lily looked down at her watch. She needed to go. "I'll see you around two Thursday, and I'll be happy to take both off of your hands."

As Livingood walked Lily out, he stopped at the door. "You know, Mrs. Pierce, something has been nagging at me. There was another case, and it involved another doctor. He worked at a different hospital than Dr. Fleischman, but he worked at a charity event with Margot. They seemed very chummy. In fact, I think I have a photo or two of them at the event, well that was on a Saturday night. Margot went missing the next Tuesday. That doctor was found in his car outside of his house. He had been shot dead at close range. I'm pretty sure he took Margot home that night. I'd always wondered if it had something to do with her disappearance."

Lily, with lemon bars in hand, stopped on the sidewalk and looked back. "Wow. That is interesting. Will you put that in the boxes too?"

He nodded and smiled. "I'll see you Thursday, Mrs. Pierce."

"And I'll see you, Mr. Livingood. And please call me Lily. You've given me lemon bars. That makes us friends." She waved in the air and headed to the car. Her father-in-law would have the police looking for her if she didn't get to his house in ten minutes.

Livingood locked his front door and shook his head. He reached down and gathered his dog in his arms.

"Ernie, old man, her husband sure has his hands full." He laughed out loud and headed to his study to begin to put together research he had long given up on.

Chapter Seven

Thursday couldn't come soon enough for Lily. She had done just about all the research she could with her laptop. She couldn't wait to dig into the reporter's boxes. She called Mr. Livingood to warn him she would have her son with her this time, and he seemed to be delighted with the extra company.

As she arrived at the house, the retired reporter was sitting in a lawn chair with two full boxes next to him on the lawn. He waved her up into the skinny driveway and began to carry one of the boxes to her car.

"I didn't want you to have to get the little guy out of the car just in case he fell asleep on the ride over."

Lily looked in the backseat. "That's so kind and thoughtful. He fell asleep two blocks out of our driveway."

"My son always did that. Pop your trunk."

Lily did as she was instructed and headed to retrieve the other box. She handed it to Livingood for him to place with the other. He shut the lid softly.

"Lily, I hope you find something in this mess. I had given up until you came the other day, but please be careful. That woman is out there. She toyed with the doc's daughter, she ruined his life, and in my heart I think she had something to do with that other doctor losing his life. Even after all these years, I believe she's dangerous."

Lily could see the fear in the elderly man's eyes. "I promise I'll be careful. I also promise to take care of your work. I'll get all of this back to you as soon as I can. Thank you so much, Mr. Livingood." She touched his arm lightly.

"It's Lawrence, Lily." He began to walk back to the house, then directed his attention back to her. "Oh my gosh, I almost forgot. Don't leave yet. I have your lemon bars."

Lily clapped. "I'll take them." She waited patiently as he hurried back with a small box in his hands.

He handed the prized gift to her. "I made you a dozen, and here's the recipe. My son doesn't bake so I want you to have it."

Lily looked at the recipe card in her hand, and then up into his eyes. "That is so kind of you. I know this is so ridiculous to get wrapped up in this, but I'm happy I did it just so I could meet you."

They both heard Andrew wail very loudly. "Sounds like he's ready to get home."

"If he's lucky, he may get just a tiny crumb of lemon bar. Thank you again." Impetuously, she leaned over and embraced Livingood. His arms took her in.

As Lily broke away, she saw him dab at his eyes with a handkerchief. *Who carried a handkerchief anymore?* Livingood waved as they drove down the block and out of his sight. *And he wears suspenders! What a dear dinosaur of a man.*

As Lily and Andrew ate dinner she began to fill out her post-it notes. Andrew was practicing his spoon exercises and managing to fill his mouth most of the time. After Lily finished her salad, she opened the lemon bar box and took in the wonderful scent.

"Andrew, mommy is getting a glass of milk, and you are going to have a bite of the most wonderful flavored bars on the face of the earth." With her glass filled and a small plate adorned with a lemon bar, Lily broke off a small piece and handed it to Andrew.

At first the little guy made a sour face, but then smacked his lips in delight. "Mmmmm."

Lily smiled. "You are my son! Now if you could say *Mama* I'd be so happy. You've said *DaDa* and *dog*, but no *Mama*. Maybe after this treat you'll love me more?" She handed her son one more crumb. This time he licked his lips.

His mother looked down at her phone. Dev had just texted a quick hello. "Daddy will be back tomorrow. As soon as I get you down tonight, I need to get some work done."

"DaDa." Lily gaped at her son. "DaDa, dog." She clapped at his success even though it would've been nice if he'd called out her name.

"I think you just said your first sort of sentence. It must've been the sugar."

Lily leaned over and embraced her son, and began to clean up his mouth, his face, his hair. When he ate, it was a contact sport. "You are such a good little man. Daddy will be very happy to see you."

The remainder of the night, she bathed her son, watched him in wonderment as he fell asleep, dressed in her favorite pajamas, and returned to her post-it notes. Lily began to form her list, focusing on a timeline, a very limited one. She began to place her post-it notes one by one on the refrigerator door. She stepped back to review as she plotted.

With her own writing blurring, she called it a night around one in the morning. If she was lucky she'd have at least six hours of sleep. She was clearly fixated on the missing woman. *And where was the FBI? No one had been by to go over the yard yet.* Lily laid her head on Dev's pillow.

Lily fell asleep quickly, smelling her husband's scent, and listening to the monitor emit the soft even sounds of her son's breathing. She wouldn't give up one second of her life as it was now, but she missed Abby, and even Gretchen. Her longing wasn't for her past life, it was for the connection she once had.

The next day, Andrew had a check-up and the doctor was running late. By the time Lily and Andrew were on their way home, Friday evening traffic had every street and interstate clogged. She might have enough time to clean up her mess in the kitchen and feed her son before Dev arrived home. But when she pulled into the driveway, she knew that would be futile. Dev's car was parked in his place.

"Holy Moly. Daddy's home, Andrew," she commented to the babbling young child in the backseat.

"DaDa." Lily smiled and sighed. "DaDa," he continued to scream. His arms and legs moved in complete joy. Hopefully, he continued to squeal that one special word when Dev saw him. It would be a good distraction for her favorite DEA agent as she hurried into the kitchen to pull down her organization artwork. Remarkably, the toddler still wouldn't say certain words on demand. Andrew had a stubborn streak. *I have no idea where he gets that.*

As they entered the house, Lily searched for her husband. "Dev, we're home. The doctor's appointment ran long. Andrew's great though. He's way ahead on his growth chart."

"I'm in the kitchen."

Lily's head bowed. *Crud.* She brought her face close to her son's. "You need to speak to Daddy to save Mommy. Please understand this."

Lily took her time dropping the diaper bag and her bag in the living room, delaying Dev's ridicule. Andrew couldn't wait on her any longer and pulled away from her grasp. He scampered off into the kitchen. As Lily finally entered the kitchen, Dev seemed calm, sitting at the table, drinking a cold beer. He placed the drink on the table as Andrew lept up into his arms.

Dev pointed at the refrigerator. "What's all that? What have you been doing? How much do you owe at the office supply store?" He kissed the top of his son's head and smiled at his son's giggles.

"I had all those post-its already, smarty. I didn't have time to clean up."

Dev's one brow rose in speculation, but he returned his attention to the small boy in his arms.

"DaDa. Car. Dog."

Those words changed everything, which was what Lily was hoping for. She loved her son so much right now. She thought about buying him a pony, but he didn't even know what a dog was yet.

"Did you hear that? I never get tired of hearing him say my name, especially when I come back from a trip, and he added two more words almost like a sentence." Dev's smile was wider than Lily had ever seen. Perhaps, she had seen it on their wedding day, on their honeymoon, Christmas when she told him she was pregnant, the day Andrew was born, yes, on so many more days.

Lily began to gather up the papers spread over the kitchen table. "He said a real sentence last night, but couldn't get out *Mama*. He said *dog in bed*. Oh, and he asked for milk yesterday morning."

Her mutterings dripped with annoyance, but she really wasn't. Lily just wondered how *milk* and *dog* beat her out. Hurriedly, she picked up each note, each photograph, until her husband reached out for her with one arm, pulling her close.

Dev leaned down and kissed her strongly on the lips. "I missed you. Please stop cleaning."

"I need to clean or else I can't make dinner."

Dev kissed her again. "You're not making dinner. We'll go out or we can order something. I want to be with my family."

Lily looked up to such a joyous expression on her husband's face that she completely put the missing woman out of her mind for the first time since she dug up that purse.

"Let's just order pizza," Lily suggested. "I wouldn't mind being with my best guys."

"Andrew and I will order the pizza. Leave your work in the kitchen. Do you want to get in a nice shower, or a bath?" Dev watched as Lily pushed hair out of her eyes as she began again to collect her papers. She stopped at the mention of the bath. He knew by now that Lily's only splurge was an unhurried bathing experience.

"Who are you? I mean you're a real nice man, but I'm not sure you're for real. No man comes home from a work trip and gives his wife time to do whatever she wants."

Dev went nose-to-nose with his son. Andrew laughed and called out his name again. Dev's laughter filled the room. "Well, when your son calls out your name, I guess I become a different person. Besides, you look like you need a break."

Lily glared, but he was right. She needed a long warm shower with that new strawberry body lotion her sister had sent her. She needed to get out of her baby stained clothing and into comfy pajamas even though it was barely six in the evening.

"I'm not going to argue with you." She hurried past him, but hurriedly returned to kiss him on the cheek. "Could you make sure there's mushrooms this time?"

"Sure. So, shower or bath?"

Lily smiled. "A shower." As she began up the stairs, she turned to her husband one more time, pointing at Andrew. "He needs a diaper, and there's chicken and peas in the fridge for your son.

Dev nodded then directed his attention back to his little man. "After you eat those peas, I'm not doing those diapers. Let's get a pizza ordered, with mushrooms, and get you fed. Or maybe you just eat pizza with us?"

Lily strangely enjoyed the pummeling of the water as it streamed down onto her back. *Lord, have I told you thank you for that wonderful man lately? Oh, and for that beautiful little boy even though he puked carrots on my favorite sweatshirt yesterday?* She closed her eyes and began to think again about her life, the missing woman, and everything that was swirling around in her life. For one brief second she allowed her mind to go blank. Her forehead rested on the tile as she closed her eyes. She was startled awake by her own snoring. Slowly, she finished and toweled dry to dress in the most comfortable set of pajamas she owned. She arrived at the front door as the pizza arrived. Dev handed off the baby and answered the door.

"Did you eat? You look awfully clean." Lily searched for remnants of a green vegetable or an errant piece of chicken. "Wow, Daddy did a good job, or you haven't eaten yet."

"Oh, he's eaten some cheese and a few pieces of peaches. He's also wearing the outfit you had in your bag, and the apron that was hanging in the kitchen needs to be washed. But Andrew wants pizza tonight. He told me." Dev walked by her, the scent of pizza leading the way.

"He can tell you what he wants to eat, but he can't say my name," Lily sighed.

In a couple of hours, Andrew was full from pizza stripped of mushrooms, sausage, and peppers. He fell asleep quickly in his bed as his father rubbed his back and placed his stuffed elephant next to him. Finally together, Dev and Lily sat across from each other on the couch, a bottle of beer in each of their hands.

Dev's arm extended over the back, rubbing Lily's neck. "You know, it's nice to have a quiet night. It would be the perfect time to go out to the refrigerator and look at what you've accumulated so far in your investigation."

Lily's attention was drawn to his eyes. Those eyes and lashes had attracted her to him from the first time they'd met. *No man should have those lush lashes.* He was relaxed. Either Dev had a great working trip, or he was completely surrendering to her curiosity.

"Honey," she began. "I can't do anything I do without the unconditional love you give me. I have gained confidence I never knew I could have."

Dev smiled slightly and moved a little closer. "That's my special love power."

Lily moved away quickly. "Geez, Dev, Gretchen says that."

He cocked his head slightly. "It's a good line, besides, they don't call me Mr. Delicious for nothing."

Lily was unable to stop her laughter and soon she snorted in delight. "What am I going to do with you?"

"I can think of a few things, well more than a few things." His voice was sultry. No longer was he focusing on her investigation. He was alluding to a different kind of search.

Lily finished off her bottle, stood, and pulled him up by one arm. "Come on, Mr. Delicious."

He toasted with his bottle. "To the kitchen we go. Let's find a missing woman."

She grabbed his bottle and placed it on the table in front of them. "Nope, not tonight."

Lily began to lead him upstairs. Dev said nothing until they arrived at their bedroom.

"You mean that line actually worked?" He turned Lily in his arms. He looked down at her attire and stifled a laugh. He did love these pajamas, but he'd never tell her. He had a reputation to uphold. No man should ever admit that he gets turned on by a cartoon character with an addiction to honey. He leaned down, held her face in both of his hands and kissed her deeply. When he released his wife, she took a step back and opened her eyes.

"Well, if the line didn't work, that kiss certainly did." She took his hand again and led him into the room. "Come on, Mr. Delicious. It's time to do a little undercover work."

Dev laughed out loud. "I've missed Schmidt and Pierce. We're back in business again."

Chapter Eight

"Good morning," Dev whispered in Lily's ear. He could see she was laying awake, staring up at the ceiling. *She's going over lists in her head!* He nuzzled her ear. His mouth moved to place a kiss on her neck. "That was a nice homecoming."

Lily waited a second as she finished up a list in her head. She turned and was flesh-to-flesh with the love of her life. She patted his unshaven face and ran a hand through his hair. It was unusually long for him. *Maybe he really is doing legitimate undercover work?*

"The only good thing about you going away is when you come home." She kissed him lightly, offering him an invitation to continue their activities from a few hours ago. As Lily enjoyed the attention her husband gave her, she realized she was missing something.

"Where are my pajamas?" she asked softly.

Dev's trail of kisses was headed way below her neck. "Mm, over there somewhere," he murmured as he continued his attention to her body. "The bear is probably visiting the bunny."

"Speaking of rabbits, we need to plant that magnolia. I've been watering it, but it needs to go into the ground. I have another place for it since the FBI hasn't been out yet to check the other hole."

Dev's face shot up over her's. "What about rabbits?"

"You weren't listening, were you? We need to plant the magnolia tree."

Dev planted himself back down on the bed, staring at his own particular patch of the ceiling. "I thought maybe, well, that old-fashioned thing about rabbits and babies."

"What?" Lily asked and then realized what he was talking about. "Heaven's no! I'm not ready for another baby, are you?"

Dev thought about it for a minute before replying. He needed to be careful. "I'm not against it. We aren't getting any younger, and if we are going to have more children--"

"Not now," Lily interrupted. Luckily, Andrew could be heard from the monitor. He was waking up and sounded completely unhappy. Dev heard him too.

He placed a hand over Lily to stop her from getting out of the bed. "I'll get him. You just enjoy the bed."

Dev hurriedly grabbed his robe and headed down the hallway.

"Another baby?" Lily asked out loud. "I'm not sure I'm ready for that. Is anyone ever really ready?"

They had felt as though they'd been particularly blessed when they discovered Andrew was coming, but the days with a baby made Lily feel older, not younger. Her lower back hurt. She had headaches, and it seemed as though her stamina just wasn't up to par. And now, Andrew was walking. *Taking care of a baby isn't harder than doing a wedding, is it? Maybe. Definitely.*

Dev returned to the room with a smiling baby, reaching out for his mother.

"Mama Mama."

As Lily took him into her arms, she began to cry. The little guy knew how to reach her heart. "Do you want a little brother or a little sister, Andrew?"

Dev grabbed her leg through the sheets. "Remember, you promised Gretchen we'd have a girl the next time."

"Oh yeah, I remember, but it's not on me to get that result, Mr. Delicious."

Dev grimaced. "She'll kill me if we have another boy."

Andrew began to crawl between his parents. Lily sat up.

"I'm not sure she'll kill you, but she'll think of some kind of punishment, perhaps the removal of some appendage?" Lily laughed at the fear on her husband's face. "Planting that magnolia doesn't seem so bad right now, does it?"

After breakfast and ample playtime with the baby, Dev headed out to the backyard dragging the magnolia tree. Lily followed with a shovel and a baby.

"I was thinking back here," Lily directed. "It's near the fence and would provide great shade. The utilities already made their marks, and Mrs. Parrot was telling me about the water and service lines that were put in a few years back so right about here should be safe." She pointed to an area about three feet away from the fence.

Dev knelt down to survey the markings. "We need to move it out just a little more. I don't want roots getting into that underground line." He rose up and pointed to another area. "What about here?"

Lily mulled the idea over. "I don't like it there, but what about closer to the corner of the yard then? They marked over there too, just in case."

Dev grabbed the tree and headed in that direction. "Just in case you changed your mind," he muttered.

"I really wanted it by the garage." Lily shouted.

Dev turned back toward her. "Not where you wanted it, but you could have it on the other side of the driveway."

Lily slowly walked toward the new location and looked back at the house. "I didn't want it there. You know that. I need to look at this and see what it might look like."

Dev sighed. One thing he had learned about his wife is if she stuck an idea in her head, it seldom became dislodged. He would hear about that place she wanted to plant the magnolia for months, possibly years. He watched her cock her head in one direction and then in another. She was visualizing how the tree looked from the house and visa-versa. *Lily, it's just a tree.* But, it wasn't to her. She could see it years from now as it grew and shaded Andrew while he played, and maybe even one or two more children. He grabbed the shovel from her hand.

"Well? Will it be perfect here?"

She turned and looked at the placement one more time. "It will be perfect. Here, take Andrew." She exchanged their son for the shovel.

"I can dig for you," Dev stated.

"No, I want to do this." Lily began to dig in, lifting dirt and grass up and throwing it to the side. Dev shook his head and decided his son and he would play in the yard while mommy dug in her dirt.

He chased Andrew until he caught him, holding his body upside down. The toddler giggled with delight.

"Dev, come here, hurry!"

Lily's voice sounded funny as though she were about to cry. He pulled Andrew up into his arms and ran to her side. "What did you do? Did you find Jimmy Hoffa this time or maybe that guy who jumped from the plane with tons of money?"

"Dev, are those bones?"

With an arm around his shaking wife, Dev looked down and indeed saw bones. He couldn't be sure if they were human. "I'm going to get someone out here today." He looked at his distraught wife. "And you, stop digging."

Lily nodded slowly. She never wanted to dig in her yard again.

She didn't know who her husband called, but within an hour, there was a police car in front of her house, and several FBI agents examining her partially dug hole. The magnolia still stood by the fence lonely and unplanted.

"That darn thing may never get planted," Lily said out loud as she watched from the kitchen. Dev was out there with them, pointing back at the house. For the first time since meeting Agent Pierce, she wanted nothing to do with any action or any investigation, especially the one currently being conducted in her backyard. She was discovering too many items as though someone was sending her on a wild goose chase. *I'm not playing anymore. Whoever did all this was either covering up something or making it look like someone did something. Either way, I'm not falling for it.*

Lily turned her attention back to her son who was eating a piece of turkey bologna. "I'm not thinking about any of it. Andrew, here's a slice of orange." Andrew took the fruit into his mouth and smiled. He grabbed another piece from Lily's hand.

Lily could see the post-it notes on the refrigerator door. They were taunting her, making her want them. "Nope, Andrew. Mommy is done investigating." She turned to see Dev talking on his phone. "Now, who's he calling? The President?"

Dev needed information only one person in his family could furnish. "Aunt Mags, I have a question. Did you or your husband ever bury a dog in your backyard here, over by the corner of the fence line shared with Mrs. Parrot?"

"Oh my gosh, Devlin. Did you find Chief? That's wonderful. I didn't know where he buried that poor dog."

Dev's head bowed in relief or humiliation, he wasn't really sure. Lily would be relieved. The FBI would be incensed for the waste of their time. And he wasn't sure what he was feeling...uneasy came to mind. Something was very wrong. He had this feeling, and that knot in the stomach was usually a prelude to danger.

"Mags, I'll give you a call later. I'm going to bag Chief up, and we can have him cremated. I've got a few people here right now. Talk later." He cut the call off as his aunt was in mid-sentence. His attention was drawn to another agent who was motioning to the others. Something had set off his detector. Before Dev could reach the back of the yard, shovels were digging into the ground. *Great, now what?*

Lily was cleaning Andrew's gooey face as he began to say his favorite word and point at his father. She looked out into the yard and viewed the frenzy of activity.

"Wonderful. Another hole, and still the magnolia hasn't found a home," she muttered out loud. She grabbed her son and headed outside. Dev stopped her before she came too close.

Dev proactively splayed his arm across her, guarding Andrew too. "Lily, just stay back here. The bones you found were from Aunt Maggie's dog, but it looks like they have something else."

"But that isn't from a dog," Lily muttered as she pointed toward a shoe and what might be a shirt. Several gloved agents placed the items into evidence bags. Other agents backed away as a photographer began to shoot down into the hole.

"Stay here. I mean it," Dev directed. Once she nodded, he walked toward the action. Out of the corner of her eye, she noticed Mrs. Parrot who was watching from her raised back deck.

"What's going on?"

Lily walked nearer to that side of the fence. "I'm not sure. I found some bones, but it's a dog. But now I think they've found something else. I saw a shoe and some material, maybe a shirt."

"Honey, how about I come over and take care of that sweet boy?" Mrs. Parrot shouted over all of the investigators.

"Would you mind? He's due for a nap."

Mrs. Parrot nodded. "I'll be right over. Meet me at your front door."

Dev nodded too. He caught Lily's eyes and smiled. *I know that look. That's the look when something is very wrong, and he's attempting to assure me that everything is absolutely fine. It's his lying eyes with those amazing lashes.*

Lily hurried into the house and met her next door neighbor at the door. The woman had her knitting bag with her and a purse. She reminded Lily of Poppins and her magic carpet bag. Lily snorted. "And she's Mrs. Parrot."

"I brought my knitting, a book, and my lunch, just in case you need me for a while," Mrs. Parrot said as she hurried inside. "I have a feeling this bunch is going to be there for a few hours. You know the government always takes too much time. Now, what can I do?"

"Really, I just need you to be here just in case I need to go out there," Lily said, pointing into the back yard. "I'm going to change him, and put him down for his nap. I have the monitor so we can hear him here in the living room."

Mrs. Parrot laughed. "We didn't have those things when my boys were little. All we listened for was the screaming."

"Well there's still that. I'll be back in a few. Make yourself comfortable. Drinks are in the fridge, and just ignore all the notes on the front."

As Lily disappeared up the stairs, Mrs. Parrot's curiosity was piqued. As she entered the kitchen, she frowned. "What in God's green earth?" She began to read the post-its, intrigued by some of the information. "Girl, girl, girl. What are you up to?" She opened the refrigerator and grabbed a cold can of soda.

"Mrs. Parrot," Dev said as he entered through the back door.

"Hello Dev. I thought your wife might need some help with the baby and a little company."

Dev patted her back. "Thank you. Is she upstairs?"

"Yes, putting the baby down. What is she up to?" The former teacher pointed at the door and the multicolored squares.

Dev sighed as he began to walk away. "She's just being Lily. Make yourself comfortable. I'll be back in a few minutes."

Dev contemplated his next move as he looked up the stairs. Dan's prediction that Lily would find a dead body had come true. He knew his wife loved a good mystery, but dead bodies and bones disturbed her. That was natural, but when he saw her shaking just because she'd uncovered a dog's burial site, it hurt his heart. She had professed how she was more confident because of him. *No, Lily, you did it yourself.* But he was fearful that his news might send her reeling. He began to slowly climb the stairs as though it was Mt. Everest.

He stood in the doorframe of Andrew's bedroom watching her sooth the now sleeping toddler. The two of them were his life. He'd known he loved her when he had walked away from her in what seemed a lifetime ago. But when he returned, she had changed his life. They were his life. He had never understood how much he had needed her and this family, but without them he wasn't sure he could survive.

Lily could feel Dev's eyes on her. She could always feel his gaze, even if they were across the room from each other. She patted Andrew one more time and turned slowly to walk into her husband's arms.

"Well?" she whispered.

"Come on, let's go downstairs." He took his wife's hand, and they headed back down to the waiting Mrs. Parrot. Lily joined the woman at the kitchen table.

"I could use a real coke, please," Lily announced. She really wanted something stronger, but until the men and women swarming her backyard departed, she'd wait. Later tonight, she was going to look for that vodka Paul and Jill had brought them as a party gift.

Dev brought her a cold can of soda and took a seat in between the women. He gazed out into the backyard and just knew this was going to be a long day. The poor neglected magnolia tree leaned against the fence near Chief's burial site. *That's just sad.*

"They've found a few things. They'll end up searching this entire yard."

"Did they find her?" Mrs. Parrot asked anxiously as she leaned in closer.

"No, well I'm not sure. So far, they've found a woman's shoe. There's stained blood on it. Then it seems as though they've found a woman's blouse."

"And?" Lily questioned. She knew her husband by now. He was winding up for the big finish. "They found more bones."

Dev looked directly into her eyes. He didn't blink. He decided he would be direct. "Yes, and this time it's a human being."

Mrs. Parrot gasped. Lily muttered that she knew it, that there was a dead body buried in their yard.

"Now, we wait." Dev moved his hand slowly across the table to grasp Lily's. "I think we should get out of here while they do their work."

Mrs. Parrot nodded. "Dev, that's a great idea. Lily, you all should take that sweet boy and go somewhere, maybe grab a few things and go for a picnic. You know, I'll be just next door. Maybe the three of you should go to a hotel for the night. You could enjoy the pool, relax."

Lily stood up quickly and walked toward her improvised mystery board on the refrigerator door. "No. I'm staying here. I just hope they don't dig up the yard too much."

Dev turned to watch Lily studying her post-its. As he turned to face his well-meaning neighbor, he grimaced. "You don't know what she's like. She's in this now."

"Like some sort of character in an Agatha novel?" Mrs. Parrot asked.

Dev chuckled. "Nope. It's more like Jessica from those old television shows. You had a great idea, but she won't budge. Besides, I said I'd help her go over all the information."

Mrs. Parrot's eyes grew wide. "You mean you're okay with all of this?" The retired school teacher swept her hand over the papers on the kitchen table and toward the wallpaper of post-its.

Dev thought about his answer. He shouldn't be, but he loved Lily. He shrugged shyly. His thin smile alarmed his neighbor. "She's good at it. She sees things. But this time, I'm going to be her partner."

"So there's been other times?"

Dev crossed his arms in front of his chest and leaned back casually in his chair. He sensed Lily was in her world, studying every small square of evidence.

"The first time we met, she helped thwart a drug dealer. Then less than a year later she served as the bait to catch the same sociopath. On our honeymoon, she discovered drugs at a gala, after that she worked with my friends to take down an international terrorist. This time, I'll be by her side."

Mrs. Parrot shook her head. "Dev, you have your hands full with that one." She pointed at Lily.

Dev saw action outside. He stood up quickly and walked past his neighbor. He patted her shoulder. "You have no idea." Lily barely heard him as he closed the back door behind him.

Mrs. Parrot studied Lily for a few minutes while she drank her diet soda. She reminded her of a student she had one time that used post-it notes to outline a term paper. That young lady eventually became a police detective. She never cared how a student organized their work, as long as it was good work. *Hmm, maybe I need to get a package of those things.*

Lily turned back toward her guest. "I'm so sorry. I thought I saw something in my notes." She stretched her neck to find Dev's form in the backyard. She hadn't even heard him leave.

"Lily, I think I'll head back home, but you yell if you need me for anything." Mrs. Parrot came over and took both of Lily's hands. "Why don't you step back and take a break? Then, think of this as a term paper, a history thesis. Outline, plot it out, and then come to a conclusion with the facts you have."

"Oh my gosh, you're right. Not today though. I need to find out what my yard guests discover, and then I can go on from there. Thank you." Lily's face was bright as though it was being lit with an imaginary hue of realization. "And I will call you if I need you."

"Lily, you've got a good partner there." Mrs. Parrot pointed toward Dev.

Lily's face continued to beam. "I know. Sometimes, he's not as much fun as his friends, but he's the best."

As Mrs. Parrot gathered up her bag and headed for the door, she wondered about Dev's friends. With her hand on the door knob, she had to ask one thing. "Who are his friends, honey?"

Lily laughed. "Well, it's sort of like a bad joke, but there's a lawyer, a priest, and a Navy SEAL. Oh, and then there's his brother, the FBI agent who hunts down international art, and my buddy, the secret agent who makes Bond look like a school boy."

Mrs. Parrot's eyes grew wide. "My, my, my. Call me when that secret agent drops by."

Chapter Nine

It was nearly six in the evening when the last van left with the agents and any evidence that had been found. Jack Pierce arrived at the door at the request of his son. It was about time Dev and Lily had a night off. He didn't understand how they had lasted this long. His wife, Bernie, and he needed a night off after six weeks of no sleep when Dev turned from the perfect baby into one experiencing colic. Bernie and he had called her mother. She entertained the baby while they went into the bedroom and slept for three straight hours.

"Your emergency babysitter is here," he announced as Dev led him into the living room. "Where's my grandson?"

Andrew looked up, smiled, and ran toward him. "DaDa."

Jack was pleasantly surprised. "We'll work on that, but what a smart boy you are. It's good that you two are getting out."

"Oh, we'll be in the kitchen," Dev answered as he headed in that direction.

"The kitchen? Okay. Um, should I take Andrew upstairs so you two can have some privacy?" *To do whatever the heck you two are going to do.*

Dev waved his hand. "No problem. You can listen to us."

Bewildered by the statement, Jack followed his son into the kitchen. Lily stood in front of a refrigerator decorated with a bonanza of colored post-its. On the kitchen table sat two filled boxes and papers strewn everywhere.

"What are you two up to?"

"Lily found a dead body in the yard," Dev answered nonchalantly.

Lily turned around and smiled at her father-in-law. "Technically, I found Chief's bones."

"Maggie's dog?"

Dev nodded and took a seat at the table. "Yep. Then the FBI found the human skeletal remains."

Jack motioned to get Dev's attention. "Son, is Lily becoming obsessed with crime?" Jack whispered.

"Not really, Dad. It just seems to find her. I'm getting used to it."

Jack shook his head in disbelief. He really didn't know what to think about either one of them. Dev pulled photos from one of the boxes and showed Lily. She directed him to place the photos in a pile. She began to pull note after note and rearrange them on the refrigerator door.

"Well then, Andrew and I will be in the living room. Has he eaten?" Jack waited for anyone's attention. "Lily, has Andrew eaten yet?" He waited. He raised his voice. "Lily, Dev, have you fed this child?"

Lily and Dev turned quickly and gave every attention to the man holding the baby.

"Jack, I'm so sorry. Yes, we fed him. Dev was going to throw steaks on the grill for the three of us. Are you good with that?"

Jack came over to Lily. "I'd be better with a beer in my hand, and you two relaxing for a bit. I'm thinking all of this can wait." He waved his hand around the kitchen.

Lily gazed over at Dev. Her father-in-law was absolutely correct. All of this could wait. The mystery of a missing woman and her identification, who apparently wasn't very well liked, a bullet, a purse, a bloody shoe, and shirt, and now the bones of a body in her backyard shouldn't be that important. Her face flushed with embarrassment.

"Jack, you're right. All of this can wait. Dev, let's stop. I'll grab your Dad's beer, you fire up the grill. It's family time."

Dev saluted, and quickly headed out the back door.

Lily kissed Jack on the cheek. "I get carried away with all of this. I'm sorry." She wiped away the tears forming in her eyes. "I don't know why I need this."

Andrew reached for his mother, and she took him quickly into her arms. She kissed the top of his head and brushed a curl off his forehead.

Jack sat down at the table as Lily grabbed his drink. He flipped through a few of the photos on the stack. "Lily, I remember this. I read this reporter's column every day."

Lily joined him and moved a stack away from Andrew's reaching hands. "Mr. Livingood gave me all of this stuff. He thinks this woman is still alive, and that she had something to do with the death of a doctor. The man died after giving her a ride home to this house."

"Margot Fleischman," Jack murmured and then took a drink. "Have you checked with Maggie and Maureen about the doc? You know, he's a big fan of their wine and visits the vineyard frequently."

Lily's confusion showed on her face. "Wait a minute. I thought you didn't want me doing all of this investigating."

"No, just don't allow it to run your life. Obviously, you're good at noticing details. Dev admits you do have a talent."

Lily laughed nervously. "A talent for getting myself into pickles."

Jack nodded. "It's not the pickles. It's the jams you get stuck in. See what I did with that?"

"Very funny. I better get your son a beer or he can't seem to grill effectively without it. Here's your grandson." She passed the baby back into his very willing hands. Andrew was soon laughing, his hair rising up and down as his grandfather bounced him on his knee.

Lily arrived outside, placing the open beer into Dev's hand. Then she reached up and kissed him.

"I'm not complaining, but what was that for?" He smiled, enjoying her arm extended around his back.

"For loving me, no matter how neurotic I get."

"That's an easy thing to do." Dev kissed her on her head. "I'll need the steaks in just a few minutes."

"You think I should drop all of this, don't you?" Lily's voice was low and measured.

Dev sipped from his bottle then laid it down on the table next to the grill. He took Lily into his arms. "I've never said that. I just worry that one day you might go too far. I can't, I won't live without you. You've changed my life."

Lily laughed and then snorted. "Not for the better sometimes."

Dev looked down into her eyes and held her closer. "I wouldn't say that. You do make my life exciting, even when I don't want it to be. I thought my job gave me enough of that. Heck, my entire adult life has given me enough of that. I'm not sure why you do what you do, but this time I'm your partner. You're not getting rid of me."

His wife placed her head on his chest. "I wouldn't want to, besides if you won't be my partner in this investigation, I might have to call Gretchen."

Dev pulled away. He gathered his grilling tools of the trade and threatened his wife. "Don't, just don't! No more Gretchen."

"Oh crap," Lily exclaimed. "I still haven't called Abby. I read the announcement, and she put a post-it note in with it apologizing for not checking in with me. She wanted me to call her. I'm losing my mind!"

"And you can't blame it on the baby brain anymore." Dev led his wife into the kitchen to look for the steaks in the refrigerator. "But maybe you can?" He had the package of meat in his hand when he turned to face her. "Are you sure you're not pregnant?"

Jack's attention was piqued. His gaze fell on Lily. Her face had gone white.

"I, I don't think so, but that would explain the tears today, and the foggy brain. Oh, and the fact I couldn't stop eating those lemon bars. But I don't know." Lily was thinking, she was counting and remembering. "Huh. That might be it." Nonchalantly, she pushed past Dev to check the potatoes in the oven.

"Honey, that's all you're going to say?" Dev was perplexed by her calm demeanor.

"I microwaved the potatoes a little, and now I'm finishing them up in the oven. I just need to mix the salad so get out there and grill." Dev was stoic and unmoving. Finally, Lily pushed him out the door, literally.

As she turned back around to her father-in-law and son, she began to laugh. "Did you see his face?"

"Do you see my face?" Jack asked. "I'm in shock. Are you?"

"I might be. That would explain everything, including this obsession with a mystery. It happened with Andrew. My body incubates a baby, and my brain goes into overdrive. But, seriously, I blame it all on Dev."

Jack shook his head in confusion. "Lily, that's usually how it works. Do I need to explain the birds and bees to you?"

Now, Lily cocked her head in confusion. "What?" She thought about it a second and then laughed. "Oh no, not that. I blame all this crime stuff on him. Before he walked into my life, the only mystery I was involved in was on the television. Dev gave me a taste of this life, and I enjoy putting all the pieces together. It's all his fault."

Jack nodded in mock agreement. "Of course it is, dear."

"Besides, I've learned one thing, always blame the husband. He has broad shoulders." Lily turned on her heel to check on the progress of the steaks outside.

Jack looked at his smiling grandson. "Andrew, your mommy has it all figured out, doesn't she? Well, she thinks she does. You may be getting a little brother or sister, or mommy may find a woman who's been missing for years."

Andrew screeched in delight as if he understood every word. Or perhaps he screeched in fear as if he understood every word.

Later that night, after Andrew had finally fallen asleep, Lily listened to Dev's breathing as he laid beside her. *How can the man just lay down and immediately go to sleep? If it really is Army training, then I need it.* Her mind was racing, but not about the mystery. She had finally called Abby. Both of them had apologized to each other. Life was definitely getting in the way of their friendship. The distance, and not just in miles, was widening. But after a few sentences of catching up and acknowledging that they needed to do better, they were right back on track. Abby even asked Lily to put together her wedding flowers. The couple were marrying the same week of Dev and Lily's wedding anniversary. Lily smiled at that. They'd celebrate their day in Kansas City where they had begun their lives together.

Lily heard Andrew cry out. She raised slowly out of bed and stopped. There wasn't another sound. *Thank the Lord.* As Lily crawled back into bed, Dev rolled over.

"Everything okay?"

"Yes. Andrew cried out, but I guess he went back to sleep. Oh, and we're going to Kansas City."

"Isn't there a song that begins like that?" Dev mumbled. He shifted the sheet over her body and allowed his arm to linger over her breasts. "I've been meaning to ask, do you really think you're pregnant? You didn't drink tonight, and the other night you didn't finish your meal."

Lily stifled a giggle. Her husband was finally concerned about the discussion they had earlier in the evening. "Wine didn't sound good to me, and I was full. That really doesn't mean anything. But, I'll take a test. I'll get one tomorrow."

"How do you feel about this possibility?"

Lily turned her head. Her lips were only inches away from Dev's full, luscious ones. She kissed him fiercely. "Frankly, I'm not sure. Another pregnant summer might just do me in, and now we have a walking, running toddler who will turn two. I may be a little nastier than the last time."

Dev nuzzled her ear. "You're never nasty."

He'd made the statement believable. "Oh, I'm so going to remember you said that when you complain about my attitude again."

"I don't complain about you."

She turned her body to meet his. "Never?"

Dev knew he was treading in very dangerous waters. Where was the Navy SEAL when he needed him? "I don't remember ever complaining about you."

She kissed him again and smiled. "Do you want me to list the times in severity or chronological order?"

Dev pulled her closer so there was no space between them. "I suppose you have a list or two?"

"Of course," Lily admitted confidently. She pointed to her head. "It's all right in here, buddy."

Dev laughed loudly. "Unless you're pregnant. Your brain gets scattered, and you can't remember a thing."

"Hmm. I have no answer for that. But I do know we'll be celebrating our anniversary back home, and you will be helping me do the wedding flowers for Abby and Jeremy."

Dev glanced his hand across her forehead, removing an errant curl. "I've been told I'm very proficient carrying boxes and doing what I'm told. Oh, and I remember no talking to the wedding coordinator, especially if it's Gretchen."

Lily smiled. "Especially Gretchen, Agent Pierce. Are you sure you're up for this?"

Dev's eyes sparkled even in the darkness. "Are we still talking about wedding flowers or have we moved onto something else?"

His low whispered question warmed Lily immediately. She kissed each of his cheeks and then lingered her lips on his. "Are we?"

There was no way to pull her any closer, but Dev did his best. He was certainly up for this, all of this.

Chapter Ten

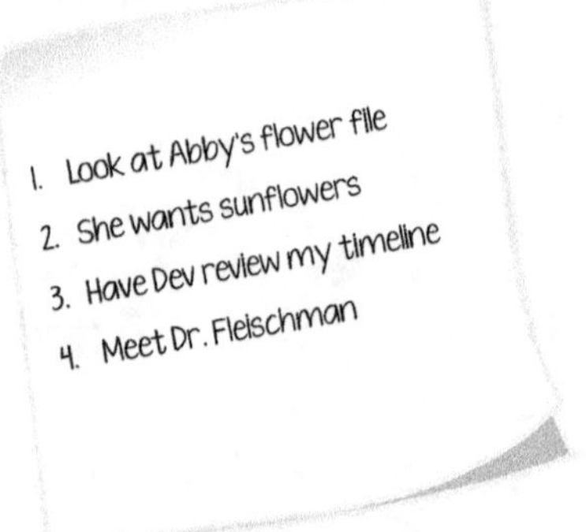

"Dev, we have to go to the vineyard today," Lily said as she attempted to pull him out of bed Saturday morning.

"No, you have to go get one of those pregnancy tests. You've been putting it off all week," Dev grumbled. Lily had managed to pull him up into a sitting position, but he wasn't budging past the bed.

"That'll wait. Your aunt said Dr. Fleischman made a reservation for around eleven this morning. I don't want to miss him."

Dev held his head with two hands. This past week had been miserable with an emergency trip down to the Texas border. He couldn't tell Lily that he'd been in a shootout with a drug dealer. He couldn't tell her that the worthless man smuggled girls, as young as eight and sold them into prostitution slavery. He couldn't tell her that it was hard to smile despite her joyful energy surrounding him. *She's dressed already! I'm going to the vineyard.*

"Fine, but I'm drinking." He stood up slowly and began the short walk to the bathroom.

"Are you going to be in there very long?" Lily asked.

Dev peeked his head out. "At least let me take a shower." He looked over at the clock. "Geez, honey, it's only seven."

"I know. I don't want to be late."

Dev closed the bathroom door and sighed. Lifting his eyes to the ceiling, Dev said a silent prayer. *She's acting like, like…crud, she's pregnant.*

During the car ride west, Lily babbled about the timeline. She figured that one key component was the weekly flower delivery. She just needed the doctor to confirm that he had **not** sent the blooms to his wife. She suspected he hadn't. That would mean that either Margot was having an affair, possibly with the doctor who went missing before her. It could also mean that the flower shop had something to do with her disappearance.

Eventually, Lily realized her husband was unusually quiet. She looked back at Andrew. Their beautiful boy was in blissful sleep. She placed her hand on Dev's shoulder and rubbed slowly.

"Are you mad because I didn't go get the test?"

Dev looked quickly over at her and then back to the road ahead. "Of course not. You'll do it when you do it."

"Then, is it work related?"

Dev winced, and she saw it. "Sorry, but yes. Of course, I can't talk about it. You'll see it in the papers."

Lily brushed her fingers in through his hair. He needed a cut, but it was nice to be able to run her hand through the dark locks now and then. Her wedding ring caught her eyes as it shined in the sun. "I love you, and I know I get carried away." *Thanks Lord, for this man.*

Dev smiled. "You think?"

"It's exciting. I blame you for my interest in crime."

Dev shook his head and laughed out loud. "Sure, it's my fault."

"Well it is," Lily responded, but she laughed too. "You walked into my life and enmeshed me in chaos."

"And took you away from your home," Dev said coolly.

Lily's face fell. "What are you talking about? My home is here with you and Andrew."

"You called Kansas City your home, that you were going back home. You know, I will transfer there for you. I will move for you. I'll do anything for you."

You dear, dear man. Lord, you gave me a good one. He was well worth the wait. Lily pulled her hand from his head and touched his lower arm. "It really was just a word, Dev. My home is where you are, and I don't regret for one second moving here, being your wife, and Andrew's mother. Heck, just a few years ago, I never thought I'd have a baby, much less a love that almost hurts because it is so unreal sometimes. I don't want you to do anything for me. I want you to be you, and you are a very good man. I think you're the best man I've ever known."

Dev answered with silence. Perhaps he was processing or just taking in the moment. "Unless Ari is around, or Danny, or JT."

Lily saw the impish grin develop on his face. "Well, that is true."

"I love you too, now let's go interview that doctor."

And that's why I love you!

Lily knew they should've left earlier, but Dev had to take that shower, and then the man had to eat for some reason. Then Andrew ate more because his daddy had to eat breakfast, and she had to completely change his outfit, not to mention change the world's most hideous diaper. *That kid loves bananas, but boy does he poop when he eats them!* Her son was now dressed in a white and blue sailor suit which Gretchen had purchased. *Gretchen and her sailors!*

Dev parked at the back of the main house at the vineyard and held Andrew in his arms. "I think I'll just keep him today. He and I can walk around while you snoop." All he was really thinking was he didn't want to lift the stroller out of the back of the car. His shoulder was still stinging after he'd hit the floor for cover during the gunfire. But Lily didn't need to know that. She'd already seen him once this morning, but he'd begged off that it was an old injury. He'd claimed that it must be going to rain.

"Honey?" He watched her scan the open seating in front of the house. In the spring, the vineyard featured long picnic tables for guests to gather around. His aunts were hosting a wine party that evening, complete with a live band. But Lily wasn't listening to him. Her neck was stretching to see something, anything. "Honey, Maggie will know him. Just cool it until we get over there."

"What?" Lily turned her head to face him. *Crud, I wasn't listening to him. He said something about Andrew, didn't he?* Dev just stood there, waiting. Her attention had been lost again.

Dev began to stalk, passing her. "Come on. Let's go find your doctor."

Lily walked behind as though she was a scolded child, but he hadn't said anything. He knew she hadn't been listening, and she knew she hadn't been listening. She walked a little faster to place her arm in through his. She saw him wince.

"Okay, what's up? That's the second time today." Lily removed her arm and stopped walking.

Dev silently uttered a profanity. "I told you, it's just an old injury."

"Which hasn't bothered you until now, after you've been away doing God knows what." Disdain dripped from her every word. "What did you do to it?"

Dev rolled his eyes and kept walking. "I slammed it down on a hard pavement. I'll ice it later."

Lily hurried her pace to walk next to him. "We need to talk about this."

"Nope. We don't. Look, there's Maureen." Dev pointed to one of his aunts as Andrew shifted in his arms. He let him down, holding onto one of his small hands. Andrew began to walk to the open arms of one of his favorite relatives.

Maureen clapped her hands as Andrew jumped into her arms. "Oh my goodness. Look at you go, little man. You are so cute. You're such an adorable sailor, Andrew."

"Dev doesn't like that outfit very much," Lily admitted as she hugged the woman. "Do you, honey?"

"Hi Aunt Mo," he said as he pecked her cheek. "Gretchen gave him that outfit. I'm not sure why she can't find camouflage."

Maureen nuzzled Andrew. "Because Daddy, camo isn't as flattering as navy blue." She ignored Dev's sullen gaze and focused on Lily. "Blue really is his color."

Dev let out a heavy sigh, and headed over to his other aunt. *Maybe Maggie will be a bit more friendly. And she is the one doing the pouring today.*

Maureen looked over at Lily. "Why is he in such a mood?"

Lily watched him meet up with his other aunt. She studied her husband. He was hurting, and it possibly wasn't just the shoulder that had been bruised. "I'm not sure. I think he's dealing with something."

Maureen shook her head knowingly. "But he can't tell you because of his job. I used to hate that when my husband used to go radio silent on me. He'd always say I'd see it on the news."

"That's what he said to me," Lily murmured. Maureen's husband had been a detective on a police force. He'd dealt with homicides. Lily could only imagine what the man had seen.

Maureen lowered Andrew down to the gravel and held on tightly to his hand. "Have patience."

Lily smiled. "You have no idea how patient I have been with him since the day I met him." *If Maureen or Maggie had seen him that day she had pushed him away, and he had left, they would've slapped him into tomorrow. But I had to let him go. Not for him, but for me.* Lily's smile faded with the memory. That day had been one of the saddest in her life. She could've been nice and submissive, but he had driven confidence into her, and she exhibited it that day. Of course, she'd also cried for hours afterward, and ordered a large pizza. *Then I went to the grocery store and bought a pint of neapolitan ice cream because I couldn't decide what flavor I really wanted. Ice cream, that's what I need, and so does Dev!*

Her eyes brightened. More life came to her face when Dev's Aunt Maggie motioned her over and pointed to a lone man sitting at the end of one of the tables. He was savoring a new spring pinot.

Lily knew the doctor immediately. She knew his face from all of the newspaper articles. She could see his crystal blue eyes from a distance. They were soft, nothing like that of a killer, well she didn't think so anyway. The police were fixated on his hiring of a hitman, but never found one shred of evidence. In fact, the doctor had freely given them all of his accounts. The IRS went over every filing. No connection was ever found.

Maggie left the bottle in Dev's capable hands, pinched Andrew's chubby cheek, and grabbed Lily. She took her to the doctor. "I'll introduce you. I told him you were doing some work with that reporter. He likes the man so he suspects nothing. I told him you were a writer."

Lily stopped and pulled Maggie back. "What? You told him I was a writer?"

"Yes. In fact, I never told your name so if you want to invent one, now is the time. How about Jessica?"

Lily frowned, her eyebrows touching. "Seriously?"

Maggie laughed. "I thought it was funny. Come on, let me introduce you."

As soon as they neared him, Dr. Fleischman stood and extended his hand to Lily. "You must be the writer."

Lily shrugged. "Actually, I'm an investigator. Thank you for talking to me for a bit."

He motioned to the bench opposite him. "Please sit down. I don't mind. I'm Leland Fleischman, of course you know that."

Lily took his hand as she sat down. "I'm Lily Pierce."

"She's our niece, Lee. Mr. Livingood gave her all his research so he must trust her," Maggie said. She patted the doctor on the back. "I think she wants to help you."

He smiled broadly. "That would be a nice change. The last couple of decades have been uncomfortable to say the least. Please, Ms. Pierce, ask me anything you want."

Lily nodded. She looked directly into his eyes and then retrieved a notebook from her purse. She also removed several photos. "Please call me Lily. I want to see if you can give me any clarification on a few discrepancies I've discovered."

As Maggie walked away, she shook her head. She patted Dev on the back. "We all knew Lily was something, but we had no idea--"

"That she was this special?" Dev focused his view on her. She immediately looked up and smiled at him. He stood up straighter with pride and regretted the motion immediately. His shoulder was hurting. "Aunt Mags, what do you have to get rid of pain?"

Maureen came up with Andrew in her arms. "He has a hurt shoulder."

Dev was surprised, but then again, he should know better. "So my wife told you?"

"Of course," she answered smugly. "We figured you hurt it by doing whatever you were doing. But you can't tell anyone about what you were doing because, well, you can't. You'd have to kill us. Right?"

Dev's eyes glared at his perceptive aunt. "Not yet."

Both ladies cringed. "We better get this man a drink," Maureen said quickly. She tickled Andrew under his shoulder. "And get this little guy some fruit."

Dev took another glance at his very intent wife as he walked into the barn. He laughed. "Oh, he loves bananas, lots and lots of bananas." *Note to self, do not take on diaper duty for the next couple of days.*

An hour later, Dev had completely forgotten about his shoulder, and his son sat on his lap eating mashed bananas. Thankfully, Dev had a very large towel over himself as protection. However, the sailor suit was now yellow, blue and white. "This sangria is so good. I can taste the cherries."

Maureen was puzzled. "How can you taste that? You are absolutely potted." She pushed a new tray of sausage and assorted cheeses in front of her nephew. "Eat."

"I have a very refined palette. My nose knows cherries." Dev laughed out loud at his own joke. Andrew joined in. His small hand reached up and smoothed banana mush all over his father's chin.

Maureen rose up and wiped Andrew's face. "Bananas are great for the skin." She grabbed his small fists and cleaned them thoroughly. "Give me the boy. I'm going to get him suitable for his mother. You can take the bib home." She had tied one of their vineyard towels around the baby's neck.

Dev casually turned around to look at Lily. She was smiling. He took another drink of sangria. *I have to take some of this home. Lily will love it, but not more than her new mystery.* He attempted to read her emotions and what she was thinking about the man she continued to interview. The doctor had to be patient to be interrogated for an hour or more by now. *Or perhaps he's intrigued and just using my wife?* Dev downed the red liquid and stood up. Lily noticed him and hailed him over.

Get it together. Don't act like you've drunk way too much. But I have. Dev walked slowly. After a few deep breaths, he smiled as he arrived at the table. Lily scooted over so he could sit by her.

"Doctor, this is my husband, Dev." Lily watched as Dev pasted a huge smile on his face and extended his hand.

"I've enjoyed speaking with your wife. She's given me renewed hope that someone might find my wife, no matter the outcome."

Dev pulled back his hand slowly. "No matter the outcome, Doctor?"

Lily saw the doctor's expression change in a second. *What is Dev doing?*

Dr. Fleischman leaned back a bit and crossed his arms across his chest. For the first time, Lily noticed that the man was fit for his age. His chest was broad, his arms were well tanned and muscled. His physique made her think he played a lot of golf, a natural thing for a doctor. Especially one who has been retired for several years now.

"Yes, sir. No matter what. Not knowing what happened to my wife does keep me up at night. If she is out there somewhere, I want to know where and why. If she is dead, well, I've assumed that's the case for some time now."

Dev's eyes narrowed, but his lips formed a thin smile. "Did you love her?"

"Yes, yes, I did," the man answered softly. "I will admit that if she is alive and did this on purpose for some reason to get even with me, then I could care less about seeing her again. Wouldn't you think the same thing?"

Lily hit Dev's left leg with her fist. He turned to her, his eyes asking why she did that. But he knew why.

He faced the doctor and shook his head. "I don't know what I would do or how you must've felt when all of this first happened. I can't imagine living all these years without knowing what happened to her."

Dev softened his tone. Lily was relieved that he had centered himself and stopped acting like the DEA agent he was. He smiled again, but this time she cocked her head to the side, peering around to see his face. *Is he drunk? He **IS** drunk!*

"What are you drinking, Dev?" the Doctor asked.

Dev smirked. "Today, just about everything. The sangria is very good."

"Lily, how about a bottle of sangria, and let's get some food," the interviewee suggested.

"Sure, that sounds great." Lily's answer sent the doctor into the barn to do the ordering. As soon as he was out of ear shot, Lily turned on Dev. "What the hell were you doing? I've been having a great conversation, and you come in like John Wayne."

Dev smiled from ear-to-ear. "You think I'm like John Wayne? That's the coolest thing you've ever said to me."

Lily didn't know whether to slap him sober or chuckle at his drunkenness. She would definitely be driving home today. *And where is our son?*

"What have you done with Andrew?"

"Mo has him. By now, Mags probably has him. I'm not sure."

"Oh great. You've lost our son," Lily muttered. She paged through her notebook to look over a couple of scribblings. Dev began to nuzzle her ear. "Stop that." She swatted lightly at his cheek.

"I want you right now."

His lips hit her sweet spot at the back of her neck. She straightened her back and planted her feet firmly on the ground under the table. She turned quickly to stop him and ran into his mouth. He'd been waiting. The long kiss took her breath away.

"Can we please wait until we get home?" she asked against his mouth.

"Must we?"

She pulled her head away slowly. "We must." They both smiled. His eyes twinkled. *I hate it, and I love it when he does that.* By now, she realized he could be the most charming of men, and one of the sexiest. *Honey, you aren't John Wayne as a soldier, you're the Duke when he plants that kiss on the redhead in that Irish movie.*

Dev smiled widely. "Promise?"

"I promise. Maybe we should wait until after you sober up," she suggested.

He shook his head. "Nope. I'm better when I've had a few."

"Alright then. Mr. Delicious, you need to cool it and let me get a few more details, please."

Dr. Fleischman returned, and Dev didn't agree or disagree. Lily just had to hope for the best.

In a few minutes, Aunt Maggie brought over three glasses and a pitcher of red sangria with sliced peaches, apples, and oranges floating through the liquid. One of her vineyard servers placed plates around and deposited a platter in the middle of the table. The charcuterie plate included various cheeses, more fruit, vegetables, assorted meats, crackers and fresh bread.

Lily's eyes widened. The vineyard did provide some fabulous food, but she'd never seen this spread before. All three of them dug in. Happily, Dev continued with idle talk, discussing golf, hobbies, and what the doctor did to fill his time. The two men enjoyed a few laughs while Lily picked through the sliced vegetables. The doctor freely began to speak of his daughter. She was an attorney now in Charlottesville. She had a small practice, a great husband, and two little girls. Dev admitted he wanted a little girl the next time.

Lily almost spit out the olive she had bitten into. *Oh geez, he sounds like Gretchen now.* Her friend had already decorated one of the bedrooms upstairs for a little girl when Lily was carrying Andrew. They would be ready for a little girl. Lily leaned her head on her hand as she listened to Dev speak tenderly about having a female sibling for their son.

"I grew up with a brother, but I can't wait for a daughter. I can't imagine what that bond is like between a girl and her dad. I'd love to hold her little hand, carry her from the car when it rains, and help her build her first snowman."

Lily watched his face and saw in her mind every picture he painted with his words. *I love this man so much. Oh crap, I'm drinking.* She quickly pushed her glass in front of her husband. "Here, you drink this. I'll stay with my water." Dev happily drained her glass.

"And I'd kill anyone who tried to hurt my little girl. Did your wife get along with your daughter?" Dev's bold statement and question stunned Lily, but it was as though the doctor expected it at some point. Lily marveled at her husband's skills. He made the victim feel comfortable, all warm and fuzzy. In seconds, he changed his direction and went in for the kill. She was learning from a master.

Dr. Fleischman sighed. "Margot didn't get along with my girl. She didn't pretend to even try. I'd gone through a terrible time after my first wife died of breast cancer. My little girl needed a mother, and frankly, I needed a woman to just be there for me. When I met Margot, I thought I'd hit the jackpot. She was the one for me. She was kind, but she told me she wasn't mother material. I thought she would change. My daughter, Laurel, was such a love. I just figured--"

"But you were wrong," Dev interrupted. "Did she hurt your daughter?"

"No. She did nothing. I had a wonderful woman who acted as the housekeeper and nanny for Laurel. She was with us since my first wife's death." The man looked away, watching two children playing in the grassy area near the bandstand. "I was questioned by the police about all of this. I gave them an honest appraisal of the situation, and I ended up in jail overnight."

"Sometimes honesty isn't the best policy," Dev remarked as he leaned over Lily to pick up a pickle and a piece of salami. "How many times did they put you in jail?"

The doctor grabbed a few pieces of cheese. "At least a dozen. I was there overnight until my attorney bailed me out. Financially, it was devastating. They built a case against me, but I was in London at a conference, and they couldn't find any payment to some hit man. They presented a murder conspiracy indictment to the grand jury, but they refused to forward it to trial. But I never let my guard down."

Lily broke the conversation, or interrogation depending on which side of the table you were on, to stand. Both men looked up at her. "I need to find my son. You two enjoy." She patted Dev on the back and smiled at the other man. As she walked away she heard Dev ask another question. *Did he just ask him if he liked football?*

Lily found her child, blissfully playing with his two great aunts. "He doesn't even miss me, does he?" she asked as she walked up. But Andrew held up his arms to greet his mother.

"Right," Maureen answered. "Look at him. We're chopped liver when he sees you. How's your visit going with Mags' friend?"

Lily looked out to see her husband talking. "The expert is at work now. He's unbelievable. I can only imagine what he does when he's working."

"We all have to imagine, don't we?" Maggie asked. "He never talks about his job."

That's the truth! "I'm realizing that I'm in the minors compared to his skills," Lily commented. Andrew turned in her arms and placed his head on her shoulder. "We're going to have to go soon. The little guy is pooped."

"He's eaten, and Dev gave him some water. He took it from the glass. He's such a good little man." Maggie pinched his cheek and kissed Lily on the cheek. "Lily, we are so happy you are here."

"Thanks. I better go out there and rescue Dr. Fleischman from Agent Pierce." Both aunts laughed as Lily walked away. She sat down next to her husband again. Her son's bottom had lowered, and he was already sleeping. That gave them a little more time.

"Who do you think sent flowers to your wife?" Dev's question came out of the blue. Lily had just reached for a piece of bread and dropped it quickly. Dr. Fleischman took a quick drink and leaned in.

"I don't know. I didn't have a clue then, and I still don't. My daughter and I did a little investigating of our own. Do you know that the flower shop closed not too long after Margot went missing?"

"I looked into that," Dev admitted. Lily's mouth was now gaping widely. *Exactly when was he going to tell me that?*

"What did you find out? We couldn't get any answers." Lily could see the concern on Dr. Fleischman's face.

"I have contacts. That flower shop was seized by the DEA." Dev's sentence lingered, seemingly electrifying the air. All three of them sat up with the mere mention of the agency. Dev searched for a reaction. Either the doctor was surprised by the information or he was a very good actor, but Dev saw something. He saw a break in the man's carefully constructed cool facade.

"So, drugs were involved?" The doctor's gaze fixed on Dev.

"Yes. That's all I can say."

Lily noticed that the man across from them was nervous. Suddenly, sweat beaded his forehead. As if in prayer, he clutched his hands on the table.

"You need to look into it. At one time, the police accused me of selling drugs, prescription drugs. I didn't understand. I think my wife was forging my signature."

"What about Dr. Tolliver, the one who was killed after he gave your wife a ride home? Did he have any prescription problems?" Dev's tone was inquisitory, but smooth.

Dr. Fleischman nodded. "How did you know? He couldn't fight for himself, but his family contended it wasn't his signature either."

Dev reached for a piece of cheese and ate slowly. "So, both of you had this problem, and both of you had one mutual acquaintance."

"My wife," the doctor murmured. "My daughter suspected she had something to do with all of that. My God, after all these years--"

"Secrets don't always stay secret," Dev said quietly.

Lily's admiration for her husband grew daily, but today it had soared. He'd learned more over one glass of sangria than she had in an hour. But it was time to go home. The mystery had to wait.

"Doctor, I can't thank you enough for visiting with us today," Lily admitted. "We've taken up too much of your time, and we need to get home."

Dev peeked at his son's face. He was down for the count. So was Dev. He'd pulled himself together enough to question the doctor, but now his head was spinning. Lily would have to drive home.

"Yes, Doctor. It was wonderful speaking with you," Dev said. He extended his hand across the table, and the man took it.

"I really did enjoy it. I mean, it's hard thinking about all of that again. I've had a good life, but I've always wondered, and I've been angry. I knew I wasn't guilty, but try telling that to the police when they are looking to wrap up a mystery." He smiled at Lily. "And Lily, I thank you for looking into this. Mr. Livingood believed in me, and that meant so much to me at the time."

"Well, it is certainly baffling," Lily admitted. "It would make a great story some day."

"Yes, some day." The doctor commented sadly.

Lily and Dev said their goodbyes to the aunts and headed to the car quietly. It wasn't until Dev opened the car doors that he said something.

"He didn't do it, but he knows more than he's admitting. He's fearful that we know more than we should. He thinks he snowed your reporter friend, and he fancies himself as smooth and much more intelligent than all of us. More than ever, I feel in my gut that Margot is still out there."

Lily slowly lowered Andrew into the car seat and buckled him in slowly. Dev started the car but jumped out of the driver's seat. He came around to the passenger side as Lily closed the door softly.

"You'll have to drive, honey."

She smiled and placed her arms around his waist. "You think?"

He winked and placed a soft kiss on her nose. "I know."

"Okay, but if Andrew wakes up, you're going to have to give him one of those juice boxes."

Dev saluted as she made her way in front of the car. "I shall do as ordered."

As Lily pulled out of the vineyard, she looked over at her husband. Another mile or two and he'd be sleeping like a baby too. "Dev, what about that flower shop and the DEA?"

"It was seized. The DEA had a sting operation. The shop was dealing drugs, mostly prescription. So the story is becoming more complicated and yet some things are clearer."

Lily's mind began to race and she visualized her post-it notes. She did some of her best thinking while driving in Virginia. "So, who was buried in the backyard?"

"The driver. That same driver delivered those flowers every week. There was a trade happening. Margot was definitely messing with those prescriptions. I'll pull the files next week when I get back into the office. I have a theory."

Lily shoved her sunglasses on her face. "Are you going to share with me?"

"When I can. Something is really nagging at me. Oh, I forgot to tell you that we have another wedding later this year. Carlos and Alise have set a date for sometime in October."

He's so good at distracting! Fine, you get away with it this time. "That is wonderful. Where are they having it?"

Dev leaned his spinning head back onto the headrest. "Some beach. Carlos said that if Angelica gets her way, it'll be held at an amusement park in Orlando."

"Alise's daughter usually does get her way. That little girl could manipulate the devil to do good, and she can twist you around her little finger." Lily glanced over at her almost-sleeping husband. Dev might be a master investigator, but she had skills too. She knew the right time to ask. "So you saw Carlos on this operation? That's interesting. What else happened? Were little girls involved?"

Dev nodded his head. "Yes."

"Honey, I know the party line of I can't tell you or I have to kill you, yadda, yadda, but what made you so upset?"

Dev's head raised up. "I saw a little girl who should be running on a playground with her fifth grade classmates. Instead, she was sold into slavery as a prostitute for a middle aged man. But there wasn't just her. There were more, but I can't get her face out of my head."

Lily continued to drive. For once, she had no words. Dev had said everything. *Maybe the little girl looked like the one from Afghanistan that haunts him some nights?* "Dev, your work is very noble. You saved her, right?"

"Yes, but the damage has been done." His voice was cold, devoid of any emotion, but obviously, his act of sharing was the admission of a hurting heart.

"But you all saved her, and all of them," Lily insisted. "I just appreciate you telling me why you are so upset. You just don't get drunk like that."

"I'm not that drunk." He rubbed her shoulder and checked on his sleeping son with a side glance. "I noticed that you didn't drink the sangria, and you stayed away from the cheese."

"Amazing. You must be some kind of secret agent." Her sarcasm was met with laughter.

"I keep telling you I have my own skills. Apparently, I'm just observant as my list-making wife. You're pregnant, aren't you?"

Lily continued to stare straight ahead as she wove her way through tree-lined streets before reaching the interstate. "I haven't taken the test. I was just being careful just in case the cheese wasn't pasteurized. You certainly don't miss anything, even when you've been drinking wine all afternoon."

"And I can interrogate a suspect too."

"Well, aren't you special?" Lily responded quickly. Yes, he had learned more in a few questions than she had in an hour. But she had gained some knowledge that he hadn't, but now wasn't the time to share. He was beginning to irritate her with his perfection.

Dev smiled that silly smile that melted her heart. She could feel his intense gaze.

"Yes, yes I am."

With the certainty that Andrew was sound asleep and couldn't understand the word she was about to say, she called her husband an ass, and she felt very good about it. Dev chuckled, laid his head back again, and this time he slept the remainder of the drive home.

Chapter Eleven

One week later, Lily talked to Abby before she began her workload for Mother's Day, checked in with Gretchen on Abby's wedding, filled in her mystery outline with a few more details, and had purchased the pregnancy test. She hadn't done anything with it except hide it in her drawer in the master bathroom. She knew what the result would be, but for some reason, she was frightened. She didn't know why, but she was.

She was also uncertain about this Mother's Day. This would be her first with Dev home. Last year, he had been called away two days before. She opened the gifts while sitting in the middle of the floor in Andrew's room. She had cried while the baby slept. Now, Lily sat in Andrew's room, rocking him back to sleep in the middle of the night after he had screamed out into the night. She kissed his head. Their lives would change if she was pregnant. *Little man, you're not going to be the star of the show if mommy has another baby.* She should be overjoyed that she was probably pregnant. *Oh great. The doctor is going to call it a geriatric pregnancy again. Or maybe ancient?*

Lily looked up to see Dev's form in the doorway. "He's asleep again. It must've been a bad dream. I was just going to put him down," she whispered.

Dev came over to her and removed his son's limp body from her arms. He carefully placed him in his bed and patted him on the back. When he turned to Lily, he held out his hand to her, lifting her from the rocking chair. He said nothing as he led her back to their room.

"Happy Mother's Day," he whispered before he kissed her softly. Bringing up his other hand to her cheek, he lifted her face up. "I love you, now come back to bed."

"Oh, I see where this is going," Lily joked.

One of Dev's brows rose in quizzical fashion. "Yes, to bed, to sleep. In fact, one of your gifts is the luxury of sleeping in today."

"We need to go to church."

"We can go later," Dev countered.

Lily's eyes narrowed. "You seem to have an answer for everything."

He released her face and took her hand again. "To bed with you, woman."

Lily climbed in on Dev's side, and as he joined her, she snuggled close to him. "Is there any news on our buried man in the backyard?"

"Yes."

She lightly hit his chest. "Come on. Give me something. It's Mother's Day, after all."

Dev reached around her body and cradled her in his arms. "Fine. You now know that the body in the backyard was definitely that of the florist delivery guy. And yes, the shop was closed and confiscated by the DEA all those years ago. But there was a serious op going on for a couple of months before the authorities swept in. I'll get the file next week when I'm in the office. So, what we know for now is--"

"Margot was involved in some capacity with drug dealing, prescription fraud, and maybe more. What I don't understand is why she married Dr. Fleischman in the first place. Obviously, she didn't want to be a mother to his daughter, and it doesn't look as though she really wanted the life of a doctor's wife. She was acting."

Dev shook his head. "You're right, of course. I keep thinking I've seen her somewhere before, and if she was involved in drugs, maybe I've seen her in the last few years."

"She's a drug dealer?" Lily suggested.

"I don't know. It looks like that, but I can't wrap my mind around this one. I saw your notes, and you've done an excellent job. Maybe do a little research on that other doctor who went missing. I think you really have missed your calling."

Lily looked up at him. "No, I haven't. I couldn't do what you do, to deal with what you see daily, weekly."

"What I see," Dev murmured. "You know, you just gave me an idea. I'm going to take her driver's license to one of our computer artists. Maybe they could run an age progression program. Maybe I have seen her, only now she's almost twenty years older."

"There you go again being special." Lily yawned before she could kiss him. She could barely keep her eyes open.

Dev turned her in his arms, leaning down to go in for a kiss. Instead, he smiled. Her eyes were shut firmly, a light snoring sound emanating from a wide-open mouth. *She's learned my secret to sleep!* He swiped hair away from her forehead and kissed her softly on the cheek. His plans with her would have to wait. He laid down again and stared into the darkness. Some of Lily's behavior had rubbed off on him. He began to make lists in his head. His wife was fleshing out the mystery of Margot Fleischman. She'd possibly uncovered two murders if not three, a drug operation, prescription fraud, and something else. He just couldn't figure out what that something was. But he had that nagging feeling that his wife might be heading into danger again.

A few hours later, Lily opened her eyes and was greeted by the sun shining into the bedroom. Dev had let her sleep in. She reached over to an empty side of the bed and sighed. *It's Mother's Day! And I'm not working.* There were no flowers to design and no last-minute deliveries to make. She often had these nightmares where she'd forgotten the flowers for a wedding or had to rush a delivery. But all that was behind her now. So instead, she stretched out like a cat, enjoying the benefit of having a devoted husband.

The door opened slowly to reveal Dev, Andrew, and a tray with food. It was adorned with a lovely single rose in a vase. "Good morning. Happy Mother's Day."

Andrew slowly ambled in, arriving at the bed for Lily to pick him up.

"Good morning." Andrew climbed onto her and did his version of a sloppy kiss on her cheek. She looked up at the food and her stomach curdled. "It looks--" She stopped and jumped off the bed, running into the bathroom.

Dev set the tray down and grabbed his son before he took a header off the bed. He listened to Lily as she threw up. He didn't know whether to smile or to frown. She sounded absolutely miserable. After a few minutes, he entered the bathroom. He placed cold water on a small towel and laid it on the back of her neck as she focused on the toilet bowl.

"Thanks," Lily answered weakly. "The food did look good. Can we warm it up in a bit?" She turned her head and looked up at her husband and son.

"Of course." Dev noticed her usually bright eyes were sunken with dark circles under them. "Honey, we don't have to do one thing today."

"Except go to church," Lily countered as she began to slowly rise up from her knees. "I want that special Mother's Day blessing, darn it! I've earned it."

"Later, we can go much later," Dev suggested. "I'll take the tray downstairs. Why don't you just go back to bed for a little bit?"

"Nope. I'm going to take a quick shower. Give me thirty minutes, and I'll be ready to eat. I remember how this works."

Dev said nothing. It wasn't the time to confirm her condition, but as he maneuvered Andrew down the stairs while balancing the tray, he smiled. He knew she was pregnant again.

True to form, Lily arrived in the kitchen thirty minutes later. She was dressed in a flowing light blue dress and sandals. "Now, I'm hungry."

Dev turned around from the sink and saw a transformed woman. "You look amazing. Do you want your gifts now or later?"

She sat down next to Andrew at the table. "Later. I'd really like that beautiful omelet now if you'd just warm it up. Oh, and I want that pastry and the fruit, please. What is the plan for our day?"

"Well, I guess we are going to church, per your orders. Then, we're going for ice cream at your favorite place. I'll be offering you a foot massage, and I'll be grilling our dinner."

Lily clapped and Andrew joined in. "That sounds like the perfect day."

Dev plated her food and waited until the microwave pinged to serve her. "It's all about you today." He kissed her on the head, but before he could move away, she tugged on his arm.

"And this is a gift for you." She placed a small item into his hand. It was the pregnancy test that she had been frightened to take. Her fears vanished.

Dev glanced down and only saw the plus sign. "And are we happy about this?"

She took a bite of the omelet and sighed. "Are we?"

Dev searched her face for an answer. He found no clues. "I'm thrilled, but you're the one who literally has to do the heavy lifting. Remember when we thought we might not be able to have children?"

Lily continued to eat. Every bite made her feel better, at least for now. "Oh, I remember. Apparently, that's not a problem, except the doctor is going to say I'm older than dirt. I just know it. And, I'm going to be pregnant during the summer again. At least I won't be **as** pregnant, but I promised Abby I'd do the flowers for her wedding. You are really going to have to help."

Dev made himself a cup of coffee and sat across from her. "You know I will. You just tell me what to do, and I'll do anything for you."

Lily had just finished a bite of the cherry and cream cheese pastry. She swore nothing could taste better. When she opened her eyes from the sublime experience, she held Dev's gaze. "You really would do anything for me, wouldn't you?"

"Yes." His answer was simple, but everything. "Well, except to travel with Gretchen. I draw the line at that. There will be no family vacation with your bestie."

Andrew squealed out in delight. Lily and Dev were entertained by his timing.

"I think," Lily said slowly. "I'll make you tell Gretchen we're pregnant. She demands a girl this time, buddy. If you disappoint her, you'll have to take her wrath. It won't be my fault."

"Why must you take the fun out of all of this by mentioning that?" Dev winced at the thought of Gretchen. It was easy to dislike the woman, and so much harder to like her, but she was one of a kind. Knowing that there was just one Gretchen in the world, set his mind at ease. He smiled slyly. "You know, I could charm Gretchen with my good looks. She's putty in my hands."

Lily defied him with her cold stare. "Keep telling yourself that, Mr. Delicious. This baby better be a girl."

"And so it begins," Dev lamented. He'd pay Dan to say an extra Mass now and then as a sacrifice to Gretchen's wishes. Secretly, she wasn't the only one who wanted to fill the frilly pink bedroom upstairs.

After Mass, and Lily's much-needed blessing, they stopped at her favorite ice cream site, and travelled to the nursery for a few plants for the edge of the back patio. She received smiles from several of the workers. They were friendly, but she had a suspicion they were actually amused by the purchase and then the return of her beautiful magnolia. No one had ever returned any plant or tree to the nursery because of a dead body in the yard. She'd give up until next year.

Lily was able to take a nap with Andrew while Dev dug the holes for the new flowers. *I don't know why he won't let me do it...something about finding another dead body?*

After their naps, Lily and Andrew slowly came down the stairs. The house was quiet. She looked out to see her father-in-law's car in the driveway.

"Your grandpa is here," she told Andrew as he carefully negotiated the steps helped along with the tight grip from his mother's hand. She walked through the living room and saw a huge bouquet of flowers on the table. Most of the blooms were white hydrangeas with touches of white and lavender lilacs. "Your daddy is so funny, and he's also so wonderful." He always managed to include the blooms that had brought them together, and her favorite lilacs. "He also paid a lot of money for all of that." Surrounding the floral display were several boxes, and a card that was obviously from Jack.

Lily saw both men, beer in their hands, sitting by the grill. She looked over at the oven and something was baking. "What is Daddy making?" Carefully opening the door, Lily saw some sort of a casserole. The aroma was amazing...potatoes, cheese, onions...what more did she need? She opened the refrigerator to grab sliced peaches for Andrew and saw a salad alongside a cheesecake. "I love your Daddy." Andrew clapped at the sight of his treat. "You are my son. You clap for food."

As she came outside, Jack Pierce got up quickly and grabbed his grandson. "Happy Mother's Day, Lily. Let me have that critter."

"Thank you. You also get his cup." She hugged her seated husband, kissing him on the cheek. "What are we eating?"

"Something a little different. I've marinated chicken breasts, but first I'm grilling vegetable kabobs. I did put on a couple of steaks too."

She leaned down to whisper to him. "Did you tell him?"

"No. Maybe we should wait?"

Lily kissed him again. "Maybe, but let's tell him."

"It's early, right?"

"Since when did you become a pessimist? I'm usually the one worried about everything, making lists to cover every contingency."

Dev looked up into her bright eyes. "You've transferred all your worries to me. In fact, for your information, I have a stockpile of post-it notes in my desk drawer at work, and another one here at home. I hope you're happy."

She laughed out loud, kissing him a third time for good measure. "I'm absolutely ecstatic."

Lily looked over at Jack and Andrew. They were so blissfully ignorant of the future, and all of the changes that would come over time. "Jack, we have an announcement. Now, this is very early, and I haven't had it professionally confirmed, but--"

Jack's face lifted in joy. "You're pregnant! That is wonderful news. I know, I know, it's early, but I hope it's true. This little guy needs someone to push around."

"Or that someone will push him around," Dev murmured. Lily playfully hit him on the shoulder.

"So no more mystery for a while?" Jack asked hopefully.

"Oh no, I'm still continuing to research that," Lily said unapologetically. "I keep finding out more information. I'm going to visit Mr. Livingood again next week. Dev suggested I look into the other doctor's disappearance. Do you two need another beer? I'm going in to get some water." Her excitement exhibited itself in her quick speech.

Both men answered affirmatively as Lily left the area.

"You suggested she look into that other disappearance?" Jack was incredulous. "Son, you're encouraging Lily's sleuthing?"

"Yes," Dev answered meekly. "It's hard to stop her when she sinks her teeth into something like this, so I might as well help her."

Jack shook his head. "And encourage her right into danger? That last time with the terrorist could have really been the last time for her. I don't like this."

"That's why I'm there every step of the way this time." Dev stood at the grill to check on the vegetables. But he wasn't always every step of the way with her, not in any of the dangerous occasions she had been involved in. In Kansas City, when he had first met her, she had to watch an old friend be involved in a lethal shootout to protect her. In Key West, she had volunteered to be used as bait, walking a dangerous path toward a meeting with a known drug dealer. On their honeymoon in Paris, he'd inadvertently placed her in danger twice. Almost two years ago, he hadn't been allowed to be with her as his nemesis was successful in his abduction of Lily while she was pregnant with Andrew. *This time, I'll be with her.* He knew enough about Lily that if he attempted to force her to stop looking into mysteries, he might as well kiss his marriage goodbye. The organized, less than confident woman he had first met had vanished, leaving him with a confident, inquisitive to a fault woman he loved more than he could tell. He knew one thing for sure, this time he would be there, no matter what.

Chapter Twelve

"How was Mother's Day?" Lily could hear the exhaustion in Abby's voice when she said hello.

"You know. I've never been so tired, well maybe I have, but right now it doesn't feel that way. Now, it's on to May and June weddings."

"And your own in August," Lily added. "Are you going to be ready for that?"

Abby laughed. "Since I don't have a man who will plan the entire thing, and then invite me to it, I guess I'll have to get ready."

"That is some kind of man!" Lily laughed. She touched Andrew's face softly. *Your Daddy did an amazing thing planning an entire surprise wedding for me.* Andrew continued to walk his way around the coffee table.

"I'll order the flowers for you and plan the way I want things so you won't have to do much, except all the work."

Lily was counting on Dev, and on Gretchen to assist her just in case the baby was draining her. She was hoping that old adrenaline charge of putting together flowers for a wedding would kick in. "That sounds easy enough. Where is the venue?"

"The Allendale Farm Estate. We had flowers for a wedding there a few years ago, and it was over one hundred degrees. I'm hoping it will be a little cooler."

Lily rolled her eyes. "You can hope, but you know how it is in August."

"Well, the ceremony will be at six in the evening on that beautiful grassy area, and then we'll head into the amazing stables for the reception."

"Oh, I remember that place now," Lily interrupted. "It's beautiful. I'll need the van to get all the flowers out there."

"Sure, anything you need. Remember, I have a couple of helpers for you too. I'm sorry you'll be here over your anniversary," Abby said quietly. "I didn't even think about it, but you know it's the slowest time of the summer."

"It's okay, no worries, but we'll also be celebrating Andrew's second birthday. Gretchen said she's going to handle it, and frankly, I'm just fine with that. God knows what she'll do." As Lily marveled at her son walking unassisted, she pictured Gretchen in fishnet stockings, a vibrant red corseted swimsuit, and top hat. The woman would probably be the mistress of ceremonies for a circus including baby donkeys, a small elephant, and tons of yapping poodles as they ran through hoops. Most guests at the party would be laughing too hard to take it seriously, but Dev would absolutely hate it. *Not for my son! Besides, he detests small yapping dogs.*

"You know Gretchen, Lily. What were you thinking giving her free rein?"

Lily sighed. "Well, for his first birthday, I just let him cover himself in cake. Dev was out of town, and it just wasn't worth having a large party just for his grandfather, his great aunts, and me. My sister and brother came the next weekend and we celebrated. As for Gretchen, she's worn me down, Abby. Besides, I think she and I truly are best friends now. It's frightening."

"You've officially lost your mind. Are you feeling alright?"

Lily remained silent for a second or two before she lied to her dear friend. "Of course. It will just be easier if Gretchen is in charge. Traveling with a little boy isn't that easy. Did you get us a room at our hotel?"

"Yes, in fact, you won't have your honeymoon suite, but you'll be on the same concierge level. I thought you might need that with Andrew. He eats real food now, right?"

"Yes. Thanks for doing that. Send me an email on what I need to know for the flowers. I'll keep in touch. I have to go. Andrew is walking into the kitchen."

"He's walking?" Abby's question went unanswered as Lily ended the call.

Lily shook her head. *We really do need to stay in touch more.*

By Wednesday afternoon, Lily had already been to the doctor, shopped for groceries, and picked up Andrew from Jack. She'd just finished putting away the dairy items when the doorbell rang. She looked out to see a friendly face.

A tanned man in khaki shorts and a black polo shirt stood on the porch. "Danny, this is a nice surprise. What's up?" Lily was already heading into the kitchen as Danny closed the door and picked up Andrew.

"He is getting big. What are you feeding this kid?"

"DaDa." Andrew pointed his finger in Danny's mouth.

Lily looked up at her son and saw Dan's shock. "You two do look a little similar. Maybe the hair?"

"Let's not let Dev hear this, Andrew," Dan suggested to the boy in his arms. But he hugged him a little tighter. "Your husband invited me over for dinner. He didn't tell you, did he?"

Lily stopped moving. *Did he tell me? Oh come on, brain. Engage!* She looked at the calendar on the refrigerator and silently said a four-letter word. "Yes, he did! I've been crazy busy, and I forgot. Remember you're a priest, and you're supposed to be forgiving." She took another look at the man holding her son. "Where did you get that great tan?"

"I flew out to see JT a few weeks ago in Coronado at the warfare center, and I played in a charity golf tournament for the high school last week."

"I guess I couldn't see it through your cassock when we were at Mass." Lily did remember that JT was working with trainees in the SEAL program. He'd be back in a few weeks. Admittedly, she needed some JT time. He was never judgmental, nor did he take too many things seriously, except for her safety and well-being.

Dan sat down at the kitchen table and continued to play peek-a-boo with his youngest fan. "Dev said you've been investigating that missing woman. He said you had the reporter's files."

"Yes. Until yesterday, the boxes were stacked up on this table. I managed to move them into a corner of the office. Mr. Livingood was the reporter who covered the story all those years ago."

"Dev also said they found a few things in your yard."

Lily opened the refrigerator and stared inside. "You could say that." She pulled out a package of hamburger and another of italian sausage. "How does Italian sound?"

"Sounds good. Um, Lily, I have some news for you."

With two packages of meat in her hand, Lily turned to face him. His tone had drastically changed. Usually, Danny was the one she could count on, always. He had a smile for her and a friendly demeanor, but his face was showing concern.

Lily placed the two packages on the kitchen counter and walked swiftly to take a seat across from him. "What? Just tell me."

"I'm doing Mr. Livingood's funeral on Friday. He had a massive heart attack Sunday evening."

Lily took in a quick breath. *Oh Lord.* She had no words. She was supposed to see him Thursday afternoon to update him on all her findings. "I have all of his stuff."

"I'll tell the family for you, and I can find out if they want it returned," Dan suggested.

Lily nodded. "Oh my God, Dan. This is awful." She held her head in her hands. She just didn't believe this was happening. She just didn't believe he was dead. Quickly, her head escaped her hands.

"Was it really a heart attack? I mean, he didn't die mysteriously, did he?"

Danny smiled as he metaphorically saw the cogs turning in her brain. "No, it really was a heart attack. His son was visiting at the time. Mr. Livingood had a history of heart disease, and I think the son said this was the man's third incident. That's hard to survive, Lily. There was nothing nefarious. Geez, you really do have to stop talking to Ari. He sees conspiracies everywhere, and now he has you doing it."

"But he's usually correct," Lily added.

"Well, there is that. Have you heard from the super spy lately?" Dan tickled Andrew under his arm eliciting the joyous noise of giggles.

"No. He's somewhere doing something. He met up with Jackson in Prague a few weeks ago. I've always wanted to go to Prague."

"It's beautiful. I met a woman there years ago, but, well, that was years ago. So, Dev's brother is still traveling?" Dan stood up with Andrew and mimicked a baby in flight. Andrew's laughter roared through the kitchen.

"The FBI apparently prefers him to stay away from the States." Lily was deflated for the day after hearing the news.

She was also extremely fatigued. She'd done way too much. But she needed to make dinner, and she was craving pasta. She stood up too fast and reached for the table to steady herself. She thought Danny had been too busy playing with the baby to pay attention, but of course, she was wrong. It was hard to pull over anything on an ex Special Forces soldier.

Danny reached out with one arm to steady Lily while he held Andrew in the other. "Are you okay?"

"Yes, I'm just tired. It's been a long day." She waved off his assistance and headed to the stove. "I'm going to fix the hamburger and sausage and put together a lasagna. It won't be as good as our favorite place in Alexandria, but mine is pretty good. I'll make a salad and garlic toast. I just don't believe Mr. Livingood is dead."

As if on cue, before Danny could ask any more questions, Dev opened the front door. "I brought dessert."

"That's what I love about you most!" Lily yelled from the kitchen. "You bring me dessert."

Dev tugged at his tie as he passed Danny and Andrew. "Hey Dan, son." Laying the precious bakery item on the counter, he came from behind his wife and kissed her cheek while holding her in his arms. "How was your day?"

Lily closed her eyes as she answered. "It was as we expected."

Despite his best friend, the priest, occupying space in the same room, Dev turned her around and kissed her. He lingered on her top lip, and then moved to her forehead with one sweet peck. He brought his forehead down to melt with hers.

"It will be okay. We can do this, and we will do this, together," he whispered.

She believed his words. With him, she could always do anything. She could see a confused guest from the corner of her eye. "Um, we have company."

"Pay no attention to the priest. Just stare into my beautiful eyes and lush lashes."

She pushed him away as she began to laugh. "Dan, entertain your annoying friend while I get dinner together."

"Oh, Dan's here," Dev joked. "Buddy, do you want a beer?"

"Are we celebrating something, or are we worried about something?"

"Both," Dev and Lily answered in unison.

The confused Danny held the baby a little closer. "Andrew, I'm very worried about your mommy and daddy. Something is up, and they aren't telling their priest."

"Because our priest is a very nosy tattle-tale," Dev said coolly as he presented his friend a bottle of beer and sat across from him. He finally pulled off his tie and threw it over an empty chair. He clinked his bottle with his friend's in a toast and took a long drink. "Washington makes me crazy, and today was certainly not an exception to the rule."

Danny examined his friend. Lily and he were too cool, pretending that nothing was going on except the usual life-numbing situations.

"Oh come on guys," Danny erupted. "What the hell is going on?"

Dev's one brow rose in usual quizzical fashion as he looked toward Lily. She turned around with a cut onion in her hand and tears on her cheeks.

Now Danny was concerned. "Oh my gosh, what is so wrong?"

Lily looked at the onion and looked up at her guest. "Onion. Onions make me cry, Danny."

"But something **is** going on." Dan just let the statement linger in the air. All three of them shared glances, dueling for who would crack first. No one did. Dan knew Dev wouldn't give so he began to stare at Lily. She wiped away the tears and smiled. *Geez, she's really becoming one of us.* Dan focused his attention on Andrew. "Well, little guy, it seems as though there's a secret. Do you know?"

With impeccable timing, Andrew uttered a new word as he pointed toward Lily. "Mama."

"Oh my God, he did not just say that again. I love it everytime I hear it," Lily gushed as she ran over to her son. She pulled him from Dan's arms and kissed him until he was giggling.

"He won't say it on demand," Dev muttered. His focus remained on Danny. He didn't intend for the comment to sound harsh, but his wife took it as such.

"Oh, it's fine and dandy when he calls your name, or points out a dog on the street, and it's no big deal when he calls for me? Really, Dev? How can you be so insensitive?

You aren't the only one who had a tough day. I did all the shopping, I went to the doctor, and my life changed. I'm fixing dinner for you and your friend, and you're just sitting there," Lily roared.

Something clicked in Dan's brain. He smiled. *Could it be?* He looked over at Dev. His friend was stoic, possibly in shock from the diatribe railed at him.

"Hormones," Dev whispered across the table.

And Dan had his confirmation with that one word. "As Andrew's godfather, I'm thinking he needs a sibling. Wouldn't that be nice?" He folded his arms across his chest and stared.

"As Andrew's godfather, you are the consultant for his spiritual upbringing. Nothing more." Dev took another drink of beer.

"Seriously? Neither one of you is going to answer me?" Dan began to laugh at both of his friends. They wouldn't meet his gaze, nor were they looking at each other. "I'm a priest. I keep confessions sacred by pain of death."

Finally, Dev turned to Lily. She nodded. "Go ahead and tell him." She brought Andrew to him. "And take your son. I have to make dinner."

As Dev gathered Andrew in his arms, he reached out for Lily's hand and held her in place. "Stop. Just stop. You're tired, and you've had a long day. Put the meat back in the fridge. Let's go out for dinner to celebrate. Tell him." His eyes pleaded with her.

"Yes, tell me," Dan added.

Lily sighed. "Dev, Mr. Livingood is dead. Dan is having the funeral." Lily began to cry again. "I'll miss him so much."

Dev's concern showed on his face. "How did he die? I mean was it natural, or something else?"

Dan hit his forehead with his hand. "What is it with you two? Do you see murder everywhere? The man had heart problems. Lily, you didn't know him that well, did you?"

Lily began to sob. "He was such a special man."

Dan shook his head. He was completely befuddled by her swing in emotions. He looked to Dev for the answers. "Were they that close?"

Dev smirked. "Nah, he fed her lemon bars."

Dan pretended to understand. "Ah, well that explains everything." He paused and searched Lily's face. She had a tissue up to her face and blew her nose loudly. "Now, tell me, Lily, are you pregnant?"

Lily nodded, ending Dan's irritation. He clapped his hands in delight. Lily began to cry. "I have to go to the bathroom. We can go to that grill off the parkway. I'll be back." She ran from the room with her hand over her mouth and tears flowing freely again.

Dev pasted a smile on his face. "We're very happy."

Dan molded his hands together in prayer-like fashion. "Oh I can tell. Should we pray?"

Dev cocked his head, and Andrew mimicked him. "It can't hurt. I have a feeling the remainder of this year will be hell. Do you have a prayer for that?"

"Bow your head. I'll fake it."

Chapter Thirteen

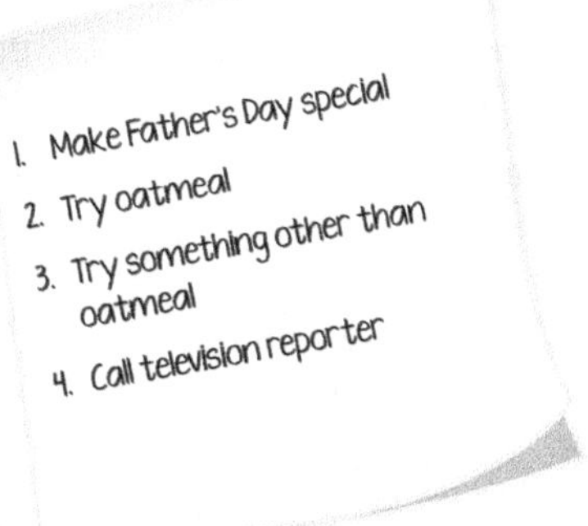

Dev had been away for two weeks, returning on the afternoon of Father's Day. Lily was dragging. There were days when she had superpower energy. The next day, she could barely heave her body out of bed to answer Andrew's wailing. He was teething again. The usual delightful baby boy became a monster sporting a red face and clenched fists.

Lily's stomach was not only betraying her in the morning, but now she was residing in the bathroom after lunch and before dinner. Andrew would sit beside her and watch her throw up. He even began to attempt the noise which only made her gag more. Andrew and she were a pair, a pair of what, Lily wasn't sure.

Andrew went down easily for a nap, and Lily spread out on the sofa to wait for Dev. He'd texted he'd be at the house within the hour. She was excited to update him on her investigation. She'd called the local television reporter who had covered the news story of the missing doctor's wife. He was now an anchor at one of the Indianapolis stations. He filled in a few details, but had nothing to add. He didn't believe the other doctor had any connection to Dr. Fleischman's wife. But, he did think Margot had no love for her stepdaughter. He had discovered a police report filed by Mrs. Parrot. She'd called the police while the doctor was away on a trip to Boston when she saw his daughter Laurel with an unusual red mark on her arm and a bruise on her cheek. She'd also heard yelling every night Dr. Fleischman was away.

Next, Lily wanted to touch base with Dr. Fleischman's daughter, if she'd even talk with her. Fortunately, the doctor's daughter met her for a quick lunch. She still needed to review her notes from that visit and figured she'd tell Dev about that meeting when he was in an extremely good mood. Lily had planned to reach the housekeeper who had dual duties as a nanny. Mr. Livingood had detailed notes about the woman, but when she did manage to track her name down it was found in the obituary section of a Maryland newspaper.

Lily shut her eyes briefly when she heard the door open. She stood up quickly, a little too quickly. She sat down on the sofa before Dev could see her sway.

She heard him go into his office, probably to drop off his laptop and anything else that didn't belong lying around the house. He peeked his head around the corner.

"Hi beautiful."

Lily smiled. *That man! He lies so well.* She knew her hair was messed up. She wore no makeup, and her shirt was marked with the sweet potatoes Andrew had eaten at lunch.

"Hi Mr. Delicious." Lily thought he looked more tired than usual after being in the field. He didn't have a three o'clock shadow; he had a seven o'clock one. His hair fell over the back of his collar, and he needed a haircut, but she wouldn't suggest that. Even his usually bright eyes were dim.

He kissed her on the top of her head and sat beside her. Reaching over for her hand, Dev brought it up to his lips. "I missed you very much. Is this your new signature style? I like the sweet potato look." He lightly touched her collar.

Lily glanced down at her shirt knowing full well what she would see. "Really? I thought you might like this. We decorated my shirt especially for Father's Day. I'm so happy you approve."

He dropped her hand slowly and placed his arm around her shoulders to bring her near his chest. Rubbing her neck slowly, he placed his chin on top of her head.

"How have you been feeling?"

"Weird," Lily whispered. "This isn't like when I was pregnant with Andrew. Morning sickness is a given, but now I have an afternoon and an evening session. I plan my day around it."

"I remember another time when you were sick in the evening. We didn't even get through a Valentine's Day dinner."

Lily patted his chest. "Right. I forgot. Oh, and I have a baby brain again. I'm leaving lists around, and then I can't find them. Little good they do me."

"Is Dad coming over later?"

"Yes. He'll be here around five."

"It smells good here. What are we having?"

Lily stood slowly this time. She touched his face with her hand, outlining his lips with her finger. "Pot roast, mashed potatoes and gravy, carrots, and green beans. For dessert, I made your favorite, pecan pie."

"Wow, I'm glad I came home." Dev kissed her finger. "Do we have any other plans except for dinner?"

"Andrew just went down for his nap. He has a few gifts for you, but no, it's going to be quiet."

Dev's eyes narrowed. He stood up and pulled her up with him. "Come on. I figure we have an hour, right?"

Lily suspiciously tugged at his hands. "Where are we going? And what are we doing?"

"Upstairs. To bed. Something and then a short nap." He pulled this time, but she willingly followed him up the stairs.

"Is this all you want for Father's Day?" Lily asked coyly as they came to the top of the stairs.

Dev cupped her face in his hands and kissed her soundly. "Isn't that enough? And I get pecan pie later. That's the perfect day. Come on."

Lily saluted her husband. Andrew was the perfect son and took an extra long nap for his daddy. Dev was sound asleep, but she'd heard their son's sounds and picked him up, bringing him into their room. Andrew saw his father and climbed out of her arms to amble toward Dev's side of the bed. He tried to climb but failed. The bed was like Mt. Everest to a baby, but there were a few times when Andrew ingeniously used the bedspread to pull himself up. In just a few more months it would almost be as high a climb for Lily.

One eye opened on the sleeping daddy. With one arm he grabbed up the child, bringing him up into his arms. Giggling ensued. "Have you been good to mommy?"

Lily sat on the edge of the bed. "He's saying no to me. He's been such a happy little guy. I'm not sure how to feel about it."

"What does he say no to?" Dev wrestled with his son.

"Me, everything about me." Lily brushed Andrew's curly hair out of his eyes. "I have this feeling he's not happy with me being pregnant."

Dev playfully blew on Andrew's face as his son grabbed at his mouth. "Honey, he can't know anything about that. You know that."

"I do, but, sometimes, I wonder." A smile crossed her face as she watched the two loves of her life play on the bed. Dev's bare chest was kicked by Andrew's small feet. Her husband's large hands cradled his son's body.

Lily wanted this day to be special for Dev, but his work had interrupted all thoughts of an all day celebration of fatherhood. Instead, they would have only hours. But the last hour alone with him had been amazing. Dev was the most passionate man she'd ever known, and she was grateful that his love fell on her. She'd prayed for him, and God had blessed her. If he fought as fiercely as he loved, no one could stop him. But today, she'd seen the mask he wore. He wasn't just fatigued, his soul was troubled. Whatever he was working on was taking him down. She wondered if he was still involved in some sort of child trafficking case.

Andrew's enthusiasm could be seen in every inch of his little body. He gave as good as he got, especially when he kicked out and hit his father's nose.

"Crap," Dev yelled out in pain. "He got me good."

"Oh my gosh. You're bleeding," Lily acknowledged. She handed him a tissue and then went running into the bathroom for a cold towel.

Andrew was still kickboxing when Lily placed the cloth across the bridge of Dev's nose. "Did he break it?"

"Maybe, but I've broken it so many times before it doesn't really matter."

Lily looked down at the bloody tissue and felt her stomach lurch. "Oh no, gotta go." She ran into the bathroom and began her usual afternoon routine.

When Dev arrived with Andrew in his arms, he saw Lily worshiping at the porcelain altar. "Honey, are you okay?"

She lifted her head briefly and continued with the disgusting bodily function. Dev watched Lily raise a hand and give him a thumbs up.

"Come on Andrew. Let's let mommy throw up in private." *This is going to be a long pregnancy!*

Dev dressed and changed Andrew's diaper. He also brought a cold drink to Lily. Color had returned to her face as she sat on the bathroom floor. He crouched down in front of her as Andrew walked around them.

Lily seemed fixated on the towels hanging next to her. "We need some new towels. How did that happen? We've just been married for almost three years."

"Those are my towels from the townhouse. I've had those for years."

"Ah, that explains it." She continued to examine the frayed edges. "Can I get rid of them or do you have some sort of emotional attachment?"

"Get rid of them. Get what you want."

"I want to go with a light shade of grey here. Will you have time to paint this summer?" Andrew ambled over to his mother and sat down on her lap.

"I should. We're going to Kansas City in August, but I can start next week if you get the paint."

"Okay." Lily's one word answer concerned Dev. Just a few weeks pregnant, Lily seemed more tired and less like herself.

"I have some information for you," Dev said. He thought that good news might perk her up. Her face brightened a bit.

"So tell me."

"I have that age progression of Margot on my computer. I can show you later."

"That would be great. I found out a few things too, but we can talk about that tomorrow. It's your day."

"I appreciate that, but I have some even better news for you. Once I saw the progression, I realized I have seen her. Tomorrow, I'll have them run the program through the computer data file."

"Really?" Lily's voice raised considerably with excitement. "You've seen her?"

"Yes. I think I remember seeing her in South America only a couple of years ago. Lily, I'm pretty sure you're right. Margot is alive."

Lily's brain engaged. *She's alive! Jessica would be so proud of me right now!* Lily began to slowly move her son, and to raise up off the cool tiled floor.

"I have to finish dinner, and I'm so ready for that pie! Happy Father's Day, Dev."

Chapter Fourteen

It made no difference if it was summer in Virginia, or summer in Missouri. Lily could feel the humidity even inside an air conditioned home. She seemed to become a hermit in July as she stayed inside and continued to search through every piece of paper in Mr. Livingood's boxes. When she needed a break, she began to throw items into luggage in preparation for their trip to Abby and Jeremy's wedding. It used to be so simple to pack, but she realized traveling with a toddler was not for the faint of heart. July soon passed and it was time to return home.

August in Kansas City was the beginning of the end of the warm weather, but the heat always took its time leaving. When they landed, the temperature was over ninety. It seemed as though steam was rising up to greet the little family. Dev searched for landmarks along the interstate as they passed through the downtown area. They were familiar streets, but after a couple of years of being away, he was uncertain of a few turns. Luckily, Lily still remembered her way to her area of the city.

"Now, you're absolutely certain that Gretchen is not meeting us at the hotel?" Dev asked as he drove the streets of Kansas City on their way to the Plaza.

"Yes, I've told you several times. Gosh, you'd think you were afraid of her," Lily commented. "Oh wow, look, that restaurant is new."

"It probably isn't new. It's been a few years since you've lived here." Dev looked over at the train tracks. "Shouldn't I turn left here at Union Station?"

"No, just keep going down Broadway." Lily looked back at a sleeping Andrew. He was growing so fast. He wasn't a baby anymore.

Dev noticed the grand memorial to World War I as they headed up the hill. It was the only one of its kind in the entire nation honoring that first world war and the men who fought it. "By the way, I'm not afraid of Gretchen. She can be wonderful, but she can be well, what's the word?"

Lily snickered. "Obnoxious? Dramatic? Condescending? Pushy? Witchy? Do you want me to go on?"

Dev smiled. "No, that's a good beginning, but she does have a heart of gold. And she loves you. She would do anything for you."

Lily noticed a familiar large Catholic church. She always loved it when she had a wedding there. She'd go early and sit in the stillness of the sanctuary. She would look up toward heaven imagining she was seeing God, and she hoped God was looking down on her. *We've spent a lot of time talking, haven't we, big guy?*

Lily sighed. "I've surrendered to the fact that Gretchen and I are best friends. It's going to be worse right now dealing with her. I can't drink."

Dev grimaced as if he was in pain. "Have you told her about the new baby?"

"Heaven's no! I thought we'd surprise Abby and her. As soon as Gretchen learns I'm pregnant, she'll start threatening your life. She wants that little girl."

"I turn here, right?"

"Yes, Dev. Then left at the next block. The hotel is up there on the corner. You'll remember it. You used to run these streets. Did you realize that Gretchen's apartment is right across from the hotel?"

Dev nodded. "I knew that, but I always tried to forget it. I had this feeling that she was going to walk in on us the morning after the wedding and ask for a rating on how it went. I can picture her with a pair of high powered binoculars, and she'd have a placard with numbers on it to rate my performance."

Lily patted his shoulder. "I would've given you a ten, honey."

"Thanks. I appreciate it. Oh, I see it. What if I help you unpack and then I hit the swimming pool?"

"And you'll take your son?" Lily asked hopefully. She wanted to call Abby, or maybe even go to the shop to look at the wedding flowers.

"And I'll take our son. You can go see Abby." Dev looked over at her happy face. "That's what you wanted me to say."

"Yep. Thank you. I'm getting excited about this wedding. I really can't wait to put the flowers together."

Dev pulled slowly into the hotel's drive and popped the trunk. They left the car doors open to allow Andrew to sleep as they unloaded the luggage. Lily went in to register, and in a few minutes, she walked out with keycards in hand.

"I have to unload the boy." Dev went to the side of the car and removed the sleeping child as Lily checked the luggage. The bellhop was already walking into the hotel with the cart. "I'll leave the car seat. They're going to leave the car over there for you."

"Thanks, honey."

Dev watched Lily as she entered the hotel. He could see her mind working, remembering how it was when she would deliver flowers here. *Maybe she's thinking about our wedding, our reception? Nah, she's thinking about that one wedding she did, or those bouquets that were all red roses.* But then, on the elevator, she grasped his hand and kissed his cheek. *No, she remembers us.*

Andrew woke up a few minutes after they began to unpack. Dev volunteered to go to the reception area on the concierge level to grab food and drinks. By the time he returned, Lily had hung up their clothes and was going through the carry-on pieces.

"Why don't you leave that for later and go see Abby? Maybe you two could get lunch. Andrew and I will eat, and then we'll go to the pool. Just lay out his suit and some clothes for after." Dev took a drink from his water bottle and handed Andrew a piece of banana.

"Are you sure?"

"Absolutely. You'll begin to worry if you don't see those flowers. You probably have a list stowed away somewhere with everything you need to do before Saturday." Dev offered a small piece of chicken to his son as he took a bite of his sandwich. "This stuff is good. Can Andrew have a pickle?"

"Sure, but don't be surprised if he spits it out. Sour stuff isn't his favorite. Okay, so do I look presentable?" Lily had changed to a flowy top. *Abby won't be able to see anything this way.*

"You look lovely, and you look like you're trying to cover up the fact that you're pregnant. Just my opinion." Dev smiled and winked at her as she glared.

Lily grabbed the rental car keys, her purse, and phone as she walked past him. "You're just very observant. Most people won't notice."

But as soon as Lily entered the shop, Abby looked directly in her stomach area.

"Oh my, you're pregnant!" She ran to Lily and hugged her. "I'm so happy you're here, and you're going to have another baby. Oh my gosh, Gretchen is going to be thrilled."

"Oh good," Lily said slowly. *Dev and I didn't do it for Gretchen!* "Show me the flowers. I can't wait to see what you want your wedding to look like. I brought all my notes."

Abby released her former boss. "I bet you did, and I have an entire new pack of post-its just for you. Come on."

Lily surveyed the shop. Abby had moved a few things around. After all, it was Abby's place now. Almost every remnant of Lily's influence had vanished. It was all Abby. Lily felt like she could cry, but this wasn't her life anymore, and she was absolutely okay about that.

Abby led her into the back room and to the walk-in refrigerator. "These will need to be brought out tomorrow to pop a little."

Lily looked over the blooms, scribbling in her notebook. "Yes, those sunflowers do need to sit out a little. The colors are great, Abby. The flowers are happy, just like you." She leaned over and smelled lavender and yellow freesia. The sweet aroma made Lily's stomach twinge. *I'm hungry.*

"Abs, have you had lunch yet?"

"No. I'm just waiting on my assistant to get back from a delivery. Oh, and the girls will be your helpers. I especially don't want you doing too much now. But, I'm also waiting on--"

Lily heard the door open. The voice, and the all too familiar clicking of heels made Lily smile, and shudder a bit. It was her!

"Hello. There better be a Lily in the house." Gretchen entered the shop.

Lily peeked around the corner. Gretchen came running with open arms, her stilettos making their trademark tapping sound on the floor as she rushed toward her bestie. Lily's entire body was captured in her hug. *Now I am going to cry.*

Finally, Gretchen released her and stood back. Her eyes became narrow as she examined her friend. "It's a girl. You're having my girl."

Lily flipped her larger-than-usual shirt. *I'm going to burn this worthless shirt, and I refuse to tell Dev he's right.* "How did you know?"

Gretchen extended a finger of examination. "Well, if you must know, your face is a little bloated, your ankles are swollen. Your skin is flawless, and you have a baby bump right there." Gretchen pinpointed Lily's midsection. "It better be a girl."

"Dev's feeling a little pressure about that," Lily said sarcastically.

"As well he should. As you will recall, it was a promise you both made."

Lily rolled her eyes as Abby made faces behind Gretchen. Gretchen turned quickly.

"Abigail, you should know by now I have eyes in the back of my head. I've made reservations at Pierre's for a girls' luncheon. We need to move or we'll lose our table." Gretchen tapped on her gold watch. Lily noticed a new ruby bracelet on her friend's wrist. *Is it a gift from the new male friend?*

"God forbid we are late for the quiche." Abby's humor was lost on the diva coordinator. Abby felt about three feet high as Gretchen stared through her. "Fine. We can go as soon as Andrea gets here." Luckily, for Abby's preservation, Andrea arrived through the back door in a matter of minutes. After a few instructions, the three women departed for lunch. Lily was only hoping that they'd have fresh bread on the table.

Lily's hopes were realized. Abby and she dug into the bread and butter as Gretchen ordered a glass of wine.

"So where is Mr. Delicious?"

Lily wiped the crumbs from the edge of her mouth and looked up at Gretchen. "He's back at the hotel with Andrew. They were going to the pool."

"That reminds me," Gretchen said as her wine arrived. "I've planned the birthday party for that dear boy. We'll have a celebration around my building's pool area."

"That's not appropriate for a second birthday," Abby muttered as she buttered another piece of bread.

"It is when Auntie G is hosting."

Lily and Abby crossed their eyes. *Auntie G? Dev is going to love this one, well actually he won't, but who is going to stop her? No one really stops Gretchen.*

"Gretchen, I told you it wasn't necessary. Andrew doesn't know the difference between green beans and beets. He just knows he puts them in his mouth. We don't need a big party. He'd be fine with ice cream and a cupcake. We have a wedding on Saturday. We'll celebrate then."

Gretchen planted her wine glass on the table. The red liquid swished within the glass. "Do not say that about your son's birthday, Lily Pierce. This is extremely important. Birthdays are important. We're having a party on Sunday, after the wedding. I won't take no for an answer."

Can you roll your eyes too many times? But Lily did move her eyes up to the ceiling. She had missed Gretchen? *Have I really?* "Is the waiter coming back to take our order?" Lily craned her neck to gain the server's attention.

Her attempt at distraction failed miserably, drawing Gretchen's full attention. "What's up with that extra large blouse? It doesn't suit you at all. I hope you haven't become some hausfrau. That would be so unlike you. I know you don't wear makeup or fix your hair, but you've been doing better since Dev came into your life, and of course, I do my part to lead you in the correct direction. You must remember that just because you're pregnant doesn't mean you throw your fashion sense out the window."

I wish I could have a large glass of wine, perhaps the bottle. I'd throw something in her direction and drink the rest. "Our flight was early this morning. I'm hungry." Lily completely ignored Gretchen's brief lesson in wardrobe. She finally caught the server's attention and waved lightly.

"And you get a little testy when you're pregnant," Gretchen muttered as she looked over the menu.

Abby giggled. "Welcome home, Lily."

"Oh, yeah. I'm feeling the love."

"You love me, just admit it," Gretchen winked at her from over her menu and smiled sweetly.

Lily bit her tongue and decided that she'd answer with an equally sweet smile. *I wish I were at the pool with Dev and Andrew.*

After lunch, Gretchen returned Abby to the shop, and Lily headed to the hotel. There was only so much Gretchen she could take after a long flight. Besides, it was difficult to be the outsider, and that is exactly who she was now. Abby and the coordinator shared a laugh about one of their brides. The bride-to-be insisted that Gretchen had the latest guest list in an email she had forwarded. Abby reminded Gretchen she needed the table count for the centerpieces.

Gretchen would make sure she had the information by Tuesday, and that the caterer knew the new count for the rehearsal dinner. The two professionals discussed a future event and a December wedding Gretchen was planning in St. Louis.

Lily stared at her water. Lily drank most of the glass, and she smiled when they laughed. She had nothing to add to the conversation. She was no longer part of their world. *It used to be my world.*

On her way back to the hotel, Lily took a side trip a few blocks away from the hotel. She drove slowly past the brick buildings that had been her high school. Noticing the new convocation building, Lily realized all of the oak and maple trees had been removed. *Gosh, I loved fall here. Those trees were so beautiful, but it seems like everything and everyone changes. Just look at me. I'm a shining example of that theory.* She turned around in the circular drive that used to feature large speed bumps that would rock the old Oldsmobile she used to drive to school every day. She took one final look and sighed. It was time to go back to the hotel.

Lily removed her shoes as she entered the pool area. Dev and Andrew were the only ones splashing about, a few others were laying around in lounge chairs enjoying the sun. She saw Andrew point at her and yell.

"Mama." Lily never tired of that kind of welcome from the little man.

Dev turned and waved. "Honey, you should change and come in."

She nodded and left to go to the room. She heard Andrew scream out, but Dev comforted him. By the time Lily returned to her boys, her son was swimming.

"How did that happen?" Lily asked as she stepped safely into the water.

"My hand is under his stomach. How was lunch?" Andrew threw water directly into his father's face.

"Tiring. I wish you could just float me like you do him." Lily kissed him as she met them.

"Get on my back and put your arms around my shoulders. I'll float you around."

Lily accepted the invitation willingly. She placed her head on his shoulder. "I'm not one of the girls anymore."

"What? Of course you are. Abby loves you," Dev said, attempting to head off the sad tone in his wife's voice.

"Gretchen took us to lunch at this chic little French place. The two of them are thicker than thieves, and I'm, well, I'm the one who doesn't live here." Lily figured if she did cry, Dev wouldn't be able to tell with the water that Andrew was throwing about. But, she did want to cry.

Dev thought for a few minutes. "Well, you are the one who doesn't live here anymore, and that happens. I mean, look at Paul. We were all so tight, but his family is his main concern, and that's how it should be. Look at us. We don't socialize very much. We work, we take care of the house, our child, soon to be children--"

"Just stop. You're making sense and making me more depressed." She kissed the side of his neck and closed her eyes. The tears flowed easily and mixed with the chlorinated water just as she had hoped.

Dev was torn. Andrew was delightfully happy, and Lily was depressed and homesick in an entirely different definition of the word. "Lily, you have a new life. You're a wife, a mother, and you do amazing work for the aunts at the vineyard. Do you want to come back here? I told you I'd get a transfer, or find another job back here. If that's what you want. I'll do anything, absolutely anything to make you happy. Including tracking down a missing woman, remember?"

"I remember." Lily's tone was flat without any emotion. *What am I feeling? This is silly. I have everything.* She was holding her everything. She saw her everything splashing happily in his father's arms. She slowly slid down Dev's back and plunged into the cool water. When she came up, Andrew's wide eyes were searching for her.

She held out her arms, and he did his own form of swimming to his mother. "I'm okay. I have so much. My home is back in Virginia now, but I miss what I used to have here. Just a bit. Being with Abby and Gretchen was just a little uncomfortable."

"Do you need girlfriends? You're surrounded by all of us guys. That's got to get old," Dev admitted.

Finally, Lily laughed. "Oh, you all are never old. In fact, I love having all of you around. Maybe I'm just missing the rest of the crazy team."

"That was never an adjective for our team. In fact, that's a very tame description." Dev winked at her and kissed her wet cheek. "I'm going to swim a few laps. Are you sure you're okay?"

"Yes, go swim." Lily moved over to the steps so she could sit down and hold Andrew easier in her arms. He was becoming a handful, and she was hitting her afternoon slump.

Dev began to swim away, but stopped and walked back to her. "Lily, just listen to me. Change is relative. I've been through so many changes in my life that I just roll with it now. I left home at seventeen. I lived through West Point, deployments to so many countries, getting out of the Army, taking on a new job that sent me to other countries, and now I'm a dad and a husband. If I didn't change, I wouldn't have you."

Lily just stared at him. Andrew splashed the water happily. "Dev, if I went missing, how long would you look for me?"

"Forever, Lily, forever."

Her mind went in another direction than her heart. *Dr. Fleischman didn't look for Margot for very long. He hired a private investigator, but he surrendered the search after six months. Maybe he didn't want to find her, or he knew where she was all along?*

Dev still stood before her, possibly waiting for an answer of some kind. Andrew flipped water up in her face. Her mind stopped wondering. Lily smiled at her husband.

"And, I would look for you too. I'd find you, you know." Lily's confident answer made Dev laugh.

"Yes, I believe you would, honey. Now that you're smiling, I'm going to swim." Dev dove into the water and was gone.

His wife looked up from her son to notice a couple of the women on the other side of the water, adjusting their sunglasses onto their noses as they watched Lily's very fit husband swim across the pool.

Just keep looking, ladies. He is all mine, thankfully. Proudly, she waved at him as he surfaced at the other end. A few more laps and Dev came up next to her.

"I touched base with Tom, but we'll just see them at the wedding. But, if you're up to it, Aunt Pat wants us up for dinner tomorrow night."

"That would be perfect. Tonight, though, I think I just want to lay around. I'm dragging. I'll need to start on the flowers Wednesday for the rehearsal dinner, and then Thursday for the wedding. I promise to take breaks, plus Abby is giving me her helpers."

Dev plunged into the water one final time. Andrew laughed as he shot out of the water. "And our anniversary is Wednesday. We should at least go out for dinner."

"Oh, Gretchen has that all planned out," Lily answered. "We apparently have reservations at the restaurant down the street, and then, wait, this is a biggie. You and I are going to Starlight Theatre. She thought that would be appropriate for our anniversary spent here."

Dev smiled knowingly. He pretended he knew nothing of the night out, but of course, he knew everything. His deception began. He wiped any remnants of water off of his face. "It depends. What's the musical?"

Lily laughed at his hesitation. She had taken him twice to the Kansas City outdoor theatre in the first few months of knowing him. "I have no idea. You'll just have to go and find out."

Dev eyed her suspiciously. "Fine, but I have the ability to leave early or to go to the bar if the show involves anything dealing with weddings."

Lily nodded. "Deal. Now kiss me so those girls over there are so jealous they can't stand it. It'll make me feel better."

"I can do that and more." Dev leaned over Andrew and kissed her long and hard. "Now, if you'll join me upstairs, I'll replace any doubts you have about the life you have as I love you like no one ever has."

Lily stood up quickly. "That's a deal. Come on, Boy Scout. I'll race you to the room."

Chapter Fifteen

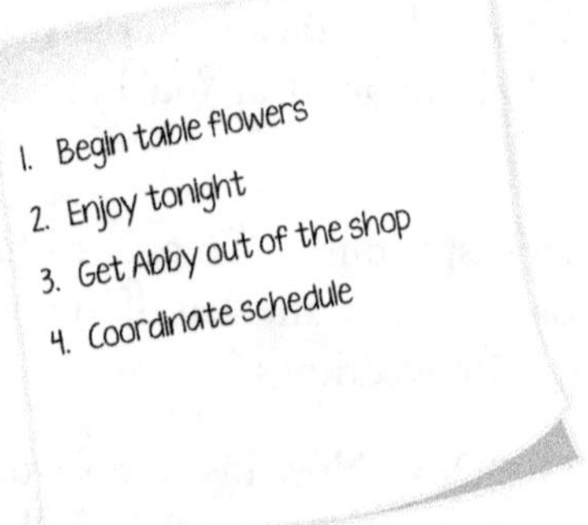

Dev held his wife's hand as they walked up the pathway into the theatre. They entered through the security area, had their tickets scanned, and received their programs. Lily was admiring the fountains and the lush flowers and greens until she heard Dev groan.

"You're kidding me. Really? Did you see what the show is?"

Lily took a glance at her program and smiled. "You are going to love this. It's your kind of show. Come on. I need some popcorn."

"We just had dinner and dessert." Dev floated the program under her nose. "A musical about a bodyguard? Really? Come on. Gretchen planned this."

"If it's any consolation, I don't think there's a wedding in the production." Lily breathed in the night air. The fountains, the flowers, and the two towers of the outdoor venue were all still there. "It's so nice that some things don't change. I love Starlight. Ever since I was a little girl, this place was magical." She ignored her husband's grumbling.

"Are you talking about Gretchen not changing or Starlight?" Dev focused on her face. She was in her element. The second show they saw together here, they had danced together and held hands as they walked back to the car. He had figured he didn't want to lose her in the crowd. When he reviewed the situation later, and when he honestly dealt with his emotions, he realized it had been a ruse. He wanted to dance with her. He wanted to hold her, and he wanted to touch her. Even back then.

Dev took her hand and raised it up to his lips. "I love you, and I especially love you here."

"This is so special. I never thought I would see this place again, and to be here with you again makes my heart happy." She looked down at the ticket. "Dev, this is my old seat."

"You said Gretchen took over your seats."

"But, I didn't think she took over the actual seats. She said she was only going to use them for clients. I hope the gang is still there."

Lily looked into the open air theatre and saw her row. It was empty. They were early. The light in her eyes dimmed a bit in disappointment.

"How about a cool drink, and I'll get your popcorn," Dev suggested.

"Yes, something cold."

By the time they'd gathered the popcorn and two bottles of water, Lily's row had filled. Her Starlight family was waiting.

"Oh my gosh, it's Lily," Julie announced.

Dev gathered the box of popcorn and the water bottle out of Lily's hands as she moved down the row hugging each and every one of them. But Dev saw that one person was missing. Lily finished with her greetings and returned to her seat next to Julie and her daughter.

"Where's your husband tonight?"

Dev saw the woman's face pull tight. Lily was so happy she saw nothing but good friends.

Julie began to cry. "Oh, Lily. I lost your phone number. John died last month. It was an aneurysm, and he was gone within hours."

Lily plopped down into the seat with a thud. Dev placed the items in his hands down on the concrete and began to rub his wife's back as she faced the woman.

He leaned his head down to whisper in her ear. "Honey, keep breathing. Don't faint. She doesn't need this. Breathe."

Lily nodded in response to his suggestion, but she couldn't stop the tears. The two women hugged each other. "He was so much fun. We had such a good time together out here."

"He enjoyed you too, Lily. Remember that show girl that came up to him that one night?"

Lily snorted with laughter mixed with tears. "She was so tall his head came up to her boobs. He was so embarrassed his ears turned red, but he loved it."

"Oh, he did." Julie looked over Lily's shoulder. "It's good to see you too. So, you two got married? We knew it after that first night."

"Then you knew before I did," Dev joked. "I'm so sorry about your husband. I certainly enjoyed my time with him."

"He knew you'd be great for her."

Lily's little family row visited and brought each other up to speed on their lives until Starlight's director came out onto the stage. Dev reached over and took Lily's popcorn away.

"What are you doing?" Her pout made him laugh.

"We'll have to stand up for the flag in just a second."

Lily maintained her pouty face. "We need to call Gretchen and make sure she hasn't bedazzled our son."

"It was your idea that Auntie G babysit tonight."

Lily hit Dev playfully on the arm. "There was no way to stop Auntie G. By the way, it isn't easy to call her that, but she loves it."

Dev cocked his head. "As long as Gretchen is happy. No worries though. I put a tracker on Andrew."

Lily's mouth gaped open. "You did not! Where?"

"That little bracelet that you all thought was so sweet has a chip in it. You can thank me later." He sat straighter in the chair. His self-satisfaction was obvious.

"And that's why I love you, and I will thank you." She added a wink. *Wait, he micro-chipped our child?* Then she heard her name called from the stage. "What the bloody hell--"

"Happy anniversary," Dev whispered.

The actor portraying the bodyguard came to their row. He presented Lily with a large bouquet of her favorite antique pink and lavender roses. He also added a kiss. He handed Dev a bottle of champagne. Now Lily was the one with the red face and a few tears. The audience clapped enthusiastically.

It was time to stand for *The Star Spangled Banner*. Lily held Dev's hand. His energy was her energy. His heart was her heart. She might question her strength, but she never questioned his. And yes, this was her home and where she was from, but her family was with him. Their family would grow in Virginia.

When they sat to wait for the show to begin, she asked if Gretchen had done all of this.

"I asked her, and she did it. That one time we were out here I remembered a couple became engaged almost right in front of us. I wanted you to have a moment like that. She did good."

"Yes, she did. It's funny that you were like my bodyguard, and it's the show tonight. Of course, I never sang for you."

Dev leaned over and kissed her cheek. "No, but you made me laugh."

"And made you eat terribly unhealthy food," Lily added.

At the intermission, Lily called Gretchen. "Is Andrew fine?"

"Yes, Lily. He's just a little boy. I can handle boys, remember?"

But the way you handle boys isn't appropriate for a toddler! "He went to sleep for you?"

"Yes, Lily." Gretchen bit her tongue. She knew her friend was just being a nervous mother, but she was beginning to irritate her. "I fed him. I cleaned him up. I changed him. We watched a little baseball. We walked a little, and he fell asleep in my arms. I put him down, and he's snoring away. He makes these little puffing noises. Did you know that?"

"Yes, Gretchen," Lily answered. *His father does too when he's completely at peace.*

"Will you be okay if we stay until the end of the show?"

"Of course, dear. Did you enjoy your little surprise?"

"Yes. It was wonderful. Thank you so much."

"I implemented it, but your husband is the one who came up with the idea. Those roses will need water as soon as you get back to the hotel."

"Yes, mother. I need to go. We'll be there as soon as we can get out of here. You know how Dev can drive."

"Take your time, Lily. My little Drew and I are perfectly wonderful. Just enjoy. We'll be here when you get back to the hotel."

Drew? She's renaming my son? "Thank you. See you soon."

Dev stood in front of her. "Is she fine? Is Andrew still alive?"

"Yes, but apparently, his name is now Drew."

Dev's brow furrowed in thought. "I like it. Drew Pierce. Geez, that would be a great super agent name. Much better than Ari." Lily punched him in the rib cage.

The second part of the show went by too quickly. By the time the main character was singing she'd always love her agent, Lily was sobbing. Dev timidly gathered her into his arms knowing full well it wasn't just the musical. He leaned down to whisper some words of comfort.

"I came back, remember? You're stuck with me." Her head nodded.

At the very end of the show, everyone was invited to get up and dance with somebody. This time, Dev danced with his wife and had no problem kissing her senseless in public.

They arrived back at the hotel room to a beautiful sight. They crept in silently to see a sleeping Gretchen, reading glasses poised on the tip of her nose, sitting on the sofa with their son on her lap. He was breathing deeply and sighing after each breath. Gretchen was snoring.

"I'm going to go down and get us something to snack on. You wake her up." Dev departed before Lily could argue.

Gretchen woke with the click of the door as Dev left. "I didn't hear you. Sorry. He woke up around ten, but I guess we both fell asleep."

Lily leaned over her friend and slowly gathered up her son. "Thank you so much. You must be done in. Let me go lay him down."

When Lily returned, she kissed Gretchen on the cheek. "You are amazing. Thank you for everything you've ever done for me."

Gretchen patted the area next to her for Lily to sit. "I'm not sure I've done that much."

"Well, you're always helping my husband pull off whoppers of surprises for me."

Dev came into the room with drinks and a plate of snacks. "Gretchen, I got you a Cabernet. Lily, chocolate milk. Oh, and they had chocolate covered strawberries and these little mini chocolate peanut butter bars. Look."

Gretchen shook her head. "Who are you? Are you some college kid in a hotel for the first time, Devlin?"

"Yep. I'm having a great night. My baby is asleep. My love is with me, and we are able to celebrate with a great friend who is more like family."

Gretchen shoved Lily. "Oh, he is good. No wonder you're pregnant every time I see you."

Lily shrugged and smiled coyly. *Well, he is very good at what he does.*

Chapter Sixteen

Lily remembered the venue as soon as they took the exit. A former horse ranch, you passed by the white fence for a couple of blocks before you arrived at the wrought iron gates. As the car negotiated the curving brick paved drive, a pond was on one side and rolling green pasture was on the other. There were three small houses near the pond, but the reception and wedding was to take place by the immaculate, grand stables.

"This place looks like it could be in Williamsburg," Dev commented. "That stable is so nice we could live in it."

Lily smiled. *I've taught him to appreciate a good venue. My job is done!* "Wait until you see the inside. The wood beams are amazing."

The two parked and quickly grabbed the items they had brought to begin the setup. But as they entered the large room, Lily stopped in her tracks. "What in all that is good is Jeremy doing?" Her view was of the groom, a dog, and a blow dryer at the ceremony grounds.

"I have no earthly idea, but it's good to see Mort again," Dev admitted. He laid Lily's bags down on one of the tables. Abby's assistants were already beginning to decorate the tables. Mort, the DEA dropout German Shepherd rolled in the grass as Jeremy leaned over. Chairs were set to form an aisle. Jeremy had a blow dryer in his hand with a long extension cord behind him. He was blowing the grass.

"I'm going to find out what he is doing," Lily announced and swiftly made her way outside with Dev in her wake.

She yelled his name a couple of times, but he didn't hear her. Mort greeted both of them immediately. Instead of walking to him, Lily pulled on the extension cord. The blow dryer immediately shut down causing Jeremy to look down at it in confusion.

"I'll never get this dried."

"Jeremy, why are you doing this?" Lily came up next to him. She knew the reason as soon as she felt the wetness enter her flat shoes. "Oh my. It is really wet."

"Abs wants to be married up here on the grass, but I'll never get it dry." Jeremy's forlorn and dejected eyes showed his frustration. His hand brushed through his hair as he looked up to see Dev playing with Mort. "Hello Agent Pierce."

Dev smiled. "Jeremy, chill. We aren't on a job. It's just Dev today."

In silence, Lily studied the situation. Her heart hurt for Jeremy. He wanted to please his bride so much. Something needed to be done. By the time she placed her hands on hips she had a solution.

"Jeremy, stop worrying," Lily said as she placed her arm around him. "I'll go talk to her. There's a lovely place by the pond near the large house where she's getting dressed."

Jeremy trailed the extension cord back to the outlet and began once more. Lily intervened quickly. "Just stop," she commanded as she pulled the dryer from his hands. "I'll convince her it'll be better down there on the concrete, but we'll have to move all of these chairs."

"We can do it," Dev said confidently. "Jeremy, bring your truck to the side over here, and I'll start piling them up. We can have this done before noon."

Lily left in the car to drive down to the bride. It was never an easy task to convince a bride on the day of her wedding that really didn't want to do something she had her heart set on. She needed to convince Abby before everyone's chairs sunk into the ground. They'd had a wedding years ago after a big rain that created flooding all over the city. The groom had insisted they be married by the gazebo, and so they were. Shoes were ruined, and his own mother's chair sunk into the mud. She fell over in the middle of the ceremony and arrived at her son's reception with a large brown spot covering her rump. The groom ended up paying thousands in dry cleaning bills on the bridal party's dresses and for the guests in attendance. Lily wouldn't allow a debacle like that for her own friend.

She took a deep breath as she entered the bridal room. The girls were laughing, and beginning their makeup preparations. Abby squealed when Lily entered.

"Where's Andrew?" She searched around for the small boy.

"He's back at the hotel with Dev's aunt, but he'll be here tonight. He wants to dance with you."

Abby turned back to her friends. "Lily has the most adorable little boy. You all are going to fall in love. Do you want a drink? Oh, sorry, you can't. How about some water?"

"I'm fine. I need to talk to you in the hallway."

Abby knew that tone. That tone meant something was wrong. She'd heard it years before when a blush rose was too pink, when the photographer was drunk, when flowers were added to the cake because it was falling over.

Abby took Lily's hand and quickly left the room, shutting the door firmly behind them.

"What? Just tell me. Jeremy isn't coming, right?"

"No, Abs, he's already here. We need to move the ceremony to the lake location, right outside the back of this building." Lily's composure was due to years of explanations, and always maintaining a professional mystique, no matter how bad a situation was. If she could stare down a drug dealer and a terrorist, she could certainly calm a nervous bride.

"But that's not where I wanted the wedding. It's supposed to be up by the stables." Her lower lip stuck out as though she were three again, and she didn't get the extra scoop of ice cream.

Lily halfway expected Abby to stamp her foot. She needed to sell this. "Come on. Let me show you something."

Lily pulled Abby by the hand as they walked to the patio below, the nice dry concrete patio that had no wet grass.

"Now, go walk over in the grass," Lily commanded. "It's squishy. Well, it's worse up by the stable. Poor Jeremy has been trying to blow dry the grass. Mort has been rolling around in it and has a wet dog smell now. The chairs are sinking in without people's butts in them. Can you imagine how bad it could be? Remember the wedding after the flood? Well, it could be your wedding. Now, let me show you what we can do."

Lily walked her around the space. There was a small trellis they could decorate. There were already urns on either side that featured lush greens. The photographer would have the perfect photo of the two of them with the lake framing the happy couple. It would be perfect. "We'll lay down multi-colored petals." Lily continued to describe the aesthetics until she saw Abby's eyes glowing with the vision. *I've got her!*

"It'll be perfect," Abby murmured. "Yes, I see it. Okay. Just do what you do. Tell the girls to do whatever you think, and I'm on board with it. You're in charge, Lily."

Lily clapped her hands. *That's all I wanted. Now, it's time to go to work.*

"Abby, I promise, we will make it beautiful." Lily spied Jeremy's truck heading their way. "You need to get back in. Your groom and Dev are coming with the chairs."

Abby placed her hands on her hips. "So you knew I would agree with you?"

"You should know by now, more than anyone, that on a wedding day I do whatever the bride needs me to do." Lily kissed her on the cheek. "Get inside."

"You do what you want to do and make the bride think it was her idea. You just manipulated me. Do you do this to Dev?" Abby continued to scamper inside as she berated her former boss and friend, but Lily didn't respond.

Of course, I do it to him. And it's called diversion. It's a Pierce trait. Lily waited until the two men came to the area. She showed them where to place the chairs, and then headed back to the stable to gather the two assistants to tell them of the changes. They would need lots of petals for this work.

With the trellis decorated a few hours later, the aisle adorned with petals from every rose in the shop, and signs posted marking the location of the ceremony, Lily stood back to make sure it was the look Abby wanted. Dev had assisted her on the trellis. He'd stepped up to help her just like he had just a few years ago. But she missed her number one helper, JT. In fact, Dev had been right. She had all those men around her and not a female friend, but she missed them. Paul and Danny were back home, JT was in California, and Ari and Jackson were God only knew where.

"I'll make sure I grab your dress and shoes, and Andrew's bag," Dev said as he walked her into the house where Abby was still getting ready. "Do you need anything else? Oh, I'm going to bring you a snack too."

"Okay, but Abby has sandwiches. I also saw several bottles of water in a cooler. Make sure you bring that bag next to Andrew's. It has my makeup in it, and a few other things like another pair of flats, just in case."

Dev frowned as he looked at Lily's feet. "You need to get off of those until I get back, and drink plenty of water," he commanded as he pointed down at her swollen ankles. "The reception decoration is finished. Everything is ready to go here. Abby's helpers will be back with the bouquets in a bit. You rest."

His comment was more like an order, so Lily saluted her commanding officer. "Yes, sir."

Dev's brow rose. "Do not make fun of me. I mean it. Get off of those feet, woman."

Lily waved him off and pushed him out of the door. "Go get my stuff, and my son, please."

Dev planted his feet. Her pushes were futile. "I mean it. Do it."

"What?" Abby asked as she entered the kitchen.

Dev looked up from Lily's glares. "She needs to rest, and she needs food and water."

"I'm not a horse," Lily muttered.

Dev leaned down and kissed her slowly. While his lips were still on hers, he whispered, "But you're as stubborn as a mule."

Lily pushed again, but he still didn't budge. There was a problem moving someone who was almost all muscle. *Darn him.* "Get out."

"I'll make sure she eats, drinks, and sits down. I promise, Dev."

"Then I'll go. Thanks, Abs." Dev kissed his wife one more time and ran down the steps to the car. "Oh, and Mort is with Jeremy. They're playing catch."

"I so like him," Abby remarked.

"Because he pushes me around?" Lily reached down to grab a bottle of water out of the cooler.

Abby smiled. "Exactly. Let's get you a sandwich. You can rest on the bed where I'm getting ready. I want you to be a part of all of this."

With her plate filled with a small sandwich, grapes, strawberries, and a couple pieces of celery, Lily propped herself up on the bed in the center of the bridal suite. The smell of hair products hung in the air as Abby's friends flitted around the room grabbing a lipstick, then a mascara, and double sided tape. *Are they taping her into the gown? They could be. I've seen it before.*

Lily munched away while Abby's mother teared up, and the photographer brought the bride out to stand in front of Lily. Abby turned to face her and smiled widely.

"Lily, just look at this dress. Isn't it amazing?"

Holy Moly! When did that happen, Lord? When did this little nut become such a spectacular beauty, a woman who can do anything? Lily swiped away a tear. "Oh my, Abs. You are absolutely breathtaking."

The bright white gown featured a scalloped sweetheart bodice off the shoulders. Abby's waist looked so thin when the tulle skirt flared away from her body in layers. She had a thin silver and pearl belt at her middle. With her hair up off of her shoulders and wrapped into a loose braided bun, you could see her simple pearl choker necklace accented with pearl drop earrings. Lily grabbed her camera and took several photos, immediately texting one of them to Dev.

As everyone in the room took in the bridal beauty, Lily seemed to be the only one hearing the heels as they came up the stairs. They all took note as Gretchen entered, clapping.

"Now, we've had the show, it is time to get these photos started, ladies. We are behind on our schedule."

Gretchen in true Gretchen Malloy fashion was dressed from head-to-toe in designer threads. Today she was wearing a flowing white dress that had large black and deep blue blooms all over it. She also had her signature cleavage showing, and of course, wore her stilettos. Lily looked down to note they were a deep blue with a crystal shimmer. At her neck hung a single topaz teardrop. Her earrings matched as did one ring, but she had the ruby bracelet still on her wrist.

Gretchen came over and kissed Lily on the head. "It is good for the baby girl to rest."

Lily grabbed softly at the bracelet that didn't match. "I have a feeling you like this man a lot if you're willing to wear red when you're in blue shades."

Gretchen's left eyebrow arched. "It's always good to be a trendsetter, Lily. A little color never hurt anyone. Besides, if you had a man give you a bracelet like this, you'd like him too." She leaned down and took Lily's left hand. "It seems you don't have a problem taking one or two pieces of good jewelry from a man either."

"Gretchen, you might have a point there. Now, help me up." The two friends shared a laugh, and the wedding coordinator lightly pulled on Lily's two hands to help her slide off of the tall bed.

Gretchen pointed at the photographer. "You. We need to start taking these photos. Let's begin outside by the pond. I have the men hiding in the other house. Chop, chop. I want the bride back into the building in twenty minutes. Then you can meet with the men."

Lily gave Abby a quick kiss. "Have a wonderful day, Abs. You deserve it and so does Jeremy. I just received a text from your girls that your flowers are downstairs waiting for you."

Abby took Lily in her arms. "This is getting real. Thank you. I couldn't do this without you here," she whispered through a few tears.

Lily stepped out to take one more look at her. "I wouldn't let you marry Jeremy without me. You are stunning. Now, go have a good time."

Gretchen had already scooted the maids and Abby's mother down the stairs. "Come on, bride. I'll help you." She grabbed the back of Abby's dress and steered her down the stairs. After they'd left, and Lily had stopped crying, she slowly made her own way down to watch the photos.

Lily watched the photography session from the back row of chairs. Gretchen made sure every photo was picture perfect, moving this tendril of hair or smoothing out a bridesmaid's dress. Abby loved her bouquet, and more importantly, she approved of the new ceremony location.

After a few minutes, Abby dropped her bouquet into Gretchen's hands and went running up the back patio steps. Lily, confused, looked in that direction to see her husband and son coming toward them.

Abby met them halfway up. "Oh my gosh. He is so cute. Look at those suspenders." Abby extended her hands out and after a thorough examination of the pretty girl in the white dress, he decided she was a friend. He willingly flew into her arms. Lily gazed over at Gretchen. Even the hardened wedding professional had tears in her eyes. *That's my boys! Both of them are ladykillers.*

Dev assisted Abby back down the stairs and spotted his wife. "I have your dress, shoes, and all of the bags in the car. I'll be right back. Oh, and he slept all the way out here."

"Oh thank God. He'll be pleasant for a while." Once Andrew saw his mother, he began to pull away from Abby. She dropped him carefully down onto the concrete, and he ambled quickly to his mother.

"You are getting to be such a big boy. I missed you so much." Lily really had missed him. It was wonderful being with the girls, and decorating a wedding again, but her thoughts had been with Andrew. Soon, a second child would completely fill up her life.

It was unusual for Lily to sit through a wedding. She never did that, well there was that one time...her own wedding! Their friend, FBI agent Tom Fullerton and his wife sat next to Dev and Lily and happily played with Andrew before the ceremony. Gretchen was in all her glory, assisting with Abby's train and making sure the ushers did everything they were supposed to do.

Gretchen Malloy always had her weddings and events begin on time. There was no excuse not to as far as she was concerned. As on cue, the ceremony began with a violin playing. The four maids floated down the aisle. There were chuckles at the back of the aisle as Mort the dog, basket in mouth and a collar of flowers around the neck, walked slowly down the aisle to stand at Jeremy's side.

As the violin's soft strings joined with a trumpet and guitar, everyone stood as the bride, accompanied by her mother, took her very deliberate steps toward her groom.

The vows were perfect until Jeremy forgot his name. The guests laughed. Dev leaned over to Lily and whispered. "Do you think we've called him nitwit so many times he forgot his real name?"

Lily chose not to answer. Dev was probably right. *Bless his little heart.* Jeremy remembered and corrected his misstep. On cue, Mort passed the basket to the officiant who removed the two simple wedding bands. In a matter of minutes, Abby and Jeremy were married. Now it was time to party.

Everything seemed to be fine. Gretchen had her clipboard in hand and was wearing her earpiece. Lily had no idea if the woman was wearing the communication device for her work or for looks. *Knowing Gretchen, she could be listening to a baseball game or receiving messages from Mars.* But for once, Lily was relieved to let Gretchen be Gretchen and for herself to be merely a guest.

"So here's the age progression photo, Tom." Dev passed the FBI agent his phone as soon as they sat down at their table for dinner.

Tom Fullerton looked closely. "You know, that does look like this woman who married a doctor in Johnson County. We were brought in when he went missing. Eventually, we found his body in a ditch up by the airport. The woman hung around for a couple of weeks after, and then her attorney informed us that she was leaving on vacation. She needed to get away. She was distraught. We never saw her again. There still might be a file on the case in our offices. I'll look on Monday and forward them."

"Well, she reminds me of a woman I ran into in Matamores. I was working a cartel investigation that involved the supply chain into Houston, Texas with a connection to a couple of banks down there. They were just beginning a trade of fentanyl and prescription drugs. It's a bigger market with the addition of codeine and heroin. If she is the same woman, I could swear that I was told she was a stone-cold killer. We may be looking at a paid killer situation or a serial murderer. I told you Lily has been investigating after they found that body in our yard, but if this woman is really a killer, she needs to pull back."

Tom laughed. "Good luck with that, Dev. Have you met your wife?"

Dev looked over at her. Luckily, Lily and Tom's wife were busy talking about siblings. "I know. That's what always frightens me when she gets involved in stuff like this. That, and the fact that she's very good at it."

"She's very observant," Tom answered. "In fact, right now she knows we're talking about her, and at the same time, she's listening to my wife." Both men stared in her direction. Lily blew a kiss. "See what I mean?"

Dev just shook his head. He knew everything about his wife. Then again, he learned something new every day. She made life worthwhile and interesting. She had arrived in his life just in time to save him.

"Dev, I talked to your friend Paul the other day. He might be in over his head," Tom remarked as the salads were served.

"I'll talk to him. I'm the one who suggested he get in touch with you. He's looking at a child trafficking situation in Maryland that might be connected to a drug case I'm working on."

Lily sat down next to her husband and son. "What are we discussing?"

Dev smiled and nodded knowingly at Tom. "We are discussing how beautiful this salad is. Oh, and our server said they'll be bringing Andrew chicken fingers and macaroni and cheese with peaches."

Lily squinted. "You are one of the worst liars ever. I always wonder how you do your job."

Tom's head tilted back in laughter. "She has you there, Dev. You really are an awful liar."

Dev stabbed a piece of lettuce. "I'm good at it when it counts. Trust me."

Thankfully, Andrew's food arrived and saved the inquiry.

The evening began to pass away. The main course was served, toasts were made. Abby and Jeremy performed their first dance to some rock song. They cut their cake, and Lily was one of the first in line for her sweet treat.

Dev had just finished a bourbon when he stood and offered a hand to Lily. "Come dance with me."

"You don't have to ask me twice," Lily answered. Besides, Andrew was happily playing with a place card while surrounded by more than one admirer.

Thankfully for Lily, it was a slow dance. She was just about done for the day. She'd been on her feet way too long. She leaned her head on Dev's lowered shoulder.

"Are you feeling better now or do you still feel like an outsider?" Dev asked. He saw Gretchen moving through the tables. She caught his eye and waved.

"I'm okay now. I'm where I should be. I know that. And I'm who I should be, and that's with you." She pulled back to stare into his eyes. "God really did answer my prayers. He took his time, and then you took your own sweet time, but waiting has been well worth it."

"It certainly has." He kissed her lightly and pulled her closer. His world was in his arms. As soon as the song was over, Lily began to lead him back to the table, but one of Dev's favorite salsa songs began. He pulled her to him. "Oh no. You and I are going to dance this last one, and then we'll go."

Lily shook her head. "But I don't know how to dance to this."

Dev winked. "Oh, but I know how to salsa, and I haven't done it in quite awhile. Humor me."

"Oh, Lord," Lily muttered.

"Just hold on for the ride. Don't let go of my hands."

Dev's tie had been long removed, and his shirt was open at least three buttons down. His gaze almost made her uncomfortable, but on the other hand it was exciting to be swaying in a fashion that wasn't what she usually would do. He did challenge her in many ways. She wouldn't let go of his hand; she thought she might careen into table five. As her husband twirled her until her back was against his chest, Lily noticed that several couples had left the dance floor leaving them one of two sets of dancers. As quickly as Lily could look over, it seemed like the other man and woman were very good at the Latin dance. But she had her DEA husband, and obviously her undercover love had done a lot of salsa dancing in his past. *Geez, did the agency have to train him in Latin dances? Note to me...ask later when I have more breath in my lungs.* Thankfully, the song ended. Lily was in her husband's arms, dipped over, gazing into his beautiful eyes.

"I love you, but I'm so done, Dev."

He lifted her up and kissed her. "I was hoping for more words of love, but I do think you are done. Frankly, so am I. It's been a long day."

Lily held his hand as they headed back to the table and to a clapping little boy. "Frankly, it's been a long week. I'll say goodbye to Abby, Jeremy, and Gretchen while you get our son together." Lily was on her way to the happy couple when Abby grabbed the microphone and pointed at her.

"I want to thank someone very special in my life. She's been there for me while I was figuring out how to be an adult. She's taught me so much, and she's given me skills that gave me a great life. She used to be my boss, but more importantly now, she is one of my dearest friends. She put together all of these beautiful flowers and made my day perfect. I raise my glass to Lily. I love you."

Lily continued walking to the bride and hugged her upon her arrival. "I love you too. I'm so proud of you and of Jeremy."

Abby spoke again into the microphone. "And Lily and Dev are celebrating their anniversary!"

"Okay, that's enough. Abs, I have to go. My body is shot. We will see you two at the party tomorrow?"

Abby giggled. "You know it. I'm not going to miss Gretchen seeing Dev in swim trunks. It'll be too delicious.``

Lily narrowed her eyes. Instead of responding playfully, she hugged Jeremy. She searched for Gretchen. Auntie G was holding Andrew and talking to Dev.

"You don't want him to go to West Point, do you?" Gretchen's question made Dev laugh.

"He's only two, Gretchen. We have time."

"What's going on?" Lily asked as she arrived. Andrew instantly stretched out to climb into his mother's arms.

"I just think that Drew should be allowed the freedom to make his own decisions. Auntie G will support him no matter what, but I'm not sure he should go to West Point."

"Okay, Gretchen. But like Dev said, we have some time. Fullertons, we need to get the little guy and me to bed. We're going to go. Will we see you tomorrow?"

"Of course, Lily," Tom's wife answered quickly. "Gretchen invited us weeks ago. I don't think I've ever been to a pool party for a toddler."

Dev casually leaned closer to Tom. "I suppose we should consider ourselves lucky Gretchen didn't plan some sort of three-ring circus with elephants, lions, and monkeys."

"I heard that Devlin Pierce." Gretchen's tone created a thread of terror down Dev's spine. She reminded him of a particularly nasty commanding officer when he was only a lieutenant. She also reminded him of a nun, only without the habit, the ruler for hitting his hands, and of course, the virginal soul. "And, for your information, my condo wouldn't allow the elephants or the lions. The monkeys were unavailable on Sunday. They have their own union."

Dev and Tom laughed out loud, but Gretchen's act continued. She seemed serious. She could see their discomfort, and that's when she finally broke her stoic demeanor.

"Gotcha," she yelled. "Of course we wouldn't have animals. They're very uncomfortable with the fireworks."

Was she having fireworks? Dev couldn't read her at all. He stood up and grabbed Andrew's bag. "It's time to go. We'll see you all tomorrow. Gretchen, we'll appreciate anything you've planned."

Loading his precious cargo into the rental car, Dev drove back to the hotel in silence. Lily and Andrew fell asleep before he even drove the car onto the interstate. An hour later, Lily heard the car door open. Her eyes were blinded by the hotel's exterior lights.

As Dev pulled his son out of the car seat, Andrew stirred a little before he planted his head on his father's shoulder. Dev lifted out the bags and flipped the keys to the valet.

"Could you please park the car? I have my hands full. Room 626. Pierce." The hotel worker nodded understandingly. By the time Dev rounded the car, Lily was standing there.

"I can park the car."

"No, you're done. Come on, let's get both of you to bed."

Once they were in the room, Lily placed Andrew down and changed for bed. Dev went down the hall to grab a snack and drinks. He was beginning to enjoy the late night treats. He entered the room to see Lily in a lovely black negligee he'd never seen before, and her feet propped up on the cocktail table in front of her.

"Am I in the wrong room?" he asked sheepishly as he brought the food and two bottles of water to her.

"Come here," Lily said seductively as she patted the spot next to her. She'd been practicing her seductive voice, one she had never had in her life. But Gretchen had insisted that she needed one. Gretchen had also told her she was taking advantage of Dev's good heart. *That isn't true, but he does do so much.*

"I'm either in the wrong room, or I'm in trouble." He hung his head down, and he sat next to her. "Nice perfume."

"It's body lotion."

"Well it's nice. I brought you some more of those strawberries. I noticed the other night that Gretchen ate all of them. There's also some celery, cheese for me, these little tomato wheels--"

Lily slowly slid her arm around his back and pressed her body to him.

Dev's hands remained in his lap. *This is interesting.* "Why Mrs. Pierce, are you trying to seduce me? I thought you were tired, but maybe we should dance more often."

"I was tired, but I just had a nap." She nuzzled his neck. "We'll have to talk about how experienced you are in all things Latin."

"Some day after I'm retired." Lily's lips tenderly tickled his neck. "This hotel really does something to you," Dev murmured. "I was once told that sex on your wedding night is highly overrated. That most people just go to sleep from the exhaustion of the day."

Lily continued to move her lips from his collar to his mouth. "Um, that's if you're the ones getting married. If you're already married, a wedding can make your wife want you more than she usually does. Besides, you've been wonderful today. You let me be me."

"I wouldn't have it any other way, even when you make me crazy with your Jessica routine." He turned and took her in his arms. "The problem is you're usually right with your suspicions."

Lily bolted from his arms and sat back. "Really? I'm right about Margot Fleischman?" Her face was literally beaming with delight, and her voice had raised higher in pitch.

Dev was torn emotionally. He relished the joy in her face, but he wanted to kick himself for ruining the mood. "Well, Tom is going to look into it, but he's pretty sure she's the same woman who was involved in a FBI case here in Kansas City. We both think she's still alive."

"Oh my gosh! Wouldn't it be amazing to solve this whole thing? I mean, the doctor's life with her would have closure, his daughter wouldn't have to look over her shoulder anymore--"

Dev grabbed one of her hands. "Wait, back up. His daughter wouldn't have to look over her shoulder? What are you talking about? Have I missed something?"

Lily's eyes showed panic. "Um, well, I didn't tell you I had lunch with her when you were gone. She was up in Fairfax for a case for her law firm, and her father set it up. Did you know she has had threatening mail for several years now? I also found out she was abused by Margot, and that's probably why Dr. Fleischman didn't pursue his missing wife. It was good riddance. Mrs. Parrot is the one who called the police about the abuse when she saw a mark on Laurel's arm."

"Honey, we've been through this before. You can't get so carried away that you're careless and place yourself in danger. Even some people who are trained get in over their heads." Dev needed to call Paul to go over details with him so his friend wouldn't be put into any danger he couldn't handle.

Dev's reprimand and reminder fell on deaf ears. "This is so exciting, Dev. Really. I mean if Tom thinks this is something, and you do too, then it must be something really big."

"Lily," Dev said quietly. He stared into her eyes. He said nothing else.

She knew. *How could Dev ruin a moment by just uttering her name? He's such a killjoy sometimes. I was trying to be romantic.* Dev took a piece of cheese from the plate and ate it as he walked into the bedroom. She was left with the chocolate covered strawberries and a place on the couch that was now empty.

Lily quickly ate a strawberry. *Oh my gosh, that's better than sex. Well...*She waited a few minutes and then joined her husband. Dev was already in bed. *The man can undress as fast as he can dress. It must be Army training.* The television was on, but was mute. Her sleeping son was out for the night.

"I'm sorry. I should've told you. I guess I just forgot."

"Uh huh."

Holy Moly. I've done it now. Lily looked over at him. His concentration level was amazing. He hadn't even sent her a glance. *This nightgown wasn't worth the price I paid for it! He's mad, or he's pretending. Could he be? And why does he have to look so good?*

She planned an alternative attack. She turned out the light and got into bed. Dev continued to sit up, watching a baseball game. By this time of night, he really needed a shave. With his longer than usual hair, he almost looked like a bad boy. He was bare chested, but as Lily decided to implement her plan, she realized that his chest wasn't the only unclothed part of his body that wasn't covered. *He's not that mad.*

"You have to forgive me. We can't be fighting at our son's birthday party."

"We never fight. We have discussions, don't we?" Dev looked down at her. "Besides, we can't be fighting when Gretchen presents the monkeys."

"There's no monkeys. Knowing Auntie G, there's probably fireworks."

Dev turned off the television and turned to his wife. Hovering over Lily, he finally smiled. "I'll show you fireworks, woman."

"I knew you weren't really mad. You love me too much."

"That is the truth, but again, you need to be careful. If Margot is who I think she is, this little hunt could become a very dangerous big game hunt. I don't trust the doctor, his daughter, not any of them. I want you to trust no one. Now, prove to me how much you love me."

Lily pretended to be completely bored. "Fine, if you insist."

Chapter Seventeen

"Oh my dear Lord," Lily exclaimed as she entered the pool area of Gretchen's apartment building. "I think the theme is unicorns and rainbows."

Dev's eyes centered on the small white pony, a real pony, adorned with a purple and gold cone on his nose. A small saddle with fringe completed the look. *Wait, are the hooves painted pink? Ah geez!* The pretend unicorn was accompanied by his trainer dressed as a fairy. Across the pool were balloons shaped and colored in the form of a rainbow. On the gift table were an abundance of presents.

"How are we getting all of these gifts on the plane?"

Lily looked up at Dev's blank face. "Close your mouth, honey. I'll find some way. Oh look. There's a little cake for Andrew, and there's another cake."

"You mean the three-tiered number under the umbrella that has real balloons sticking out of it? What the hell was she thinking?"

But Andrew was in awe of the colors and of the pony. As soon as Auntie G joined them, he immediately jumped into her arms and went off to the unicorn.

"I'm speechless." He gazed at Gretchen in her best ensemble to replicate Auntie Mame. With her signature animal print stilettos, she had on a black jumpsuit with harem-style pants, and a gold tunic top. Her accessories were all gold from an ankle bracelet to drop earrings that Andrew liked to touch. But his son was more intent on his perch atop the pony. Dev could see all of his teeth in his wide smile.

Lily nudged him in the ribs. "Look at him. She's made him the happiest little guy in the world."

"If you got me a pony, I'd love you too. But this is too much, too--"

Lily laughed. "Over-the-top? So Gretchen?"

And it was. Guests began to arrive including Dev's Aunt Pat, The Fullertons, Abby and Jeremy who were delaying their honeymoon until the winter, a couple of acquaintances from Lily's time at the flower shop, and two surprise guests. Dev was beyond surprised when his father showed up. The other surprise came in the form of a man jumping into the pool, swimming under the rainbow balloons, and emerging yelling *Go Navy, Beat Army.* JT bobbed up from the water and yelled out *Cowabunga.*

"No wonder Gretchen had a pool party," Lily remarked to Tom's wife. "She's been trying to see JT's pecs for three years now."

It was Gretchen's lucky day when Dev dove into the pool to join the former SEAL. Lily glanced over at her friend, and Gretchen seemed more amused than the birthday boy. The food served was phenomenal including small puff pastry filled with macaroni and cheese, appetizer pizza wheels, cold shrimp, crab rolls, filet mignon bites, and petite stuffed potatoes. Gretchen had arranged for one of her favorite chefs to grill lobster and steaks. Thankfully, there were no monkeys, and Jack and JT's presence were the only other surprises... except for the fireworks when the skies became dark.

Gretchen held Andrew and pointed up at the sky. The first round of pyrotechnics illuminated the clay tiles and the towers of the Plaza. America's first open-air planned shopping and restaurant area never looked so good as each round of fireworks brightened the night. Auntie G oohed and aahed with her small charge as she pointed at each sky design above them.

Dev watched the two of them, marveling at how much Andrew was listening to the woman. His arms hugged her neck, and his head pillowed under her chin. Andrew's calm demeanor meant one of two things...he would be a pyromaniac, or he loved Gretchen. *Perhaps she really is Andrew's Auntie G?*

As Dev watched the two, their forms lit by the fire in the sky, another man joined them. He lightly kissed Gretchen on the cheek and placed his arm around her. Dev splashed water at his wife's feet and pointed at the sight.

"Is that him?" Lily mouthed. Dev's nod gave her an answer. It was the detective, Gretchen's man for the time, but this seemed different. Lily analyzed the couple. Detective Daniel Williams had once accused Gretchen of a murder she didn't commit, but now he was holding her as though she was a priceless piece of china. The man was younger than Gretchen, but that was probably a good thing. Lily had trouble keeping up with the woman when they used to work on weddings together. He was handsome with just a little silver in his hair.

Dev came to stand by his wife. "Well, what do you think?"

"I think they actually look good together."

Dev pulled his towel around his shoulders. "He's a really nice guy, and he's wealthy, but he works as a cop. He also works with urban kids. He's almost too good to be true."

Lily looked admiringly. "He really loves her, and it almost looks like she's in love with him. She looks so soft and less Gretchen right now."

Dev, like his son, continued to be mesmerized by the show. "How much did she spend on this?" Lily wiped away a tear.

"Too much, but that's Gretchen. God bless her."

"We'll have to do something for her," Dev suggested, but Lily cackled.

"Oh, I think she's been rewarded enough for one day. She's seen JT and you in nothing but swim trunks. She's good for a while."

After the show in the sky ended, the detective came over to meet Lily. After the introductions, they sat down at one of the tables to watch the party.

"She goes a little above and beyond, doesn't she?"

Lily did a double take. "That is an understatement, detective."

"Daniel, please." He laughed. "But strangely that's what really entertains me. Plus, the woman is honest. She may be many things, but she doesn't lie. It's refreshing to not play around."

Lily almost spit out her lemonade. As it was, she had some of the liquid lodged in her nostrils. *Gretchen is the queen of playing around.* As if she'd heard Lily's thoughts, Gretchen touched JT's shoulder and tried to wrap her hand around his very ample bicep. *Yes, Gretchen is one happy woman tonight.*

"Daniel, I have to ask since no one else will," Lily stated. She stopped. *Should I ask? Go ahead, you'll never get another opportunity like this.* "What are your intentions with our Gretchen?"

The detective took a drink of his beer. "Truth be told, your husband already asked that after I met him. My intentions are very clear. I just want to make her happy."

Lily nodded. "That's all I wanted to hear. It is wonderful that you are in her life."

"Lily, you know she misses you every day," he said quietly.

"No. She has such a life." Lily giggled nervously.

"But she doesn't have you here. You mean so much to her."

Lily wiped away a tear. "That's nice to know. Thank you. I miss her too." *Oh, Lord, I really do miss her and all of her insanity.*

Dev took Andrew in for one final dip in the water. The birthday boy was yawning, but he was persistently attempting to not close his eyes. Lily figured his stimulation level was off the charts. He'd eaten cake, opened gifts of stuffed animals and clothing which he promptly threw on the ground. He had been propelled across the water by his Uncle JT and caught by his father. His grandfather had proudly helped him blow out his candles, and all the adults in his presence were surprised at his good behavior. Now Lily was yawning. It had been a long week, and it was time to go home.

Andrew was handed off to Abby. Her new husband Jeremy, Dev, his father, and JT began an impromptu volleyball match. Lily looked over at Gretchen. The pool lights lit the men as though they were in a movie. She thought Gretchen wiped a tear or two from her eyes. *Maybe Gretchen is so happy to be with everyone? Nah!* JT went up to block Dev's wicked spike and Gretchen clapped furiously. *Gretchen has created her own volleyball scene from a certain Navy movie!* But, as if she could sense that she shouldn't enjoy this too much in the presence of Daniel, Gretchen blew him a kiss. The detective just shook his head as she sauntered over to him. She laced her arm through his.

"Gretchen, you do realize the volleyball scene with Maverick was with Navy pilots, and not an Army guy and a Navy SEAL?" Lily nudged Gretchen's arm to bring her back to reality, hopefully.

"Navy, smavy, it doesn't matter. They're servicemen. That's good enough. Oh, and they have muscles." Gretchen's attention was on the pool. She hugged Lily while still keeping her eyes on the men. She stole a kiss from Daniel, who seemed amused by the entire situation. "Lily, I don't know how you did it, well, I do, but you got him. You are a very lucky woman." Gretchen nudged her own man. "And it seems I am too."

Dev rose up out of the pool, his upper body completely exposed, spiking the volleyball into JT's face. Lily smiled. "Yes, yes, I am, Gretchen." *You have no idea, nor will I ever tell you!*

While the boys played in the pool, Lily said goodbye to all her friends and Kansas City family. It was definitely time to kiss this lovely city goodbye. It would always be where she was from. She'd miss the fountains, the football Sundays, the Plaza lighting on Thanksgiving night, and even driving around the Meyer Circle on Ward Parkway, but she had a future beyond here.

Gretchen broke from her detective and slipped her arm around Lily's waist. "Thank you for allowing me to do all of this. It was just the best day. I noticed you even got in the water for a little bit."

"Yes, but we should be the ones thanking you. This was beyond anything we would've done."

"I know," Gretchen admitted freely. "But that's why God put people like Auntie G on this earth. I will never have a child. I'll never know what you feel, but I can offer something, even if it's just what I can do with my money."

Lily turned and hugged her friend. She patted her tenderly on the back. "Gretchen, you are so much more than just your money. As Andrew grows, he will love you, and this new baby will too."

"I know I go a little crazy."

Both women were tearing up a bit as they pulled out of the embrace. "You think? We thought the cake was too much, then the horse, but then the fireworks really were outrageous."

Gretchen carefully patted under her eyes. "But wasn't it fun?"

"Oh, it was fantastic. I need to get that little guy to bed."

"Which one are you talking about?" Gretchen purred. "If I could take my pick--"

Lily tapped her foot. "The baby, Gretchen. Well, and the very attractive dark haired one too."

"He is still Mr. Delicious." Gretchen said as she admired the man who fell in love with the little florist with the frizzy hair and the curves. "But," Gretchen added as she nodded back to Daniel. "I seem to have my own Mr. Delicious now."

"We'll agree that Dev is the first Mr. Delicious, and Daniel can be number two. He's nice. Don't blow this. We need to call it a night. We will fly out tomorrow afternoon."

"And then I won't see you until next year when I meet that little girl."

Lily waved at Dev. Jack saw her and left the pool. He grabbed a heavy towel. He and Abby wrapped up Andrew. "We can virtually call until we see you next. And don't put all your hopes in a girl, please. The baby could be another boy."

Gretchen waved her words out of the air with her hand. "Pish, posh. That will not happen. I designed a little girl's room, and Dev and you promised."

Lily knew it was a losing battle attempting to convince Gretchen of the facts of reproduction so she surrendered quickly. Sometimes giving up was the only way, and with Gretchen, it was usually the only way to make her happy.

"Lily, Jack and I are sharing a room, and flying out with you." JT was dangerously close to Gretchen as he dried himself off. He'd come from SEAL training. Every muscle was perfect; his hair was almost non-existent.

"Wonderful. I can't believe you both flew in just for today."

"Actually, we came early on Saturday, but you all were busy with the wedding. We played with Andrew while Dev's aunt took care of him, and Jack and I had a great dinner last night. It was worth it to see all of this." JT looked around the pool deck and smiled. "I wish I were a baby again."

Gretchen heard him and didn't miss a beat. "I could arrange that, dear."

The mental image that Lily was forming began to turn her stomach. JT looked a little frightened, as well he should be. The man who had survived terrorists dand the Taliban informed both ladies that Jack and he would be leaving with the happy family. Together. No man left behind.

With impeccable timing, Daniel and Dev joined them. JT seemed more than a little relieved when Gretchen's male friend placed his arm around her shoulders. Dev shook the detective's hand and promised to stay in touch if only to hear about Gretchen's further adventures into investigating. One of Daniel's stories kept Dev amused for hours.

The Fullertons said their goodbyes, as did Abby and Jeremy. Some of Gretchen and Lily's friends remained, drinking signature blue martinis. Lily's longer than usual hug with Abby sealed the end of the trip. They pulled apart from each other, both with tears staining their faces.

"And I'll see you next Monday," Tom said, pointing at Jeremy.

"What?" Lily exclaimed. It seemed like she was the only one who didn't get a memo.

"Jeremy will be joining our office next Monday. He's been assigned to Kansas City," Tom explained.

"That's wonderful!" Lily hugged the newlyweds one more time. "So, is Jeremy moving into my house?"

"We wanted to talk to you about that," Jeremy said quietly. "Lily, we'd like to buy your house instead of renting."

Lily's mouth gaped open. Dev grasped his wife's hand. "We can talk about that after you get settled," he suggested.

Abby agreed. "I want to see Jeremy's first pay stub before we do this, if it's okay with you, Lily."

Lily took in a deep breath and then smiled widely. "Of course. If I'm selling the house, I'd prefer you two started your married life there. We'll talk. I'm just a little overwhelmed, but I think it's a great idea."

Dev let go of his wife's hand. He knew, absolutely knew

what she was thinking. This trip was emotional for her; it had shown her that her decisions and choices had led her away from everything she had in Kansas City. Of course, she'd return now and then, but Lily's past truly was in the past now. He put his shirt on to walk back to the hotel. With their bag in his hand, he walked over to Gretchen.

He hugged her warmly and kissed her on the cheek. "Thank you, for all of this Gretchen, and for being such a good friend to Lily and me. And now, thank you for being an amazing aunt to Andrew. We love you."

Gretchen Malloy remained speechless. Lily saw the twinkle in her husband's eyes. His satisfaction showed. Dev had finally silenced Gretchen.

The next afternoon, Lily's gaze out the plane's window offered her one more look at her hometown. Dev turned his head to watch, but not at the view. He loved to study her face, to see her emotions in real time before she had the opportunity to mask her feelings. He knew what she did because he did the same thing. For most of his adult life, he had to fight the willingness to express his feelings. His outright survival in many situations was an excuse to hide how he felt, his anger, and his joy. But Lily broke him down. At work he had to turn it off, but as soon as he entered through their home's door, he was broken, but in a good way. She could read him, and he could read her.

"Why was it so much easier to get on the plane today?" Lily asked as she turned away from the window. She'd already scraped away a tear that had escaped.

"We had JT and Dad help us."

She shook her head. "That is so sad. We need four adults for one baby."

Dev looked down at the sleeping Andrew in the seat between them. "Does that mean we'll need eight when the next baby comes?"

Lily smiled. "I'm sure we can round them up." She leaned forward from her seat to see JT and her father-in-law sitting across the aisle. JT instinctively looked over at her as if he could feel her watching. He smiled.

"I'm glad Dev's the one who has to get out of his seat this time if you have to pee."

Lily placed her hand up to her ear. "I didn't hear you. What?"

JT laughed out loud and shared his joke with Jack Pierce. But Dev wasn't laughing. *Great. I gave her the window seat!*

Chapter Eighteen

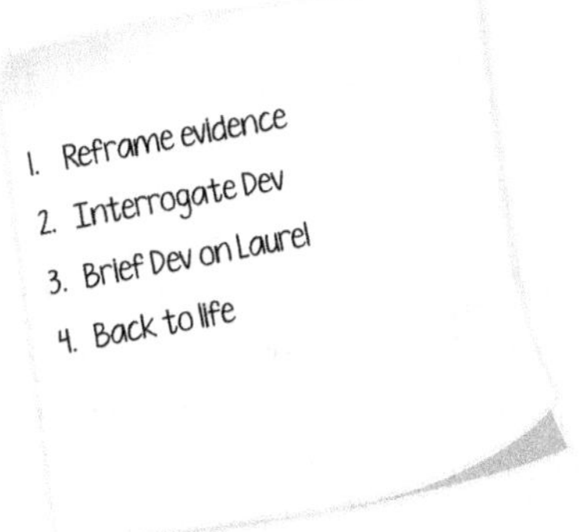

"Welcome home." The door of their house opened and a man stood in the doorway as he lifted a glass of wine in Lily and Dev's direction.

"What the hell?" Dev lifted Andrew out of the car seat as Lily ran toward the door. "Ari?"

"What are you doing here?" Lily asked as she greeted her very special friend. She kissed him quickly on the cheek and shoved him out of the way. "I've got to get to the bathroom. Talk later."

"What are you doing here?" Dev asked cooly as he stood in front of the international agent. "May I come into my own home?"

"Well, of course. And I'm bearing gifts for Andrew, Lily, and even you."

Dev rolled his eyes. "How kind. By the way, how did you get in?"

Ari nonchalantly followed Dev into the living room. "I told you Pierce, you need to upgrade your security system. I can upgrade it for you while I'm here."

Dev placed Andrew on the floor and dropped one of the bags onto the couch. "We didn't invite you in. You can't just come in if we haven't invited you in."

"You're babbling. I'm not a vampire. I can get in just about any facility. Houses are elementary." Ari walked confidently into the kitchen and poured another glass of wine. "What will you be drinking?"

"Something stronger than wine," Dev muttered as he freed Andrew. Of course, his son followed after his godfather.

"I brought you bourbon from Scotland. Will that suffice?"

"Seriously? Why would you do that?" Dev huffed his displeasure at Ari's appearance. He didn't mind the man if he had given some warning. With no warning, Ari was an interloper, a menace.

"Because we're friends? I have no idea why I did it. I was in Scotland. I saw the bourbon, and I thought you might like it. If you don't, the priest will." Ari pulled a large bottle from a box and opened it. He opened several cabinets until he found the proper glass. He handed a full glass to Dev.

"And are you cooking?" Dev picked up Andrew who was about to place Ari's billfold in his mouth. "Don't leave anything expensive on the table."

"My, we are cranky." Ari grabbed the billfold, wiping off the slobber. "We are having baked chicken in a bath of wine with a reduced mushroom sauce. I have a grilled vegetable pasta salad cooling in the refrigerator. I'm also serving roasted parmesan potatoes." Ari stopped to listen to the sound emanating from the downstairs bathroom. It wasn't a good one. "Is Lily okay? She doesn't sound okay."

"She had onions on her hamburger."

Ari didn't understand. "Is she allergic to onions? I don't recall that."

Dev smiled at his son, now on his lap, as he sipped the expensive liquor. He looked up at Ari. "You don't recall that because she isn't allergic to onions, but they make her throw up now. She's pregnant."

Ari poured more wine in his glass and sat down at the table. "Well, how did that happen?"

Dev chuckled out loud. "The old-fashioned way, you goof."

"I realize that, Pierce," Ari said, his voice just a little higher. "I mean, did you two plan another baby?"

"We aren't planning anything, Ari. At our ages, we're blessed to have this little guy, and if we can have another, we'll be a complete family."

Ari looked at him over the rim of his glass. "So, we're happy about this?"

Lily arrived to answer his question. "Ecstatic. When I'm not sick. Sorry about all of that." She reached out to hug her friend. Ari stood and took her in his embrace.

Lily looked like she'd been through a war as Ari examined her. He led her to a chair quickly and sat her down. Her sunken eyes and swollen face made him wonder about her health. "What can I get you? Crackers? A soda of some kind?"

"Did you happen to purchase milk?" *I bet the ladies at the grocery store stopped everything to check him out. Literally. I wish I'd been there.*

Ari smiled and pointed his finger up in the air. "That is one thing I always get. I'll pour you a glass. What about a banana?"

Lily sighed as her stomach calmed. "Peanut butter and jelly on toast for me, but Andrew would love that banana."

Ari began to pull items from the refrigerator and the cabinets. He knew them well from his adventure at the Pierce house. "Your wish is my command."

Dev rolled his eyes. "I'm going to get the rest of the luggage into the house. Take our son, and allow your servant here to take care of you." He kissed the top of her head as he handed Andrew over. *She's awfully warm. She's usually cold when she's pregnant.*

Dev and Ari shared a look between them before one man left. Ari saw the concern in the husband's eyes and the nod of his head in his wife's direction. Something wasn't right. Ari knew Pierce long enough to know when the man thought something was out of sync.

"For you, my friend and your small attachment there." Andrew's hand instinctively latched onto his favorite food item. Lily took a bite and then a drink of cold milk.

"Thank you, Ari. Can I ask? Why are you here?"

"I couldn't make it to that grand party you had for Master Pierce, but I thought I'd drop in to welcome you home. And, I came bearing gifts. I'll present them after dinner. Oh, and we're having roasted potatoes, baked chicken in a wine and mushroom sauce, and a vegetable pasta salad. Will you be okay with the wine?"

Ari was crouched before Lily, his deep-set eyes focused directly on her. She patted his tanned face. "Of course, I will, friend. You are too good to me."

"I'm never too good. I'm bad or some have found me fantastic, and the best they have ever had. But never too good." He flashed his signature mischievous smile.

Lily leaned over and kissed him on the cheek. "Whatever."

Dev could've just ignored what he saw in the kitchen. He knew it wasn't anything he should be concerned about, but as the husband, he felt as though it was his job to act jealous. He dropped the two pieces of luggage climatically on the floor with a loud thud.

"You two do know that I'm here, right?"

Ari's eyebrows furrowed in concern. "Did you hear something, Lily, dear?"

Lily turned to see her husband, his arms folded in pretend dismay. "I think I heard something. Maybe it's thunder?"

Dev shook his head. "I'm taking all of this upstairs, and I'll sort it for the laundry while you two play house."

"Excellent idea, Pierce," Ari admitted. He clapped his hands in satisfaction. "So, Lily, how was the party? I want to hear all about it. Excuse me while I continue preparing the potatoes."

Lily watched Ari remove foil from a tray to uncover quartered potatoes with some kind of seasoning on them. He removed the roasting pan from the oven and placed the potatoes within. "Well, it was crazy. Gretchen, well Gretchen was Gretchen. It was a pool party complete with a horse costumed like a unicorn, rainbow colored balloons extending over the pool, and fireworks at the end of the night."

"Pool party for the little guy? JT was there, right?" Ari asked as he checked the chicken.

"Yes, and of course, Dev. She had her fill of abs and pecs for a while. JT was flying back from Coronado. I don't know if it's possible, but I think his arms are getting larger."

Ari chuckled. "He really will be Popeye if he gets any bigger. And the man swears he's never taken steroids."

Andrew had eaten all of his banana. Lily reached for a towel on the side of the counter and began to clean him up. "Ari, did they ever give you a nickname? You should have one."

"No. I'm not part of their team." Ari's cold and abrupt answer made Lily stop.

"But you are, besides, JT wasn't either. You're just as much one of them as he is."

Ari returned the lid on the roasting pan and turned around. "I am not, Lily. I will never be. There will always be an element of non-trust between all of us. That is the way it is."

His face said it all. He totally believed what he had just said. And he knew for certain it would never change.

Lily released Andrew down onto the floor. "I'm sure after all of these years, that's changed."

"No. Just drop it." Ari turned back to his food. The conversation had unceremoniously ended.

Lily was shocked. Her heart hurt for him. The feeling was so similar to when her father would say that a discussion was over, when he said it was over, not really when she wanted it to end. *What the heck don't I know? Was there some betrayal or miscommunication? Surely, it's not because of Ari's lineage or country of origin?* She wondered if she asked Dev what kind of a response she would receive.

"I'll leave you to cook. I'm going to get Andrew into a bath. Thank you for the wonderful meal." Lily retreated from the kitchen before Ari had the opportunity to answer her. She refused to cry in front of him.

Ari bit the inside of his mouth. *I shouldn't be that way with her. I shouldn't talk that way, but the past is always with me.*

As one Pierce left, another returned. Dev had changed into shorts, a tee, and sported sandals on his feet. "Honey, it smells fantastic."

He poured himself another glass of bourbon. Ari's back was to him. The usually talkative super agent remained silent. "Did I do something?"

"No. I did."

Dev was confused. He hadn't been gone that long. "You do know I wasn't really jealous of you two, right?"

"I know." Still Ari stared at the stove, basting the chicken over and over.

"What happened? By the way, thanks for this. This is the finest bourbon I think I've ever drunk."

"No, we had that bourbon in London, remember? You were coming back from that awful deployment when everything went wrong."

Ari finally turned around. He watched as Dev sipped his drink.

Dev slowly placed his glass on the table and leaned back. "I remember that. We were in that pub down the street from the Embassy. You were headed back to finish things off."

"I headed back home to see my wife."

Dev sat straight up. "What the hell is going on? You were you when I went upstairs, and now you are someone I don't recognize."

Ari took a deep breath. "I made Lily cry."

Dev shot out of his seat. "What the hell did you do?"

"It was nothing, really. I just gave her a shot of reality. She wondered why your band of thieves never gave me a nickname. She said I was part of your team. I told her I wasn't, nor would I ever be."

Dev stopped in his tracks. He'd been willing to go hand-to-hand with him only seconds before the explanation. "Oh. She wouldn't understand that."

"Exactly," Ari admitted plainly. "If I tell her about the past, she'll hate me. I'm not sure my heart could take that."

Dev's crooked smile made Ari wonder what he was thinking. "I understand that. After I left her when my job was finished in Kansas City, I have to admit that there were nights when my heart actually hurt. I had disappointed her. I've attempted to make it up to her every single day."

Ari reached out for Dev's arm. He grasped it strongly, desperately. "I can't tell her. Will you explain it to her? She won't stop until she finds out. I saw her eyes light up with the prospect of solving my mystery. I just can't be the one to tell her that I betrayed you all."

Devlin Pierce shut his eyes briefly, opening them in realization of what he had to do. He had to help Ari forgive himself. He reached around him and embraced the usual nuisance of a man. "That was a long time ago. Ari, we have forgiven, and in some cases forgotten. It was a war. We all did what we were ordered to do. She'll understand."

"I better pull away from you for this one." Ari dabbed at his eyes. "I love your wife." He saw Dev's jaw clench. "Not in that way, but she has changed me. She has made me realize that life isn't that bad, well not all the time. I don't want to lose her friendship."

Dev reached for his forehead. "This gives me a headache." He lowered his hand. "But I do understand. You two are great friends for some reason, and I respect that. But you need to be the one to explain why you said what you did. By the way, you are totally wrong. You should have a nickname, in fact, I think we did name you."

"No, you all named the blasted donkey."

Dev cocked his head to the side. "Did we? I don't remember."

Ari opened the stove's door to check his potatoes. "You remember. Ask Daniel."

Dev snapped his fingers. "You jerk. You do have a nickname, and I remember it. Solomon, we named you Solomon."

Ari flipped a kitchen towel onto his shoulder. "What? That was my name? I thought it was an insult."

Dev shook his head. "No. Danny came up with it. You are Solomon. You live in two worlds. You have to be wise. Remember, Danny was talking about the *Songs of Solomon*, and you started spouting scripture."

"I know the Old Testament, Devlin. I am part Jewish."

"I know, but you two began discussing when Solomon had to decide which woman the child belonged to, and he decided to split the baby down the middle. He realized the mother was the one who shouted for him to stop, and to give the baby to the other woman because she wouldn't allow her own son to be killed. That's you, Ari. You sacrifice for the greater good. You follow orders unconditionally, until you just can't. But you always protect your friends."

"Pierce, I appreciate what you're doing, but I betrayed your team."

I remember. "But, you came back and saved us. Ari, let it go."

Ari held Dev's eyes with his. "You know why I'm not a team member."

"Because you're a very special agent," Dev murmured as he grabbed for his bourbon. "And you think if you're part of a team, you'll get the team killed." Dev took a drink. "Because it has happened before."

"May I add something?" Lily stood at the edge of the kitchen island. She'd changed into baggy sweatpants and one of Dev's larger Army shirts. Andrew, now wearing his favorite pajamas, walked off into the living room to play with his missed toys.

Dev extended his arm in invitation. Ari shook his head. He removed the potatoes, golden and sizzling, from the oven. Then he returned the chicken into the heat to brown the skin.

"I've been listening to this discussion. Ari, I love you too. You are someone I never even dreamed of meeting, much less gaining as a friend. You are like an elusive unicorn, or that guy who makes it big as a heartthrob in movies, and you knew him back in high school when he snorted glue. Then the big star comes into town and takes you out to dinner. You're a fantasy for someone like me." Lily glanced at her husband and knew what he was thinking.

"Fine. I married that guy, but you are so different. You are a good man. Whatever you did or didn't do, whatever happened in war, I know by now that's not who you are in your heart. It's the same for Dev, JT, Paul, Danny, my brother, and anyone who serves for his or her country. Now, I only have one other question, Solomon."

Dev and Ari both smiled. Ari stood up straight and stretched his neck proudly. "Yes, dear lady."

"What's for dessert, and how long until dinner? I'm starving."

"Dinner should be ready in about twenty minutes, and sadly, I didn't have time to make dessert, but the bakery had this lovely lemon meringue pie. One of your favorites, yes?" Ari smiled as he presented the pie for her approval.

Lily nodded frantically. "If I can't wait twenty minutes, can I have dessert as an appetizer?"

Dev noticed her swollen ankles. Simultaneously, Ari and he yelled. "No!"

After an amazing dinner, Lily was on her second slice of pie as Ari carried in a large bag filled with tissue. Lily dropped her fork when she saw the designer's name. "Good Lord, Christian Dior?"

"That bag is for Andrew, but you can open it."

Andrew sat on his father's lap with a towel around his neck. He was licking off meringue from a spoon.

Lily pulled out several sheets of tissue until she removed two stuffed animals, an elephant and a giraffe.

"They are *Toile de Jouy*. I loved the blue for Andrew."

Lily marveled at the toile stuffed animals. "How much did you pay for these? You shouldn't do that. Besides, he'll just slobber all over them."

Ari smiled widely. "I should, and I don't care how much or what bodily function happens to them. I liked them, and I thought he would like them, or maybe the new baby will."

I'll look this up later, but I have a feeling these toys are worth more than my first car."

Ari placed another Dior package in front of his friend. "This is for you."

"Ari, you shouldn't." But Lily pulled off the ribbon and opened the box revealing a beautiful navy shawl. "It's gorgeous."

"It's a Dior oblique shawl. My sister and I thought you'd be able to use it this fall when you help with the weddings at the vineyard." Ari sat back down in his chair and sipped his coffee. "And for you Pierce, I have a file from INTERPOL on that mystery woman."

Lily's face lit up. "What? You know about my mystery woman? What did you find out? INTERPOL? That is so amazing. Tell me."

"Thanks, Solomon," Dev said as he stood up with his son.

"It's Lily's mystery woman?" Ari was completely confused. *Why is Pierce still allowing her to get involved in crimes?*

"It is since she found the dead body in the yard." Dev's tone was nonchalant, which frightened Ari even more.

"What on earth is wrong with the two of you?" he asked loudly.

Andrew squealed as Dev washed his hands and face.

"Even the baby realizes you two are nuts," Ari quipped.

Lily patted his hand. "It's okay. It began when I wanted to plant this magnolia tree. You see, I wanted shade on the edge of the front porch, but Dev wanted to move it to the other side of the garage. I didn't want that look. I'm trying to add color to the yard, but I wanted a little fragrance. We have a swing on that side. Don't you think that would look nice? Well, we found the driver's license, and then--"

Ari nestled his head in his hand and listened to his friend describe the last few weeks. He looked up briefly to see Dev laughing hysterically. It would be a long night now that he had awakened the novice mystery investigator. *Agatha would be so proud, Lily!"*

Chapter Nineteen

"They call her Gilda," Ari explained as he opened the file on his laptop. A blurry photo popped up of a woman. Lily leaned over his shoulder. Dev's disapproval was quite obvious. He scowled. He growled. Lily didn't budge.

"I see why. She does look like Rita Hayworth. Is her hair red now?" Lily scribbled down a note.

Ari looked over at her. "Yes, yes it is. It's a deeper red than your handsome son's."

"So why Gilda and red hair?" Dev's question made the other two stare at him. "What? What did I say?"

Ari shook his head in disbelief. "You need to educate your husband. Is he so ignorant?"

"I didn't realize it. That's embarrassing. Dev, *Gilda* is an old movie, and Rita Hayworth was the actress who portrayed her. Margot does look like her."

"Margot?"

Lily waved her hand for him to move the screen. "Margot Fleischman was her name here. Does INTERPOL know her real name?"

"No, well at least they don't say if they do. Spies are that way, Lily."

"Oh, I know," Lily said as she rolled her eyes at her husband and her friend. It had taken her nearly five years to have a more open relationship with her husband, and obviously, Ari had secrets in abundance. It was like pulling a layer away from a very pungent onion.

Ari searched the next page and closed the laptop quickly. It snapped shut, almost capturing one of Lily's fingers. "Why did you do that?"

"Because, that's all you see, Lily. Dev can review the file, but you're done." Ari's tone was superior and very alpha male.

"Wait a minute, are you telling me that I put all this information together, and now you're shutting me out? You two are taking your ball and going home, and not allowing the little woman to play. That is ridiculous." She stamped her foot for emphasis.

"Well, you are acting like a spoiled little girl," Ari said as he looked down at her foot.

Dev winced as soon as the statement filled the air. He was actually happy that Ari was the one to say exactly what he was thinking. *Let Ari receive the wrath of Lily.* But, he'd explain to her later, much later, that Ari was risking whatever career he had by even allowing her to see any screen from INTERPOL. Ari had requested access for Dev, and it had been granted reluctantly. They'd requested the information as part of a DEA operation in Columbia.

"You disappoint me, Ari."

Lily's pouting mouth made the super agent laugh. "Oh, darling woman, the longer you know me, the more I will disappoint you. I admire your skills, Lily, I truly do. If I didn't, I wouldn't have involved you in the entire escapade to capture Khalid. But this is completely different. This isn't personal. It really doesn't concern you."

Dev turned away and closed his eyes. He knew she was going to blow. Ari had just cut her down in so many ways. But instead, Lily began to leave the office slowly.

"Goodnight, gentlemen," she said quietly. "I need to check on my son, and then the little woman here who is the incubator for another lovely human will put herself to bed. A woman's work is never done, but I have to get my beauty rest, right?"

Before either one of them could respond, she was gone. Ari looked at Dev who was locking his laptop away. He handed his own in his direction. "That went well."

Dev chuckled. "Oh sure! You really explained everything to her and so concisely."

"Will you have to sleep with one eye open?"

"I don't know. I think I will hide all the knives, just in case."

"But this woman means nothing to her," Ari explained. "Gilda is an international criminal. Most likely she is a contract killer. Lily doesn't need to be involved with this."

"You tell her that. The woman's stuff was found in Lily's yard. A gun was found in Lily's yard, along with a bloody shoe, shirt, purse, and finally a dead body. As far as my wife is concerned it is her business. You, above all people, should know that if Lily cares about something, it is personal for her. Now, I'm heading up there." Dev pointed to the second floor. "Wish me luck."

"May Allah protect you, my friend."

Dev stopped and turned. "Thanks, Solomon. If you don't see me tomorrow, check the backyard."

Dev reached a darkened bedroom. The television was on. Jessica and Mort were finding another killer in the small Maine coastal town. *Geez, that place is a murder magnet.* Lily appeared to be sound asleep, as well she should be. It had been a long day. She seemed to have a lot of discomfort on the flight, but she insisted it was nothing. It appeared that she was having some kind of cramping, and it wasn't back pain. He put on his lounge pants and slipped under the sheets. Lily instinctively folded into his body.

"You two are in so much trouble," she mumbled. She spread her hand across his chest and sighed. "If I didn't love you and him, you both would be bunking at Dan's parish rectory."

"I know. Just in case, I've hidden all the knives. Go back to sleep," Dev directed. He moved his arm around her and rubbed her back. He heard a soft giggle, but she didn't move.

"You silly man," Lily whispered. "I wouldn't use a knife. Poison maybe, but never a knife. Ow." Dev felt her body contract, moving her hand to her stomach area. Then she relaxed quickly. She was asleep now, yet her body was betraying her. *There's something wrong. I'll be going to the next doctor's appointment. Besides, she didn't argue like she normally would.*

Dev watched Jessica solve another murder. He turned off the television and fell asleep. He'd really hide the knives before Lily woke. He'd also be smelling his food and drink for the scent of almonds. Her nonchalant behavior frightened him.

The next morning, the aroma of coffee woke Lily. As soon as she opened her eyes, she shielded them with her arm from the sunlight flowing into the room. *How late is it?*

Lily turned to see the vacant side of the bed where Dev should be, and the clock showed a hand on the numbers twelve and nine.

"Oh my Lord," she yelled out loud. She threw back the covers and began to jump out of bed. She stopped. "Holy Moly." Her head spinned. Her vision was a little blurry. "Stop. Just stop whatever this is." Her stomach cramped so much it made her gasp. *I'm just hungry, but I can't make it down those stairs. Oh my gosh. Andrew!*

Slowly, Lily slid from the edge of the bed. She navigated her way around the room, touching furniture to bolster her balance. Her hand slid along the wall of the hallway on the way to her son's bedroom. As she arrived, her balance was better, and her head was clearer. She walked toward the rocker and sat down to catch her breath. This pregnancy wasn't feeling like the last one.

"I'll see if she's up." Lily heard Dev's voice as he bounded up the stairs.

"I'm in Andrew's room," she yelled out.

His smiling face peeked around the edge of the door. "Good morning, sunshine." The look on her face drew him in quickly. He knelt in front of her and held her hands.

"Lily, honey, what's wrong? You are very pale."

She swallowed hard. "I don't feel very well, I mean there's something really off."

"Then, I'll call the doctor's office, and we'll get you in. Ari can take care of Andrew. What are you feeling?"

Lily could see the concern in his eyes. He wasn't even trying to conceal it. "I'm dizzy with a little blurred vision. There's some cramping, and I'm so tired."

"You could just be a little dehydrated," Dev suggested. "Let's get you back to bed." Instead of assisting her out of the rocking chair to walk her back, he raised her slowly by her hands and pulled her up into his arms.

"Oh my gosh. What are you doing?"

"Taking you back to bed," he whispered and kissed her on her cheek. "I've only done it one other time, and that was on our honeymoon in Paris."

Lily nudged her head under his chin. "I remember. I thought you were crazy then, and I know you're crazy now."

Dev didn't say anything until he placed her lightly on his side of the bed. He covered her up and retreated to the bathroom. He returned with a bottle of water. "I knew I had one in my carry-on. Drink this. I'll make the call and see what they say. I'll bring back some toast and more water." He kissed her on the forehead and left.

Ari continued to fix breakfast and entertain his small charge while Dev made the call. Ari heard a few words and understood that something wasn't right. He nodded to Pierce that he was good with Andrew in his care.

As soon as Dev ended the call, Ari yelled out. "Do you need to take her to see the doctor?"

"He's actually at the emergency clinic today so I'll take her there. I think she's dehydrated, but something else is going on. Are you good with him? I mean, he still needs to be changed out of his pajamas. I can do that before we go."

Ari waved him off. He smiled at Andrew, knowing full well a child could sense fear. "Go, brother. I had a girl, remember? A boy will be easier. Just call me when you can to make sure he hasn't taken over the house."

Dev began to run up the stairs. "Thanks, Ari. Dad's phone number is by the fridge if you need additional troops."

Andrew threw his spoon in Ari's direction. He laughed. Ari squinted. "I'll not have trouble with you. That is not a question, it is a direct command, *bubala*. Don't make me regret staying behind." Andrew's face sobered as if he understood. Ari messed up his red locks. "Ah, I was only kidding. We will have a fine time, you and me. Now, would you like to learn how to drive Uncle Ari's rental sports car?"

Later that afternoon, Lily returned through the front door of her home to the delight of her friend. Quickly, he came to her side and guided her to the couch. "Here, sit. Put your feet up. What did the doctor say?"

"Geez, you're worse than him." Lily pointed back at her husband who followed with her purse and medical file.

"I never became nervous. I was intense," Dev answered. He mouthed to Ari that she was okay.

"You yelled at the bloody nurse." Lily allowed Ari to prop her feet up on a pillow he'd placed on the coffee table. "You scared her to death. It was like some kind of scene from a World War II movie when the drill sergeant yells at the new inductee."

"She was talking to her boyfriend for fifteen minutes before I informed her I wasn't going to wait any longer." Dev's precise words warned Ari that his concern had obviously thrown rational behavior out of the window.

"So, Mr. Cool lost it?" Ari joked.

"Oh yeah. It was a thing to behold," Lily acknowledged. "Every day I see more and more of what he must've been like in the Army. It's quite frightening."

Ari looked up at Dev. They shared a look. If Lily knew what they had been like, or what they had done, she said she would forgive, but she would never forget the awful stories. They both blinked away the memories.

"I thought she was dehydrated, and she was. She's also having some blood pressure problems. It was high with Andrew, well now it's low with this one. The baby is good, just cooking away."

"Allah be praised."

Lily was confused. "I've been meaning to ask you about that. Sometimes, you talk about God, and at other times you mention Allah. I've even heard you quote Budha and talk about Jesus Christ. Are you confused?"

Ari smirked. "No, just covering my bets. Now, what can I get her?"

"Something healthy," Dev muttered. He looked around the living room and into the kitchen. "Where's our son?"

"Happily taking his afternoon nap. He has been changed, diapered a couple of times, walked around the yard, fed, and is now sleeping. You two should consider potty training. I had forgotten how much work little people are." He headed into the kitchen. "I'll fix you both something, but dinner will be early tonight."

"It's so nice to have a nanny and a cook," Dev said. He handed Lily's purse to her and laid the file on the table. "I'm going to go up and check on the little guy. What do you need from upstairs?"

"My house slippers? Other than that, I'd love to have a diversion, perhaps something about Gilda?" She smiled sweetly up at her husband's face and fluttered her eyelashes. It was the perfect time to push the subject of the mystery, while his heart was still beating a little faster in fear.

Again, Ari and Dev both answered no from their respective positions in the house. Dev left while Ari was busy in the kitchen.

Lily sat alone. "Well darn. That didn't work on either of them." They were forming a defensive line against her. That was a first.

Ari arrived back in the living room before Dev. He placed a glass of iced water in front of her, along with a plate.

"This salad has everything in it. There's chicken, lettuce, grapes, tomatoes, cucumbers, no onions, well just about everything. I made the dressing from olive and balsamic oils with crushed walnuts. I hope you like it."

Lily's eyes widened. "This looks amazing. You should've been a chef, or had your own restaurant."

"I do own a brasserie in Paris, and we have one in Nice. We feature some of my family's recipes."

"I didn't know that."

Ari's clear eyes stole through her soul. "You don't know a lot about me."

She touched his arm softly. "But I know more than most do. Thank you, friend."

"You are most welcome, my dear Lily. Now eat, and you need to drink."

Dev arrived just in time to agree. "Yes, you have to drink at least six to eight glasses of water every day. Wow, what are you eating? That looks great." Dev checked a text he'd just received. His search into Dr. Fleischman's nanny was a dead end according to the FBI. He'd tell Lily later, much later. With his luck, she'd probably already found out about the woman.

Ari nodded. "I'll get you a plate. By the way, your son loves figs."

This time, Dev and Lily questioned him in unison. "What?"

"I hope you two like them because we are having fig and ginger chicken tagine tonight."

"Is that what smells so good?" Dev asked as he joined Ari in the kitchen.

"Yes. I began it in the slow cooker after you two left. It usually takes around six hours. Pierce, you probably had it sometime in your travels."

Dev lifted the lid on the cooker. The fragrance rejuvenated him. "I think I had this dish in Turkey. They made it with lamb."

"Well, in Virginia, I think it would be difficult to put a lamb on a spit in the backyard, so I substituted chicken. It's very good and very healthy. Here's your salad. Now that she can't hear us, is that all that is wrong?"

"Yes, for now. The doctor is going to keep an eye on her. There may be some issues, but until she's into the third trimester we may not know," Dev whispered. "She wants to look at that file."

"You should allow your wife to see her own medical file," Ari said, his whisper becoming louder.

"Not that file. That INTERPOL file on Gilda."

Ari cocked his head in thought. "She can not see that file, but you could tell her about it. She could take notes and fill in some of the facts. She's already built a pretty reasonable case to insist that the doctor's wife is indeed alive. Now, Lily is seeing that the woman may not have married the doctor for the most altruistic reasons. There may have been a larger plan, one that extends into drug trafficking and murder. Your wife can connect the dots, but she isn't allowed to color them in."

Dev looked directly at Ari. "Agreed. I'm happy to hear you say that."

"By the way, Devlin, your neighbor yelled over at me and asked if I was the super agent. She seems to be a lovely woman, but I just smiled and laughed. What has Lily been telling people?"

As if Lily knew exactly what they were planning, she yelled, "You two better not be bonding in there."

Dev almost spit out a bite of food as Ari stifled a laugh. Ari shook his head in despair. "My friend, you do have your hands full with that one."

"You have no idea. Pray for me, and I don't care which deity you use."

Chapter Twenty

"You're like a nun restricting my every action," Lily complained as her husband sat her down in his office a few days later.

"Shush. I'm not hitting your hands with a ruler. Enjoy not having to do as much." Dev turned around the dry-erase board in his office. He'd fixed dinner and put Andrew to bed. He added some of Lily's notes to her board and the ones he could from Ari's file. He almost envied Ari as he said goodbye on his next secret mission. Right now, Dev's life wasn't that exciting. Except for the argument earlier at lunch.

Ari had asked if Dev had ever made Lily go to the shooting range. Dev had threatened that activity from early on in their relationship. But Lily always had her excuses.

"All Israeli women serve in the army, and they know how to shoot. My wife knew how. She had her own gun," Ari acknowledged.

"See? Ari's wife did it. It's just a layer of protection," Dev chimed in agreement.

Lily glared at Dev. "First, his wife was an American living in Israel, and she never served in the army. He got her that gun as an anniversary gift. And sadly, we all know it didn't protect her." Lily reached out for Ari's hand as she uttered the hurtful truth. "I'm sorry. I don't want to hurt you, but I'm not sure a gun is the answer."

Ari's eyes darkened. He knew of his friend's sincerity, but her comment still creased his heart. "Point well taken. I still think it's wise to just have that option. I am supporting your husband on this."

"I can't. Guns frighten me." Lily's voice had quivered with the admission. "I won't go into why, but I just can't. You two bullying me won't make me change my mind. I promise to consider it someday. Maybe."

Dev had watched the two friends admit fears, but he knew Ari's. Lily's was another story. Something happened to make her detest guns. It just wasn't a television advertisement depicting the killing of some little bunny or deer.

For Lily, she contended that the two of them were consistently ganging up on her. Somehow the leverage of power had moved to the two alpha males, eliminating the little woman. She didn't like it one bit. Now that Ari had left, it was just down to Lily and Dev. She liked it better this way. *And I do love him doing everything, but I can't wait until he goes back to work next Monday.* She sipped her water as she looked over the board.

"What's that?" She pointed at a timeline entry with a date posted.

"She was spotted by an agent in Mexico City on that date. This next date marks the death of a very high-powered attorney in Mexico. The correlation of timing and facts is very familiar. Your mystery woman, Margot, was dating the man and disappeared the next day. The police figured she was taken by the kidnappers. The condo looked as though the attorney fought them off, and he was killed. However, on second look, by international agents, it seems she was the hit man, well woman."

"Wow, Dr. Fleischman was lucky." Lily took another sip of water. She reached for her bag of almonds and munched away while looking over the timeline. "So, are they thinking she's responsible for two murders already this year?"

"Yes, but over the past years, she could be responsible for so many more killings. It's frightening." Dev added in a couple of items from Lily's post-it notes.

"So, who is paying her, and how?"

Dev held up his marker. "Ah, that's how INTERPOL became involved. Money transfers alerted them. She used to have Swiss bank accounts, but now she's moved onto the Caymans. It can be the wild west down there when it comes to hiding money. She also has some links to Cuba. And yes, the doctor and his daughter were very lucky. If they had come home at the wrong time, they would have been collateral damage. That's what happened to that delivery mule. She needed to tidy up all the loose ends."

"So what's next?" Lily asked casually as if they were discussing which dress she should wear to an event.

"We just keep filling in the blanks. We can forward all of this to Ari, and he'll send it on to his contacts. They'll get her."

Lily stopped munching. "No way. Why does he get to have all the fun? Why can't we get her?"

Dev looked up at his wife. *Is her baby brain losing it? What the hell is wrong with her?* "Honey, you've done enough. There is no more for you to do."

Lily straightened her back and crossed her arms in defiance as a barrier to her husband. "Yes, there is, and they'll be here in an hour."

Dev took two large steps and stood in front of his wife. His tone wasn't pleasant. "What have you done?"

"The doctor and his daughter are coming to see us. I want you to talk to her. When I had lunch with her, she explained some things, but you need to do that agent thing you do to get to the truth." Lily's hand lifted and made a circle in the air.

Dev shut his eyes and breathed in slowly. His anger was forming into rage. "What the hell is wrong with you? Why? Why do you need this? You aren't Jessica, or Agatha, or Mata Hari. You're you, and I love that woman, but if you continue to do this kind of crap--" He stopped before his anger was out of control.

"We never used to argue," Lily muttered.

"You never used to get involved in mysteries that didn't concern you. I didn't like it, but I understood when you wanted Khalid gone. You were protecting me and our family. But this--" Dev pointed back to the board and shook his head.

"But it's okay for you to do it," Lily added. She placed her hand over her mouth as soon as the stupidity left her lips.

"It's my job, Lily."

"And you don't share anything with me. I understand, but I guess I don't."

"I can't share. I really want to sometimes. That mission where we rescued those girls is something I'll never forget, but I can't tell you any details." Dev sat down behind his desk, his hands stuck to the desk.

"I saw it on the news, you know," Lily said softly. "That was awful, and I'm so proud of you and what you do." They both stopped talking, stopped arguing. "In Paris, I did nothing. I left it all to you super agents, but yet, I was still in danger."

Dev remained silent. *What is going on? Is it because it's just the two of us? Do we need JT, Danny, and the gang?*

Lily broke the silence. "We don't play well together, do we?"

Dev drummed his fingers on the desk. One eyebrow rose. "Lily, we do play well, but it's usually just upstairs." He pointed up to their bedroom. "I don't think it's that. Just think, this is how we began. We bantered back and forth all the time. You didn't appreciate my job. I didn't trust you. You didn't trust me. I used you as bait. I wanted to kiss you. You sent me away. I figured it out, and I came back for you."

"You left out one very valuable thing," Lily said softly. She unclenched her hands and relaxed. "You opened my eyes to another world, and I like living in it. I like helping people. I used to do everything for my clients. When I see something that isn't right, I want to fix it. I understand your concern. But let me be me, and I'll let you be you. Deal?"

Dev placed both arms up in a surrendering motion. "I give up, but you can't place yourself in danger. We have too much to lose if you do stuff like that."

"I kind of like it when we have discussions like this."

Dev laughed out loud and moved around the desk to her side. "It's called an argument, dear."

He kissed the top of her head. Lily reached around his waist and beckoned him down for a full kiss. "You know what they say about making up?"

Dev pulled away from the kiss. "But we have visitors coming because someone invited them."

Lily winced. "I did that. Sorry."

The doorbell rang once. Dev ran before they hit it again and possibly woke a sleeping baby. Dev pretended to be happy when he opened the door, but he saw two people in fear.

"Mr. Pierce, my daughter and I were almost killed coming over here," Dr. Fleischman said, still gasping for breath. "We were threatened today that if we kept looking for Margot they'd kill us and anyone else who tried to find her."

"Get in here," Dev directed. He looked out onto the street. Nothing looked out of the ordinary, but they weren't dealing with ordinary criminals.

Lily greeted her guests and led them into the living room. The doctor's daughter was visibly shaking. "Please, sit down. I'll get us something to drink. Would you like wine or something stronger?"

"No, just water," Dr. Fleischman answered for them.

Dev sat opposite the man and his daughter to evaluate them, and to ask some very important questions as Lily left to grab their drinks. "What happened today? Begin with the threat."

"I was home and my daughter was visiting. Her husband is in Charlottesville. He decided to stay with the kids. Laurel went to court. Around ten this morning, I received a call on my home line. It was a man's voice. All he said was to leave Margot alone. Then every hour on the hour, I received the same phone call."

"Did you get a number?" Dev asked. Lily came in with four glasses of iced water on a tray. The doctor's daughter held her glass with two hands as she brought the liquid to her lips. Lily looked over at Dev. The woman seemed to be completely undone.

"After the second call, I called the number back, but it said it wasn't a working number. I don't understand that."

Dev shifted uncomfortably in his chair. The hair on the back of his neck was standing straight up. "It was probably a burner phone. Did you call the police?"

"Yes," Dr. Fleischman answered. "They said until something really happened, or if I knew who was harassing me, they couldn't do anything. Is that right?"

"Yes." Lily answered for Dev. He smiled at her slightly, and returned to his questioning.

"So the calls continued. What happened on the way over here?"

"My daughter ran into the house saying that a car had followed her from the courthouse to my house. Since the police wouldn't do anything, I suggested we go ahead and come see you two. Maybe you know someone who could help us?"

Dev nodded to Lily. "Yes, I do. Um, Ms.--"

"Laurel is fine. My married name is Culver." The doctor's daughter placed the glass carefully on the tray and sat back on the couch. Her hands continued to shake.

"Fine. Laurel, did you see anyone at court who didn't look like he or she belonged? Maybe the way they were dressed was a little outrageous, or they looked different than your clients, or the audience there to watch or testify?"

She was definitely attempting to review the scene in her mind. She closed her eyes for a minute. "We had a closed court so the only ones there were pre-approved. There were two men at the back of the courtroom who were in dark clothing. It's odd since it's so hot. They also had dark glasses and gold watches. They waited to leave until my team and I were ready to head out. They may have been the ones following me."

Dev smiled. "That's good. The courtroom has cameras. We can check them and see who we're dealing with. Now tell me about the drive over here."

"The car began to follow us, but then they left once we hit the parkway. That's when another car came from a side street and swerved in front of us. Dad had to step hard on the brakes. We dropped back, trying to stay away. The car dropped back. They shadowed us at every turn and lane change, and then we saw the guns."

"Do you know what kind?"

Both guests shook their heads negatively. "Sorry, I'm not a gun person." Dr. Fleischman answered. "They shot at us and yelled to leave Margot alone. I'm sorry, but they mentioned that my friends needed to stop butting in. They shouted different things. One time, I heard a man say that more bodies can be buried in your yard. I don't think I have bodies in my yard. Margot didn't even live in my house."

Dev didn't look at Lily. He hoped she was taking all this in. This is what he always feared. Danger could come to them because of his job, but his wife had added to the level of intensity.

"No, but she lived here," Dev said slowly. Neither one of their guests understood his comment, but Lily did. She smiled, attempting to comfort the doctor and his daughter, but she was chilled to the bone. Fear was creeping in, and Dev's nonchalant manner only proved that he was acting. He was worried too.

"I'm not sure what is going on. What can we do?" Dr. Fleischman pleaded.

Dev sat forward, his hands almost in a prayer-like action. "First, I'll make a couple of phone calls. Please write down your husband's name, address, and cell phone. I'll make sure your family is safe. Lily, can we make them comfortable so they could stay here tonight?"

Before Lily could answer, the doctor said that wouldn't be necessary. Dev insisted and left the room to make his calls.

"You really need to stay here tonight. We have plenty of room," Lily insisted. "Now, can I get you both something to eat? A friend has left us some amazing leftovers. Come on into the kitchen while Dev contacts some people."

Both guests followed her into the other room. Lily began pulling food, placing them on the counter. "We have buffet service only tonight. Please help yourself, and if you don't see something, just look in the fridge. It's probably there."

Laurel admitted she was hungry. Neither one of them had eaten dinner. "Your husband, he's a federal agent, isn't he?"

Lily nodded coyly.

"I could tell. I've seen those men operate before. They have this look, a certain demeanor. Lily, I think your investigation broke this whole thing open, and now we're in the crosshairs."

Lily understood her fear, her anger. Lily had been there a few years ago too. For a while, you just don't see a way out into safety. But she trusted Dev then, and she trusted him now more than ever. "I'm sorry, but we found things in this yard.

"Laurel didn't mean it that way, Lily," Dr. Fleischman said softly. "She's just upset. You are being too kind, feeding us, and setting us up for the night. We're strangers, and you are taking us in. Thank you."

Laurel didn't look at Lily. Clearly, the woman was embarrassed, but Lily was suspicious. *Is she embarrassed about her behavior or dropping her guard?*

"Lily, I'm sorry. It's just that this is the most significant threat we've had. You know I told you that a few years back I was sent some threatening letters. They couldn't be traced, and the police in Charlottesville figured it might be connected to a case I was working on or to someone I was defending. I knew they were wrong. I knew it was just Margot terrorizing me like she did when she was married to my father."

Dr. Fleischman's face flushed. He reached for her hand. "I'm so sorry I did nothing, honey. I'm sorry I didn't believe you when you told me what she was doing to you."

I knew it! She was abused. I'll have to share all of this with Mrs. Parrot. Lily poured her own glass of milk and had a small snack with her guests. She tried to steer the conversation away from the agony they were experiencing. She could distract and divert. She did have the Pierce family trait. But that nagging feeling had returned. The two reminded her of a past client and her mother. *Oh, I remember. They came in with this large budget, played me along for months, and then canceled the wedding at the last minute because they took my ideas and budget to another florist who did the work cheaper. Money makes people do funny things, but could it be at the root of this?*

They were finished eating when Dev finally arrived with news. "Well, you are staying the night here. I've contacted your husband, and there's already police watching your home. The film from the courtroom is being pulled as we speak, and they'll want you to look at it in the morning. There are also police at your home, doctor. In a few minutes, the FBI will be here to talk to you both. They'll have photos for you to look over. They'll take your statements. They can check cameras on the parkway and a few of the other streets. I'll be with you through all of this."

"Are you FBI or CIA?" Laurel asked boldly.

Dev grinned. "Actually, neither. I believe all of this actually extends into a world I know very well so I'll sit in on the interview. It will be a long night, so we'll show you your rooms right now and that way you can collapse when we're done. Doctor, there's a large master over here, and Laurel you can take the guest room next to my office. Let's get you settled before the FBI invades."

Lily began to shuffle behind them, but Dev turned and stopped her. "You, go to bed!"

"What?"

"This is non-negotiable, honey. You can't sit in with the FBI. You need your rest." He pointed down to her ankles. "Your feet are swollen. You're pale, and Andrew will need you upstairs if he wakes up with all of this commotion. They're probably bringing about six agents."

Lily pouted. "This isn't fair. And yes, I know I'm acting like a baby."

Dev smiled down at her. His hand lifted her chin. "But you're my baby, and I need you upstairs."

"You always say that." She nudged him playfully. "You always want me upstairs," she whispered. He pointed to the stairs. "Wow, you are self-disciplined, Pierce. Fine. I'm going." She said her goodnights to the doctor and his daughter and plodded up to the second floor. She checked in on Andrew and found a wide-awake boy playing with the very expensive Dior elephant.

"How did you get that? I put it on the shelf above your bed." She changed his diaper, and then lifted him into her arms. "Come on. You're with me tonight. I don't trust anyone right now, and I need to look over that stuffed animal to make sure it isn't bugged." She retreated to the master bedroom and closed the door. The lights from two cars flashed on the wall.

Looking outside the window, Lily counted the agents as they walked up her driveway. Subtle, they were not. She counted six agents, two black sedans, and one white van.

The FBI was definitely here, and they were swarming.

Chapter Twenty-One

Dev stood over the bed gazing down at the two figures blissfully sleeping away. In the midst of the chaos in the last hours, he attempted to be dispassionate. He did his job. He sounded like the agent he was. Ari would be proud that all of his international knowledge had significantly added to the FBI's case. The doctor and his daughter were in trouble. Yet, he knew full well that the woman sleeping upstairs could be in just as much danger. She opened a can of worms, a huge can. As he looked down at Lily, and Andrew at her side, everything seemed at peace again. But it wasn't.

There was something missing. Lily was so good at putting together the puzzle, intricately moving every piece around until everything was complete. Dev felt like he was missing something. The doctor and his daughter seemed believable. *Surely they couldn't be involved in all of this? But Lily had a point. If Gilda left behind doctors in her wake, why did she allow this doctor to live? And what did Lauren have to do with all of this?* She was a defense attorney to several bad actors. She visited the jails and penitentiaries. Tomorrow, he would begin looking more closely at her clients and their interaction with her.

Slowly, he lifted the covers and slid in. Andrew's little arms stretched out briefly. Dev placed his hand on his son's stomach, and the baby calmed again. Lily sensed the movement. She placed her hand over his. Dev moved his hand out and extended his arm across the two greatest loves of his life. He slept for just a few hours before he felt a small fist hitting his nose. Andrew was awake.

"Little man, what are you doing?"

Andrew babbled away as he tumbled onto Dev's chest. Lily stirred, turning onto her side.

Dev placed a finger to the boy's mouth. "Shh, we have to be quiet. Mommy is sleeping." Andrew grabbed the digit and stuck it in his mouth. "Ow." Andrew giggled as he bit hard.

"He'll bite your finger if you even get near his mouth," Lily mumbled.

"Too late for that intel."

His wife turned over slowly and smiled. "When did you get to bed?"

"The final bunch of agents left around three this morning." Dev lifted his son into the air and lowered him quickly. "This is better than the gym."

"Yep." Lily scooted her body next to the two men in her life. "So what is happening with the doctor and his daughter?"

"They'll have security. His daughter is working on a high-profile case right now, so the FBI is assessing the risk. But, they think this involves the missing wife. I believe the INTERPOL file completely changed how they were looking at the case. They are taking this very seriously now."

"And you?" Lily's question was met with Dev's eyes seriously meeting hers.

"I've always taken it seriously. We may be looking at the DEA getting involved so it may actually become my case too."

Lily leaned up on her elbow. Her smile was intoxicating. "That's wonderful! Maybe we'll be the ones to solve it."

"Maybe, now that it has something to do with my job, but there is no we."

"You are kidding, aren't you? You can't do this to me."

"I can, and I will. You're off the case, Lily. This thing is way above your pay grade."

"Dev, I have nothing to say to you. Actually, I have a lot to say to you, but if I say it right now, we won't see our next wedding anniversary." She scurried out of the bed and to the bathroom, slamming the door. She regretted the action as soon as she heard the noise, but hopefully her husband understood her frustration.

Dev flinched. "Andrew, don't you think that went well?" His son looked strangely at him and promptly spit up all over his chest. "You too, son?" He held Andrew with one hand as he headed to the bathroom for a towel. As he entered, Lily's head lifted from the toilet bowl. "I just need a towel. You okay?"

She turned her head back into her target area and lifted her usual thumb's up sign. As Dev cleaned off Andrew and himself, he dampened a washcloth and came over to Lily. When she lifted her head, he wiped her forehead and her mouth.

Lily smiled up at him. Undaunted by her morning

sickness, she decided to take a stand. "Dev, I am involved. I might not have an alphabet organization behind my name, but I put you on this path to capture someone who is an awful human being. I understand that you can't tell me about your job, but I'm still going to keep looking for clues, and you're going to listen to me each and every time I figure out something. You'll protect me, and I'll be careful. That's the deal. Take it or leave it. Because I'm not going to fight with you."

Dev nodded. "I didn't think we ever fought. We just have discussions. You know, I'll always worry about you and need to keep you safe. That was my job in the very beginning when we met, and it's one job I'll never stop performing. I'm going to throw some clothes on and check on our guests. This little guy needs food. Rest. Don't rush this morning. I've got this."

"You always do. I love you for that." She blew a kiss. "Now, get out of here. I've got to throw up again."

Dev threw on some clothes while Andrew crawled on the bed. The two of them headed downstairs. They were greeted by Dr. Fleischman and his daughter.

"Dad and I wanted to make coffee or something, but we didn't want to search around in your kitchen."

"No, that's what I usually do," Dev said with a charming smile. "Let's get the coffee on and get us all some much needed breakfast. Please join us in the kitchen."

"I'll be happy to help," Laurel offered. "How about scrambled eggs?"

Dev placed Andrew in his chair and headed to the

refrigerator. "Perfect. I'll get the sausage out. We have fruit." He opened the door and searched inside the shelves. "Wow, we have a coffee cake too." *Ari must have bought this.*

By the time Lily had showered and dressed, she arrived in the kitchen to see three smiling adults and one child who had smeared apricots all over his pajamas. Empty plates filled the kitchen table. Coffee actually smelled good to her this morning. After salutations, Lily eating, and attempting a cup of decaf coffee with lots of milk, the subject of the future was brought to the forefront.

"And what's next for all of us?" Lily asked as she ate the last bite of toast. She directed her question to her husband, the DEA agent.

"They'll be going back to the doctor's house with an FBI escort. We will be staying in today while everything gets set up. The U.S. Marshals may take over the protective detail for them. We catch these guys threatening you, we'll be able to figure out why this is happening."

Lily knew why. She chewed away slowly as if she was the only one who knew. *We're getting close to solving this mystery.* As soon as she could, she'd head into the home office to close up a few holes on the board. But she did need her husband's valuable assessment on the two people sitting across the table from her? *Am I sensing fear or suspicion? Are they innocent or guilty? Do I see uncertainty in their eyes or is it arrogance?*

As soon as the doctor, Dev, and Andrew headed into the living room to go over a few details from last night's statement, Lily made her move.

"Laurel, would you like a little more coffee?" The

fragrance of the brewed, caffeinated liquid made Lily dream of better days when she wasn't pregnant. *I miss coffee so much. Oh, and I miss wine, onions, and so many other things.*

Laurel glanced into the other room. Her full attention seemed to be on her father and what he may or may not be admitting. "Yes, I'd love another cup." Lily reached over and poured her cup full. "Lily, you have been so kind to us."

"You have been through so much for so long. I just want it over for you. I can't understand how a woman can abuse a child."

Lily sat down across from her and sipped on her iced glass of water. She could see Laurel tense; she noticed how she glanced into the other room almost every other minute. *What is she so worried about?*

"What?"

"Margot, what she did to you."

Laurel took a slow drink from her cup and feigned realization. "Oh yes. That's right. Well, she was more verbally abusive than anything else."

Okay, maybe that makes sense? "But you still didn't deserve that. You were just a girl missing her mom and thinking that maybe this woman could be a substitute to give you the love you deserved."

Laurel's laughter stunned Lily. "Oh, I gave as good as I got. I'm not someone who will just take crap."

As soon as the last word left her mouth, Lily noticed that Laurel realized she had broken her playacting. *Gotcha!*

Laurel stood up quickly. "I'm sorry. I'm just upset.

I really need to be with my Dad. This business has really brought up a very dark time in our lives, and it is so hard on him. Excuse me, and thank you, Lily, for everything you've done to us."

Lily nodded in understanding. *Everything I've done to you? That's either a huge grammar mistake or you have something to hide, Laurel.*

Chapter Twenty-Two

The discussion with Dev about her suspicions about the doctor and his daughter received the usual nonchalant interest, except he completely agreed that Laurel knew more than she was letting on. A few days later, life had relatively returned to normal and Lily needed, really needed, fresh baked bread and cherry pie from Barney's bakery. It would be a drive out of her way, but Andrew could use the trip. He'd probably take an afternoon nap in the car. Her morning appointment with the doctor went well. She dropped by Jack's to pick up Andrew, and headed back out onto the interstate to go to Barney's. She was correct about her son; Andrew was asleep when she turned onto I-95. He woke up long enough in the bakery to receive his complimentary cookie. As she began her drive back home, he fell into peaceful slumber one more time. *This is bliss!*

Lily sang along to the light music on the radio. Her son was napping, she was singing to one of her favorite songs, and she could smell bread in her car. *Life is good.* It was very good until a car began weaving in and out of traffic. She noticed the blue sedan in her rearview mirror when she heard an eighteen wheeler's horn. Eventually, the car sped up next to hers.

"This isn't good," Lily said out loud. She looked over to see two men, two very unsavory looking men. She wasn't sure she could describe unsavory, but she knew it when she saw it. Actually, they perfectly fit the description of the two men who had threatened the doctor and his daughter. She slowed down. The car slowed down. They paced hers. She had two options. Driving down the interstate at seventy miles an hour, pregnant, and with a toddler in the back seat was not the perfect scenario. She could fight or she could flee. *Thank God I've learned to drive in Northern Virginia.* "Crap." She looked forward into the traffic and safely cut in front of an RV, hopefully hiding out. Andrew began to stir. *No, no, no, little man. I need you to be quiet.* Andrew seldom accommodated his mother these days. He was quickly becoming a Daddy's boy and had already hit his stride in the terrible twos.

She was at least two exits away from the road she took home. She had no idea where a police station was, and she had just passed the last truck check-in before the metro area. Andrew began to cry. "Come on, baby, please hang in there." Lily made her way to the farthest lane. She'd at least have the highway's shoulder for a path to escape. Where to, she had no idea. She called the speed dial on her wheel. The first number was Dev's. He didn't pick up. She left him a message and a location. She hit another.

"Hey, momma. What's up?"

"Danny, I'm in trouble. I'm on the interstate, and I'm being followed. I'm in my car. Their car is a blue sedan with D.C. plates." Lily recited the license number and that the car was occupied by two men.

"I'm going about seventy-five and driving in the slow lane. I haven't been boxed in yet. I've passed the last truck check-in, and I'm heading north for home. Andrew is wailing in the back seat."

"Okay, I'm calling the highway patrol on the other line. Slow down, keep in that lane, exit as if you were coming here to the rectory." Danny looked out at the church's parking lot. He could get Mrs. Lane and the church manager out of the way before Lily arrived. "Get here. Always stay in the right lane, even when you hit the parkway. You might have to speed when you hit the two-way road up to the church. Just do it. I'll stay on the line with you. Yes, this is Father Dan Parsons. There's a woman--"

Lily could hear him giving information to a patrolman. She took a couple of breaths to calm her heart, but the adrenaline was pumping. She could hear her fast heartbeat, and she swore she could feel the baby's. "Baby, just hang in there. Andrew Michael, will you please be quiet? Mommy is trying to save us from a couple of killers."

Andrew chose not to listen to his mother. "Danny, how are we? Danny?" She couldn't hear anything on the line. *That crappy cell tower is killing my call.* She was on her own. She'd do what Dan recommended, but she'd take the other road into the church. She might be able to lose the Toyota off of the parkway. She remembered hearing the guys talking about a time in Afghanistan where they took the back way. It was longer, but it got them out of trouble.

"That's what I'm going to do. Andrew, you just hold on. Mommy is going to get us out of trouble."

As she took her exit, three cars behind her, the thugs followed. Andrew screamed a pitch only heard by mothers and a few dogs on patrol. "Andrew, damn it. Mommy said to shut it!" She'd never yelled at her son, but his crying stopped immediately. She looked back to see a frightened child, wide eyes and open mouth. Lily brushed away tears. "I'm so sorry, baby, but you just need to be quiet while mommy drives like daddy would if he was being tailed by terrorists in the streets of Damascus." *Holy Moly, Dev is going to kill me...if I survive.*

Lily looked ahead at the intersection. Thankfully, traffic was light, and school wasn't in session. Her light was turning yellow. She kept driving at fifty miles per hour, and blew through the red light. A ticket would be better than being caught by whomever was following her. She turned down the back road to come up from behind the church. She redialed Danny.

"Lily, where are you?"

"I'm two blocks from you. I'm coming in hot. I'll be landing this car. What do you need me to do? I have to get Andrew out." She talked quickly with no quiver in her voice. *I can do this. I have to do this.*

"All the vehicles are out of the garage. You pull in there, and I'll take care of the rest. Gun it up the hill." *Coming in hot? She's been around us too long.*

"I'm on the back road."

"Better. Just make a hard right, and you'll be in the garage. I don't care if you hit the side of the wall." Danny had run out into the parking lot by now. He had the police on the way, but they were at least three minutes out. The highway patrol had lost the car when it had cut off a pickup truck in traffic. The driver couldn't stop in time. Four cars were wrecked and impeding any rescue of Lily.

Father Dan, dressed in his collar, black shirt and pants, held a cell phone in one hand, and a Beretta in the other. He placed the phone in his pocket. He could still hear Lily talking. He prepared his stance. His heart began to race. He pictured Lily swerving at the corner at the bottom of the hill. She'd be racing up the neighborhood street. He took in a deep breath and began to count. This would be like so many nights in Afghanistan. His gun had been bigger then, but the fear had not.

He heard Lily's car first, her wheels squealing as she rounded the corner. He saw the intent on her face as she careened into the garage. Lily placed the car in park and opened the back door while still crouching for protection. She pulled on the latch, but it didn't budge.

"Shit," Lily yelled as she tussled with the buckle. Andrew held up his hands and yelled too. "Shit, mom." Miraculously, the buckle opened. Lily lifted her son out quickly. She hid behind the car and took a defensive position.

The sedan was only seconds behind. They missed the turn and came in up the main drive. Dan went down on one knee and began to fire, hitting the radiator area of the car first. He stood, held one arm with the other, and in the next three shots, he hit both men and rolled to the side onto the hard concrete. The car sped through the parking lot until it hit one of the large trees near the playground.

Dan slowly rose to his feet near the garage door. He looked back to see Lily holding her son in her arms with a basket at her feet. She was also holding a hammer.

He smiled, still holding the gun in his hand. "What the hell were you going to do with that?"

"I was going to throw it, but first I was going to hide Andrew under the basket you use for palms." Lily smiled half-heartedly.

Dan cocked his head. "It worked for Moses. Oh great, the cavalry's here." Three police units stormed into the church's compound. Dan pointed to the crashed vehicle. The passenger had fallen out of the car and was trying to get to his feet. "I'm losing my touch. I must've just winged him."

Lily came up from behind him and patted his back. "Where were you aiming?"

Dan's focus was on the car. "Oh, I was aiming for their heads. I got one. One shot probably hit the backseat. I need to go to the range."

"Please don't mention the shooting range, Dan." *It's inevitable I'll have to go now.* "Dev and Ari have been on me to go." She held tightly onto her son, but Andrew wanted to go to his favorite priest.

Dan placed his gun behind him, sliding it into his waistband and reached out to take his favorite baby. "You need to go to the range, Lily. There's no debating it now." The priest looked at the sweat on Lily's lip and forehead, yet she was very pale. "Lily, right behind you is a lawn chair. Get it, and sit in it, now."

Lily felt unsteady. She grabbed the chair and managed to sit in it as the world began to spin. *And I'm starving. I have bread!* She opened the passenger door and pulled out the bakery item. She tore off a chunk and began to eat as the police questioned Dan. By now the paramedics had arrived and one began to check her vitals. Her sight was fine, her hands were still shaking, and her blood pressure was off the charts. She was handed a bottle of water and ordered to drink.

Television crews began to arrive. Dan still held Andrew as he turned over his gun to a detective who had just taken him into the garage, away from the nosy reporters. They didn't need to know that the area priest with a heart of gold was a marksman and had killed one criminal and sent the other to the hospital in critical condition. He had missed his forehead, but he had hit the man somewhere in the face. The police weren't specific about the location.

Dan and Lily looked at each other when they heard the rather loud bellowing of a man they both knew very well. Dev's form crossed in front of the garage. He looked in and walked past, but soon returned.

"Lily," Dan yelled over at her. "You did good today. Just know that, but now you're going to catch hell. He's just worried."

Lily toasted the priest with her bottle of water. It almost made her cry when her eyes met with her husband's. She could tell he'd been crying. *Oh my gosh, he's been crying! He cried when Andrew was born and on our wedding day.* But the romanticization of Devlin Pierce was over quickly as he strode toward her. He was fuming.

"This is what happens when you get your nose into someone else's business. I told you. I warned you. Are you happy now?" Dev stood over her like a menacing bear. *If Gretchen saw him right now she wouldn't think he was Mr. Delicious! Mr. Ogre might be more appropriate. But, crud, he's right.*

Lily remained silent. She bit her lip so she wouldn't cry. She took a drink of water. She looked down at her wedding ring. If she waited long enough, perhaps he would cool down? Dev finally couldn't wait any longer, and her evil plan had worked. He crouched down in front of her and held her hands, water bottle included.

"How are you feeling? Any damage to you or the baby? Oh, God, what about Andrew?"

"I'm fine. The baby is fine. I've been checked over. My blood pressure is way up, and I need to take it easy. I'll check in with the doctor tomorrow morning. And your son is in Dan's arms right over there. He's giving his informal statement to a detective. Dan, not the baby." Lily snorted in amusement. "We're trying to stay away from the news crews. Oh, and I love you too."

Dev lowered his head in relief. "We'll talk later, but I thought the worst when I heard your message. Then Danny called me, and I was out the door, but it took me a while to get here. I was doing a hundred at one point."

"I drove like I've lived here all my life. I drove defensively, but aggressively, just like you do when we go downtown, you know, by the Kennedy Center, and when we go to Arlington Cemetery. That darn memorial bridge. You'd be so proud," Lily admitted. Her speech was rambling with excitement, or another adrenaline surge. "Um, Dev, could you look at my ankles? I have this feeling they've become--"

Dev was looking at her swollen feet when she touched his shoulder.

"Dev, I don't feel very good." She placed her head on his shoulder. He felt her go limp as he gathered her in his arms.

"I need help. My wife just fainted."

Danny stopped talking, looking over toward the couple. The detective ran over until a medic came to Lily's side. In a matter of minutes, Lily's eyes were clear. She knew what the day and date was, and even the name of the president of the United States.

Lily noticed her son chewing his fists, a telltale sign that he had missed his snack and really needed dinner. "Dev, there's a fruit pouch in the bag in the backseat. Could you feed Andrew before he goes for Danny's nose?"

"Of course, darling."

Darling, wow. He only calls me that after, well, that's so nice. Lily watched him as he crawled into the backseat and found the food item. That's when she noticed he still had an identification badge and shoulder holster on, gun included. *I wonder how long before he mentions that shooting range again?*

Danny and Andrew walked to Lily's side. "How are you feeling now?"

"Much better. Adrenaline can really mess you up especially when you're pregnant," she answered as she looked up at them. Andrew yelled momma and attempted to hurl himself down to his mother. Danny held on for dear life. "It's okay. I'll take him."

"Is this what you wanted?" Dev held up a small bag with a colorful peach on the front. Andrew held out his hand. "Okay, I guess it is. Let me pop this for you."

Andrew took it quickly in his hands and began to eat through the opening. He leaned his body against Lily's, and the other baby kicked. Andrew looked down briefly questioning the feeling then went back to filling his stomach.

"So, what's the plan, Major?" Danny asked. "The detective said they're going to tell the news crews that they had a shootout with the two men. They're running identification on them right now. The one guy may not make it to surgery."

"You're losing your touch?"

Dan shook his head. "It looks like it. And I had one complete miss." He saw Lily's pleas with her eyes, and he knew what she didn't want him to mention. There'd be a time for that, but not now. "Let's get you all home. We could go out the back door and get the two of them to your car. I can drive her car over later tonight, after all of this dies down."

"And my pie," Lily interrupted. "I have a perfectly good cherry pie with a crust to die for, and I want it tonight. I'm having vanilla ice cream on top of it, with a glass of milk."

"You have pie?" Dev asked. "Where?"

"Ah, now you're interested. In the front seat."

Danny looked through the window and frowned. "Well, you have pieces of pie. I think your last maneuver sent it sailing."

"My pie isn't perfect?" Lily's eyes began to fill with tears. "Is there one piece left?"

Dev craned to get a look. "We can probably scrape some off of the seat."

Lily sniffed. "That's good enough. Save whatever you can. I'm having pie tonight!" She began to cry harder. "They killed my pie." Andrew looked up at his mother and joined her, his eyes welling with tears for no reason at all. Of course, he wanted pie too. Whatever pie was.

"Oh, and we need to stop cursing," Lily said between sniffs. "Andrew said a new word, and it wasn't a good one."

Dev and Dan shared a look. "I don't curse when Andrew's around, do you Dan?"

Both men folded their arms and looked directly at the crying woman. Lily sniffed. They were blaming her. "What? So? Traffic sometimes requires cursing now and then."

Dan leaned over to his friend. "We should probably cut her some slack. She did some great driving to get here, and she parked the car in here without hitting anything."

Dev shook his head and whispered, "But she can't parallel park to save her soul. Unbelievable." He looked at the perfectly parked car. "You do have security film, right?"

"Yep, and it'll be the pre-game entertainment for this year's Army-Navy game."

Lily knew they were talking about her, but she couldn't hear them over the din of the other voices in the garage. "You two better not be talking about that shooting range."

Dev's brow arched. "We weren't, but now that you mention it--"

Lily closed her eyes as her only attempt at escape. "Well, sh--" She slammed her mouth shut as her husband and one of her best friends laughed hysterically. They laughed harder when Andrew repeated the curse word. He smiled and clapped as though he had uttered the best word ever said in the English language.

Chapter Twenty-Three

Priests, at least ones like Dan Parsons, are always true to their word. Dan arrived an hour later with Lily's car, and a perfectly acceptable cherry pie he'd picked up at the grocery store. He also picked up the dinner order Dev had called in at the restaurant down the street, Lily's beloved Taco Heaven. To complete the meal, he ran to the grocery store and picked up a gallon of vanilla ice cream. He was confident Lily would be pleased with the quantity.

The dinner discussion was usually at Lily's expense, but she even managed to laugh at Andrew's expanding vocabulary. They all agreed Dev needed to tell Jack that there'd been a shooting in the church's parking lot before he saw it on the evening news. But Dev would wait until he saw his dad in person to tell him of Dan and Lily's true involvement.

Lily put the little man down after dinner. Before she even left his room, his eyes were shut, and his arms cradled Ari's designer elephant and giraffe for security. The great adventure for Mommy and Andrew was over, at least until tomorrow. She was yawning as she came down the stairs slowly. Her ankles were better, but it seemed as though the rest of her body was rebelling, especially around the baby. Her balance was off. Dan watched her take the last step carefully, and stood up.

"I think I better get going. Dev, I need a ride," Dan announced. "That woman needs to get some rest." He pointed at his closest female friend.

Dev grabbed his keys off the table. "Let's roll. I'll be right back." Dev kissed her on the forehead. "You need to go to bed."

"Uh huh," Lily muttered through another yawn. "Night Dan. Thank you."

Danny's eyes became softer than usual as he held her hands, merely inches away from her. "I would do anything to protect you and your babies." He kissed her cheek and placed his hand on her belly. "God bless you, little one. I'll call you tomorrow to check in on you."

And she knew he would. Lily noted that most women, well her specifically, didn't much like people laying their hands on your pregnant belly. A priest and his prayer was another thing. What she had put her children through today deserved a papal blessing. Lily watched from the door as the two men drove off. She noticed the unmarked car a few houses down. *He's got the DEA guys watching the house? Geez, Dev. But, that's nice of them.* She waved to the darkened vehicle. In a matter of seconds the front lights blinked back. "I love that man so much."

Lily shuffled to the kitchen, her bedroom slippers sounding as though they were made of sandpaper. She grabbed another bottle of water, turned off the lights, and headed slowly up the steps for bed.

Lily stood there in the silence of the house and looked at her profile in the mirror. She caressed her baby bump. This pregnancy was so different. She didn't seem to be carrying the baby at the same height. Jack told her, according to what his mother always said, it looked like they'd be welcoming a little girl in January. Gretchen and Dev would be happy. And she wouldn't be the only female anymore. *That would be nice! But today, I needed that testosterone, even if it was from a priest.* She saw it all so vividly. Dan had stood straight as an arrow, and he had shot so quickly. She heard the popping noise of the gun. She heard the car racing, finally crashing into the tree. She saw Danny's hands shaking later as he ate his taco.

"What have I done? I know, I've placed everybody in danger," Lily said out loud. She felt Dev's eyes on her and quickly turned to see him watching her. "You still need to work on giving me a head's up when you're here. That stealth stuff scares me to death."

He leaned against the doorframe as though he was bored to death. But Lily knew better. She was waiting for the yelling, the comments. "This isn't the first time we've all been in danger, honey. We're big boys. We can handle it."

"I saw Danny's hands. His hands are so perfect. I watch them during Mass. Did I ever tell you that? There used to be this old, old saying that you could tell a priest by his hands. A man who had beautiful hands was always a priest, or should be one. Now, I've made those beautiful hands kill one, maybe two men."

"If it will make you feel better, there's no way he wouldn't have done it, no matter what vow to God. How's this pregnancy?"

Lily caressed the bump again. "This isn't like Andrew. We really may be having a girl. Look, my boobs aren't even as big."

Dev smiled a smile Lily knew very well. "Um, well they look good to me. Come here."

His arms opened and she fell into him. His body became a cocoon for her. Right now she felt like a furry caterpillar, and not much like a butterfly at all. "When are you going to yell again, or talk about the shooting range? We might as well get everything traumatic over tonight or are you going to let me languish in self pity?" Lily murmured into his chest.

Dev kissed the top of her completely frizzing hair. *And she wondered where Andrew got those curls? Really, Lily? The boy had no choice. I'll take the blame on the color, the same as my mom's.* "Not tonight. You do the self-pity thing pretty good all on your own. Let's get you to bed."

He led her to the bed and helped her in. "I need you," Lily whispered as he kissed her on the cheek.

"I'll be there in a second," Dev said as he began to unbutton his shirt.

Lily leaned up on her elbow. "Um, I **need** you."

Dev looked up from his buttons. "What? Really?"

Lily giggled. "It will make me feel better."

Dev threw off his shoes and socks and undressed quickly. As he joined her in bed, he took her in his arms. "Well, it's not like you can get more pregnant."

Later, in the darkness of their bedroom, Dev played with his wife's hair. "Are you feeling better now?"

Lily settled in on her husband's chest, her usual location after they'd made love. "It always makes me feel better, especially when I'm pregnant. That's so weird. My stomach isn't bothering me at all. I was thinking. The first time you took me to your Dad's, and we pulled up in the drive, I saw all those hydrangea bushes across the front of the house. I asked Jack, and he said they really were your mom's favorite flower. But I knew you lied when you came into the shop that day we met. You were so bad at lying."

Dev pulled the sheet up on Lily's shoulder. She snuggled closer to him. "I couldn't remember the name of the darn things. I knew that the shipment of drugs was in the hydrangeas, but you confused me with all your questions."

"Little old me made the big bad DEA agent confused?" Lily leaned her chin onto his shoulder so she could see his expressions, even in the dark.

Dev looked away. "You bothered me."

Lily snorted. "Itty, bitty overweight florist bothered you? I wasn't your type."

Dev tightened his hold around her. "No, you weren't. That was the confusing part. You didn't have long, wavy hair. Your legs weren't long enough to get you out of the kiddie pool at most hotels. You had no makeup on. You were wearing jeans and sneakers with that apron over you. And you just kept pushing."

"And yet here we are."

"Yep. So, I guess you were my type afterall."

"Dev," Lily whispered. "Your dad said your mom used to stick her nose into everyone's business in the neighborhood. He said she found Jackson's bike, oh, and your baseball glove."

Dev chuckled lightly. "That is true. She tracked them down. Jackson cried for a week until she found that Tommy Pascoe had stolen the thing, and it was in Pascoe's garage. Mom would walk the neighborhood twice a day, and about a week after it went missing, she spotted it. She brought it out of the garage and rode it home." Dev laughed harder. "My glove was taken by old man Mr. Foster. He was a real piece of work, and seriously hated kids. I'd left the glove down on the grass when we were called in for dinner. He came out of his house and took it. What a jackass. Well, mom asked the neighbors. She waited to talk to Foster. He wouldn't invite her in just to talk, so she barged in the next day with a peach cobbler. She handed him the dessert, saw the glove in the living room, grabbed it and ran."

"So your mom made a difference by not leaving things alone?"

"Smooth, Lily." Dev patted his wife's bottom. "But Mr. Foster came after my mother with a rake. Mom was fast. She came running into the house, said she found my glove, threw it at me as she went by, and yelled for my dad. I see what you're doing. Well, the truth is, we are in this now. You and me. I hope you're happy."

"Dev, I know this may sound bizarre, but I think Laurel put this hit on me."

Lily's husband closed his eyes. He placed a kiss on the top of her head. "Honey, that sounds really crazy."

"I told you what she said. I think she was being honest then. She's wrapped up in this more than she is letting on."

Dev decided his only response was silence. In the darkness, he could hold his list making, post-it note writing, obsessive wife and know that she was safe in his embrace. "Let's leave that for another day. I'll look into it. Now, is there anything you want?" His seductive tone humored his wife.

He's trying to distract me so I must be on the right track. Two can play this game, buddy. "I just want justice," Lily murmured playfully.

Surprisingly, Dev laughed. "You did not just say that. That sounds like something I would have said about four years ago."

"And what do you say now, Boy Scout?" Lily kissed her husband's lips slowly, tenderly.

"Life is never boring with you."

Lily kissed him again and slowly moved down to his neck. "You need to shave."

Dev sighed. "Honey, I have a problem. I'm not feeling very good. Do you think there's something you could do to make me feel better?"

"I suppose you have something in mind."

Dev gently turned her onto her back, looming over her. "Anything to make me feel better, right?"

She caressed his cheek. "You do seem to be my type."

Dev's lips ran a trail from her forehead down to her lips. He murmured against her mouth. "And what type is that?"

Just a few years ago, Lily would never have thought she would be with a man like her husband, yet here she was. She was grateful for that in so many ways. "The delicious type."

Dev threw his head back in laughter. "And that's why I love you. You make me laugh."

As Lily caressed his back, she knew that tomorrow and the next day would become more serious. Her meddling had put all of them in a very precarious situation, and no amount of protection would do until they saw this through.

Chapter Twenty-Four

"He's okay. He's one of the good guys," Lily announced to the two agents on either side of the priest. They immediately removed their hands from his arms. Danny smoothed his black jacket's sleeves.

As he approached the front door, he smiled. "You know, I could've taken them."

Lily scanned his face. He didn't flinch. "Crud, you really could."

"I just figured they were supposed to be protecting you." Danny turned and yelled louder. "But you shouldn't have allowed me to get up this far in the driveway." He greeted Lily with a kiss on the cheek. "Rookies. How are you, and how is that little potty mouth son of yours?"

"He's down for a nap. I really don't know where he got it."

Dan glanced sideways at his friend. "Really? You really don't? Gee, Lily, you say it all the time when you're driving especially if you're on the beltway. So, how are you feeling today?"

"Good, really. I checked in with my doctor and filled them in on everything. They just said to rest. I've been looking at options to go to Carlos and Alise's wedding. The doctor suggested driving might be less stressful. I'll be six months pregnant by then, but we'll have to stop frequently for me to walk around. But, he said I could fly. I just have to stay hydrated, and take care. You know my husband will do enough caring for the two of us."

"That's true. By the way, I'll be going as the unofficial officiant," Dan announced. "I'll wear my robes and bless the marriage, but Alise and Carlos are legally marrying that morning."

Lily began to think. "Right. You can't perform a Catholic service on the beach." Lily paused. "So, we could fly if you were with us. Andrew thinks you walk on water."

Dan chuckled. "No, my boss does that."

Lily made a face at the bad joke. *Sorry, Lord.* "Let's fly then?"

"You line it up," Dan suggested. "I'll text you how many days I can take off once I get back to the office. That's been a zoo with all the reporters calling. I'll have to do something for the police. I don't know what the press would do if they found out a priest took out two drug cartel thugs."

"So, the other guy did die?"

Dan bowed his head and looked up slowly. "Yes, before he even made it to surgery. The DEA will know more now that they're able to check the database for the two. They'll discover what cartel they work for, if they did. Maybe they'll figure out who gave the hit orders on the doctor, his daughter, and on you. I'm sure that's why they're watching your house."

"I'm going to check on the doctor and his daughter."

Dan's hand flew up in the air. "You are **not** leaving this house today. I won't even let you do it. Dev told me about all of your suspicions with those two."

Lily fluttered her eyes. *I can't lie to a priest.* "Fine. I'll call them. Is that fine with you, your eminence?"

"Yes, but make sure you don't begin to interrogate them." Dan made the sign of the cross over her. "I'm really blessing you. You need it, and so does that baby."

"She's doing fine." Lily clapped both hands over her mouth.

Dan jumped up. His face lit up with a smile a mile wide. "Really? We really are having a girl?"

"I'm having the girl, and you all will spoil her just like you do Mr. Potty Mouth." Lily smiled at his happy reaction. "You can't say anything. Dev doesn't know yet. I called in to talk to the doctor, and his big mouth nurse told me. They'd run a sonogram when I had that episode after we flew, but I didn't ask for the results. She just assumed I knew."

"My mouth is sealed." Dan crossed himself. "I am the only one who can keep a secret in this gang."

"By pain of mortal sin," Lily added.

"Well, there is that. Gretchen will be thrilled." Dan sat back down and laughed to himself. "At least the room is ready. You'll just have to dust."

"I'll admit that this pregnancy has been totally different. I was just thinking it was because it was the second one, but maybe it is because it's a girl. Poor Andrew doesn't know what's going to hit him after the first of the year."

"So, January, huh?"

Lily grimaced. "Just thinking about the weather, I'm comforted by the fact my husband can drive in all sorts of conditions."

"Let's talk about driving," Dan added. "You did some fine driving yesterday. The highway patrol pulled some video from the interstate and sent it to Dev this morning. That detective came over to the rectory and showed it to me. Dang, girl."

"I listen and watch you guys."

"And that's what we're all afraid of," Dan added. "Lily, I can't hold back the raging tide that is Devlin Pierce if you get yourself in trouble again."

Lily waved him off and pretended everything was fine. "Don't worry about that. We worked all that out last night."

Dan smiled. "Really?" *What game is she playing now on my old friend, and thinking she can do it to me too?* "Lily, don't push it. You have a full life. A great marriage, a son, and a baby on the way, you work at the vineyard and on weddings out there, so why this mystery stuff? If you want to do something, maybe go back to what your degree was in. I don't think I ever heard what that was."

"No, none of you even asked me, not even my husband. You all just assumed I was a florist, and always had been."

Dan pushed. "Well? What did you do before the flower shop?"

Lily stood up and walked to the edge of the stairs. She thought she heard Andrew. "You can be the first to know, Daniel, and I'll even let you tell my husband. I received my degree in journalism, and I was a political reporter before I took over the family's business. So I guess I just come by asking questions naturally."

Dan grabbed his head. "Oh no. A reporter? We used to hate reporters in the sand box."

Lily's smile was as wide as her face. *So, finally, they know what I started out wanting to do!* "Yep. And my lifetime goal was to be a writer, a mystery novelist, just like Jessica."

Dan stood up. It was time to go. "*Oy!* You do know that Jessica is a fictional character, right?"

"Don't be silly. Of course, I do! But one can have lofty goals, can't one?" Lily was having the time of her life messing with the priest. She knew that before he hit the stop sign at the end of their street, he'd be on the phone to Dev. The man could keep a secret, but he could fuel the rumor mill with the best of them.

Lily waved at the nice DEA agents as she shut the front door, and promptly locked it. As long as Andrew was asleep, she'd take advantage of the quiet time to check on the doctor.

She poured herself a glass of milk before Dr. Fleischman answered the phone.

"Doctor, Lily Pierce. I just wanted to check on you and your daughter." She took a seat on the soft couch, laying her feet up on one of the cushions.

"Lily, thank you for calling. I've heard that those men who threatened us are dead. Did you hear anything more?"

Lies-R-Lily! Geez, I hate doing this. "I did see the news coverage. I haven't heard anything."

Dr. Fleischman cleared his throat. "My daughter did some checking over the years." He paused and cleared his throat a second time. "Well, we were looking at her notes last night, and she discovered that Margot had been married before, to a doctor in Kansas City, Missouri. I guess doctors were her type. Isn't that where you're from?"

It was Margot in Kansas City! Tom must have a large file on her with the FBI. I don't think I mentioned where I was from. Laurel certainly became interested all of a sudden. Fine, I'll play. "Yes, that's my hometown. Unbelievable. So now what for you all?"

"I'm talking to the marshalls and the FBI, but we're thinking of getting out of town, far out of town, maybe heading on a cruise. It will be a great excuse for the whole family to spend some time together. My grandchildren can take a week off, or bring their schoolwork along, but we need to leave. I can't count on the police to protect us twenty-four, seven."

"I completely understand." *I really do. If you are afraid, getting away would be a good idea. If you're feeling very uncomfortable because someone is getting close to one of your secrets, I'd be flying out on the next plane to an island.* If Lily didn't have her very own special forces unit, would she still be alive? She sighed and turned off her suspicious mind for a few minutes. She needed to go to the shooting range. She'd have to get over her fear, if only to protect Andrew and the baby. *Dev will be happy!* But she really didn't want to see the satisfied look of superiority on his face when she finally agreed to learn to really shoot a gun.

"Please be careful, and maybe we can all get together at the vineyard when everything calms down. Goodbye, Lily."

She understood his meaning. For now, he was telling her he wouldn't be talking to her. It also seemed like he would not be searching for his missing wife ever again. Perhaps she was reading too much into his words, but then again maybe she was reading exactly the correct words. At least she now knew in her heart that Laurel was involved in some capacity.

Andrew woke up just a few minutes later after the call, happy and ready to play. After their snacks, they went out on the front porch to swing. Lily noticed her detail pulling away as her husband's vehicle came from the other direction. The two cars stopped and words were exchanged.

Lily pointed out at the cars. "Look, Andrew, those cars are talking. It's the handing over of the troublesome pregnant woman. Oh, and it's Daddy too." Andrew saw his father and clapped as he realized his favorite playmate was home. Dev pulled into the driveway and parked. He gathered his backpack and began to walk up the sidewalk.

"DaDa home," Andrew yelled.

"Little man."

As Dev came up the steps, Andrew bolted from Lily's lap to amble slowly into his father's arms. Dev knelt, dispatching his pack onto the porch. Andrew pressed his head on his father's chest. Dev rose up, still holding his child in his arms.

"Now, that's a greeting," he said happily.

"Come swing with me, and I'll give you another greeting." Lily crooked her finger to beckon him to the space remaining next to her.

As soon as he sat down, Lily reached over and kissed him. "It has been a very uneventful day."

"Thank God. Danny updated me on his visit, and he tells me you have something to announce? But first, is there a reason why the priest knows something before me?"

"Well, that's on me," Lily admitted freely. "I goofed. I blurted out some information."

"Such as?" Dev peered into her eyes, attempting to read his wife. That was becoming increasingly difficult. Her "tells" were disappearing. He refused to teach her poker.

"When I talked to the nurse this morning, she gave me the results of the sonogram they gave me. I didn't ask her for it. She just assumed I knew. While talking to Danny, I let it slip that--"

"We're having a girl."

Lily tapped Dev's leg. "Dev! Did Danny tell you?"

"No, I just knew it." He leaned over and offered a kiss, which his wife returned.

"Of course you did," Lily muttered. "You know a lot of stuff, and you don't share pieces of information with your wife, although you know she wouldn't tell anyone--"

Dev swept his hand up. "Stop. Just stop. When you begin speaking this quickly, you're nervous about something. Just tell me."

"I need to do something." Lily's resolve was wavering. She'd made the decision, but her fear continued to get the best of her. "Dev, I need to go to the shooting range to at least know how to point the gun."

Dev sat quietly. He'd done that before in Key West. When he was leaving her in danger. But this was different. She said she needed to go. "I noticed you didn't say you wanted to go."

Lily offered a half-smile. "Well, I don't want to go, but I need to go. I know that now. I mean, I know where the guns are in this house, but you're the one who uses them. I might need to someday. That's the only reason why I'm doing it."

Dev nodded. He wouldn't pretend to be happy. She was acknowledging she had to do something she found reprehensible. But that was half the battle with his wife. "We'll go, but in the meantime, I'm going to show you again all the parts to a gun, and how to aim. And if the safety is on or off. Deal?"

Lily nodded. "Deal." Lily chuckled as Andrew tried to stick his finger up his father's nose. "Can we go out for dinner? I really am too tired to do anything tonight."

"You're probably exhausted after your race yesterday."

"So you enjoyed the film?" Lily stood up to look down on him. *He's going to drive this into the dirt!*

"Oh, yes. Frankly, the guys are thinking you've missed your calling. Perhaps you should be a DEA agent, or maybe a driver for some ambassador. Dang, girl. From now on, you're driving in D.C., not me."

"I've learned from the best," Lily said as she bowed in his direction. She realized the pants she was wearing were a little snug. "I need to change. I think I grew today, I mean really just grew in the last few hours."

"Andrew, is that even possible?" Dev asked his curious son. "I mean if your momma can get bigger in just hours, what's that mean for the next months? You and I better be very good or we'll be in big trouble because she gets so cranky when she gets bigger. Do you understand trouble, little man?"

His son giggled and said his favorite new word that shouldn't be said by a toddler. But Dev nodded. "Yep, that's the kind of trouble we'll be in."

Lily thought she could get more information about Margot/Gilda at dinner, but Dev's mouth remained shut. He did offer a pinch of information admitting that Tom sent a complete file, and definitely Dr. Fleischman's wife was indeed alive. In the past years, she'd been very busy. Dev also assured her that they were checking Laurel out.

She had numerous contacts in the drug world, but most of them had been her clients. If she was involved with Margot, that would put an entirely different spin on this whole mystery. If she had been the one who ordered the hit on Lily, Laurel posed more of a threat than a missing hit woman.

Later that night, Dev volunteered to give Andrew a bath and put him down to sleep. Lily was supposed to be resting and folding laundry, instead she stood in her husband's office staring at the white board. She moved a couple notes around now that she knew for sure the woman was alive. *Surely, Laurel really couldn't send two hit men after me? Did Margot/Gilda do it? The woman has the power to send two men after her prey. She has to have money too, perhaps in the islands somewhere. But in the beginning, she was collaborating with someone with more power, and definitely more connections. Perhaps she put together some trade with prescription drugs? She could easily forge signatures of her husbands, or paramours.* Lily snorted. "Paramours. Such an old word." But crime never aged, and it was never ending. Sadly, because of the ever enlarging illegal drug trade, her husband would always have a job.

Eventually, Lily sat down in the corner chair and gazed at the board, not thinking of any details. Possibly something might just jump out at her, but it didn't. Dev found her in the office. Her face was devoid of any emotion. She was contemplative. Dev leaned against the doorframe, his usual position for watching Lily. He was cultivating a real talent in watching his wife.

"What are you missing, honey?"

Lily glanced at him and then back at the magical white board. "Was she setting up some sort of system to funnel drugs? And who on earth was she working for?"

Dev moved away from the door and kissed his wife. He sat on the corner of the chair with his arm around the top of the chair. It was time to offer Lily a very important detail. "She was ahead of her time. She was one of the first to funnel fentanyl into North America. The synthetic forms are deadly. That's what we have on our plates now. They're laced in everything, and they're killing people. As for who she was working for back then, I'm not sure, but she had an American contact. He is someone very familiar to us, Bernard Notte."

Seldom was Lily speechless, but this was one of those times. "No!"

"Oh yes. Bernard was in this stuff way before his son was. He said that the kid involved him, but the dad had his own agenda. I don't think he realized how serious the prescription drug scheme was and thought the pain pills were legitimate. He was just looking at making easy money. Instead, the drugs were mixed with another chemical, or were actually doses way over the limit. Most of these drugs hooked their users, and on occasion, became murderous cocktails. Bernard was also into smuggling art, jewelry, and funneling money to the Caymans and Switzerland. He's a really classy guy."

"Will the Nottes ever go away?" Lily lamented. She leaned against Dev. "I'm tired. How's Andrew?"

"Snoozing away. He makes these little puffing noises. Is that normal?"

Lily looked up shyly. "It is. He comes by it honestly from his father."

"I don't do that."

"Yes, you do. Ask your friends," Lily quipped as she attempted to raise herself out of the deep chair. Her lower back was on fire. "I need some help here."

Dev lifted under her shoulders, and gently raised her. He turned her around into his arms. "Tell me something about Margot/Gilda that I need to know."

Lily contemplated which item she should offer. "Her ego can do her in. She thinks she's hot stuff, probably still almost twenty years later. But, whoever put her down this path was some man that she really loved, or idolized."

"That's pretty spot on," Dev admitted. "And she's the one who has used that moniker on more than one occasion."

Lily nuzzled her head against his chest. "Honey, did you tell Dr. Fleischman that I was from Kansas City?"

Dev perched his jaw on top of her head. "Nope. I don't share anything that I don't want to share."

"Well, he apparently looked me up. He knew where I was from. His comments made me feel uncomfortable." Lily didn't dare look at Dev. *He'll look at me with those dagger eyes. He'll be the one that was right about placing myself in danger.*

Dev thought a second before he answered his wife. There'd be time to reprimand her later for always pushing just a little too much. "The doctor and his daughter seem to be cooperating with the FBI. Of course, he did years ago too. He had the perfect alibi when Margot went missing. There was no record of a payoff, or any intake of huge sums of money. But, if you have your suspicions about the doctor and his daughter, and I have mine, then this may all be a smokescreen."

Lily finally pulled back to look up at him. "You are suspicious too? Oh, I'm so happy. I thought I'd have to convince you." Her back wasn't hurting anymore.

Dev held her shoulders and leaned down. "Look, for now, we have to take them at face value. We can have all the suspicions and concerns, and none of that energy will help if they are involved and they run. Do you understand?"

Lily nodded. "So, we continue to pretend to believe them?"

Dev rolled his eyes. "I suppose it's a waste of time to tell you there is no *we*, right?"

Lily chose to completely ignore the man she loved. "Let's go to bed." Lily took him by the hand and headed slowly up the stairs. "By the way, I received a text from Dan a little bit ago. We'll have a house to stay in for Carlos and Alise's wedding. The place is huge, and drumroll please--"

They'd reached the landing. Dev shrugged. "What? Just tell me."

"We've been invited to stay with the owner, Mrs. Notte."

Lily giggled, but Dev rolled his eyes. "Why can't we get away from that family?"

"I'm actually excited to see her, especially if her son and grandson stay away."

Dev agreed. "Well, the grandson is still in federal prison, and old Bernie is in protective custody somewhere. It'll be laid back and quiet?"

Lily laughed out loud now. "Do you really think we can go anywhere where the Nottes are involved and nothing happens?"

Dev began to remove pillows off the bed. His wife continued to rub her lower back area, looking more uncomfortable tonight. By the time they made it to the wedding she wouldn't need any extra stress. He better get the priest to start praying for peace, quiet, and safety. *Heck, Danny better begin a Novena! Maybe I should too, if it'll do any good.*

Chapter Twenty-Five

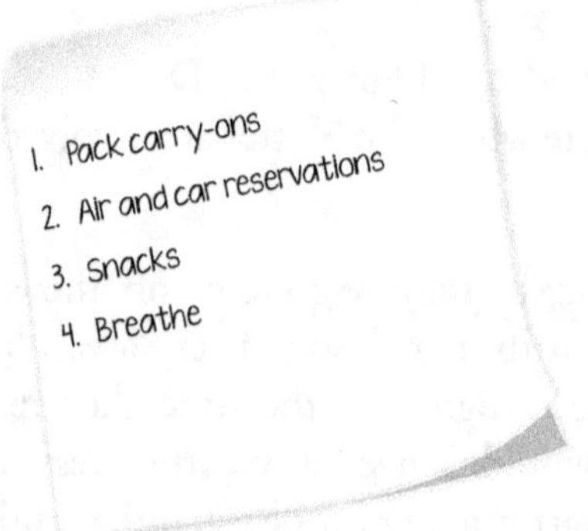

"Danny, why are you in full priest garb today?" Lily watched the priest as he chased Andrew in the airport waiting area.

"Frankly, it's to my advantage. When I flew home to see my mom in February, the flight attendants gave me three free drinks, and two extra bags of those little cheese-filled crackers." Danny flashed a smile. He picked up the toddler. "We're going to take a walk. I love to see people's faces when they see a priest with a baby. It'll be grand if Andrew calls me DaDa."

Dev looked up from his phone. "With your luck, he'll say his favorite profanity. We're attempting to stop that, so don't encourage or laugh if he does it. Tell him no."

Dan searched Lily's face. "Oh come on, guys. When did you become real parents?"

Lily chuckled as she searched her bag. She was getting hungry already. "Um like two years ago." Dev continued to read something on his phone. "Has Dan always been this way?"

Dev continued to read. "What way? I haven't noticed anything different about him."

Lily elbowed her husband. "Look at him. He's taking great delight in shocking the people who think the baby is his. Dan has always been the stable one. Well, Paul is more stable, but he's married. That always helps most men get their acts together."

Dev threw her a side glance. "First, Dan isn't the stable one, and I hate to burst your bubble, but no woman really makes a man more stable. If anything, some wives make their husbands even crazier."

Lily smiled sweetly. "Are you talking about Jill?"

"Paul's lovely wife? Absolutely not. I'm speaking from personal experience."

Lily stuck her tongue out at her loving husband. "It's a good thing you're so pretty or I wouldn't keep you."

"Yes, honey." Dev smiled widely. "You just keep telling yourself that."

Before Lily could respond, Dan herded Andrew closer to them. The toddler yawned. "Do I keep him awake?"

Lily and Dev answered simultaneously. "Yes."

"I want him to sleep on the plane," Lily said. She removed a bag of apple slices as though they were hidden treasures. Both men looked at her in amusement. "What? I'm trying to eat healthy. You two should be happy about it."

"I was hoping she had chocolate in there," Danny said sadly.

Dev glanced up again. "Oh, she does. Don't let her fool you. She has enough food in there to feed all four of us for a couple of days with no problem."

Lily smirked, but her husband was right. He was wrong about one thing. *I could feed us for a week! But, we'll have to ration the cookies.*

Thirty minutes later, they boarded. Danny carried Andrew and his own carry-on. At the ramp, Lily checked the stroller and carried her bag of food and other essentials onto the plane. Her husband carried everything else including the carseat and two more carry-ons. Lily sighed when they finally found seats. *We look like a caravan, a circus one!*

Lily took the seat nearest the window with Dev taking the aisle so he could stretch his legs. Andrew was strapped into the seat in the middle. The priest, standing to allow an elderly couple to move into the row, would take the aisle seat across from his friend.

"Hey, Dev, remember when your wife is pregnant, she has to use the restroom several times on a flight. JT is still complaining after he flew with her." Lily now stuck her tongue out at the priest.

Her husband shook his head. "We didn't have a problem when we went to Kansas City, but that was a few weeks back. I'll just do what I have to do."

Dev's statement made her heart flutter as Lily smiled widely at Dan. "And that's why JT and you aren't married." She knew as soon as she said it how ridiculous she had just sounded, but there was no taking it back now.

Dev smiled, but Danny looked down the row at his favorite woman. "Um, I'm not married because," he pointed at his collar as he continued, "I'm a priest. JT isn't married, well, who do you know who would marry him?"

Lily held her own. She knew who. "Ace."

Dev and Danny were shocked. Finally, Danny's row companions were settled in, and he was able to sit down while the flight attendants checked the over-head storage.

"How does she know?" Danny whispered to Dev.

"I have no earthly idea. Do you think Ace told her?"

Dan thought for a second. "Lily met her briefly last year. I don't think Ace would just sit down beside a stranger, even if she is your wife, and say hey, JT and I married years ago, and we forgot to get a divorce. Do you?"

Dev was about to answer when Lily's head appeared in front of him. She was able to almost stand erect. "JT and Ace were married, and they still are? How did I not know this?"

"We got played," Dev muttered. He looked into his wife's mischief-filled eyes. "Lily, you set us up?"

"I suspected something was going on with her and JT, but I didn't know what, until you two just told me. For two men who keep secrets, you certainly are lousy at it."

"And sometimes, you're too smart for your own good," Dev admitted half-heartedly.

Dan shook his finger at the amateur detective. "You, woman, say ten Our Fathers and ten Hail Mary's, and don't you ever, ever say anything to JT, or to Ace. Seriously."

Thankfully, the flight attendants began their safety instructions. Lily was the only one of their party to watch. *For two men who are used to taking orders, they sure don't do it on an airplane. JT was the same way.* As soon as the plane was up in the air, Lily looked over to see a blissfully sleeping baby. She leaned her head against the plane's wall and shut her eyes.

Dev noticed both of his loves were completely asleep before the drinks were served. Danny tapped his arm. "Hey, the first round is on me."

"I can't believe we let that secret out. Man, we are losing our touch," Dev admitted.

"Lily should've known years ago, but it was for JT to tell her. You know, I had forgotten all about it."

One of the flight attendants stood between them, taking the order from the couple next to Dan. She then looked down at him. "I'll have a bourbon and a cup of ice, and I'll get his too." He pointed at Dev.

"I'll have the same."

Dan reached for his billfold, but the attendant stopped him. "Oh no, Father. I've got this, for both of you."

Dan expressed his thanks and nodded to his friend. "See? What did I tell you?"

What are we? In college again? "Unbelievable. You can drink. One will be my limit. I want to drive out of Tampa. Lily needs to sit in the back with Andrew, and she doesn't need the stress of driving through downtown Tampa. Besides, the Skyway Bridge would make her too nervous."

"Does it get old being the Boy Scout all of the time?" Danny flashed a toothy smile, full of sarcasm.

"I'm not that good, and you know that. It's not like you're a saint, either."

"No, but I portray one in my parish." The men shared a laugh. "Hey, we didn't get Lily anything to drink."

Dev shook his head. "I'm not waking her up. I have a couple of bottles of water in my bag if Andrew or she needs a drink. She's starting to have some more symptoms. But once we land, we're going to get lunch before we begin the drive. I know this little seafood restaurant off the causeway toward Clearwater. You and I will be happy with any kind of seafood, and they have the best chicken parmesan on their menu so Lily will be thrilled."

"Seriously, when did you get so daddy-like? You always did take care of us all, but you have certainly become a professional at it."

Dev touched Andrew's little hand and watched his wife sleep. He knew when. "Dan, thanks for helping Lily get through the TSA. I had to do my thing."

The priest nodded. He understood what Dev had to do. Just going through security could be overwhelming, but checking on a gun could be a daunting task. "I hope you brought more than one thing."

"Yes, I did, just in case. I'm sure Carlos did too. I updated him on what's going on."

Their drinks came and they saluted each other. 'Here's to Boy Scouts," Dan said as he lifted his cup.

Dev touched his cup to his friend's. "And to always be prepared for everything."

"By the way, Dev, did you get her to the shooting range yet?"

Dev took another sip of his liquor. "No, not yet, but Lily has promised that after the baby is born, we'll go on a date night. In the meantime, I've given her a refresher overview. At least I got it into her hands, and she knows how to use it to scare someone away."

Dan's partners in the row wanted to talk with him about the Catholic church. Dev only smiled. Dan slipped into his priestly self without missing a beat. *If those poor people only knew we were just talking about guns, and using those guns if necessary.*

Andrew's eyes opened and searched for a parent. Dev held his small hand. His son smiled and closed his eyes once more. "I'm here, little man. I only hope I'm prepared for whatever heads our way," Dev whispered.

After landing and packing up the rental vehicle, the group arrived at one of Dev's favorite restaurants. Lily enjoyed the warm breeze, but the seafood being served turned her stomach. She had Dev order her a grilled chicken salad while Dan and he enjoyed fresh gulf shrimp. Andrew flirted with the server and ate his fill of fruit and some of his mother's chicken and avocado.

"How did this place become one of your favorites?" Lily finally asked. *How did he find this place? Was he on some sort of DEA raid?*

"I've been down here now and then for work, and MacDill has central and special operations commands." He stopped abruptly before he said too much.

"Ah," Lily answered. *Will I ever know everything about my husband?* Lily knew her life was a short story, and she was way past some editing and a re-write. Her epilogue would be stellar. On the other hand, Dev was a great American novel, filled with twists and turns.

After a last restroom stop, they headed on their way to Anna Maria. Lily had been there once to visit friends who lived on the island. It was a quiet, old-Florida small town with piers where you could glimpse dolphins breach the water and manatees beg for food. She couldn't wait to get her son on the beach, and walk him into the gulf so his toes could feel the water. *Heck, I can't wait.* She needed a break, and she especially wanted to be near friends with nothing on their minds but a happy occasion. She could handle that. She could control that. But she didn't have to do the work. She was more than happy to be a guest.

By the time they pulled onto Manatee Avenue, Lily was anxious to see where they'd be staying. *Who am I kidding? Just seeing palm trees is exciting.* But she was ready to stop traveling for the day. They turned off of Gulf Drive and drove slowly. In front of them was a modern white house. It loomed as a shiny beacon of rest.

"Are you sure this is the house?" Dan asked as they pulled into the massive driveway. The three-story structure loomed in the clear blue Florida sky. There was room for at least six cars to park in the driveway, with a carport under the house on the left, and an open area on the other side. A small trail on that adjacent side gave access to the beach. "Man, I'm not sure I've ever stayed in something like this."

Dev dipped his sunglasses and furrowed his brow at his friend. "Yes, you have. We stayed in a palace once or twice."

Dan suddenly realized where he was describing. "Ah, that doesn't count. There wasn't a beach and there was rubble everywhere."

Lily could barely hear their lowered voices. *A palace?* "Well, darlings, I have stayed in a few places that would make this look like a dump," Lily joked with her version of a snob's accent. She saw Dev's sunglasses in the rearview mirror as he smiled. "Let's get in there and start having a great time."

"I'll go up and see where we need to go," Dev offered. He put down all the windows in the car, allowing Lily to feel the ocean breeze. She watched him knock on the door, greeted by Carlos, and the two men returned.

"Danny, Lily, it is so good that you're here." He greeted Lily with a hug and quickly did the same with one of his oldest friends. "You need to ditch that collar and get some sun."

"As soon as I get in. It's so good to see you, Carlos. I'm ready to have a wedding."

Carlos smiled. "Believe it or not, Daniel, I can't wait."

Lily was in charge of her son. Between carrying Andrew, and her own tired body up the first set of stairs, Lily was done when she entered the large great room. Straight ahead of her were a bank of windows, and the Gulf of Mexico. There was also a woman standing with open arms while leaning on her cane.

"Mrs. Notte," Lily screamed in delight. "I am so happy to see you." She took the embrace as if it was a warm blanket wrapped around her. "Thank you for having us."

"Of course. I'm happy to be able to have you. And look at this little one, and another one on the way?"

"Yes, we're trying to make our family before we get too old." Andrew grabbed onto Mrs. Notte's finger. Lily pulled him away before he bit her. That was his new thing. If anything came close to his mouth, the item went into the mouth, and he bit down even if it was his mother's fingers and ear. "This home is amazing." Lily couldn't take her eyes off of the water and the fantastic view. They would have just a few steps past the swimming pool to the white sandy beach.

"Carlos can show you to your rooms. There is an elevator when you don't want to do the stairs, dear. Carlos is a wonderful man, and I'm so happy for Alise and Angelica. They deserve every bit of happiness."

Lily nodded. "Yes, they do." There was a sound to the left of Lily. The elevator contained Dev with all of the luggage. Dan and Carlos came up the stairs.

"One more floor, Agent Pierce," Mrs. Notte directed. He nodded and shut the door.

"Come on Lily. I'll show you the rooms." Carlos led the way; Dan grabbed Andrew to relieve Lily as she navigated the stairs.

As Lily arrived into the large living room, she immediately realized that the view was even better one flight up. The floor-to-ceiling doors revealed a view that Lily only had in her dreams with turquoise blue water and undulating waves. In addition to the view, the room featured a large sectional and several chairs with a television that filled one wall and a lovely kitchen. Dan's suite was on that side of the floor. She looked behind her at double french doors that probably led to their bedroom.

Dev arrived with their things, and the men passed off luggage from one side to the other of the communal living area. Two bags were placed on the counter of the kitchen. Lily placed Andrew down on the floor so he could roam as she unloaded her stash of food with some items placed directly into the refrigerator.

"Honey, where do you want the pack 'n play?" Dev stood holding Andrew's collapsible playpen.

Lily looked up. "In the bedroom. He can actually sleep in that if we need him to."

She winked at her husband. Dev's mouth gaped open with complete understanding.

"We definitely may need him to do that."

Lily grabbed a bottle of water and headed to Andrew. Both of them needed hydrating. She kicked off her sandals and grabbed her son. She opened one glass door and headed out onto the white deck. She sat down on a cushioned lounge chair with Andrew perched next to her. He shut his eyes when the wind was a little more than he could handle. Lily breathed in deeply and felt every nerve in her body relax. Until there was a kick around her liver area.

"Ouch, baby hurt." Andrew looked startled. He touched his mother's belly. "Yes, ouch. Your sister just kicked me just when I was having a moment."

"This is a place for moments," Dan said as he joined the mother and child. He'd quickly changed into shorts and a t-shirt, now looking nothing like the priest he was. Beach, water, and a view of the Sunshine Skyway Bridge was in his sight line.

"Isn't it? This is a dream. I may never want to leave." *Holy Moly! Thank you God for getting us this far.*

Dev arrived with two bottles of beer in his hands. "Dan, Carlos thought you might need this." He handed off one bottle and kissed his wife's head. "I put away some of the clothes. I'll do the rest later. Wow, this is something."

"Uh huh." Lily held Andrew a little closer. He rested his head against his mother's growing stomach. Slowly, his little hand patted.

"Baby."

All three of the adults looked at him in shock. Lily pushed away a tear. "Yes, Andrew, baby."

Dan shook his head. "He picks up so many words. Is that normal?"

Lily laughed. "It is if you're around adults all the time. I need to find him some friends."

Dev leaned on the railing and took a drink. "He'll have an instant friend next year." They needed this break, and in a place like this, one might believe that you were safe and at peace. Of course, no place was ever that safe or peaceful.

But for now, all is good. "Carlos and Mrs. Notte are lining up the dinner reservation for tonight, now that we're all here. The lady's nurse is with Alise and Angelica getting some supplies."

"I'd like to get to the grocery store tomorrow," Lily suggested. "I can go by myself."

"No," Dan and Dev said forcefully. Andrew looked up at both of them to see if he was the one in trouble.

"One of us will go with you," Dev demanded.

"So that's how it's going to be?" Lily looked from her husband to her priest.

Neither of the men answered, but she wouldn't allow anything to disturb her well-being right now on this deck overlooking the Gulf. "I'm going out to the beach. Who's with me?"

That was an idea that all of them could agree upon.

Dev swung Andrew in his arms as they all walked slowly on the beach. He heard his name. A young girl came running toward him. "Dan, take him, please." He handed off Andrew and began a slow run toward the small form.

He grabbed the girl and held her up into the air. "Angel. How's my girl?"

"Good, but I'm bigger now."

Dev set her down safely on the sand. "You're right. You're getting so tall." He looked past her to see Alise and Carlos walking hand-in-hand. "You'll be a bridesmaid this time."

"I'm the maid of honor. That's even more special. I was a baby when I was your flower girl." It had only been three years, but she was almost four inches taller. "I've missed you."

"I've missed you too. Come on. Say hello to Lily and our son."

Angelica smiled widely. "Momma said I could play with your little boy."

Dev grabbed her hand. "He can't do too much, but I bet he'll love playing in the sand with you."

She saw Lily and ran ahead. Carlos and Alise greeted Dev.

"She's so tall." Dev hugged Alise as they watched her daughter run to Lily.

"She'll soon be older and smarter than us," Alise stated. "I want to see that baby boy of yours. Carlos says he has red hair. How did that happen, Agent Pierce?"

"It's my mom's fault. Lily's been wondering about that too. So how are you, bride?"

"I'm good. I guess it's about time we get married."

Carlos hugged his future wife. "It is past time."

Alise scolded her future husband with a condemning finger. "That's all your fault. You have been too busy with work to put a wedding ring on you. If you don't show up on Saturday night, I promise I'll track you down."

Dev chuckled. "Carlos, I believe her. Alise, you would've made a great agent."

Alise snapped her fingers. "You know it. Sorry, men, I've got to get to that baby."

She ran ahead on the sand, and immediately Andrew was in her arms. Carlos stopped Dev short of the group. "So what's up? I've been looking at the file you sent me. The funny thing is, I swear I saw her the other day at the Tampa airport."

"Carlos, no way. She'd be an idiot to step foot on American soil. When we ran that operation about five years ago, I shot her lover at the time. But she was the one funneling those bad drugs. She's good though. We never put together all the pieces or else we would've realized she's a hired killer. Lucky me, my wife figured it out, and it almost got her and my son killed on the interstate. Dan killed both of the guys after her."

Carlos nodded seriously. "Good. I'm happy that the priest is here. I have an extra piece for him."

"I do too. But let's not get too involved in this. It's your wedding."

Carlos placed his arm around Dev's back. "I am blessed to have my friends here, and yes, we'll enjoy every minute, but I think we need to be prepared just in case that really was her I saw."

As they approached, Dev surveyed the area. Lily and Alise talked away with Andrew sitting on the sand at their feet. He was fingering each particle in his hand, studying them as though they were gold. *What if Carlos really did see Margot? Why would she be here?* Dev's eyes fell on his wife, and she looked up as though she could hear his thoughts.

She saw the concern in his face. She knew something was wrong.

Lily smiled as the two men joined them. She put her arm around Dev's back and leaned into him. "Everything okay?" Her head tilted up to watch his reaction.

"I don't know, honey. I really don't know."

His truthfulness sent shivers down her back even though it was wonderfully warm on the beach. "Then we'll figure it out together. Right now, let's have a good time."

Dev placed his chin on top of her head. "Yes, we need a good time."

But he knew something was coming.

Chapter Twenty-Six

"When were you on Longboat Key?" Lily asked as Dev drove on their way to Sarasota. Mrs. Notte had planned a very nice dinner for the first night of the festivities. Even her nurse and caretaker Barb was invited as were Angelica and Andrew. Lily only hoped the restaurant was baby friendly.

"We had a DEA operational training program with the special response team here. It was the perfect place with water access. It's beautiful here."

Lily looked back at Danny and Andrew. They were playing a giggling game of peek-a-boo. "Dev, what is it? You seemed distracted after you talked to Carlos."

Dev thought about it for a second. "Distracted is a good word. Oh, that's a great restaurant on the beach. We should come back and eat here if we have time." He pointed at an outside eatery with long tables. "Carlos thinks he saw Margot at the airport the other day. He had been part of the special response team to take her down."

"Do you think she's after us?" Lily's voice lowered. She was making an attempt to conceal her fear.

"If she is, then she's going for revenge, and it has nothing to do with you, and everything to do with me." Dev sighed. He briefly looked at his wife. He had to tell her. "I shot her boss or lover. He went missing, and we assumed he was dead, but the body was never found. I'm still not sure who he was to her. We could never really figure out that part of the equation, but if she's here, it's because she knows who I am."

"How would she know that?" Lily rubbed his shoulder. She glanced toward the backseat at the giggling little boy and the amusing priest. *How long can Danny keep this up? He has the patience of Job. Oh, right, it's his job. He should have patience.*

"It wouldn't be that hard. Those thugs followed the doc and his daughter to our house. They probably discovered the name, and maybe she put it together. Or, they sent her a photo of us. She knew what I looked like even though I was undercover back then. Or, remember when that ignorant congressman released our names to the newspaper? A lot of bad people would be very interested in getting access to track down any number of us."

"Or our suspicions about Dr. Fleischman and his daughter are correct, and they tipped her off. Maybe they weren't even chased." Dev stared straight ahead. He chose not to answer his very perceptive wife. His contacts searching through traffic video hadn't found one tangible piece of evidence that corroborated the chase.

Dev smiled slightly. *But we have all had a look at Lily's attempt at Grand Prix driving. My wife is amazing!*

They stopped at a traffic light at the end of a bridge. Lily saw a sign for an aquarium. "What's that?"

"Mote Marine. They do a lot of research, and their aquarium is great. There's a boat ride too. We can go tomorrow, unless the wedding group has something planned for all of us."

"Great." *No wonder Dev looks so concerned. He thinks he's brought danger to us again.* Lily rubbed his neck. "Don't worry. It will be fine. We will be fine."

Dev didn't answer. He kept driving until they entered St. Armands Circle, offering a view of specialty shops and glamorous dining establishments.

Lily spotted the restaurant. *Wonderful! It looks more casual than the others. When Andrew puts his macaroni up his nose, no one will freak out.* After parking, they were led up to the rooftop where Mrs. Notte, Barb, Carlos, Alise, Angelica, and a few others were already seated. There were large plates of appetizers on the tables. This was the Cuban night of the week, in homage to Carlos' heritage.

Dev wrestled with Andrew's chair as Lily reached for a bite of food. "Oh my gosh." She clapped after the first bite.

"Cuban empanadas," Carlos said. "Here, try these yucca fries Lily, with this sauce."

"I always love food," Lily admitted. "When I'm pregnant I **really** like food." She tore off a small corner from the doughy appetizer and handed it to Andrew. Danny and Dev poured glasses of sangria for themselves. *Thankfully, it's pretty easy to get back to the island. I'm pretty sure I'm the designated driver.* Carlos was drinking beer while Alise had a peach colored drink of some kind.

"Lily, I ordered you a non-alcoholic punch, and it's very good," Alise said as she threw a kiss to her across the table. "Angelica loves the drink."

When her drink arrived, it was decorated with an umbrella, a pineapple spear, a cherry, lime quarter, and a good chunk of mango. She could just eat her drink. She watched as Mrs. Notte served as the hostess with the mostess. She fawned over her great granddaughter, and then expressed her joy over Carlos and Alise's marriage.

"As I've grown older, I thought that life would be just sitting in a chair in my library, looking out on my garden. It was peaceful and beautiful, also very well manicured. But, thanks to all of you at this table you've made my life messy, loud, and full of joy." She paused and motioned at Dan. "You, priest, I suspect will provide me with more entertainment this week than the rest of them."

"You have no idea what fun you're in for with me, madam," Dan said as he toasted her with his glass. He wore a small pink umbrella behind one ear, and a flower behind the other. The group laughed and quieted for her to continue.

"As I was saying, thanks to all of you, my life has become rather messy, but I wouldn't have it any other way. You all bring such happiness to me, and to be around these children this week will simply be divine. I believe Carlos and Alise have an announcement for all of us at this table."

The couple stood as Alise began to speak. "Thank you all for coming. You all are our family. Both of us have lost our parents, and now we have a wonderful woman in our life to help us fill that void." She nodded to the matriarch at the head of the table. "When my grandparents came from the Bahamas and when Carlos' parents came from Cuba, they had no idea that their children would do so well in America, and that we would be so blessed. We met under such unusual circumstances." She winked at Dev. Those days of assisting in a DEA sting seemed so long ago, but she'd met the love of her life in the form of an agent who smiled at her.

Carlos took her hand, lifting it for a kiss on the inside of her palm. "It wasn't unusual; it was meant to be. I just want you to know that all of you hold a special place in our hearts. We've wanted to marry before now, but timing has been an issue. But now, it's perfect. Let's have a wonderful week together."

Alise nodded. "And, we have one more announcement. We want you all to be the first to know that we're expecting, and the baby is due next year. We have so much to celebrate, but Lily and I will do it without alcohol."

The group clapped, Danny adding, "That's wonderful news for the rest of us. Everyone, we now have two designated drivers!"

"Dan, you always know how to make wine out of grapes," Carlos joked. The priest stood and bowed.

Carlos nodded. "And thank you to Mrs. Notte for everything she has done for us, and for hosting all of us this week. We have excursions planned, but if someone comes up with a better idea, we can always change the schedule."

"May we go to the park? I want to ride the railroad roller coaster, or even the dog one," Angelica yelled out. Her mother's glare told her the odds were out of the question.

"Next time, daughter."

"I'm with Angelica," Lily added. "But not this year. In the future I'll be the first one to ride with you."

Angelica posed her arms in defiance across herself. "At least Lily wants to do something with me."

Carlos rescued his step daughter from her mother's wrath by offering another toast. He knew the girl was feeling a little left out now that there'd be a baby in the family. Carlos had even changed his life taking a promotion away from field work. It was a necessary adjustment if they were to go forward as a family. He needed to talk to Dev to see how he was balancing it all. The only danger Carlos might see in the future might be an odorous diaper.

The table quieted as Carlos stood and pulled up Angelica with him. "I have another toast. Please raise your glasses to this beautiful young lady. Secretly, I've always wanted a daughter, and I'm blessed to have this one. She will be the best sister ever, and the prettiest maid of honor. You are our Angel. To Angelica." He hoisted his glass and the guests repeated her name. Tears fell down Alise's cheeks as Carlos kissed her daughter on the cheek. She was his daughter now.

Later that night, Lily drove back to Anna Maria with two asleep in the backseat, and her husband looking up at the sky.

"We need to go out and look at the stars when we get back to the house."

Lily laughed quietly. "Not tonight. I'm directing the priest to his bedroom, and putting Andrew and you to bed."

Dev's head turned quickly in her direction. "I love it when you talk that way."

"You've had way too much sangria, and whatever that drink was you all had toward the end."

"*Cuba Libre*. I think I was fine until then. Who knew rum and coke could pack such a punch?" Dev returned to his view out the car window.

"Even Carlos was feeling no pain." The baby kicked. *I wish I just didn't feel that.* The baby was stretching out side-to-side in the last few days. *The stretch marks will be visible from space!* "We don't have to go to the aquarium tomorrow. I think Carlos had some plans for Dan and you already."

Dev saw the aquarium sign. "But I do want to go. Andrew will love the fish. Maybe not tomorrow, but we have a few days."

Lily sighed. They did have a few more days, but time always seemed to run out when you were having a good time. "I'll be on the beach in the morning, but you sleep in."

Dev had nodded off. His head pulled up. "What? Sure, okay."

"We are definitely taking the elevator tonight," Lily mumbled to herself, but her husband heard her.

"Isn't that so cool that there's an escalator in the house? Who knew you could put those things in a residential home." He leaned against the window and was out like a light.

"It is pretty hard to put an escalator into a private home. Now, on the other hand, you can have an elevator, and that's what I'm pushing you into." She looked quickly to the backseat. Dan remained slumped against the carseat, his hand holding onto Andrew's. Andrew's head touched his godfather's. It was quiet in the car. *This never happens. What's going to happen now? What if Margot/Gilda is here?*

Chapter Twenty-Seven

"He likes digging in the sand." Angelica assisted Andrew with her red bucket and purple shovel. Lily and Alise sat next to each other on the beach just enjoying the peace and the sound of the waves.

"Just don't let him eat it," Lily suggested.

Alise nodded. "I remember those days. You can be watching them, and they'll put sand in their mouths. Angelica once looked like a stuffed chipmunk, and I swear I was hovering over her the entire time."

Lily's hand covered Alise's. "I'm so happy for you and Carlos. A baby? Dev says Carlos has always wanted a family."

"Dev," Alise murmured wistfully as though she was remembering some idyllic time between the two of them. "By the way, how did you get those fools upstairs last night?"

Lily saw something in Alise's eyes, but she'd ask her later. Now was not the time to break a perfect moment. "Well, I managed to wake them up enough to get them to the elevator. I had to push them on. Andrew was not the problem child last night. I directed the priest toward his room, and I pulled Dev into ours. Thankfully, he passed out."

"Carlos too. They had a good time. He has a deep sea fishing trip for them on Thursday."

Lily crunched her toes deeper into the sand. *But sometimes I just can't help myself.* "Alise, you and Dev were undercover together, right?"

"Yes," Alise answered slowly. Lily's tone made her wonder where she was going with the question.

"Normally, I wouldn't ask. I mean that's his job and it's completely separate from real life, but I'm hormonal, and I just noticed that when you said his name--"

Alise slipped her hand over Lily's. "Nothing happened. Your husband was always professional, but I'm going to be honest. Dev was intoxicating. He's gentle, he listens, he's honest to a fault, he is great with kids, and he's extremely handsome. But, his thoughts were with you, and I knew it. I harped at him. Angelica told him how she felt. We were so happy he'd found you. You make him even a better man. If that's possible."

Lily wiped away a few tears. "I know, but crap gets into my head, especially when I'm pregnant and on the beach. You know, someone might mistake me for a sea turtle if I linger on the sand for too long."

"And Carlos explained you found a body buried in your yard? Lily, that's crazy. He said you've been investigating a missing woman, who probably isn't missing. And you mentioned this pregnancy is different, almost too different?"

Lily nodded. "Yes, it's all true. The doctor told me to watch it. My blood pressure has been plummeting, and I've had some very unusual cramping. I'm staying hydrated and eating as healthy as I can. By the way, that guava flan was amazing last night."

"It's a little bit Bahamian and a little Cuban. Tonight, we have grilled steaks, shrimp, chicken, chorizo, and vegetable kabobs. I'm going to keep us well fed. If we can't drink, we're eating, girl!"

Lily nudged Alise. "You are my new best friend." A form walking slowly on the beach caught her eye. She knew her husband's body. His hair was mussed, he hadn't shaved, and it looked as though he'd thrown on whatever shirt and shorts were laying in front of him. He had buttoned the shirt incorrectly. His sunglasses hid his ailment. *If he were in British Intelligence instead of MI-6, he'd be MI-0.* Lily giggled. "Watch out. Here comes Mr. Delicious. He doesn't look so good."

Alise giggled. "Isn't that what that crazy friend of yours calls him?"

"Oh yes."

Alise turned and watched him approach. "He looks so non-delicious."

"Hey you two," Dev said slowly. His words could barely be heard. "I was looking for coffee, lots of coffee."

"It would be in the kitchen," Alise offered. "Not on the beach, Pierce."

Angelica's voice lifted into the air in a squeal that brought Dev down onto his knees in the sand. The little girl had put too much water into the castle's moat. She didn't realize she had just felled a man who had put too much liquor into his body.

Dev held his head and adjusted his sunglasses. "What are we doing today?"

"We are going to go in and get us all some breakfast, and you your coffee," Alise began. "Then the four of us are enjoying the pool. Hopefully, you all will be able to watch Andrew while Lily, Angelica, and I go for our spa afternoon."

Dev lowered the glasses onto his nose. "There's always Mrs. Notte's lady to take care of him."

"Dev Pierce, you don't think you're going to be able to take care of your own son by two o'clock today? What's happened to you?" Alise pretended to be disgusted. Lily remained delightfully entertained.

"I think I got old." He returned his glasses to their proper place. "I really need help with the coffee."

Lily leaned closer to Alise. "I think he's still drunk."

"At least he's upright, sort of." Both women laughed at Dev's expense. He slowly rose up, one knee up and then the next.

"Alise, I just need some coffee," Dev growled.

Alise shoved off the sand, and offered a hand down to Lily to help her up. Lily gathered up Andrew, and Alise told her daughter they had to go in for breakfast. Angelica wanted Dev to carry her on his back, but the groan as he placated the little girl was too much for the two women. Laughter ensued. He didn't even have the energy to glare back at them.

Angelica placed her chin against Dev's. "Aren't you feeling good?"

"No."

"How can you feel bad when it's such a beautiful day, Dev?"

"I'll feel better with coffee."

"Then, after your coffee, will you spin me in the water? Carlos does that."

Dev gulped. *Oh dear Lord! Spinning?* His stomach gurgled. "Angel, all I can do right now is coffee."

She patted the top of his head. "You are silly. You can't **do** coffee."

"Oh yes, I can. I'd fill a hot tub with it and lay in it for hours if I could."

"You know she's making him crazy peppering him with questions?" Alise asked Lily.

The smile on Lily's face was her answer. "He loves me so much when I do that, or when I speak quicker than usual. I can only imagine what all of that sounds like in his head right now."

"Well, we better get him coffee, and breakfast for all of us. I guess we should see how the other two are doing?" Alise opened the door for Lily, but before she could answer, they found Carlos with a large cup in his hand.

"I made coffee," he said quietly. "This is my second cup."

"Have we seen a priest wandering around?" Lily asked as she opened the refrigerator door to find the milk.

"I believe the priest is in prayer," Dev answered as he poured himself a large cup of coffee. "I heard him saying *oh, Lord* before I headed out to see you."

Lily snorted. "Oh, I pray like that a lot while I'm pregnant." As she poured her glass of milk, Dev came behind her.

"Sorry about last night," Dev murmured as he kissed her neck. Lily turned quickly to peck him on the cheek.

"You owe me. So does the priest, but I'm glad you had a good time. This afternoon, you'll watch Andrew. It'll be his nap time. I really am looking forward to getting my feet and my hands done, before I can't see my feet anymore, like next week."

Dev took another drink. He didn't care when anyone was going to the salon, but he nodded. "I'll watch Andrew. Tomorrow, just the three of us, unless Angel wants to go along. Let's see the aquarium and take the boat ride, if you're up to it."

"Anyone who wants to come can." Lily began to pull out the eggs and fruit. "But thank you for saying that. I'm all in with the group this week. Besides, there's safety in numbers, right?"

Alise looked over at Dev. He glanced at her. They shared a quiet concern. "Honey, we're safe. Don't worry about all that other stuff."

"I'm not worried." Lily continued to move around in the kitchen. She found a box of pastries and her eyes lit up. "I just know that she's out there somewhere. I'm just being realistic. Alise, can we open this box?"

"Sure, Lily." Alise touched Dev's arm. "Is she okay?"

Dev nodded, but he wondered. *What was she thinking in that pretty head of hers? He could hear her thinking. It was hurting his head.*

When the ladies were away, and Andrew down for his nap, Dev sat across from Mrs. Notte that afternoon. Her nurse, Barb, had thought a nap sounded like a great idea and went to her own room. Danny and Carlos continued to recuperate as they laid out by the pool.

"Mrs. Notte, I need to warn you about something," Dev began.

Mrs. Notte placed her book down next to her on the sofa. "Devlin, what is it?"

"First, I was wondering. Will your son be visiting with us this week?"

"Oh, heaven's no. You above all people should know that." Her thin smile proved she knew more than she let on. "I know how much you played with my grandson's incarceration. As for my son, well let's say I'm sure you've had a hand in his detention by the authorities."

Dev clutched his hands together as he leaned over, nearer her. "Yes, ma'am. We also have another issue. Lily was planting in our yard and--"

"What was Lily planting? She has such an eye for blending colors."

Dev stopped. "Well, she was trying to plant this magnolia on the one side of the garage by the front porch."

"Oh, the fragrance would be like memories of a long lost summer day."

Dev began again. "Yes, well she uncovered the mystery of a missing woman. It's been almost two decades, and then a skeleton was found in the yard as well."

Dev was shocked at Mrs. Notte's reply. She clapped. "How absolutely, delicious, Devlin! What about the magnolia? Where did you plant it?"

Patience, man, patience. "I wanted to plant it on the other side of the garage, but she decided there was a place in the back yard she preferred. But I returned the tree after we found the bones of my aunt's dog and--"

Mrs. Notte's face feigned sympathy. "Oh, that's a shame, but how did you find the skeleton?"

"I called the FBI, and while they searched the yard, they determined the bones were from a dog, but the detectors found a few other items involved in a crime, and that's when they found the skeleton of a man."

Mrs. Notte nodded. "Wonderful. Now, I'm all caught up. What else do we have?"

Dev frowned. His worry lines had worry lines. *What's wrong with these women?* "We may have this same missing woman following us. She's dangerous. She was a drug mule of sorts, and now, I believe she may be a serial killer."

Mrs. Notte's smile disappeared. "Oh my. That's not good. Is she after our lovely Lily?"

Dev nodded regrettably. "I believe so. Two men followed Lily on the interstate. I believe they were trying to hurt or kill her. But a killer could be after me too. About five years ago, Carlos and I took out a man who meant something to her. After that went down, I think she took off to lick her wounds, but Lily's curiosity may have opened up Pandora's box."

"Then we all must be vigilant. You see, last night I spoke the truth. You all brought life to me, and if you add a little danger, well then, isn't that something? I used to read Agatha Christie. It seemed as though the years after my husband died, I was a spectator, but now I'm a participator. After all these years, Devlin, I have stories to tell the other women at the club. In fact, since you rounded up my grandson and my son, I visit the country club. I shop. Lily, Alise, Carlos, my little Angel, and you saved me."

The English called it *gobsmacked. I'm gobsmacked.* Her lack of concern was a surprise. The fact that he had another amateur mystery investigator gave him pause. *At least she's not another Jessica lover!*

Mrs. Notte reached out and took one of his hands. "Dear boy, don't fret. We have this. Besides, don't the good guys always win?"

Dev nodded, but he knew better. In reality, there were so many times that the bad guys prevailed. But, as in every situation involving Lily, he wouldn't allow anything to happen to her, not to anyone in this house. And now he had to add an elderly wealthy woman who thought crime was delicious. *Holy Moly!*

Chapter Twenty-Eight

The remainder of the week flew by with an excursion to the aquarium, fishing trips, boat rides, parasailing, jet ski, and kayak adventures. There had even been time for quiet moments for Lily and Dev to hold hands and walk on the beach to take in the magical sunsets of Anna Maria Island. Andrew walked everywhere with his new-found friend, Angelica, and she said he gave her practice for when her baby came. By the night of the rehearsal, everyone was family.

Alise handed over the directing to Lily, and of course, to their officiant. The couple planned to share their ceremony on the beach in front of one of the best wedding venues on the island. After just one run-through, Dan concluded they were ready. "Now let's go eat."

They walked into the pavilion to greet other wedding guests. The festivities were fairly uneventful until Mrs. Notte motioned to a couple walking past her as they entered the restaurant.

"Armand, how are you? And is this your lovely wife? You are joining us tomorrow, aren't you? Oh, wonderful."

Carlos searched the area. He could hear Mrs. Notte's voice. He nudged his future wife. "Darling, who is she talking to?"

Alise tried to see through the crowd. "Oh, that's a doctor friend of hers. We ran into him the other day when we went to get more wine. She's known him on the island for years."

Carlos threaded his view through those mingling in the pavilion. His eyes fixed on the doctor, a very distinguished Latino. Beside him was a striking woman in a flowing halter dress. She wore a large diamond and ruby wedding ring. Carlos finally caught a view of her face. Immediately, he waved at Dev and pointed toward Mrs. Notte.

Dev turned in his chair and looked toward the matriarch. He saw the doctor. The man was familiar to him. He'd have to search his memory, but the woman he knew. It was Margot/Gilda. She was here, not just on the island, but within fifty feet of them. As Dev turned back around, Lily touched his hand.

"Is everything okay?"

As Dev nodded and smiled, he lied. "Of course. Everything is perfect." He glanced toward Carlos. They shared another one of their looks. They spoke without speaking. Carlos only hoped he had understood correctly. Nonchalantly, Carlos stood up, walked over to the priest, and whispered to him. As soon as Carlos returned to the side of his bride, Dan strode over to Mrs. Notte and introduced himself to the couple. It was several minutes before Dan pulled Mrs. Notte back to the celebrating group.

As the priest sat down at the table once more, he nodded at Dev. *A priest can get away with murder.* Dan had managed to pull Mrs. Notte, the doctor, and more importantly, the man's wife into a quick photo. The woman was apprehensive, but she couldn't extricate herself from a memory for Mrs.

Notte. Dan also took a few quick photos while pretending to check his text messages.

All three men having served in combat together, knew they would meet later to discuss their mission. Going forward, the wedding would take center stage for the next twenty-four hours, but planning an operation of attack or for defense would be utmost in their minds. For Dan, he would support in any way he could. Carlos would do reconnaissance, gaining more information from Angelica's great grandmother, and Dev would make his calls. Perhaps this was bigger than just one woman gaining revenge on a DEA agent, or reigning terror on a woman who meddled in her past.

Dev threw down his bourbon in one drink. Lily glanced sideways at him.

"Are you sure you're okay?"

After a deep breath, Dev kissed his wife. "I don't know. That's as honest as I can be."

Now, I'm scared. If Dev isn't sure, then I can't be sure. One of us has to be sure. Sure about what? What could possibly be so wrong? Oh, Holy Moly. She's here. She's really here. Lily moved her chair back quickly. "I need to stand for a second." She patted her stomach. She took a few steps back and looked around the facility. Restaurant diners were eating on the patio. Past that, the Friday night crowd filled the bar. But in the doorway, she noticed the woman in the flowing floral beach dress. Ironically, her black gown was printed with large white magnolias with hunter green leaves. It was as though she had marked herself so Lily could see her. But she didn't see Lily.

Lily patted Dev's shoulder. "I'll be right back. I need to go to the restroom. Could you get me another one of those virgin pina coladas?"

"Of course."

Lily walked away as though she was stretching her legs or taking another trip to the restroom. Dinner hadn't been served yet, but Andrew was happy with a piece of buttered bread. Dev now nursed his second bourbon. Lily locked her sight on the woman speaking with an attractive gentleman. He was wearing a very expensive linen suit with a light blue shirt, open to expose his tanned skin and a very large gold cross. As soon as her companion walked further into the restaurant, Lily made her move.

"Oh, excuse me," Lily said as she bumped into the woman she'd been searching for.

The woman looked up and then down at the shorter pregnant interloper. She smiled sweetly. "You must be unstable carrying around that load." She pointed at Lily's belly.

"That's probably it. When you're short like me, my balance gets out of whack. It's not because I've been drinking." Lily laughed. The woman laughed. "I absolutely adore your dress."

"Thank you." Her tone was cold. She had no accent, unless haughty was a language. But her look was even colder, and void of any emotion.

I know women like you, heck, my friend pretends she's like you. But Gretchen isn't a killer. She's a lover. "Funny thing. I was trying to plant a magnolia a few months ago. I tried two different locations, and I kept finding things that had been buried in my yard."

"Really? That's very interesting. Did you find anything of importance?"

"Nothing really," Lily commented effortlessly. "I found an old driver's license, a few other things, and a dog's skeleton."

The woman didn't avoid Lily's eyes. "If you keep looking, I bet you'll find more treasures."

"My husband thinks I'll find Jimmy Hoffa one day. He's joking, but I bet I could find someone who was missing, and who had left behind some ridiculous red herrings in an attempt to implicate her husband. It doesn't work though, if someone like me just puts together all the clues."

"Are you an investigator?"

"No, I'm just very observant. I've learned over the years that if someone tries too hard, they usually fail. And if someone takes something too personal, they're the ones who end up getting hurt. Revenge really is a dish best served cold, or I'd say never served at all. Order something else."

The woman threw her red locks back and laughed. "You are a very interesting woman. I'm so happy you bumped into me, Lily."

"Ah, there you go. I never told you my name, Margot, Gilda or whatever your name of the day is. Leave us alone. Go play crazy somewhere else."

The woman's eyes narrowed. "I will after we go to a wedding tomorrow night."

The woman's companion was approaching. Lily smiled. Her heart raced. She held her hands behind her to prevent the woman from seeing them shake.

"Darling, our table is ready." The gentleman greeted Lily. "Ah, are you with Mrs. Notte's party?"

"I am. I better get back. I'm sorry again for bumping into you."

The woman nodded. "By the way, what happened to the magnolia?"

"Oh, we never planted it. The nursery will replace it in the spring. It's a shame when something beautiful dies, don't you think?"

The woman's male companion took her hand in his. They began to walk away, when the woman stopped and added a comment. "You know, it is a shame, but it is a tragedy when a small sprout is eliminated. Take care of yourself and that baby." She turned on her espadrilles and sauntered away as though she didn't have a care in the world.

Lily unclenched her trembling hands and returned to the pavilion. Carlos and Dan had their eyes on her the entire time. She saw the disapproval on their faces. *What was I thinking? I'm not Jessica confronting the murderer, almost killed before Mort gets there and yells freeze.* She sat down next to her husband, pretending that all was perfectly wonderful. Andrew was excited to see her and began to tell her in his own language about the centerpiece in the middle of the table.

Dev's left hand enveloped her right hand. She looked down at his wedding ring. He curled his fingers around hers. "I don't know what the hell you thought you were doing, but we will talk about it later."

Lily turned her head ever so slowly, finally capturing his gaze. "I'm pregnant. I don't know what I was doing. Besides, I have a baby brain this time. I guess I was waving her off."

"And what did she do?"

"She was quite pleasant as she threatened our unborn child. Before you yell at me now, or later, no I didn't know what I was thinking or what I was doing. I realize I shouldn't even pretend to play with the big boys and girls. Are you happy now?"

Dev clutched his wife's hand harder. "I'm not sure what I'm feeling. I'll let you know later."

"Could we postpone the discussion until after the wedding?" Lily offered a weak smile.

"I thought you were a stickler for schedules."

"I can be flexible."

Dev's hard demeanor faltered as he shrugged. He moved his hand as Lily's drink came. The server assured her it was non-alcoholic. He thought about what he should say, but it was too late. She'd already confronted a serial killer.

He placed his arm around the back of her chair, tickling Andrew's neck. He leaned in to whisper to his wife. "And whenever have you ever been flexible?"

Lily nuzzled his face. "There was that one time when I kissed you at the same time I itched that mosquito bite on my leg."

Dev's eyes twinkled. He laughed out loud, but as he brought his arm back next to him, he began to pop his watch's wristband. Lily saw the nervous habit had resurrected. She talked a good game, but if the professionals were concerned, she knew how very dangerous this had all become. It was one thing to fight on your home turf, but here, in this magical place, there was no advantage and perhaps her actions had just put them on the defensive even more than when her behavior had caused Dan to kill two men in the shadows of God's church.

Later that evening, Lily put Andrew to bed and grabbed the monitor. She went downstairs to visit with Alise. Dev, Dan, and Carlos were finishing the night smoking Cuban cigars on the deck. She confessed to Alise what she had done. To her surprise, the soon-to-be bride completely agreed with Lily's aggressive behavior.

"Lily, I understand they can't talk about their jobs. But if someone ever threatened my happiness, I'd take them out. Heck, that's why I helped the DEA. That, and I wanted a fresh start away from the drugs, the cartel, and all that went with that bad behavior."

Lily noticed that Alise was rubbing the locket around her neck. Alise's dad had told Lily about that special piece of jewelry. The locket held within it photos of Alise and her deceased brother, along with a photo of her mother and father.

"I miss your dad so much. He always told me when I was being a little nutty," Lily said as she moved for Alise's hand. As she held it, Alise began to cry.

"I miss Momma so much. Tomorrow I'll miss him. He won't be there to walk me down the aisle."

"Alise, he'd be so proud of you. He would love, absolutely love Carlos."

Alise pointed at Lily. "He'd be so proud of you. My Dad liked Dev, and I believe he knew he was the one who would solve everything, including my mess."

Lily nodded. Now she was the one crying. "Thanks for sharing your dad with me."

"Thanks for being his buddy when I wasn't there."

Both women had destroyed any mascara still remaining after a long night. It was time to go to bed. They had a long day tomorrow, but tonight might even be longer. Lily was already in bed with the lights off when Dev entered the room. She heard him undress and brush his teeth before the mattress bent with his body. He immediately placed his arm over her.

"Lily--"

"Just a second. Hear me out. If you haven't noticed, I can get by without you. I'm not a damsel in distress, and I wasn't waiting in some castle for you to ride up on a white horse. I survived an international terrorist attempting an abduction. I survived a car race on the interstate while followed by two thugs. Dan had to save me, but I got away from them, didn't I? I drove like a nun being chased by the devil. And I was good at it. I kept my cool through all of that insanity, and I did something no one else was able to do for years when Khalid was placed in handcuffs. No, I don't know what I was thinking tonight, but I did it, and she knows that I will fight back."

"Are you done, honey?"

Lily still hadn't turned to face her husband. "I guess so, depending on what you're going to say."

Dev cleared his throat. He hadn't smoked a cigar in a while. It was heady stuff. "All I was going to say was that I love you, and I understand why you did it. That's it. You know the danger, and you know it's better if professionals handle the situation. But I get it. What you don't understand is criminals like her just don't walk away. They don't become afraid, and they certainly aren't intimidated by Kansas City florists who have peculiar and sensational observational skills."

Lily finally turned toward her husband and touched his face. She circled her finger around his lips. "I'm not too thrilled by the peculiar moniker, but sensational is nice."

Dev pulled her body closer to his. With no space between them, he kissed her long and hard. "What am I going to do with you?" He continued his trail of kisses to all his favorite locations.

Lily held his head with both hands. "Oh, I'm pretty sure you know exactly what to do."

Chapter Twenty-Nine

1. Check flowers
2. Check photographer
3. Check band
4. Check cake and food
5. Enjoy

Lily and Danny arrived at the venue early. Lily would've preferred to have done all the overseeing by herself, but there was no way Dev was letting her go alone. Danny was the likely sidekick. No one would suspect that the pseudo officiant shouldn't be there for anything but the wedding. She inherently knew that he was a priest who was packing. She thought Dev would've given him one, but it was Carlos who offered Dan his choice of three different guns. They hadn't noticed her watching as the man in the cleric's collar checked each firearm, weighing one after the other in his hand. She was shocked when he selected two of the three and hid them on his body.

The island's florist was almost finished with the table arrangements when they arrived. The seafoam tablecloths were adorned with ivory china and fine glassware with silver place settings. The flowers were beautifully done upon pieces of driftwood. Tropical flowers were blended with pale blush roses. The designs had the beach feel with a Miami vibe, and oozed with romance.

The cake had been left in the restaurant's cooler, and Lily checked in on the dessert. In white and ivory, the three layers of tasty cake featured icing seashells cascading down the front. Lily clapped at the thought of eating cake. *And icing!*

As Lily exited the cooler, the warm sea breeze actually felt refreshing. "Does the ceremony area look okay?" she asked as she joined Dan in the pavilion.

Dan pointed at the wood trellis out on the beach. A simple ivory swag of material floated in the gulf breeze decorated the vow area. The white chairs were already set to form a short aisle in the sand. "It's simple. Actually, it's perfect."

The two sat in the back row of chairs as they stared out onto the Gulf of Mexico. The band began to set up their equipment. "The restaurant is ready, the cake is ready, and all the flowers are here. The florist is delivering the bouquets and boutonnieres to the house right now." Lily checked the list she'd placed on her phone. She deleted each line until none were left, except one. "Do you have the rings?"

"Yes. Carlos handed me the rings after they were married this morning. Oh, and the local pastor is allowing me to do this. I lied and said they were family. My bishop would've had a fit."

Lily giggled. "You lied. Wonderful. Well, I'm happy you did. Alise and Carlos deserve a beautiful ceremony. No one else needs to know they're already married. And if you create a scandal in the church, you can handle it, right?"

Dan grimaced. "I suppose I can. I'll get those robes off as soon as I can. By the way, I have everything in the car, and the car is locked in valet parking. I need to leave here by three-thirty to get to Mass at the local church. Are you coming with me?"

"Of course," Lily answered quickly. "My dress and shoes are in the car. I'll put on a little makeup, but that only takes me seconds. I'm the low maintenance one if you'll recall. Dev and Andrew will come later with Mrs. Notte."

Dan took a drink from his glass of water. *This might be the perfect time to talk to Lily.* "Lily, what were you thinking? Did you think when you confronted that woman last night?"

"Please understand I don't always think before I do something. Case in point, I became engaged at the scene of the arrest of a major drug dealer. I admit I wasn't thinking last night, but I guess I thought I'm a woman, she's a woman, and if I'm able to deal with Gretchen, certainly I could deal with a serial killer."

"Or she's a contract killer. Judgment is still out on that one," Dan added. "Either way, it was a dangerous thing to do."

Lily sat quietly, sipping on her lemonade. The baby liked this drink and loved the virgin pina colada last night. She'd be drinking those tonight as a treat for surviving the day, in more ways than one. "Look at us, sitting here talking about murder and mayhem as if we're discussing a new cooking show on a cable channel."

Dan rolled his eyes. "Well, Jessica, what will we be cooking today?"

"Just a wedding, hopefully." Lily's wish ended their discussion about her actions, but in her heart she knew that nothing was finished when it came to Margot. She also knew that somewhere on Dan's body, he carried two guns just in case Lily's wish didn't come true.

Dan and Lily's arrival at the local Catholic church created a buzz throughout the congregation. *Was he a married priest? Oh my gosh, she's pregnant!* Lily desperately wanted one large post-it note she could stick on her forehead that said--**We're just friends. My husband stayed back with our son**--but since it wasn't possible, she just smiled and maintained a healthy distance from the priest.

Dan came out on the altar as the visiting priest. The pastor began Mass. Lily felt like a pageant contender with her prayers for peace, but that's exactly what she wanted. A good mystery was a good mystery, but when the resurrected person was found, and was a murderer and some sort of a drug contact, that was another thing. *Why can't I just find lost dogs? Maybe I could occasionally notice someone's wallet being stolen at the grocery store? And maybe I could just call 9-1-1, and they'd apprehend the perpetrator?* Lily attempted to rationalize why this was happening, but the more she analyzed the dilemma she blamed one thing...the magnolia tree. All she wanted was a little fragrance when a Virginia breeze blew on a warm summer night. She just wanted a little shade by their porch swing. Her need for a magnolia had begun this whole crazy adventure. *Do I even want the stupid tree now? Such a dilemma!*

Toward the end of Mass, she resolved that it was Dev and his gang's fault. If they had been engineers or plumbers this wouldn't be happening. Even though Lily was praying, her head bowed and her hands folded, her inner struggle consumed her. *But, where would be the fun in that? Plumbers aren't chased by terrorists, and I've never seen one dressed in a designer suit.*

After Communion, Lily knelt very carefully and talked to God. *Lord, you put this wonderful man in my life after all my years of praying. Thank you. Please keep us safe. Also, I'm thinking I'll need your help. I need to be a little less Angela Lansbury and a lot more Doris Day. Oh wait, she did get in trouble in several of her movies. Crud, I can't think of a wimpy woman I like. Maybe that's my problem?*

Dan and she hurried out of church as soon as he had disrobed. As they headed back to the wedding pavilion, they remained quiet in the car. Lily figured Dan was finishing his prayers; Dan figured Lily was taking a rest before tonight's festivities. About a block away, before Dan turned down to the valet parking, Lily spoke up.

"I'm sorry I was so stupid last night. I just thought one woman talking to another might be a good approach. I guess I should've begged her."

Dan's head pivoted swiftly. "Don't you ever say that. Don't beg anyone. You are who you are. Don't you think Dev knows that? Do you really think he'd still be around if he disapproved of what you do and how you think? We all respect you. You are one of us. But, we act as a team. If you're going to be part of the team, then you don't go rogue. Got it?"

Lily's eyes widened. "Yes, sir. Do I get a rank or something?"

Dan finally smiled. "You probably are the general, but we allow Dev to think he's always in charge. He always has been. We follow his lead."

Lily had no witty comeback. It was hard not to follow the man she loved.

Andrew ran, not walked when he saw his mother after a long day of her absence. His hair flew in the ocean air as he bounded into her arms. "Mama."

Thankfully, she was still able to bend over and gather him in her arms. "I missed you so much, little man."

Dev greeted her with a kiss on the cheek. "He missed you too, but Mrs. Notte is becoming his best friend. They had a milk and cookies party this afternoon." Dev surveyed his wife's demeanor. She seemed relaxed. *Of course she is. She's in her element at a wedding.* He also did an examination of her ankles and her legs. Nothing was swollen. He rubbed her back, and she winced a bit. "Ah, you've been on your feet."

"Actually, this just happened in the last hour. I knelt at church, but I've been very good. I've been resting and sitting down a lot. I am also fully hydrated. Dan and I had time to have lunch. I feel good."

Dev's brow rose in speculation. "Are you convincing yourself or me?"

Lily passed her son off to his father. "Both. I can't hold him for very long while standing up. I'm just happy we're all here." Lily noticed a beach walker examining the decorated trellis while guests were being seated. "Excuse me. I've got to do my job."

Before Dev could say he would go, his wife was gone. "There goes Mommy being the person she'll always be." His explanation to Andrew fell flat. His son was too interested in the sandpipers looking for dropped food as they walked through the restaurant area of the beach. Dev knew deep down she'd never change. She'd always be the one to go headlong into a situation when something needed to be righted. He would always be the one to overplan, and only initiate the plan once it had been vetted and rehearsed.

"Andrew, I overthink things too, but I almost lost Mommy because of that. Be like her. Love, laugh, and definitely eat like she does. You'll have a great life."

He watched as Lily graciously dispersed the looky loos. Mrs. Notte and Barb were ready to take their seats, but the matriarch came over to Dev first. "Devlin, I'd like Lily, Andrew, and you to sit next to me as my family during the wedding. I won't take no for an answer."

"Yes, ma'am." You didn't argue with a woman like her. He was beginning to understand that with his own wife. "I'll tell Lily to join us after she directs the ladies down the aisle."

A few of Carlos' cousins arrived, as did an aunt and uncle. Carlos happily greeted them, and then Lily banished him down the aisle to where Dan was standing. The priest's robes blew in the breeze, but his mere presence made the ceremony official. Guests quieted. Even the restaurant crowd began to watch. Dev and Andrew kissed Lily goodbye and took their seats.

Angelica came forward, her bare feet showing under her dress. She held a small bouquet of blush pink roses.

Her smile couldn't be any larger. Lily showed her where to hold her flowers and checked her one more time to make sure her bow in the back was straight, and every hair was in its place.

"It's time for you to go down the aisle, Angel. Take your time, and don't forget to smile, Sunshine."

Angelica kissed Lily's cheek while she was close enough. "There's no way I can't smile. My Mom is finally marrying my Dad. Oh, I know he's not my real one, but from this day on, he's mine."

Lily's eyes filled with tears. She brushed them away and guided the young girl forward to the aisle, but Angelica stopped. "Lily, I'm the happiest girl in the world, but I'd be happier if we were seeing a certain castle and a large mouse."

Lily nodded. "Me too. Next time, baby. It's time for you to go down the aisle."

Angelica acted like the bright star she was. She waved and blew kisses to those guests she knew. She hugged her great grandmother and blew Dev a kiss before she bowed to Dan for some reason, and then shuffled through the sand to hug Carlos.

Lily watched and knew everyone was now in tears, happy tears. But as she turned to see the bride appear, Lily began to cry heavily. She took Alise's hands in hers and shared a short moment.

"You look as though you fell from heaven," Lily whispered. Both sets of their hands were shaking.

"I miss Daddy so much right now," Alise whispered. "You're the only one who really understands. You loved him as much as I did. And Momma. You knew what a wonderful woman she was. I don't deserve this."

"Oh no. You **do** deserve this. I think that the best thing we can do for them is to live our best lives. There's ups and downs, but we love, we laugh, and most of all we're going to have wedding cake in just a few hours. Get down that aisle so I can get my cake."

The two women's shared laugh brought the guests' attention toward them. Alise saw Dan motion her down as the music changed for her walk. Lily blotted Alise's tears and handed her the bouquet of white orchids. Alise grabbed Lily's hand one more time, nodded, threw her chin up, and began her walk to her future.

Carlos' eyes filled with his own tears. He didn't hide his feelings. Everyone else saw a tall, thin, caramel-colored woman. Her hair was knotted up with a few loose tendrils cradling her face. Her strapless gown caressed every thin curve, even her ever so slight baby bump. There was an audible gasp at the beautiful woman who could stride down any Paris runway with confidence. But Carlos only saw the woman he loved. His wife was his everything.

Lily slid in next to Dev and took his hand in hers. His glance revealed his glowing wife, her tear-stained cheeks, and her soft smile.

"Welcome tonight friends and family," Dan began. "We are here to celebrate Carlos and Alise, and to witness the birth of a family who love each other very much."

"Was Dan this windy at our wedding?" Lily whispered.

"I don't think so. Your local priest reigned him in." Dev shifted Andrew in his lap. His young son wasn't impressed in the least by his Uncle Dan's words of love and wisdom. He wanted to run on the beach.

Lily nudged him. "Look at the sunset. It's absolutely perfect."

"And now you want another wedding, is that it?"

"Absolutely not. Our day was perfect. And this is perfect for them."

"Love is patient, love is kind." Dan began to recite the entire passage from memory. He paused afterward and smiled at the couple in front of him.

"I can tell you that these two human beings are perfect examples of St. Paul's description of love. They are two of the most patient people I've ever met. They are kind to each other and to others. They place others' needs ahead of their own, and I'm not sure they've ever had a fight."

Alise and Carlos began to laugh hard. "I'm Latin and she's a Miami diva. Of course we fight," Carlos admitted.

Dan smiled knowingly. "I stand corrected. They are imperfect humans who have found each other after years of searching. We rejoice in their love; we celebrate this union. We pray God will continue to bless them. Now, Alise and Carlos will recite vows and exchange their rings."

After the couple finished, Dan blessed them, and before he could offer his congratulations, Carlos kissed his bride in dramatic fashion as he dipped Alise passionately backward. Finishing the kiss, the couple walked down the aisle, with their daughter in the middle, their hands connecting them as a family. Dan announced that everyone should move for the cocktail hour while the couple greeted them. As the guests moved happily to the bar and appetizers, Lily, Dev, and Andrew headed to Dan.

"Well, Father, that was lovely," Lily complimented.

"Lily is right. It was one of your best," Dev added. "I needed a paddle with a 'ten' on it to rate you perfect."

Dan was suspicious of the good words. "What? Did I blow something? You two are never this nice, well not together, and at the same time."

"No, it really was beautiful. It was almost as nice as our wedding. Almost," Lily kidded. "I'm always amazed at what a wonderful priest you are."

Dev began to laugh at her back-handed compliment. "All of us guys are amazed too Danny, if that will make you feel better."

"Okay, kids. Daddy is done with the jokes. Let's go have a good time."

Lily saluted. "I'm going to check on the cake." As she walked away she sang.

Dan tried to hear the words. "What is she singing?"

Dev raised his eyes to the sky. "She's singing, 'I get to eat cake. I get to eat cake.' You know she loves wedding cake."

"The woman loves weddings, and it's not just the cake." Both men could agree on that.

The evening was full of laughter and romance. The sunset painted the full sky as a gift to the couple. Once darkness enveloped the setting, candlelight, music, and dancing filled the remainder of the night. Lily took it all in. She also noticed that her husband and the priest were nursing the same drink for the last hour. Even Carlos hadn't touched a drop, except for the champagne in a toast to his wife.

Dan had godson duty while Lily and Dev danced to one of their favorite slow songs. It was an old song from the World War II era, and several other couples joined them. She felt Dev hold her closer in his arms. She just knew that he must've seen Margot/Gilda and her doctor husband. *What was with this woman and her doctors?* Dev barely turned her on the dancefloor, but she managed a side glance to see the attractive killer. *The woman can give Gretchen a run for her money in the fashion department.* Tonight, she wore an elegant black jumpsuit that featured palazzo pants and a bodice that showed off her perfect breasts. A flashy diamond necklace covered her neck and matched her ring and bracelet.

"I love you," Dev whispered near her ear. "Let's call it an early night and go back to the house."

Even though Lily was tired, she wasn't about to run away. "In a while."

Dev rubbed her back. "I want to take you home."

Lily pulled back in his arms and looked up at her husband. "I know what you're doing. Just stop it. I'm not running. You wouldn't run if I wasn't here. If you worry about me, you won't be at your best. Got it, soldier?"

Dev blinked twice. *What the bloody hell?* There was only one tack to take. "You are right. If Andrew and you weren't here, I wouldn't run. You are my Achilles Heel, but you're the target because of my job, my past life." Lily wasn't the one who placed herself in danger, he placed her in danger. "Maybe you should leave me."

Lily's feet stopped moving. Both of them stood motionless in the middle of the dance floor. Her heart froze. The baby kicked her. She studied his face. She couldn't read him. He was the man she loved, and she couldn't figure out what he was saying. She had no recourse; not a thought in her head or direction of where to go. Lily grabbed Dev's tie and pulled him through the tables. As they passed Dan, she motioned that they'd be on the beach.

Lily released his tie as her feet touched the sand. The only light came from the pavilion. She could barely hear the waves crashing onto the sand. "Stop whatever you're doing. Don't even think that the messes I get myself into are your fault. Don't take on my mistakes and make them yours."

The silence between them lasted just a few minutes. Dev ran his hand through his hair. "Lily, we can't live like this the rest of our lives. It was my job that brought us together. You were targeted because of my job. Khalid came after you to get to me because of my service. I did something to this woman, and now you're a target again. So many field agents don't have families, and now I completely understand why. What's next? Maybe some drug lord is going to capture you and take you--"

"Is he a good looking drug lord? We watched that movie the other night where the criminal kidnapped the beautiful woman he'd seen in passing years before, and gave her a year to fall in love with him. She did it in three months after hours of lovemaking. Then she was pregnant, and his enemies blew her up right before they were married. That bad guy was so hot."

Dev sat down on a wooden bench and held his head. "Is that how your brain really works all the time? You know, there are nights when I think I can hear you thinking?"

Lily smiled. She sat close to him and grabbed his hand. "Yep, and you love me for it. Pierce, just do your job. We'll do what we always do, and we'll do it together."

Dev nodded. "Fine. You've broken me. I'll always worry about you, but I'm done trying to hold you back. Fine, look up old mysteries. Fine, investigate the neighbor down the street who is having an affair with that widow in the house on the corner."

Lily pressed his arm. "Wait, is that true? Is Mr. Palmer fooling around with Mrs. Davenport? How did I not know this?"

"I don't tell you everything," Dev admitted. Lily frowned. "Fine. Mrs. Parrot told me. She figured it out. You two should start some sort of the club." As soon as the words were out of his mouth, he regretted it.

"That could replace Schmidt and Malloy. We could be Pierce and Parrot." Lily snorted. "The club is a great idea, but I think it's been done before, and the group always gets in trouble when they investigate. The police frown on that sort of behavior."

Dev wanted to laugh. Instead, he frowned. "I frown on your behavior, yet you still do it. Is it because you're bored?

I know you're busy with Andrew, now the baby is coming, and you help at the vineyard, but do you need something more? Is that what all of this is about?"

Lily grasped Dev's hand tighter. "I've been thinking about that. You've offered me a new life filled with so much. You and our family will always be my main priority. Your aunts and I are talking about expanding some of their services to do more events at the vineyard. I'd be in charge of all of that. But, I'm going to start writing again. After talking to Mr. Livingood and going through all of his notes, I miss being a reporter."

"Excuse me? When were you going to tell me that you used to be a reporter?"

"I just told Dan the other day. I'm surprised he didn't tell you. It got me thinking of why I put my nose in places where I shouldn't. Newspapers aren't what they used to be, but I'm thinking about what I might do. For now, I'm going to be a mother, and I'll begin writing on my own. That should be safe enough. I'm sure you have some stories from some of your former ops, right?" Her face glowed with hope.

"I should've run a more thorough check on you. It didn't show up on your record," Dev murmured. *No, I'm not giving you material for your stories and getting you in even more trouble.*

"I stopped reporting just a couple of years out of college. Mom was sick. My brother was away in the Army, and my sister just couldn't do everything. She had her own family to raise. But, don't think I didn't want to take over the shop. Every day was different, and the clients were the best part." Lily stopped. She removed her hand from her husband's. "Wait, you ran a check on me?"

"That was before I knew you. You could've been involved in the drug case for all I knew."

"But, after meeting me, you knew I'd never do anything like that, right?" Lily moved her face under his and crossed her eyes. She needed a quick response.

Dev laughed at her antics and her question. He didn't answer.

"Devlin? Right?"

Instead of answering, Dev decided an offensive attack was the best maneuver. He reached around her and pulled her gently up into his arms. His lips barely missed hers. "I knew from the moment I met you that you had nothing to do with the drugs, but I had to have proof. I couldn't listen to my heart."

"Oh, Pierce, that was good. In addition to my observational skills, I also have a fantastic memory, and I know for a fact, you didn't even love me--"

Dev began kissing her. He pulled her closer, his embrace enveloping her. He broke off slowly. "I came back for you. I'll never leave you. This has nothing to do with that woman in there, but I want to go back to the house. I know you're tired. Andrew is almost done in, and I want to show you just how much I do love you."

Lily leaned back on the bench to catch her breath. *My husband can be very persuasive. I'm thinking we're both finished with overthinking.* She stood up and reached back for his hand. "Well, why didn't you just say that?"

"Lily."

Dev pretended irritation, but Lily knew better, and she knew how to pull his strings. "Do you think you could pretend to be a bad guy tonight? You could be the evil cartel guy who works for Carlos, and you picked me up at the wedding because you think I'm a rogue DEA agent who could help you with your supplyline in Florida."

Dev stopped in his tracks. Lily nearly lost her balance. "Lily, I think you may have put the pieces together for me again."

Lily hadn't seen him have more than one drink. *What the heck is he talking about?* "Were you listening to me?"

Dev waved her off. "Yes, role playing, got it. And you seem to be talking faster than usual. I'll work on the whole Margot/Gilda thing tomorrow, but I'm feeling better about it."

Usually Devlin Pierce was a vanilla sort of guy, but tonight Lily had seen him transform into mint chocolate chip. "Let's get Andrew and go to bed."

Dev came from behind her and held her in his arms. He leaned down so only she could hear. "And I don't work for Carlos. I'm the rich cartel bad guy in charge of the entire operation. I don't even care if you work for the DEA. We should get your cake to go."

My husband actually listens to every word I say! I'm not sure if I should be relieved or worried. This should be some night.

Lily said her goodbyes as Dev made a phone call. "Are you near Florida? My friends are already here. I'll text you info. We're going on the offense. I'm not going to wait for her to hit."

Dev watched to see Lily coming toward him. He gathered Andrew from Angelica's lap. "Angel, do you want to go home with Lily and me? Dan?"

"I'm going home with my granny," Angelica answered then promptly yawned.

"Do you two need me? If not, I'll go home with Mrs. Notte too," Dan answered.

Dev shook his head. "No. We'll talk in the morning. But we will talk in the morning."

Dan's eyes fixed on his friend's. He knew what and who Dev needed to talk about. *So, it's going down? Good. I hate waiting, especially for an attack.*

In only a few blocks back to the house, Andrew fell asleep. Dev carried him up the stairs while Lily took the elevator. Dev felt unsure about all three of them in the elevator now that he knew there was indeed a threat on the island. Lily already had the lights on in the bedroom and had kicked off her shoes along the way.

Andrew's limp body was cradled in his father's arm. Dev smiled. The baby was making those puffing sounds again. *I think Lily is right. I do make those same sounds, but I'm not admitting it to her.* He laid the small form on the bed. Lily waited to undress Andrew.

"Take off his little shirt, please," she whispered. Dev did as he was told. Lily removed the seersucker pants. Andrew didn't stir one bit. "He'll sleep through this just like you can sleep through the television."

"Unless it's the Caps playing an overtime hockey game." Dev's head was so near his wife's he could smell her hair and the fragrance of the coconut from the shampoo she used. Lily was intent on changing Andrew's diaper when Dev kissed her bare neck.

Lily turned her face. "What was that for?" It was too late to receive an answer as Dev kissed her softly. The intensity left her breathless.

"I just wanted to," Dev whispered. "Here, let me finish that. Just the diaper and shirt?"

"Yes. He gets so hot. I'll lay a light blanket over him. I'm going to change and get a snack. Do you want something?"

"I'll meet you in the living room." Dev finished his job while Lily changed and walked into the outer room. Dev looked down on his baby boy and sighed. *It would be so nice to be that innocent again.*

Lily stood behind the kitchen island eating a cracker with peanut butter and jelly on it. She had a full glass of milk in front of her. Dev pulled his shirt out of his waistband while he looked inside the refrigerator. "I shouldn't be hungry, but I want something. That meal was amazing."

"Uh huh. I wanted that lobster tail so much, but just one bite did me. I hope you enjoyed it."

Dev pulled out the deli plate and removed a roast beef sandwich. "I did, and the shrimp cocktail was amazing. My steak was perfect too. It was probably the best food at a wedding since ours."

"Jeremy and Abby had great food. The barbecue was so good. Those baked beans were to die for, and I know my baked beans." Lily pulled another cracker out of the box. "The coleslaw was good. The fruit dip, well I could've eaten that without the fruit."

"I just don't think about picnic food for a wedding," Dev admitted. He pulled out a bottle of beer and twisted off the top.

"I think it's a great idea to have food from your area, and nothing is more Kansas City than barbecue. Besides, let's be thankful that Jeremy didn't insist on pepperoni pizza with green peppers."

Dev leaned on the counter. "Well, there is that." He raised the beer in praise. "When are you eating your cake?" He pointed to the small box on the counter.

"Tomorrow. It'll be my afternoon treat. Anticipation is half the excitement. Speaking of anticipation, Devlin, do you want to tell me about the two cars parked less than a block away?"

Nothing that Lily noticed ever surprised Dev anymore. "Why should I tell you about them? You already noticed them."

"Are they the cavalry?"

"I told you I don't always tell you everything."

Lily stamped her foot. She absolutely hated when he did that. Dev continued to eat his sandwich, washing it down with the beer. She reached her hand out for the beer.

"What?"

"I desperately want a drink, and it settles the baby. She is kicking up a storm by the way." Dev handed the bottle to her, and Lily slowly savored the small sip she took. "That was so good. Now what about all that romance I was promised?"

Dev's eyes didn't twinkle, they sparkled. *So she's not going to pepper me with questions about the agents watching the house? She'll make me pay for this.* "Did I? I don't recall that."

Lily didn't answer him. She put away her snacks and cleaned up her crumbs. "Okay. Then I guess I'll go to bed. I'm really tired." She yawned and stretched in exaggeration. As she shuffled across the living room floor, her husband suddenly appeared and placed his hands on her shoulders.

"Remember, I'm the cartel lord and you're the rogue DEA agent. I'm going to seduce you to the dark side."

Lily shook her head playfully. "No, that's not right. The dark side? We didn't bring a black helmet. If you're going to be the cartel guy, you should be romancing me in a foreign language, promising me jewelry, trips around the world, and a full time nanny for my children."

"You're a pregnant DEA agent?" Dev questioned with a smile as they entered the bedroom.

Lily smoothed her nightgown, showing her baby bump. "We can't pretend in any world that this baby isn't here."

Dev removed his shirt and looked over at her. He slowly walked toward her. In Lily's eyes, he almost appeared like a tiger stalking his prey. *But it's Dev. He's my Boy Scout.* He took her in his arms until there was no space between them. "That baby is there, and yes, I am her father."

"We're back to the black helmet guy?" Lily giggled. She stepped out of his embrace and got into bed. "Why don't you just be you, and I'll just be me? It seems to work pretty well that way."

Dev removed his shoes and finished undressing. "Don't you want me to talk to you in a foreign language?"

Lily turned out the light next to her side of the bed. "That would be nice. Which one?"

"Well, let's see," Dev whispered as he joined her. "We have the Latin languages. I can do a bit of German, but that's a bit harsh. How about Pashto?"

As Lily snuggled against her husband, she murmured, "Surprise me like you always do."

Dev touched the side of her face tenderly. "I always obey a direct order, honey."

Lily swept her hand over his lips. "And I love surprises." Dev's low laughter touched her heart.

Chapter Thirty

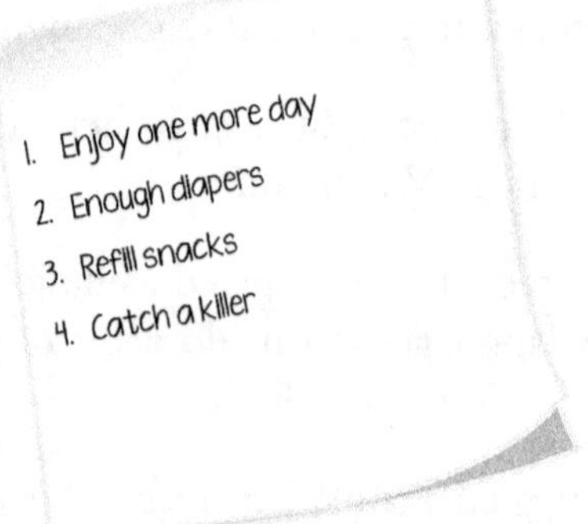

Lily and Dev woke about the same time the sun flooded into their room. They'd forgotten to close the curtains before they went to bed, but thankfully, Andrew hadn't stirred.

Dev played with Lily's hair as she massaged his shoulder. "Is he okay?"

Lily nodded. "I checked him right before you woke up. He is just a tired little guy. He's had non-stop attention, and he's eaten very well on this trip. If he was older, he might not be going back home with us. He'd stay with Mrs. Notte and her nurse."

"I think we'll take Margot/Gilda down today," Dev said casually. Lily's eyes widened quickly, and she shoved his chest.

"When were you going to tell me?"

Dev smiled. "I just did. At least I'm telling you. Oh, and you might be the bait, again."

Lily sat up quickly, eyeing her husband suspiciously. "Why are you so relaxed? You hate me being in danger, remember?"

"This time, I'm calling the shots. I hate to give you credit, but some of the information you cultivated got me thinking, and frankly, triggered my memory. Margot/Gilda is a contract killer. The doctor she's with is the man I thought I killed. He's Armand Miserli, Dr. Misery. Obviously, these two characters don't stay dead."

Lily snickered. "Now that's a dilemma."

"So, years ago Margot and Miserli established this illegal prescription operation. This was the beginning of illegal synthetic drugs. They figured doctors could be a viable route into the country. The DEA currently has a Diversion Control Division that handles that. It's a complicated system now, funneling into the United States from China and South America. At the time I was involved, we were going after a network headed by the doctor in Bogota. Carlos was there too. We saw Margot with the man time after time so when we began following her, we realized her involvement. She wasn't just his lover. She was his trusted employee. The doctor and Margot received money from one of the wealthiest and deadliest cartels out of Columbia. Over the years, Margot became an international hired gun, perhaps engaging more trafficking channels along the way through blackmail or favors."

Lily leaned on her elbow. "This is fascinating. Why are you offering me all this information, Agent Pierce? Isn't this highly inappropriate?"

"It seems inappropriate is currently appropriate. And, I think you deserve to know. Because of your investigation, we will be able to capture one of INTERPOL's most wanted, and one of ours, even though he was supposed to be dead." Dev reached out and flicked one of Lily's wayward frizzy curls. "We've set a trap today. I just hope they show up."

"Here?"

"Yes. Mrs. Notte is having a luncheon today, and they're invited."

Lily shook her head. "When exactly was all of this planned?"

"Yesterday, but the particulars were completed last night after you slept, my love." Dev kissed her ear and then her cheek.

Lily reached over to touch his face. "You were very busy last night."

"Yes, I was," Dev laughed.

Andrew began to stir. Lily listened. She kissed Dev. "The party is officially over. Your son is awake."

Lily began to leave the bed but was pulled back by her husband. "I love you, Lily."

After one more kiss, Lily scrambled from the bed. "And I love you, but your son is going to scream in a minute if I don't grab him."

They had enough time to dress and begin fixing breakfast before the elevator door opened to reveal a surprise guest.

"Honey, I'm home." Ari stepped into the room, a wide smile on his face, and open arms proclaiming his arrival.

Lily was shocked, but for once, her husband seemed very happy to see the super agent. "You're just in time for breakfast."

"Wonderful. I've been flying all night, and I'm starved. Lovely Lily, how is the pregnancy?" Ari came to her side and kissed her on both cheeks and on her forehead. He touched her belly and said a short prayer in Hebrew, and another in Arabic. He mussed up Andrew's curly red hair and shook Dev's hand. "I could use a very large cup of coffee, and please no decaf. Perhaps you have some Cuban coffee?"

Dev poured the dark liquid of energy into a large mug. "No, just regular, and Lily is doing better. She still needs to watch the blood pressure. She was feeling absolutely wonderful last night." Her husband winked in her direction.

Lily's mouth gaped open from the Ari surprise. Her face reddened at Dev's description of their intimacy. *He's right. It does make me feel better. That is so weird. It's almost like going back to the scene of the crime! Ha!*

"Why am I always surprised when you just show up?" Lily asked as she broke another egg into the bowl. "Are scrambled eggs with cheese and peppers good for you?"

"Add in some tomatoes, and I'm in," Ari answered. Ari blew Lily a kiss, and she pretended to catch and then kiss it, holding it over her heart.

"I should be upset by this behavior, but I know you both mean nothing," Dev muttered.

Ari cocked his head in quizzical fashion. "Do we, Pierce?"

Dan finally made an appearance, walking out slowly to the coffee, pouring a cup, and turning around. He looked at Ari, took a drink of coffee, and then another. He closed his eyes and then opened them again. The vision remained. "Nope. You're still here. Why are you here?"

"I am General Custer," Ari proudly announced. All three of the other adults in the room groaned. "What? Oh, right. I am the cavalry."

Dan shuffled to Ari's side of the island, sitting on the most distant seat across from Lily. "We need more than just you."

Dev nodded. "We do. Ari is just an accessory."

Lily snorted. She knew what was coming.

Ari pretended to be wounded. "I am a handsome accessory. Is this everyone?"

"No," Dev answered. "Carlos is downstairs, and there's more outside. I'm not telling you everything."

"Now you know how I usually feel," Lily said slowly. She looked up from the skillet to see Dan laughing. "Well, it's true. Dev, I need that ceramic bowl on the second shelf."

The agent became a sous chef immediately. "We'll go over the details during breakfast. You, Ari, are just an accessory. You aren't officially on American soil."

"But it appears I am here." Ari's aloof persona was wearing thin on Dev and Dan.

As Dan helped Lily with muffins and a plate of bacon he nudged her arm. "I know you are friends with the egomaniac, but I just can't take him this morning."

Lily nodded. "This morning, I tend to agree with you. Between fatigue and my hormones, Ari is just a little too much right now." They all sat down at the table and began their breakfast. Lily couldn't take Ari's gleeful nonchalance any longer.

"Ari, you're too charming even for you. I'm not sure I trust you right now," Lily admitted.

"*Moi?* You don't trust your friend? Lily, I am hurt beyond reason." He began to eat his food. "These eggs are perfect."

Lily dropped her fork onto her plate. The sound made all three men stop in motion.

"You are either on something or you're hiding something. You're just too, too happy. Spill." She looked directly at the man who had become her friend.

Ari's tone changed. "I'm not on anything. I'm here to tone things down, and to add a very real adult perspective. This is dangerous to pull these two monsters into a web you believe you have weaved. INTERPOL has been after them for years. They've evaded them in France, Belgium, Italy, and I could go on country after country in South America. Fine, you get the doctor and Gilda here in this house. You have now placed everyone downstairs and Andrew in danger. Have you thought this out? Allow me to take them in. I'll go to the house they are staying at and apprehend them. It will be clean."

"No." Dev's one word answer startled Ari.

"That's it? No discussion?" Ari questioned. Dev reached for a muffin and began to butter it. "I believed my charm would make you see reason."

"There's no debate, Ari. It's been planned out. End of discussion."

Ari tilted his head. "I don't believe we even began a discussion."

Dev put his knife down and stared into Ari's eyes. "I know what you're trying to do. You'll take them in your magic plane. We won't be allowed to question them. We won't be able to prosecute them for their many crimes. I won't get any intel, and I believe others are involved. You, and whomever you're working with this week, must have some agenda--" Dev cocked his head. "Wait, you, the collective you, want their secrets, perhaps their chemistry, or maybe where the lab is?" He saw Ari's eyes blink and knew he was correct.

"It seems, once more, Devlin, we are at an impasse."

Lily and Dan watched the sparring. If she didn't love one of them, and love the other one almost like her own brother, she'd swear they were going to get up and duel at twenty paces.

"Ari, put your smile back on," Dev suggested. "You're an accessory. When I'm on your ground, I'm the accessory. We've been through this so many times before, remember?"

"I remember, but it doesn't mean I like it. Jurisdiction is a funny thing. They have committed crimes all over the world. You Americans need to understand it's not just about you."

Dan's snicker caught both men's attention. "But it is about us. Two men went after Lily and Andrew. I had to kill them. This is most definitely personal when Lily is under threat, and I have to shoot again. I need more coffee. Actually, there's not enough coffee in the world to deal with you, Ari." Dan stood up quickly and headed into the kitchen.

Dev watched Dan as he stated his admission. Dan was hurting, and Dev hadn't noticed until now. *He had to kill, even if it was to protect Lily and Andrew. He's not up to this.*

"Ari, you need to understand it isn't just about you either," Lily said quietly. She noticed Ari seemed perplexed at her rebuke.

"Lily, perhaps it is too personal for you and this happy band of white hats. Have you thought about that? Your opponent seeks revenge, but mistakes can be made when you feed that feeling. But, I am here for all of you. I will step back. But, you will all call for me. Lily, you know nothing, my little flower girl."

"And you, above all of us, should know that revenge doesn't heal the heart or soothe the loss," Lily murmured. Briefly, Ari's eyes met hers.

Ari needed to answer, but this was Lily. She knew his story. Searching for the man who had killed his wife and daughter hadn't righted his world. He softened his tone. "Fine. I'm sorry, Lily."

Now, Dev was even more suspicious. *Ari had given up too easily. He only does that when he has his own agenda. Maybe I need to make a quick call to the State Department? But he has no power to apprehend or detain. Or, did he give up because Lily is upset at him? And why did he feel the need to demean my wife? She's his only real friend in this room.*

Dev searched Lily's eyes. He could see them filling with tears as she contorted her body to sit straighter and away from Ari. Dev wondered if Lily was going to be sick. Ari's distance with her was palpable. As they had become fast friends, Lily now understood Ari like no one else he knew. Jackson, his brother, might know the man more, but it was on a different level. Dev watched his wife as she left the table, took her plate to the kitchen, walked through the living room, picked up Andrew, and retreated into the bedroom.

"I'm going to dress Andrew," Lily said dispassionately as she shut the door.

Dev took his knife and flashed it in the air. "What the hell was all that crap? You're hurting Lily by being the Ari we all loathe."

"I suppose honesty is the best policy."

"There's a first time for everything." Dev searched Ari's eyes. *Will he tell me the truth?*

Ari pushed back from the table. "I need to take that doctor back to Lyon. INTERPOL believes he has invented a new synthetic form of a normal prescription drug. The painkiller is now deadly. If it hits the open market, it could be devastating. After I looked at Lily's notes, I began some digging, and realized the doctor was still alive."

"You could've told me. You have had several opportunities to tell me, but nothing. I saw the man the other night, and that's the first I knew he was still alive, and he's with Gilda. Ari, the woman threatened Lily and the baby the other night."

"Seriously?"

"Yes. Of course, your dear friend in there, went right up to the woman and spoke to her." Dev pointed toward their bedroom.

Ari smiled, genuinely smiled. "Your wife amazes me. Obviously, she shouldn't do things like that, but that's something you and I would've done."

"Exactly." Dev smiled too. "And that's why she shouldn't."

Dan returned to the table as he saw the mood lighten. "Are we playing nice again?"

Ari looked directly at Dan. "I had no idea, Daniel. I'm sorry you had to kill again. But it was a worthy endeavor."

"So? Are you in?" Dan took another drink of coffee. In just a few hours, all hell was going to break loose.

"I'm here, aren't I?"

Dev looked over at Dan. "When he answers a question with a question, he's usually lying."

Ari relaxed. "Pierce, you can't say that."

"Yes, he can," Dan answered. "Because it's true, at least it always has been."

Chapter Thirty-One

Mrs. Notte's guest was right on time. Everything was in place. The plan was easy and perfect. But one ingredient was missing. Gilda wasn't with the doctor.

"Doctor, it was so good to see you these last few days. I remember the martinis in Palm Beach so many years ago." Mrs. Notte was spot on. She relished playing the game with Devlin and his boys.

The doctor nodded. "But it wasn't so many years ago. Maybe ten? I always enjoyed tennis with your son."

"You and he were very close as I recall," Mrs. Notte commented. Her nurse, Barb, brought in a pitcher of iced tea and poured two glasses. "Barb, we'll have lunch in a little bit, after we reacquaint ourselves."

"Will anyone else be joining us?" Dr. Miserli's eyes followed Barb as she headed to a back room.

"Oh, I suppose. You never know who might pop up." Mrs. Notte's flippant comment was added with the flip of her hand. "At my age, I don't keep track of the comings and goings of my family."

"I haven't seen Bernard in a few years. I believe we met for a lovely dinner in Barcelona."

"Ah, yes." Mrs. Notte nodded. She added lemon to her drink. "He loved that city. Garrett, his son, was fond of South America for some reason."

The doctor said nothing. He looked around the room again. His suspicious nature had him wondering about the charming octogenarian. He heard a door open, and Mrs. Notte smiled widely.

"Well, there he is. The groom has arrived. Were you able to meet him last night?"

Dr. Miserli stood immediately and held out his hand. "No, we weren't fortunate to do so. It was a lovely wedding with a beautiful bride."

Carlos smiled and shook the man's hand. "Thank you. Please, sit. My wife won't be joining us. Our daughter and she went to the pier to see manatees and dolphins. My little girl is fascinated by them."

As the casual conversation proceeded, Dev and Dan stood on the second floor deck looking out onto the Gulf. Ari remained inside, listening to the downstairs group.

"What's Lily doing down on the beach?" Dan watched her walk slowly, picking up a shell now and then.

"With Alise taking Andrew to the pier with Angelica, Lily wanted a little alone time. I didn't think it would hurt." Dev's binoculars steadied on his wife. He saw a few other people strolling on the white sand. Lily stopped suddenly. "What is she doing?"

Ari flew out to his two friends. "Gilda isn't with the doctor. She's on the beach."

Dev focused again and saw another woman a few feet away from his wife. "She's there with Lily. She took the bait, and it is my wife." The binoculars were thrown aside as the three men ran, using the exterior stairs. It was a race to the beach.

Ari relayed information to Carlos as the chase began. In the middle of a discussion about arts in Sarasota, Carlos stood up and pulled his gun. "Doctor Armand Miserli, stand up."

"What is this?" He looked toward Mrs. Notte who simply smiled.

"Armand, dear, I believe they call it a sting." Barb came back into the room to stand behind the elderly woman. Mrs. Notte clapped. "This is so exciting."

"I don't understand," the doctor complained. "You don't need to steal from me, sir. How much do you need?"

Carlos motioned. "I need you to turn around, put your hands behind your back."

Two other agents entered the living room. Dr. Miserli saw their DEA jackets.

He yelled out. "No. This isn't possible. I won't go this easy. You people are idiots. You missed the shipment, and my colleague is taking care of a couple loose ends right now."

Carlos said nothing as he cuffed the fugitive. The satisfaction of taking him in was overwhelming, but he wouldn't let anyone, even Mrs. Notte see how he really felt. Dev would feel the same way. They'd need to talk about some missed shipment. Obviously, they'd overlooked something.

Dev arrived near Lily first, the sand flying as he skidded to a halt. Gilda's gun was pointed directly at his wife's belly.

"Pierce, just stay there. I know you have a gun so toss it. And tell those other two to stay back. In fact, tell them to go away or it ends very badly for your wife right now."

Lily attempted to turn and see her husband's face, but Gilda yelled. "Don't move an inch. I swear I'll shoot. First, your unborn baby and then you, Mrs. Pierce."

Dev pulled his gun from behind his back and laid it down carefully on the sand. With his reach, he was able to land it only inches from Lily's right hand. After years in the desert, he knew how to place a gun down on sand.

Gilda waved her gun. "Now, the other one. Tell them to get back. Send them back to the house."

Dev removed a smaller gun from his ankle and placed it on the left side of Lily. He turned to Dan and Ari. "Go back to the house. Now."

The two men complied. Dan went through the carport area as did Ari. As soon as they turned the corner, they dropped and crawled back to the dunes. Ari pointed his gun in Gilda's direction.

"I can't get a shot on the woman without hitting Lily. What about you?"

Dan brought his gun up through the sea oats. "It's tight. I'm not sure. These aren't perfect conditions."

Ari was incredulous. Dan could make any shot. "What do you mean? Daniel, don't think about anything I said this morning. Just do your job."

"Can you hear Dev?" Dan continued to focus his hand gun. He realized that even more agents wouldn't help the situation.

"No, but I can talk to Carlos. Carlos, we're in trouble down here. Do you have anyone who can take a shot from up there?"

Dan began to crawl away. "Ask if anyone has a long range rifle, a Winchester, or something up there. I'll be there in a minute."

Ari knew what Dan was doing. Taking the higher ground always worked in battle. "Carlos, Dan is coming up. He needs something to take this woman out."

Back on the sand, Gilda smiled. "Somehow, I knew this was a setup, Pierce." She motioned for him to keep his hands up.

"You mean you sacrificed your great love? That's rich." Dev laughed for emphasis. *I need to buy time. Time for what? I'll know.*

"Of course not. You'll release him or I'll kill your pregnant wife. It's that simple."

"After all these years, I don't think we'll release him," Dev answered calmly. "And if we do, breaking every procedure, INTERPOL is here to take him in. I can't stop them. You aren't going to win this time. You've left so many dead in your wake. I won't allow you to kill one more."

Gilda threw back her luxurious red hair in true movie star fashion. "What? You have nothing. You rush me, and your wife dies. Agents attack from the water or the beach, and your wife dies. There's only one other possibility. Does your wife have a gun?"

"No, she hates them. I wish she would pick one up."

Lily blinked twice. She knew what she had to do, but in her current state she needed a little more room to drop and roll. *I'm so sorry, baby. You better be a tough little girl for Daddy and me.* She began to rock back and forth on her heels.

"Stop that," Gilda demanded.

"I can't help it. When I'm pregnant, it's hard to stand in one position for very long. And then I need to pee." Lily succeeded in moving herself closer to the gun.

Behind the sea oats, Carlos crawled to Ari, handing him a pair of binoculars. "Dan has an earpiece now."

"Daniel, our Lily has managed to move over, but I fear Devlin may be in the way." Ari waited for the priest's voice. "Daniel?"

"I'm here. I'm in place, but Ari you're going to have to help me."

Ari didn't understand. "You have the best view. Just shoot at something." He heard silence.

"I don't mean that." Dan could see very well. He could shoot at the sand and maybe he'd get lucky. This wasn't his gun, but it wasn't the gun that was the problem. It was his doubts. *Lord, I trust in you. You say do not be afraid. You are with me. I'm sorry.*

"Daniel, this is our girl. And Devlin is our friend. You must. Lily will let you know when it is time. Trust in her, and in God. He is with you in all things, even this."

Ari couldn't see the perspiration forming over Dan's brows or his suddenly dried lips. But he knew the feeling when the adrenaline coursed through your veins and made your body feel as though it would burst from the energy, from the fear.

Dan repeated Ari's words. "Lily will let me know."

Ari could lip read a few words in Gilda's rants. She wanted the doctor.

"I'll have to send word to the agents to release him," Dev explained. "Let Lily go, and she can tell them. She goes in, and he comes out."

"No, you tell them. You bring him out. She stays here. Our boat is coming in, but I have time for you, Agent Pierce."

Dev looked out to see a speed boat, and a small motorized dinghy with two armed gunmen heading their way. He knew the federal agents by Bean Point wouldn't wait much longer. Nothing good was going to come from this. He doubted Lily and he would survive no matter the outcome. He couldn't think about that right now.

It was time to stop the insanity. "No, Gilda or whatever the hell your name really is. I can't do anything for you. You're the one with the gun. Both of mine are on either side of my wife, and you know she won't pick them up. We're at a stalemate."

Dev's composure only stoked Lily's fear. He was acting like the agent she'd met, not the man she loved. But he'd told her the plan. She just needed to execute it. *When?*

"Seriously? You're going to sacrifice your wife, if not your life too?"

"He's a stickler for rules. He's a Boy Scout," Lily muttered. Gilda had some uncertainty on her face. She shrugged.

"My, Pierce, even your wife thinks you are a tough one. Too bad you're on the good guy side of the equation. You know, you'll never win. We Americans always think we can fix everything. You'll never stop the drug trade. You haven't stopped the shipment we just handled, and you'll never stop people like me from adding to our bank accounts. So Agent Pierce, this is it."

"You're so willing to sacrifice the doctor?" He hoped she didn't realize he was buying time. From the corner of his eye, he could see men moving through the sand dunes near the Point.

"It's a price that needs to be paid. I will miss him. We had a good run, but I didn't have time to plan this all out, and he just had to have lunch with that old lady."

"Mrs. Notte can be very convincing," Dev acknowledged. He noticed Lily moving a few more inches away from his gun, but toward the smaller one. *What is she doing?*

"He wanted to gather information about her son and grandson. Bernard and he have some business to do, and that little idiot owes us money. I'll find him myself."

"Bernard is dead and Garrett is in federal prison." Dev's openness surprised his wife. Lily bowed her head down to look at the gun. She needed to pick it up. She had to pick it up.

"Wonderful. So all of this was for absolutely nothing? We thought Bernard would show up to see his mother. Our contacts told us about the wedding, and that the old lady was opening up the house. It was our chance and a good place for a drop down on Longboat."

A drop? A drug shipment? "I figured this wasn't just about my wife or me, but you should know Mrs. Notte has no idea where they are. Call off your dogs."

Gilda changed her stance. She held the gun tighter and at the ready. "Pierce, you have no power. Frankly, I'm bored with you. It's done."

Dev saw the dinghy within feet of the beach. Guns were pointed at them from the water. Gilda heard the motor slowing.

"I love you, Lily. Do what you need to do," Dev said calmly.

"I love you too. I hate this."

Gilda laughed. "We all hate this, Mrs. Pierce, but it's over. Enough."

As soon as Lily took this as her chance to drop to the sand and roll, a distracting shot whizzed by Gilda's head. Lily grabbed the gun and slipped it like a boomerang to Dev who was already down on one knee. Gilda pressed the trigger, but missed her mark when the pregnant woman dropped. Dev shot, clipping Gilda's hand. Her gun was sent flying. She writhed in pain, but in that split second, her head snapped back. She fell dead in a heap on the sand.

As the two gunmen came even closer to the shore, Dev ran forward, shooting furiously. He was aided by fire from above and from agents running down the beach. Quickly, the gunmen punched the motor and turned away. More shots rang out and the dinghy came to a stop. The other boat sped away into the Gulf. In a matter of minutes, the Coast Guard was giving chase with another DEA speedboat capturing the two armed guards.

Dev looked behind him to see Lily sitting in the sand with his small gun in her hands. "I think I fired it. Take it." She held it up.

He knelt down and kissed her, holding her face in his hands. "Arc you okay? What about the baby? You went down pretty hard."

"I'll hurt tomorrow."

Dev nodded. "We'll have you checked out." He looked up to the house to see where the gunfire had been coming from, but he saw nothing. He did see Ari and Danny running toward them. "Let's get you up, slowly." Dev lifted his wife up carefully. He brushed off the sand from her clothes and kissed her again.

Ari, binoculars around his neck, still had a gun in his hand. Danny had a rifle as a new accessory on his shoulder.

"Is she safe?" Ari asked.

"How's Lily?" Dan asked.

"I'm fine for now," Lily answered. Dan thanked God, Ari thanked Allah, and Dev thanked them both. The four gathered together with arms around each other for a group hug.

"Okay, guys. Can we go somewhere and sit before I fall down?" Lily suggested. She thought she could feel the bruises forming near her abdomen and hip. *Oh, baby girl. Please be okay.*

Chapter Thirty-Two

The DEA had Lily examined by a health professional as quickly as they brought her up to the house. She remained on the sofa, a pillow behind her back, her legs and feet propped up, and a glass of milk and cookies in her hands. Mrs. Notte and Barb sat with her. Alise had been told that it was safe to return to the house, but possibly she should take the children out for ice cream to postpone their return. Agents swarmed the beach and the living room area completing their forensic examinations.

"Isn't this exciting, Lily?" Mrs. Notte's face lit up as though she was expecting Santa Claus. "Oh, I'm sorry. It's exciting except for your grave encounter."

Lily dropped part of a cookie into her milk until it was just soft enough. She lifted it out and relished every chocolate chip. "Thankfully, it didn't end up with a grave."

"Oh my, you are witty," Mrs. Notte exclaimed. "Dear girl, what else can Barb get you?"

"I'm fine. I can't wait to hold Andrew though."

Carlos sat on the edge of the couch near Lily's feet. "Alise says they are having a great time. They'll be back in an hour or so. Andrew is being a very good little boy, and now Angelica wants a baby brother."

"Oh good." Lily sighed. They'd almost left Andrew an orphan, yet her hands weren't even shaking now. "Carlos, when will Dev be finished?"

"Soon. When he gets back to the office he'll have a lot of paperwork. Heck, I'll have my own in Miami. They are taking Ari and Dan's statements right now. Are you sure you are feeling fine?"

Lily nodded while she chewed another piece of cookie.

"It's just that your ankles are swelling up," Carlos said as he pointed down.

"I fight that," Lily admitted. "Could you get me some ice water? I'm really getting warm."

Carlos immediately got up and waved Barb off. He returned quickly with a large glass. "Drink."

"Yes, sir. I'm so sorry this has happened the day after your wedding." Lily carefully lifted the cold water to her mouth, the fluid sloshing side to side. *Now my hands are shaking.* She grasped one hand over the other. *I need my husband.*

"Why? Alise is having a wonderful time with your boy." He motioned toward Mrs. Notte. "This one is having the time of her life. We've taken out a killer and a cartel doctor is finally in custody. He's not dead, but now he'll be in prison."

"But, he got away with some drug shipment," Lily lamented.

Carlos smiled. "No, he didn't. The Coast Guard checked the GPS on that speedboat. They've grabbed a boat with cocaine and hundreds of bottles of illegal meds near the Keys. They've picked up a few of their soldiers in Longboat. Some of these agents will head down as soon as they are finished here. I would too, but Alise and I are going to take a couple of days. I'll return to the office to sign off on all of this, and then in a couple of weeks, we're taking Angelica to the mouse house before Alise becomes too uncomfortable."

Now Lily's face lit up. "Oh my. Angelica is going to be so surprised. I'm jealous."

"Come with us," Carlos suggested.

Lily looked down at her belly and the two cookies anchored on top. "Um, that won't work. I can't ride anything except the monorail or the ferry boat on the lagoon. Can I take a raincheck?"

"Of course. In fact, let's plan a group trip for about five years from now?"

"Perfect," Lily answered. She could feel Dev, sitting on the sofa's arm behind her.

"Where are we going?" He rubbed her shoulders softly.

Lily stretched her neck to look up at him. "They're surprising Angelica with a trip to the mouse house in a couple of weeks, and we're all going five years from now."

"Wonderful." His tone elicited a disingenuous response.

"I know you don't really feel that way, but thank you for lying," Lily muttered.

"You'll need to give a formal statement, honey. I've written one for you, but I need you to look at it, and you can add in anything I missed."

Lily nodded. She finished off another cookie. *I missed lunch! No wonder I'm hungry.*

Dan sat down in one of the chairs opposite them. "Lily, how are you?"

"Hungry. What are we doing for dinner?"

"I have a surprise for all of us," Mrs. Notte answered.

Dan held his head with his left hand. "I don't think I can take another surprise."

"You'll love this one, Father," Mrs. Notte explained. "I have a fantastic chef coming here. No need to move or to dress up in our finery."

"That shot was from heaven," Ari said as he joined the group. He lifted Lily's legs, removed the pillows and sat down, placing her legs back onto his lap. Lily eyed him suspiciously. Dev became interested in his wife's demeanor. Her hands were shaking, and it seemed as though she wasn't that comfortable with her friend Ari.

Dan said nothing. "I was aiming for the sand." He looked as though he had lost his best friend.

"It was a miracle shot, Danny," Dev said quietly. He understood what his friend was feeling. Protecting Lily required the priest to kill. "Danny, without you, I'm not sure we'd be here."

"I'm not sure God is going to see it that way," the priest lamented.

"Daniel, your talent came from God. Obviously, God condemns us when we take a life, but you were acting as an avenging angel. You must remember that God allows the bad so we can know the good. You are good." Ari sounded so certain of what he had just told the man he'd known for many years now.

Lily snickered in the light of the serious conversation. "Geez, Dan. You better get back to being a priest or this one is going to take over your pulpit." She kicked at Ari's arm. But then her smile faded. Dev noticed the sudden change again. He also saw her wince as she brought her leg back.

Dan finally smiled and lifted his head. "I just have to come to terms again. It brings back memories I thought I had vanquished."

"Those memories pop up when you least expect them," Dev began. "If not for Lily jogging my memory with something she said, we wouldn't have had a successful operation today. Sometimes, memories can help. Like what you do. Wow, that was a shot, and that warning one gave me enough time to protect us. As soon as I heard it, I knew you were the only one who could miss that close and not hit the target."

Dan sighed. Lily looked over to see a despondent friend. She needed to break this up. "So, Mrs. Notte, exactly what will the chef be creating? I really deserve a treat. I've been a very good girl today."

Before Mrs. Notte could answer, Dev interrupted. "If you'd been a good girl, you never would've begun a search for a missing stranger."

"But where's the fun in that, Devlin?" Mrs. Notte's pointed question made everyone laugh. She had broken the ice. "Lily, dear, he'll have lobster, crab, steak, chicken, pasta, potatoes of some kind, and something for dessert. Oh yes, baked Alaska and chocolate lava cake with cream cheese and strawberry icing. It's my favorite, and I believe you'll love it. That will be your treat."

Lily clapped. Ari seemed delighted. Dev rolled his eyes. Dan and Carlos smiled.

"By the way, could we order a pizza or something right now? I'm starving," Dan commented.

Lily pointed at her friend and agreed. "Yes, that's the best idea I've heard all day."

Dev studied his wife quickly. Her smile, and her conversation seemed forced. *She's happy, but...*

"Pizza it is." Dev went to order a well-deserved lunch. The swarm of agents began to diminish as the pizza delivery van pulled into the driveway. Dev and Dan went down to receive their food. On the way up in the elevator, Dev broached a subject that they usually left in the past.

"Dan, do you need to talk to someone?"

"Again? Yes, probably. I'll definitely talk to Monsignor McGinnis. He's an Army chaplain. I think you remember him from Fort Benning. He was there with us."

The pizza fragrance filled the small elevator. Yes, Dev remembered him. "Danny, were you thinking about being a priest way back then?"

The priest leaned against the wall. "I had thoughts. I was torn. I wanted a family, a wife, someone who loved me."

Dev shoved Dan's body. "You don't have a wife, but you have all of that. I hope you know that. And I'll go with you, if you want me to. I can use some debriefing of the God kind."

"I do have all that." Danny's voice was low. "I didn't realize that until you just said it. I mean, we've always been our own little band, but we are a family. You know, I would do anything to protect any of you, especially your wife."

Dev frowned. "Even Ari? Really?"

Dan chuckled. "Maybe I spoke too soon. Maybe not Ari. It really depends."

Finally, Dev could see that Dan's demeanor began to lighten. Of course, it had been at Ari's expense. *Why not? Ari is always good for a laugh.*

"I would appreciate it if you came with me, Dev."

The elevator door opened, and the two men were greeted by cheers. As Dan and Dev set the pizzas out on the island, a small boy walked over to Dan and reached up with his arms. "DaDa."

Dan picked up Andrew, but turned to wipe a tear away. Dev embraced his shoulders. "See? He picks you before me. Again, I should be jealous. My own son." Dev shook his head in feigned despair. Andrew peeked around Dan's arms.

"DaDa." He leaned over for his father to take him.

"Great, my son is calling everyone his dad."

Dan smiled. "I wouldn't worry until he does it to Ari."

Dev reached for a slice. "You have a point. By the way, where is your mother?"

Andrew only wanted his pizza.

On the other side of the wall, in the master bathroom's large tiled shower, Lily allowed the water to blend with her tears. Blue splotches formed on her lower stomach, leg, and hip. To see the damage that her behavior had created on her body, on her baby stunned her. She leaned up against the side of the wall, standing in silence. Lily began to shake and cry uncontrollably.

"Oh God."

God didn't answer her directly, but her husband appeared in the bathroom. Now, he realized what was going on. Dev couldn't wait to comfort her. He threw off his sandals and walked completely clothed into the rain shower. Lily was in too much distress to shove him out. Instead she allowed him to gather her in his arms. Dev just held her. No words passed between them, but he soothed the shock.

Dev was soaked within a minute, but it didn't matter. "Honey, you're fine. I'm here."

Lily pulled away from him, trapped in the corner of the shower. "Look what I did to our baby. What if I've hurt her?"

Dev wiped away water from his eyes. The bruising was extensive, over her stomach area and down her hip. "You did what you needed to do."

"But I didn't need to start this entire business, did I?" Lily's screams shook Dev to his core. "What is wrong with me?"

Dev reached out and pulled her away from the corner and into his arms once more. "Absolutely nothing. You care, that's all. I wouldn't change that about you. It's who you are, and you're the woman I love."

When the couple finally joined the group, no one asked why Dev's hair was wet, and he had completely changed his clothing.

Dinner was truly entertaining. With a touch of cognac added to the filets, fire rose from the pan. The chef was delighted by the cheers from his spectators. Even Lily clapped at the display. It seemed as though Dev's arm had not left her shoulders since he rescued her in the shower. Andrew never left her lap. He clapped along with the others, but leaned back against his mother and yawned

"He's needy tonight," Dev commented to Lily. "Do you want me to take him?"

Lily kissed her son's head. "No. I need him as much as he needs me."

Lily didn't see the looks between Ari and her husband. Dev nodded and reached for his son. "Why don't you go get some air on the deck? Just take a breath for a minute."

"I'm breathing just fine," Lily answered abruptly, but Dev had already turned her chair.

"Take a break. It's been a long day."

Lily slid carefully down from the tall bar chair. "Fine. I will take a break. I need to listen to the ocean one more time anyway."

Once she arrived on the deck, Lily leaned against the bannister and listened to the roar of nighttime waves. The full moon offered enough light for a view of the Gulf. She felt that she wasn't alone anymore, but chose to not turn around, or acknowledge the other guest with her.

Ari came up on her left side and leaned on the same bannister. "I thought we should talk. I feel I've disappointed you today."

"You were just being you," Lily mumbled. "That's not always attractive."

Ari hung his head down. "I sometimes wonder why I care so much about how you feel about me. Lily, I am not like the Boy Scout."

Lily laughed nervously. "Oh that's for sure."

"You married the last Boy Scout."

Finally, Lily looked at her friend. "Really? That's a movie. Do you always have to turn everything into a joke? Oh wait, you do that when you want something."

"I thought the movie reference would make you laugh." Ari wanted to make her laugh. *Why do I need her to like me?* "Lily, I have a very difficult job. I walk lines where there aren't even lines. The world is not always black and white, and you should know that by now."

She touched his arm. "Don't you think I know that? Every time my husband leaves for some operation, I know that. I realize he may not come back. I don't know what I would've done if I'd been his wife while he was in the Army."

"You would've handled it."

Ari's quick response made her smile. Lily shook her head. "Yes, I suppose. I thought you'd have more loyalty to your friends than you did this morning. I was shocked and yes, very disappointed."

Ari sighed. "Devlin and I have had a very sordid history. He has loyalty flowing in his veins. Because of my lineage, my background, I have to dodge between groups and cultures. I can't always say I work for the better good." Ari turned and placed a hand on each of her shoulders. "Lily, forgive me. Now, let's discuss you. You always see people as they are, not how they really are. You see the best in others. That's not always the case. Just ask your husband."

"Well, in the end you did the right thing." Lily smiled softly. She embraced her friend, and he pulled her close. *But, I'll always look for the good in others. But sometimes I will still wonder and question.* There remained a doctor and his daughter that had her doubting her intuition.

"It was fifty-fifty for several minutes." As Lily pushed back from him they both laughed. "You keep trying to make me a better person, and I love you for that. Friends again?"

Lily reached up and kissed him briefly on the cheek. "Friends, but I certainly won't have my children coming to Uncle Ari for ethics lessons."

"Completely understandable." Ari kissed her on the forehead and then on one cheek and the other.

"Oh, and I'm not going to be investigating anything from now on." Lily had made a decision.

Ari's eyes widened, but he began laughing quickly. "Of course. You'll be back questioning why your neighbor put out the trash a day early as soon as you return home."

"Don't be ridiculous. I'm done. Really. I endangered the baby, and that has scared me straight. No more mysteries for me." *I'll have to have Dev continue my investigation when we get home.*

Despite the serious look on Lily's face, and her hands placed defiantly on her hips, Ari didn't believe a word that was coming out of her mouth. He took her hand and patted it. "Whatever you say, Lily."

"Don't placate me. You still don't believe me," Lily said indignantly. "Fine, but you'll see."

Ari chuckled. "I suppose I will."

The two walked hand-in-hand back into the living room. Dev stood waiting. "Everything back to normal, well as normal as it can be with you, Ari?"

Ari lifted Lily's hand up to his lips and kissed it tenderly. His eyes danced with delight as he watched Dev's jealous response. He thought he could see steam coming out of his ears.

"Once again, I should be jealous," Dev muttered. "Honey, they're making the potatoes with gruyere cheese."

Lily shuffled off quickly. "Carbs get her every time." Dev's statement of fact created a light moment between the two men.

"She is a foodie," Ari said calmly. "May I hold Andrew for just a while? I'm not sure when I'll see him again."

"A new op?" Dev handed his son off.

"I need to go home. Lily always makes me think. She's very dangerous to my psyche."

Dev patted Ari on the back. "It's funny how that happens. You look at her. She's very unassuming, very normal, and yet, beneath that surface is a heart and soul that can make you a better man. She does that for me every morning when I look over and see her face."

"I suppose that's what I need," Ari admitted. "I need someone like her."

Dev watched as his wife clapped in delight as melted cheese mixed with Yukon gold potatoes. Andrew traced Ari's lips with his hand. "You need a home. Maybe you need to make a decision about who you really are, Ari?"

Andrew managed to stick his finger into Ari's mouth. The super agent was relegated to almost looking like a normal human being. "Devlin, where would be the fun in that?" He removed Andrew's finger and kissed the boy's forehead. "Many blessings to you, little man. You don't know how lucky you are."

Dev smiled, but he noticed Ari's pensive focus on the little boy in his arms. The usual enigmatic Ari had tiny cracks of fallibility. His frailties were exhibited on public display. Dev always knew they were there, but now others would be able to see them too. That was very dangerous for a man like Ari. "Come on, let's make sure the pregnant woman doesn't put herself into a carb coma."

"You mean you can stop her? You have that kind of power?" It was either Ari's grin or his unshaven face that made Andrew laugh as the toddler patted his chin. "That's right, my child. You don't believe your daddy either, do you?"

"Sadly, you are right. Lily has the power of a hurricane sometimes, and I'm that plane that flies into the calm of the eye, but it's a bumpy ride until you get there."

Ari patted Dev on the back. "But the ride is worth it, isn't it?"

Dev didn't answer. Instead, as he approached his wife, he brushed her neck, replacing his hand with a quick kiss. Loving Lily was a humbling experience that had changed his life completely. *Yes, it's all worth it even when she's doing her Jessica thing.*

Chapter Thirty-Three

It was good to be home. Dev insisted Danny stay for dinner and the night. He'd drop him back at the rectory tomorrow. Dev threw the priest's luggage in the downstairs guest suite before he could protest. Dan, Lily, and Andrew lounged on the couch as they watched Dev take care of them. Every one of his actions had a purpose. He brought them water and insisted they hydrate. He disappeared for a few minutes. When he returned, Dev announced he had sorted the laundry. He even brought down a load and began the washer. He asked them for their orders for dinner and went to pick up Chinese food. Lily especially wanted a large container of egg drop soup.

As the front door closed, Dan touched Lily's hand. "I didn't realize he was such a mother hen."

"Yep. Welcome to my world." Lily ran her hand through her son's hair. His long day of travel was almost over. She doubted he'd still be awake when Dev returned with the food. "Dev gets like this when he's nervous about something."

"But it's all over," Dan murmured as he straightened up on the couch. "Isn't it?"

Lily shook her head negatively. "I have this nagging feeling. We've missed something, or I don't know how to prove what I'm concerned about, and maybe Dev has?"

"But he's not telling you?"

Now, Lily nodded affirmatively. "I need to learn one thing. There are some mysteries that only my husband can solve. He has to do his federal agent thing. I'm realizing he'll tell me when he can...when it's all over."

Before his father had returned, Andrew was carried up to bed by his Uncle Dan. After dinner, Dan and Dev were watching hockey as Lily came from checking on Andrew.

"Poor little guy was hungry when he woke. I gave him a cookie. He ate it, and he was asleep before I could even kiss him." Lily sat down next to her husband and nestled into his chest. Dev's arm came around to hold her.

"I think we're all done for today. I'll have stacks of paperwork on my desk when I get back in a few days." Dev turned down the volume of the game.

"And I have an entire parish and a school to manage," Dan added.

"I want you both to know that I really am giving up sleuthing," Lily said. Dev's arm came away from her so he could look down at her face. Dan spit out his soda.

The two old combat friends waited. She said nothing else, and so they began to laugh.

Lily pushed away from Dev and became indignant. "I mean it. You've all taught me a lesson. You should be happy."

"I would be happy, if it were true," Dev admitted. Dan nodded in agreement.

"You two are incorrigible. You get around Ari, and you begin to act like him. It's rude, very rude."

"Oh, my Lord. Ari laughed too when you told him, didn't he?" Dan clutched his stomach as his laughter became uncontrollable.

Lily stuck her tongue out at the priest. "You think you're so smart."

"Did he laugh?" Dev calmed down and attempted to remain serious. Lily was angry.

"Yes. He treated me like the little woman. I didn't like it." Her pouting mouth and bent head reminded Dev of a little girl who had just lost her puppy. He'd soon be dealing with this kind of behavior once his daughter was born.

"Honey, you've had a big shock. This one was bad, but you know you love the intrigue, figuring out clues, or finding missing people. It's okay. We'll deal with it."

Lily's mouth opened wide. Now her husband was the king of placation. "What? You'll deal with it? I can do what I want. You're not the boss of me. If I want to investigate I will. If I want to write about it, I'll do that too. I'll be freaking Jessica if I want to be. Gentlemen, I'm going to bed. I'm sure we'll all feel better in the morning."

After her brief lecture, Lily rose slowly off the couch, grabbing the channel selector and clicking. The television went to a dark screen. Dev and Dan sat speechless as she slowly made her way up the stairs. She paused. "Devlin, are you coming?"

Dan mimicked her question. Dev winked. "Yes, dear. Goodnight, Daniel. Apparently, I am going to bed. You can stay up as long as you want."

"No he can't," Lily ordered. "Dan, go to bed. You need your sleep."

As Dev headed up the stairs he mouthed "help me" to his friend.

"She's worse than you when you were in charge of a mission," Dan said. Soon he was alone in the living room, finishing his soda. "Lily will stop being Lily when I stop being a priest, and that isn't happening." He took his bottle out to the kitchen, and grabbed a glass of water. He walked to the guest room and closed the door. Then, he did as he was told and went to bed.

The next morning the sun was barely up when Lily snuggled closer to her husband. His arm wrapped automatically around her lower hip.

"Ow."

Dev's eyes opened. His arm shot up into the air. "What? What's wrong?"

"My leg hurts. That's all." Lily moved closer and buried her face into his chest.

He lowered his arm carefully. This time his arm landed around her shoulder. "Maybe you should call the doctor today?"

"And tell him what? Oh, hi doc. Over the weekend, I was held at gunpoint by a contract killer. I had to drop to the sand, throw a gun to my husband, roll, and grab another gun." Lily's sarcasm seemed heightened this early in the morning.

Dev chuckled. "You forgot the wedding. You used to always tell me about the weddings first, remember?"

"That's what I need to go back to. I just need to help out at the vineyard and coordinate a few weddings, a few events, and I'll be good as gold. No matter my suspicions."

Dev felt Lily's heart beating near his. She was very talkative this morning which meant she had a lot on her mind. They still had almost three months before the baby came. She didn't need to decorate the room. She didn't need to prepare for anything. There were no lists to make, no post-its to attach on any mirror or board. *This isn't good for Lily. Wait, what suspicions? Does she have more? I need to ignore her comments right now.*

"Besides, I see the doctor on Wednesday, and you're going with me. Unless, you have other plans."

"I wasn't going into the office until next week, but I thought I'd drop Dan off this morning and go in to see what I need to file and fill out. Since this wasn't a usual DEA operation, I'm not sure what I need to do."

Lily snorted. "The great Devlin Pierce isn't sure about paperwork? Wow, alert the forces."

Dev looked down but only saw the top of her head. "Honey, what is going on in that pretty head of yours? Are you just tired?"

Lily shoved off of his chest to look down at him. "Nothing is wrong."

Dev rolled his eyes. "Crud. When you say nothing is wrong, something is wrong. What?"

Lily placed her hand up to her mouth. "You know I have this nagging feeling we've missed something. Hold that thought. I'm sick."

Dev watched his wife scramble from the bed and walk quickly to the bathroom. He grimaced as he heard her. Throwing back the covers, Dev's day officially began. He found her sitting on the floor with a wet towel on her head.

"I need help getting up," Lily said slowly. "I don't feel very well."

Dev tenderly picked up his wife and steadied her before heading her back into the direction of the bed. "I'll get Andrew. You just rest. I'll call Dad to see if he can come over. I'm sure he wants to see his grandson."

Lily climbed into the bed but stopped. "Is that bacon? Do you smell bacon?"

Dev breathed in. "Dan found bacon? I've heard of the story of loaves and fishes, but I don't know how he made bacon."

"I could eat some bacon and eggs. Wait, do we have eggs?" Lily lowered her legs back down onto the floor. "I'm hungry now. I feel better." Lily grabbed a robe and headed out of the bedroom.

"She's more difficult to keep up with than some drug dealers," Dev muttered. He went back into the bathroom, showered, shaved, and dressed to go into the office. Before he headed down the stairs, he heard his son yell for him. Andrew sat in the middle of his bed, his arms outstretched at just the right height for the taking into his father's arms. "DaDa."

"Little man, your smile is worth everything. Every morning I wake up so surprised with how blessed I am."

By the time Dev and Andrew arrived in the kitchen, Dan was drinking fresh coffee, and Lily was chowing down on eggs, bacon, and a toasted muffin.

"Where did you get the food?" Dev poured a large cup of coffee and grabbed Andrew's cereal from the cabinet.

"I was up early so I went to the store. You also have milk, and there's some fruit in the refrigerator." Dan took another drink from his mug.

While picking up a piece of bacon, Dev began to eat while preparing Andrew's cereal. Lily was unusually quiet. Dan was silent. As Dev placed Andrew in his chair, he studied both of them. Finally, he stopped. "What? What the hell is going on?"

"Lily has a theory," Dan said frankly. "You need to listen to her."

Dev smiled. "Ah. So, we haven't officially stopped our Jessica thing yet?"

Lily looked up, wiping a muffin crumb from the side of her mouth. She scrunched her face. "No, Mr. Smarty. Do you want to hear what I have to say or not?"

"Sure. Why not?"

Lily finished her bite, and took a drink of her glass of milk. "Something has been nagging at me. It's just bothering me that Margot/Gilda didn't kill Dr. Fleischman."

Dev began to spoon feed his son. "Yes, I know."

"Margot didn't kill Dr. Fleischman," Lily repeated.

Dan nodded. "Right. Margot didn't kill Dr. Fleischman."

Dev dropped the spoon down. His irritation was showing. "Fine. My hearing is still pretty good. I heard both of you."

"So, why didn't she?" Lily waved her muffin in the air. Her smugness began to put thoughts in Dev's head. His forehead creased.

"Maybe she loved him?"

Lily waved the muffin back and forth. "She supposedly abused his daughter. Laurel seems nice, but then she doesn't. I felt threatened by just her words."

"She's an attorney. They talk like that. Her father didn't know about the abuse, right?" Dev's question made Dan and Lily exchange glances. He couldn't share his suspicions about Laurel so diversion was his only move.

"Did it really happen?" Dan added his question into the mix. "Maybe it was just a girl who didn't like sharing her father with a new mommy."

"We have to go back to the reports to see if a teacher saw bruising, etc." Dev began to feed Andrew again. "You should have all those reports in the office."

Lily's thoughts returned to her original problem. "But she didn't kill him. She killed all those other men. Maybe she offered them a cut when they were developing their web of prescription drug trafficking? Maybe they said no, and that sealed their fate? And where does Bernard Notte come into play? You need to interrogate him."

Andrew fought with his father for authority over the spoon. Finally, Dev surrendered to the independent toddler. "I don't even know where the blasted man is, Lily."

"Does this all mean that Dr. Fleischman did participate? Maybe those weren't all forged prescriptions?" Dan asked Lily and not his friend. Dev was in his own battle with a small child who wanted control over his food and was reaching for a piece of bacon. Andrew, successful, smiled as he ate the slice. *Wow, kids sure do want to have control over their world at an early age.*

Dev took a slow drink of coffee and shifted his eyes from his wife to his friend. "We've been looking at this all wrong, then? I'll admit that maybe those two thugs weren't chasing them that night. Honestly, traffic footage doesn't show one ounce of proof. I'll even admit that maybe Gilda didn't hire them to chase you either. Maybe it was to send us on a wild goose chase. I even have crazy thoughts that Laurel may be the one who had those goons follow you, Lily. But I've been wondering why the daughter goes along with all of this if she is involved. She's a defense attorney."

Lily laughed. "Yes, for some very unsavory people, right? Can you remain clean when you're defending some of the worst offenders? I looked over her case lists and most of them involved drugs. Besides, you don't have conclusive evidence that Laurel and her father were followed over to our house, do you? We just took their word for it. Maybe they wanted to set me up, or you."

Dev kept his own thoughts and conclusions to himself. "Maybe you're overthinking all of this? Maybe it is just as it is, Lily, nothing more? All that is left is the paperwork, honey." *I'm saying that as a fact, but I have this feeling it isn't. Maybe she'll just believe me and let it go this time? Holy Moly, when has she ever done that? I need to wrap this up first before she--*

Thankfully for Dev's own preservation, Lily nodded. "Perhaps. If you could call your father to come over that would be great, honey. I do need to rest." She grabbed her plate and walked over to the sink. "I need to get the house back in order too."

Dev and Dan studied her. Dan patted Dev on the arm. "You know, as soon as we leave she's going to be in there going over every piece of evidence and every file."

To his chagrin, Dev agreed. "I wouldn't expect anything less from her. But, I hate to admit it, she's got me thinking. Lily may be right again. Something has been wrong with this entire thing. One thing through all of this has been bothering me. I told Lily I would search for her forever. Why didn't the doctor who claimed he was so much in love do the same?"

Dan took another sip of coffee. "Dev, you know your heart. You have a point. Why did the man stop looking for his wife?"

As soon as Dev and Dan pulled out of the driveway, they saw Lily's form pass by the office windows. Apparently, she sat down in the chair.

"That didn't take long," Dan said.

"Did she tell you why she started thinking about all of this again?" Dev continued to focus on the back of his wife's head.

"Believe it or not, it was something Ari told her about how she only sees what she wants to see, not how things are sometimes." Dan saw a change in his friend's face, but instead of addressing it, he preferred to allow Dev to think about the statement.

Instead of more discussion, Dev drove down the street. *She's looking at that darn board and trying to figure out what she missed.* His only hope was if there was something to be found, he found it before she did. *Lily always figures out who a person is. It may take her a while, but she always does. And she's never wrong.*

Chapter Thirty-Four

"Mrs. Parrot, do you remember where the doctor met Margot? Did he ever talk about it?"

"Lily, honey, are you sure you don't want some of my apple crumble?" The neighbor passed the dessert under the pregnant woman's nose.

Lily measured about two inches with her fingers. "Maybe this much?"

Her neighbor smiled. "And would you like a cold glass of milk to go with it?"

"Yes, please," Lily answered quickly. When she was with the former school teacher, she always felt like a student. She sat up a little straighter, she answered very properly. She respected and liked Yvonne Parrot.

In a few minutes, Mrs. Parrot came back out to the porch with a tray filled with a glass of milk, a glass of iced tea, and two pieces of apple crumble topped with ice cream. "I warmed it up a little. You have to have vanilla ice cream on top, don't you?"

Lily nodded quickly in appreciation of how her neighbor addressed a dessert.

"Now, you were asking about how the doctor met Margot, right?"

"Yes, ma'am." Lily took her first bite and savored the apple morsel. She closed her eyes, even thinking she could see a bit of heaven. It tasted like Kansas City in the fall. The apple orchards all provided tours and featured festivals of all kinds. They also had the best apple cider, cold or hot. It was wonderful how the taste of apples and cinnamon could take you home in one bite.

"Oh my," Mrs. Parrot exclaimed after her first bite. "That is good. Well, I believe he met her at a conference."

Lily clapped. "I knew it! She cultivated those doctors at large conferences. When she went missing, the doctor was at a conference in London. This all makes sense."

Yvonne reached over to touch Lily's hand. "Dear, are you feeling well? I know you get a little flush when you're eating a dessert, but you aren't making much sense."

"Yes I am," Lily admitted confidently. "He met her at a conference. He was gone at a conference when she went missing. It's beginning to make sense. I just have to figure out if his daughter was involved."

"Laurel? She was such a sweet girl. She just didn't like Margot, and you already have confirmed that her stepmother didn't like her."

Lily licked her spoon clean, avoiding Mrs. Parrot's statement. "Where was Laurel when Margot went missing? Was she at the house?"

"Oh, heaven's no. The girl always stayed with friends when her father was out of town. They had that housekeeper, but she couldn't keep track of that girl. Laurel could be sweet, but she was a little wild. Margot didn't want to be seen around that school as a mother figure. I believe Laurel was staying with her friend Bridget. Those two were inseparable. I saw them at school every day. It was such a shame when Bridget died."

"Bridget died? When and how?" Lily asked quickly.

"It was a drug overdose." Mrs. Parrot grasped her hands as she recalled. "It was so sad. You know, I remember now. It was poor Laurel who found her."

Lily gulped. "Laurel found her when?"

"Well, it wasn't too long after Margot disappeared. The girls went hiking for the weekend. Teenagers always want something new to do. Bridget and her entire family hiked, and Laurel wanted to try it out so the girls went out on their big adventure. But it turned into a tragedy."

"A drug overdose? Did the high school have a problem back then?" Lily probed.

Mrs. Parrot closed her eyes. A small tear fell. When she finally looked at Lily, she dabbed at more. "We did seem to have a problem. The police were involved, but no one could ever figure out how the drugs were coming into the school. One investigator walked the school's halls for three weeks in an attempt to discover who the inside dealer was. It made me sick to think that one of the staff might be dealing drugs to our children."

Lily finished off her treat. She stood up to gather the dishes. "Let me do this. I need to move." Her bruising made her more stiff than usual. Of course, her neighbor argued, so they both walked into the house. "You know, it might not have been a member of the staff. It could've been one of the students." *It could've been Laurel. She had direct access to drugs, didn't she?*

"You know, Lily, one detective did think that, but he could never get the goods on anyone. One thing is for sure, Bridget's death devastated Laurel. She never returned to school. I believe she had a private tutor until she went off to college."

Lily just smiled. There was no need to worry Mrs. Parrot about anything. *How could you go back after you killed your best friend? But did the doctor know? Why do I have all these questions and not one blasted answer? Lord, I need answers.*

Returning from the kitchen, Lily wandered into the living room and to its wall of photos. The assorted frames were a legacy of Mrs. Parrot's family, from a tin type to black and white, and then to color portraits. Yvonne followed her neighbor.

"My family is always with me," she murmured.

"I understand completely." Lily saw photos of Mrs. Parrot's students, photos of teacher friends, and of course, her family. Family wasn't just blood. It was a shared connection. She had that with all of Dev's friends. And they had it with her. "We are blessed."

Yvonne placed a comforting arm around Lily. "When it gets colder in a few weeks, I'll come over to your house so you don't have to get out. I'll bake you a few favorites. You just have the tea kettle on."

"That sounds like a great deal to me. I need to get back before Andrew does his grandfather in, but thank you for the apple crumble and for the information." Lily kissed the woman on the cheek and walked slowly back to her own home. Jack and Andrew were playing on the floor with building blocks.

"I think he's going to be an engineer," Jack said proudly. His daughter-in-law looked tired, but she feigned a lovely smile. "Why don't you take a nap? We're having a good time, and I have nothing else to do."

Lily grimaced as she accidentally hit the side of the couch. "Really? I do need a break. That trip was more than I needed." *And I need to do more thinking.*

Jack handed his grandson a blue block. Andrew whacked the other blocks creating a construction disaster. "Oh, Dev called. He's in some meeting and might be late tonight. He also said he didn't want you doing anything about anything. Does that make sense to you?"

Lily shrugged. "Yes, he's being motherly again." *Or he knows something.* Slowly, she pulled herself up the stairs to their bedroom. Lily laid down on the bed and opened her phone to see a new text from Dev. She sighed. He just said to do nothing. *Really? How do you know I'm doing anything?*

Lily steadied her phone on her stomach and went through her emails. There were several for future dates at the vineyard. One bride was reserving for the last open weekend in May. Another contact expressed interest in a holiday party the first of December. *The aunts are going to have a great fourth quarter, hopefully with me.* She needed rest, but she didn't need sleep so it was the perfect time to delete some unnecessary phone calls. She came across Laurel's number and pressed the call button. *Lord, we can't tell my husband I just did this.*

"Laurel, this is Lily Pierce. I just wanted to touch base and see how you were. Give me a call if you can. Take care."

Before Lily placed the phone next to her on the bed, it rang. It was Laurel. "Thank you for returning my call so quickly."

"No problem, Lily. Thank you for checking on me. I'm surprised to hear from you. How are you?"

"I'm good. Getting more and more pregnant." Lily's nervous giggle masked some of her fear, fear of the problems she was having carrying this baby and of the questions she needed to ask of the woman on the other end of the line. *And are you surprised to hear from me because you thought I'd be dead by now?* "Laurel, how are things for you and for your dad?"

"Well, everything seems to be back to normal here in Charlottesville. My kids are good, and my husband has been super responsive to the fear I've been having because of Margot."

"That's why I'm calling. I hate for you to relive this, but what did your dad do when you told him about Margot's abusive side?"

"He didn't know at the time. She threatened me. The police talked to me because someone from school had called them, but I told them I'd fallen off my bike. I didn't tell anyone the truth, well my friend Bridget knew. I think she told her mother. I spent so much time over there. Their house was like my own sanctuary."

That makes sense. The day Margot went missing, the housekeeper was taking her day off. At Margot's request. "Your friend, Bridget? Do you still keep in contact with her?"

"No. My friend is dead."

Lily bit her lip. *Should I? Of course I should.* "Oh no. Was it recent?"

There was silence on the other side of the phone. "No. She died when we were in high school. Why do you care?"

Lily snapped her fingers. Laurel's biting tone enlightened the amateur detective. *Gotcha!* "I'm so sorry. I just thought if your friend was around, these are the times you really need them. By the way, how is your dad?"

There was a pause again as though Laurel was calculating her next response. "I really don't know, Lily. He has left for a conference. Even though he's retired, he was asked to be a speaker. I can't believe with all that is going on that he actually went, but the FBI allowed it."

Lily patted the bed beside her. *What? Really?* "Where's the conference?"

"He said he was heading to the Miami vicinity. He also said he gave all the contact information to one of the agents."

"Where's he staying?" Lily asked quickly.

"Lily, I don't know," Laurel answered sharply. She cleared her throat and her voice softened almost to a whisper. "He seemed very secretive, but I just thought he was somehow being protective of me. Margot's re-entry into the world has been a lot to take in."

"I am sorry about that." Lily answered the way she used to reply to a nervous mother on her daughter's wedding day. *Just kill them with kindness. Holy Moly, poor choice of a word, Lily!* She rubbed her belly and felt another bruise. *Is this a new one?* "I bet it was hard for you while they were dating."

"Actually, they had a whirlwind romance. He met her at a conference in Kansas City. She was acting as one of the event coordinators. They flew back and forth around the nation, and I only met her a month before they married. They had a small ceremony at the club. That was it. Margot moved in with three pieces of luggage. She was never a mother to me."

"Amazing. I'm so sorry, Laurel." Lily was expressing her concern, but her thoughts were back in Kansas City. *A second gotcha!*

"I'm okay now. I have a wonderful family, and I made sure my kids had the childhood I didn't. But I have great memories of my mom. That carries me through."

Lily heard the hitch in Laurel's voice. *You are such a good actress. I hope your kids didn't have the childhood you had!* "Laurel, I'll let you go. I just want you to take care of yourself, and keep enjoying your family."

"You too, Lily. Take care, and I really do mean that."

Lily grimaced. *Laurel is a real piece of work. Dev thinks she talks like a lawyer? She speaks like a sociopath!* As soon as Lily ended the call, she made another call. She needed a few more pieces of the puzzle. "Gretchen, it's Lily, are you there and not just picking up?"

She knew her friend. In seconds Gretchen was answering. "I'm here. I was, and am taking an afternoon bubble bath."

Who does that? "Fine, whatever, I need some information. About twenty some years ago, there was a medical convention in Kansas City. Supposedly, there was an event planner by the name of Margot. Do you remember that name at all?"

Lily heard the splashing of water. "Let me think. It's lucky for you that I remember almost everything. I did forget to buy beer for Daniel the other day, but that's just a glitch. Beer isn't my style, but the man just seems to love it. He suggested we use it in the shower the other day on my--"

"Stop. Gretchen, please focus," Lily interrupted. *I'm not sure I like her being in love. The visuals right now are making me a little ill.*

"What's the last name?"

"I don't know. She married a doctor named Fleischman from Virginia. They actually used to own our house."

"Dr. Leland Fleischman! What a personality and such a flirt. We drank Cosmopolitans at a downtown hotel. It's the bar with the red wallpaper. We had the Sheldon wedding there. You had large bouquets of pink peonies on each table. The doc had rented a Jaguar. Who rents a Jag?"

As Gretchen continued talking, Lily was wondering again why this woman and she were friends. The woman was describing the car, how the blue was the same color as the shoes she was wearing. *Gretchen, focus! Wait, who rents a Jag? Someone who wants to draw attention to himself? Ari would do that.*

"Wait, Gretchen, did you say he put the moves on you?"

"Of course, dear. But I think he was trying to make someone jealous. She was a redhead."

Lily pushed off her cushioned pillows. "That's her. Margot had, has red hair."

"Oh, I remember her now," Gretchen admitted. "She

was an event planner for one of the doctors. The man had invented some synthetic drug, and was intent on signing up as many doctors as he could. The drugs were going to be cheap. But not many doctors were taking the bait."

"Why say that?"

"There was something slimy about the guy. First, his name was very European, but I think he was from Mexico. Then my doctor friend, Dr. Percy Wilton, I play tennis with him occasionally at the club, insisted on seeing the clinical studies. He never did get those results. The doctor was very vague, and that redhead was there with him every step of the way. I could tell they were closer than just co-workers. You know I know those kinds of things."

"I know," Lily mumbled. "Anything else?"

"I could put you in touch with Dr. Percy. He's retired now, but he might have some notes, or remember something. Are you investigating a case without me?"

"I wouldn't ever do anything like that without you," Lily lied. "I'm just laying here being pregnant."

"Good. You need to take care of yourself and that little girl. Sorry, but I have to get back to my bath, dear. My water is getting tepid, and all my bubbles are disappearing. Tell Mr. Delicious hello, and give that sweet little baby boy a kiss from Auntie G. Ta."

A click ended the call before Lily could say any cute goodbye words. "Ta. I hate ta."

Dev is not going to believe what I've discovered! Yes, he will. And then he'll growl.

Chapter Thirty-Five

Agent Devlin Pierce twirled in his chair as if he were a grade school kid visiting his father's office. He hated waiting for information, but that's what he needed to do right now. After one full rotation, he saw a body in the chair across from his desk.

"Are you pretending you're on an amusement ride?"

Dev stopped abruptly. "JT, what are you doing here?"

"Just checking in and wondering if I can crash in your guest room downstairs for a couple of weeks."

Dev was surprised to see JT in his Navy uniform. "Have you been at the Pentagon?"

"Yep. I was called in, actually debriefed on something very hush hush. What's wrong with you?"

I hate how they all know me so well. "I'm waiting on some intel. Your friend, Lily began an investigation into a missing woman, and it's led me in some different directions, actually tying up some loose ends."

"I remember back at that party for Andy you mentioned something."

Dev ignored another new name for his son. "Well, I've found a drug dealer, a contract killer, and a few other crazy things. I'm waiting on a passport search right now and info from the FBI."

JT studied Dev closely. His friend was on edge. He always did get this way when he was just about to close in on the enemy. Dev would have his ducks in a row first. *Yep, the Boy Scout is ready to pounce.* "So you never said if I can stay at your house."

Dev flashed a soft smile. "Of course you can. If I have to leave town, I'll feel good with you being there with Lily and Andrew. She has a doctor's appointment tomorrow."

JT grimaced. "Uh, what kind of doc? One that checks her parts and stuff with the baby?"

Dev laughed. "Yes. But you don't go in with her, you nut."

JT was relieved. "Oh thank God. I'd throw up if I had to see that stuff."

"But blood never bothers you," Dev mumbled. An agent knocked on his door and brought in two files.

"Agent Pierce, you can access the passport and flight information online now, but these files are from the FBI on Bernard Notte."

Dev received the files. "Thanks, Don. I really appreciate you doing this for me. Thank your FBI contact for me. I think they'll get something out of this too if I'm correct about my suspicions."

Don saluted. "Just let me know, and the FBI will be there for you."

JT watched as the other man left the office. "That'll be the first time they've been there for us."

"No, that's the CIA. Remember your part time employer?" Dev began to pour over the file. He flipped one file into JT's direction.

"What am I looking for, boss?"

"Bernard Notte in London about twenty years ago. Maybe he's at the Savoy, or another hotel. Just yell if you see anything around that time. And if someone goofed up and put in the file where he is now. That would be helpful."

"You mean government officials sometimes make mistakes?" JT and Dev shared a laugh and began to search through document after document. Dev turned to his computer screen and pulled up passport records.

It didn't take long to find the information he had suspected was there. "Bingo. Notte was in London at the same time as Dr. Fleischman."

JT weakly cheered him. Now, Dev turned his attention to the bank transfers he had requested. He saw enough in just two pages of documents. One fund was surprising though.

JT looked up. "You're making that face."

"What face?"

JT pointed at him. "That. You make that face when you're disappointed that you've figured out something. You look like you're constipated. You know, like that time you thought the only one who could be the informant was that sweet little Afghan guy who was our guide. You didn't want it to be true, and then you set that trap, and he took the bait. You made that same face. You always do."

"Thank you, Doctor Perceptive." Dev began to pull items out of his desk, throwing them into his leather bag. "Do you have a car?"

"Nope."

Dev stood up quickly. "Bring the files and read in the car. I'll take you home, and then I'm leaving for Miami. I'll have to make a few calls in the car."

JT followed obediently. "I'm good with that. I have a bag down in security. Do you think you can get it for me?"

Dev stopped quickly in the hallway. "What exactly did you have in the bag?"

"It is just a souvenir."

Dev glared. "What kind of souvenir and from where, SEAL?"

"I can't tell you, but it's a very big knife that has a very big curve."

"JT." Dev continued to walk briskly. JT continued to talk, attempting some explanation that included bartering for a motorcycle and an extraction by a chopper on a rooftop in Turkey. *And I don't miss that world one bit.*

Don ran up to Dev as he hit the elevator button. "Agent Pierce, we just got a hit on that attorney's number from your home phone. Do you know what that's all about?"

JT began to laugh as Dev lowered his head. "Yes. She's at it again."

"Excuse me?" The man was confused at the special agent's answer.

"Nothing." Dev looked up. "Thank you. I understand what is going on."

As Dev's hand reached again for the button, the agent stopped him. "And, we have no concrete evidence, but they did suspect the teenager. Also, we've scheduled an agent to visit the Cardle home this afternoon. The mother was more than willing to talk about her daughter's drug overdose."

"Suspected overdose," Dev countered. "Thank you. Text me with the information. I'll be heading out." Finally, the elevator door opened. Once inside, JT glanced at his friend. That nervous muscle in Dev's jawline was pulsing.

"This is some serious stuff," he murmured.

"Yes, it is. You're going to have to act like a junkyard dog to keep my wife safe, and no one that is an outsider comes near her. Understood, SEAL?"

JT saluted. "Yes, sir. No one will pass." Dev only nodded. This was serious stuff indeed.

On the drive home, JT confirmed Bernard Notte's trip to London, and that he stayed in the same hotel as Doctor Fleischman. Bernard had also visited with the doctor in Virginia, Kansas City, Las Vegas, Mexico City, and in Venezuela over the years. There were also visits to the Caymans. The United States government was continuing its pursuit of the funds in Notte's accounts in the Caribbean.

As Dev opened the front door of his home, he turned back to his guest. "So the beginning of Notte's relationship with Fleischman was either in Kansas City or London."

Lily greeted them with cheering and answered instead. "I knew it. I knew it. Notte was involved, and the doctor was also trafficking drugs! Supposedly, his daughter wasn't involved, but I'm more convinced than ever that she was, or she knew more than she's told us."

JT and Dev stood silent. "Hi honey, we're home." Dev kissed her on the cheek. "You don't need to call Laurel ever again. You will not call her ever again." He hugged her and ran up the stairs.

"Hi JT."

"Hey, Lily. What's new?" He dropped his bag on the floor and grabbed Andrew in his arms. "How's Andy?"

"Andrew is fine. What's Dev doing, and why did you just drop your bag here in the house? And what is up with the instructions?"

JT smiled widely. "I'm staying in your guest room for a couple of weeks. Daddy said it was okay, and I can watch over you while he's gone. Laurel is not a good person. How's that for a recap?"

Instead of complaining, Lily began to dance around the house. "I knew it. I'm not thrilled that he knew about my call, but I got it right again."

JT planted himself in one of the oversized chairs. "I'm happy you're happy."

Lily planted her hands on her hips as she faced him. "What is going on?" She watched as Dev brought down his own "to go" bag. "And you're headed to Miami, right?"

Dev was jolted. "How in the blazes do you know that?"

"Because I'm brilliant," Lily said smugly. "And as you apparently know, I talked to Laurel today. Supposedly, her dad left very quickly and secretly to go to some conference or convention in the Miami area. He's running, isn't he? And do you know about her best friend who supposedly saw the abuse in high school and ended up dead from a drug overdose?"

Dev kissed her quickly. "Have I told you how much I love you? Yes, he's running. He has accounts in the islands. He's known Bernard Notte for years, and they've maintained contact. Yes, I know about the drug overdose. We have an agent talking to the friend's mother today. I'm thinking she had to go because she knew too much about Laurel. I have to go, but--"

He kissed his wife one more time. This time he drew her up against him with one arm. Lily touched his cheek. The nagging look had been replaced by a cold dense stare. Her husband was going somewhere dangerous, and this was not the time to push him to validate her suspicions. He had put all the pieces together. "Please be careful."

Dev pulled away. "Of course, always. Now, you will promise me that the SEAL goes everywhere with you. And, I'm going to sound like the worst husband in the world, but you are done with this mystery. It's time to have trained professionals step in." As his voice caught, he whispered, "Lily, please."

Lily couldn't love him more than she did right now at this moment. "I absolutely promise. I can't afford any more bruises. But you have to come back to me. That's the deal."

Dev nodded. He kissed Andrew on the head and on his way out of the house, he kissed Lily one final time. "And JT goes with you everywhere, even the doctor tomorrow. I'll call or text when I can."

Lily remained on the porch watching her husband hurry off into an unmarked car parked at the end of their driveway. She felt JT's hand on her shoulder. "He'll be fine. Don't worry, Sweet Pea."

Lily nodded, but she didn't go back into the house until her tears were dry. She entered the livingroom to see JT heaving Andrew up into the air, and very close to the ceiling.

"JT, those are high ceilings, but watch it. You really are throwing him up there pretty--" It was too late as they both heard the thud. Andrew's laughter became cries.

"I broke your kid."

Lily sat down on the couch, holding her son tightly. A bump was already rising on his head. "He's not broken, but don't you ever do that again."

"But the kid loves it."

Lily rocked her son back and forth. Very quickly, his cries became giggles as he watched JT's funny faces. "The kid loves to pee in his bath water too, but I don't let him drink it."

JT cocked his head. "You do know you can if it means survival. It's good for ray stings too." The highly decorated, brave in battle SEAL shivered to his core as Andrew's mother shot daggers at him with her eyes. "I won't do it again, promise."

Andrew's sobbing ceased, but he held his mother close. Lily watched as JT walked into the kitchen, opened the refrigerator and pulled out a beer.

"Isn't it early for that?" Lily yelled out.

JT was already holding the bottle to his lips as he sat in the chair across from her.

"Not really. My body is still in another time zone. What are we eating tonight?"

"I fixed a meatloaf. All I need to do is stick it in the oven."

JT nodded. "If you add mashed potatoes to that, I'm in."

Andrew finally slid off Lily's lap to find his building blocks and tow truck pull toy. "We could go ahead and have an early dinner, and yes, I can fix mashed potatoes."

JT stood up. "We could and we should. I'll get that oven preheated right now. You can oversee my KP duty."

"JT," Lily called after him. "You usually don't just show up out of thin air. Well, you do, but there's some motivation. What's up?"

JT returned. "The priest contacted me. I really came for him, but it seems as though I need to be here for you too. Should we invite Dan to dinner?"

"That's a good idea. I'll call Dev's dad and have him over too." Lily rose from the couch and plopped back down. She held her stomach.

JT quickly was at her side. "What was that?"

"I'm having this weird cramping. I think I was just too active. I fell on the sand during that whole Margot thing on the beach."

JT pushed a pillow behind her back. He picked up another pillow and placed it on the chair in front of them, lifting Lily's legs on top of it. "You mean the part where she had a gun on you? You have to stop doing this. And, don't worry about Devlin Pierce. I've seen him in tough jams, and he's the best at getting out of them safely."

"I just think I can help, and frankly, I can't even help myself or my own husband."

"You make Dev crazy." JT chuckled. "That's the part I like about your investigating. It's good for him to be a little unsettled. But, you can't keep scaring the snot out of him either. Let us, literally, do the heavy lifting."

"I know." Lily's lament created silence in the room except for Andrew's made-up words he recited as he marched around. Her thoughts were with her husband. "JT, what is Dev headed into?"

"I imagine he has plenty of backup, and if he is going after that doctor then it won't be too dangerous. Don't worry about it."

Lily crossed her eyes in protest. "When you all say don't worry, I do. I've learned that much about every single one of you, even Paul." Paul was the most settled of the bunch and married the longest to dear Lynn. Lily had heard the man explain to his wife that their daughter would be absolutely fine at college. He said she had a good head on her shoulders, and nothing bad ever happened away from home if you'd provided your children with the needed skills. *Paul is the smoothest talker of all of them. He could even give Ari and Jackson a run for their money.* He didn't tell his wife he'd put a tracker on their daughter's cell phone.

JT's phone received a text. He picked it up and smiled. "The priest is in, and he's bringing ice cream. He says you didn't have any in the freezer."

The oven buzzed. JT was more than happy to interrupt the conversation with Lily. He patted her hands and got up. "Lily, I don't know how you did it in such a short time, but you know too much about all of us." He left her side before she could answer and headed to the kitchen. *We've all lost our touch. Lily reads us like a book, more like a comic strip.*

Lily glanced around the table a few hours later. Jack Pierce held his grandson on his lap. He was offering the child another helping of mashed potatoes, and Andrew sighed after he swallowed. As her son swallowed, sighed, and then begged for another bite, JT and Dan laughed harder and harder. They clapped when Andrew yelled for more.

"Remember that time we had steaks and lobster at the camp for Christmas, and Dev made that same exact noise?" Dan asked of his brother in war.

JT nodded while finishing off another beer. "I was just thinking about that. I think he ate more than me that day."

"Well, it had been a long walk." Dan's smile faded. Lily winked at him in hopes of making that smile reappear, but it didn't. She saw him thinking, perhaps dark thoughts, or memories that should remain lost and distant. She kicked JT under the table and directed his attention to the priest.

"Danny, let's get that ice cream. And who is in for coffee and pie?" JT stood up and headed over to the kitchen counter, followed by his cohort.

"Pie? No one said anything about pie," Lily said.

"Didn't I tell you? I brought vanilla ice cream and this nice little pecan pie here." Dan lifted a box holding the dessert.

"Oh my," Lily sighed. "That looks delicious. I would like that and the ice cream, please. No coffee for me."

"We do have decaf," JT commented.

Lily sighed again, but for a different reason. "Geez, Jack, they know my kitchen better than I do."

Jack Pierce agreed. "I'll have decaf. How about it, Lily?"

"I am a little cold. Decaf would be great, JT."

"Your order is our pleasure." JT bowed deeply from the waist. Andrew smiled and broke out into laughter when Dan curtsied deeply.

"I keep them around for entertainment," Lily whispered to her father-in-law. "They think they are protecting me."

"Seems like all of you are in a winning situation. I, for one, am relieved they're here while Dev is gone."

Lily looked up at the kitchen clock. "I wonder what he's doing right now."

Jack reached for her hand and held it. "He's doing his best. Don't look at the time. It'll make you crazy. Bernie would wear two watches, one with our time, and the other set in Dev's time zone. She couldn't sleep through the night. The news reports were making her crazy with fear. I turned the television off more than once so she couldn't watch. I took her on a trip to the Bahamas hoping that would help her stop worrying."

"But she didn't, did she?"

Jack shook his head. "Nope. Lily, I've never told anyone, but a part of me believes Bernie gave up fighting cancer so she could protect her son."

Lily choked back tears. "I understand."

Dan arrived with their pie, the ice cream topping it. "There's no tears when eating pie. Your other server will have your coffee here in a minute." He patted her shoulder as he returned to his partner in the kitchen.

"I hope Dev's mom has the security shift tonight."

Jack eyed Lily strangely. "The guys said this should be an easy one. What are you thinking?"

"I'm thinking that the easy ones are the ones that trip you up, and our two servers are professional liars," Lily said slowly. She reviewed the pie and took a breath. For once, she really didn't want dessert. She realized that JT, Dan, and Jack were all watching her. If she passed on the pie they'd know something was wrong. She picked up her fork and dived in. Once the sweet treasure entered her mouth, she remained worried, but instantly one piece of her life was suddenly better. *I'm counting on you, Bernie. Protect your son so he can come back to me.*

It was almost two in the morning when Lily heard her cell phone beside the bed. She wasn't sleeping; she was waiting for him to call.

"Are you okay?"

"I knew you wouldn't go to sleep before you heard from me," Dev answered. His voice was low and seemed deeper than usual. Fatigue had settled in.

"But are you safe?"

"Yes. I'm in one piece, and there's no extra holes."

Lily sat up and placed a pillow behind her back. The baby was moving around. "That's not funny, but I'm so happy you called. Did you get him?"

"Yes, honey. That's the good news. The bad news is I'll be gone for a few more days. I'm going along with a FBI task force, but there's absolutely no reason for you to worry about anything. It really is just paperwork and dotting all the *i's*."

"But I have this feeling you'll have an amazing tan when you get home." Lily rubbed her belly to calm the baby down. *Little girl, I'm beginning to read you like a book.*

"I love how intelligent my wife is. It's late. You and I both need some sleep. I want you to text me after the doctor's visit tomorrow. I mean it."

Lily could hear the concern in his voice. "I'm fine. This baby is just different. Girls can be difficult."

Dev laughed. "That means I'm in for an even bumpier ride."

"What? I don't get it."

"Nothing, honey, really. I will call you when I can tomorrow once we get settled. I love you." Dev began to end the call.

"Dev, is Laurel involved?"

Her husband answered slowly. "I can't say yet, but we do think she's involved in more ways than one. She is under surveillance. Once she knows her father is in custody, it could get messy. You do nothing, but take care of yourself and that baby. Kiss Andrew for me. Goodnight, honey."

"Goodnight, baby." She held the phone for a few minutes before turning off the lamp and sliding down into the sheets on her husband's side of the bed. As she smelled his scent on the pillow, some of her fears instantly dissipated. The baby within her quieted, and within minutes she was asleep. In South Miami, Dev Pierce was headed to an unmarked van. He'd be on a plane headed to the islands within the hour. He only hoped that Lily would actually do what he asked.

Chapter Thirty-Six

By the time Devlin Pierce reached Grand Cayman, he and one of the FBI agents specializing in bank transfers, had followed every dime of Dr. Fleischman's money. Many times, the transfers came from an account in Kansas City, Missouri. Dev was familiar with the bank; Lily had used the same financial institution. There were other deposits from an account in Belgium. The DEA's unmarked private plane landed near customs where British and American officials stood waiting to wave them through.

In a secluded, secure area, the other agents and Dev changed into fresh shirts. One man chose to shave, but Dev kept his almost three-day shadow. His hair was longer, well longer for him. His eyes were dark from lack of sleep. He was tanned from their days on Anna Maria. He looked more like he used to, before Lily, Andrew, and one more child on the way. He looked more like a drug dealer.

Before they exited the building, Dev added a gold bracelet and rolled up his sleeves. He placed black designer sunglasses on his face. As he exited to the waiting limousine, he became his hidden persona. He was an independent facilitator checking on one of his traffickers. In predatory fashion, he smiled at a very attractive woman waiting for her hotel shuttle. He lowered the glasses to offer a wink then returned them to hide his eyes. The smile faded once he entered the vehicle. He had noticed the two men to the left of the tourist, and they were watching him. The darkness overtook him. It had to be this way if he was going to be successful. It would just be his luck to run into a former contact.

As they traveled through Georgetown, Dev watched as tourists were arriving from the cruise ships. Many were smiling, some laughing. Dev realized that Lily gave him laughter and light. In past relationships, he never spent the night with a girlfriend, preferring to leave before a shared sunrise. He'd never really talked with a lover, but he couldn't get his wife to be quiet to save her soul. In fact, Lily picked the darndest times to talk while in bed. And to laugh. She made him laugh more than any other human being in his entire life. When she snorted, they laughed even harder. He craved returning to her, to just sit on the couch and rub her feet, or to just lay his head on her growing belly. She played with his hair; he waited for the baby to kick. She gave him unconditional love. He missed his son, and he couldn't wait to have bubbles kicked up on him from the bath water. But right now, he had to forget them. He was not that man today.

A meeting had already been scheduled at the bank. They offered their identification, every piece a fake so good that embassy officials wouldn't catch them. Dev led the group. He was the man in charge. He gave the number of one of the bank accounts.

"You are not the doctor. He is in our room with his safety deposit box."

Dev offered a nod as though he knew. He smiled and blandly answered, "He is my associate, and he's also my physician."

"Ah, that explains it. I'll take you to him, but your associates must remain here in the main lobby."

Dev waved off the other men and followed the very proper official. This was a bank procedure, but Dev looked around the area memorizing the location of each security camera. Something didn't feel right.

The official opened the door to a small room. Dev stood in the hall facing "the doctor".

"You didn't wait for me, doctor. Hello Bernard." Dev finally removed his sunglasses and stared into the eyes of Bernard Notte who was busily sifting through pouches of diamonds. "Are you looking at the box for Fleischman or Miserli, or perhaps that belonging to a certain woman?"

Bernard Notte was numb. Several diamonds slipped through his fingers and flowed onto the table near the deposit box. His hands were shaking as he smiled nervously. "I, I didn't realize you would get here so quickly," he stammered.

Dev turned to the bank official. "You can go now, and I'd like my men brought here as soon as possible, if not, I am very prepared to shoot you where you stand."

As the man ran away, Dev entered the room. "Notte, you just couldn't take the deal the government offered you and live a pseudo-normal life, could you?"

"Agent Pierce, I just couldn't. When I realized that you had Dr. Miserli in custody, and figured out Fleischman's job in all of this, I knew all these diamonds were just sitting here waiting for me."

Dev sat nonchalantly on the edge of the table. He picked up one of the wayward jewels and looked closely at it. "I'm assuming you paid off Margot/Gilda in diamonds. You also set up the accounts for Fleischman. I always knew there was way more to you. If you had just waited a couple of years."

Notte threw the pouch down into the box. "Do you know where the government wanted me to live? Butte, Montana. How would I survive in Montana?"

Dev laughed. "Oh, I don't know. Maybe you could get a job as a barista? You could mess up everyone's name on their coffee cups. You could've been a cowboy cleaning out horse stalls." The other agents magically appeared at the doorway.

"I never liked you," Bernard Notte said smugly. "I don't like your little wifey either. She's a nosy b--"

Dev stood before Notte could finish the word. "Step away from the table and put your hands behind your back."

Notte smirked. "You have no jurisdiction here."

Dev pointed past his cohorts to two local policemen and two other suited gentlemen. "No, but they all do. You'll be transferred by the Brits back to London where INTERPOL, and a certain agent will be interrogating you this time. The agent is a very complicated man, one who won't take forgetfulness as an answer. He knows you very well, and if you don't give him what he wants, he mentioned something about a bad art deal in Jordan that you profited from a few years back. He'd be happy to take you back for trial, or maybe he'll just deposit you on the doorstep of your very disgruntled old client. You do have one way to make it just a little easier on yourself. You can tell me about the other deposit boxes, and who they belong to and when they were established."

"Why would I want to do that? What's it going to get me?"

The two officers entered and began to take custody of Notte. Dev nodded at them. "Well, you may not end up in Butte. You'll travel in comfort to London and then to Lyon. You'll be busy for some time outlining your network, your network's trafficking paths, who paid Margot, how you cultivated all those doctors around the nation to push your synthetic poison, and then after all of that, you can come back to the United States."

Notte shrugged as he was cuffed. "I'll take my chances with the Europeans."

The officers began to walk him by Dev, when Pierce stopped him. He looked down at Notte. *How did a lovely lady like Mrs. Notte end up having a son like this?* He came within inches, choosing to whisper. "Did I mention I'm meeting Javier after I leave here? I'm sure he'll be very surprised to hear about all the money and diamonds sitting in this bank, all under your control."

"I didn't do all of this, Pierce. You know that. You tell him, and I'm a dead man," Notte screamed. "It's not true. I'm not the one with access to all of this. I just swept in to grab it up before--"

"Before she came and took it for herself?" Dev folded his arms and sat back down on the table. He was the one in control now. "You can take your chances with the Europeans. I'm sure Ari will love to see you again after that entire Khalid episode. That terrorist and you were pretty tight. I'll tell Javier you said hello. He'll be sad when he learns you were here, right here, and you didn't stop in and say hello or goodbye." Dev frowned in feigned sympathy.

"Fine. Don't send me to the Europeans. I'll tell you."

"Bernard, that boat has sailed. As you so aptly explained, I have no jurisdiction here."

"Pierce, if I tell our government how it all began, you won't tell Javier, will you?"

Dev's half-smile comforted Notte. "You tell us how it all began, and this time, we want everything. I don't want just your part, and more information about your international smuggling. I want new stuff. I want the labs where the drugs were and are created. I want the mules. I want the doctors and their practices around the nation. I want to know who gave the orders to Margot/Gilda and how you got the diamonds to whomever paid her." Dev pointed down at the diamonds. "And I want to know who you were stealing those from. You probably know Miserli has been arrested. Margot is finished. That was a nice touch giving us information on them so you'd have enough time to get down here and away from your handlers before Fleischman could." *Someone else is running this show and those diamonds belong to them.*

"And then you won't tell Javier?"

What a miserable little man! Butte would be too good for him. "I'll tell him you're in federal custody, and you won't be available for a very long time. How's that?"

"Deal." Notte bowed his head in defeat.

"Good," Dev answered. "You'll be going with the British, but one of our guys will go with you. "We'll be seeing you soon after INTERPOL is through with you."

Notte yelled every profanity he knew as he left the room as a British official greeted Dev. "And now what is on your plate, Agent Pierce?"

"I need to see a man about a woman."

"You'll enlighten me on the way there?"

Dev stopped. "You won't be going with me. Javier doesn't like strangers. My men and I will be going. We'll drop by your place on our way off the island."

"Here's a burner to use." One of the FBI agents turned over a phone to Dev once they were in the limo.

He quickly made the call. "Good. I'm glad you answered. Yah, we got him. Now I need to visit with an old nemesis. I need you to make sure Lily doesn't meet up with anyone, not even our neighbor. She is to stay at home. She goes nowhere, do you understand? Good. What? Yes, there's some bleeding when the baby comes out of the birth canal. No, we aren't planning on eating the placenta. Geez. You have your orders, now execute them, SEAL. It could be life or death, and I'm not kidding."

The ride to the house was short. Once through the heavily secured gates, Dev was required to walk alone down the long driveway lined with palm trees and tropical plants. He was greeted by a man dressed in linen from top to bottom, sporting a large straw hat, and with a cigar drooping from his lips.

"Duncan, my good friend. Welcome." He opened his arms wide to envelope the man he knew as a connector for one cartel to another. "It has been too long."

Dev kissed him on one cheek and then the other. "Javier, my friend. It's been since Mexico City."

"Come. It is too warm to stand here in the sun. My grandchild is now a beautiful little girl, thanks to you. She'll celebrate another birthday soon."

Dev removed his sunglasses and looked around the extravagant beach house. There was a living rain forest in the center of the massive open social room. An industrial kitchen was to the right. In front of Dev was a massive wall of glass offering only a view of the water. On the floors were imported tiles, and there was marble on the exterior walls. It was extravagant yet homey. But it was a drug lord's house.

"Javier, I just knew where to take her."

"Exactly. You were the difference in her living or dying. She is only on one medicine now. We will go to Geneva for her checkup next month. I hear there's an excellent specialist in your country I might want to take her to someday." Javier snapped his fingers and a woman appeared with a tray of two glasses and what appeared to be a pitcher of margaritas. "We will sit by the pool." His hand directed to the lanai.

The woman quickly disappeared as Dev and Javier sat at a table. The host poured the drinks. "You can take the man out of Mexico, but you can't take the margaritas out of the man. I have tequila, if you would prefer. Or something else?"

Dev placed his glasses on the table, closer to Javier. The sound of the waves might distort the sound on the microphone placed in the nose piece. "This is fine. You have a beautiful place. I'm happy I dropped by."

Javier slid a drink over to his friend. "Do you really think you can land on this island, and I won't know? I would've been very disappointed if you hadn't visited."

They saluted each other. "Javier, I dropped by a bank too, as I'm sure you know. I've been cheated by that Bernard Notte fellow."

"He is a snake," Javier said flatly.

"On that we agree. I believe the police have him in custody. It may have been something I said."

Javier slammed the table with his hand. "Good for you. Good riddance to him. I heard he was on the island, but I have few men with me. I am virtually retired. Besides, a dead body on the beach is a big thing here. There is hardly any crime, so let the government have him. What do you need from me, Duncan?"

"I need the woman. I need the counselor. He was stealing from her, and I was thinking I could get some of my money back from her." Dev looked directly into Javier's eyes. The man had aged significantly in the years Dev had known him. His granddaughter's illness had directed his attention away from drugs and danger, sending him in his own form of retirement before the man was ready. Surprisingly, Javier was still alive. Most cartel leaders never retired before their deaths.

Javier moved his head back and forth as though he was in a battle of his own conscience. "She is a counselor for many of us. I'm not sure I can give you the information you seek."

"Could I just ask a few questions?" Dev's thin smile made Javier laugh out loud.

"You know, you are the son I never had. Go on. It will be entertainment for an old man."

"Was she brought in by the woman known as Gilda?"

Javier nodded.

"Is she an American? A younger woman?"

Javier nodded again.

"Is she an attorney on the east coast?"

One more nod made Dev smile. "Finally, was she related to a doctor by the name of Fleischman?"

Javier paused and took a drink. His eyes danced over the rim of the glass. "It seems as though you already know all the answers, my friend. You either have become fixated after you were cheated, or I would say you have sources for information that surpass my small brain."

"You know me. I always do my homework." Dev picked up his sunglasses and put them on. He took one more drink. "I should go."

"Duncan, are you not going to tell me you are married?"

Dev froze. Even though it was a warm day with a warm sea breeze, his body went cold and rigid. "I keep my private life private," he growled.

Javier's crooked brow warned Dev. "And you have two lives, I fear. Your secret is in my heart. No one knows. Be happy, Duncan, or whoever you really are. Come back to Grand Cayman sometime and bring your wife to visit an old man who used to do some very bad things."

Dev, in an attempt to relax, smiled as though he wasn't bothered by the realization that his cover for so many years was now blown. "You'd like her, and she'd make you crazy asking you all sorts of questions."

"I like an inquisitive woman. So many women these days are boring. They only worry about how they look, what and when they wax whatever they wax, and if their butt looks too big. Oh, and so many of them want a large bottom now. I'm happy I'm too old for all of that."

Dev saluted him. "I'm pretty sure you're not that old yet. *Adios*, my friend, until we meet again."

Javier raised his glass in the air. "I will look forward to that day when you bring that chatty woman here to meet me." He patted his friend on the back and pulled him closer into his arms. "And you should know that the woman you've asked about is the one who put the hit out on your wife. You were followed here from the airport by two of her men."

Dev nodded knowingly. "Thank you, my friend." He pulled out of the embrace feeling something that his mother had always talked about. It did feel like someone had just walked on his grave.

He nearly ran down the driveway to the waiting car. *What the hell had just happened?* He threw his glasses off into the backseat as he closed the car door. "Call the agents in Charlottesville. She's the one. Let's get the hell out of here and get back home. He knows who I am." *And get me back to my chatty wife.*

Chapter Thirty-Seven

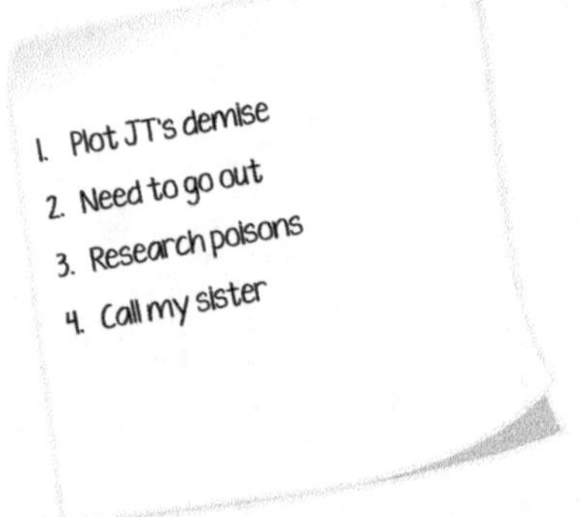

"He's like an armed guard without guns, well his muscles are the guns, but he's intolerant. Yes, that's the word. You must save me." Lily's frantic phone call to her sister was after JT didn't allow her to get fresh air on the front porch or on the back deck for the third time today. Fall was her favorite time of year, and the SEAL was ruining it for her.

Elizabeth laughed heartily. "He's protecting you. Dev must've told him to do it, don't you think?"

"I know, but I don't care. He's making me insane." Lily was alone in her bedroom. She sat in one of the chairs by the window seat, looking longingly out the window into the real world. "I feel like I've done something wrong."

Elizabeth sighed. "It sounds like you've done quite a bit of investigating from what you've been telling me. Why don't you just take a rest? Just be a mom and be pregnant. By the way, how is everything?"

"I'm okay, not great. This little girl is really messing with my brain and my body."

"Ooh, that's not good. That means she'll do the same thing for the rest of your life. I guess my niece will be trouble."

Lily noticed a delivery van pull up in front of their yard. "Hey, I think we have a delivery. This could be more excitement than I've had since my jailer came to live with me."

"I'll let you go, oh, and I'm good to stay with you in January for a few weeks when the baby comes. This is going to be fun. I haven't taken care of you in years, baby sister," Elizabeth commented.

Lily trailed the delivery man longingly with her eyes. She heard the doorbell. "It is a delivery! Beth, I've got to go see what is. Great on January, and tell your husband thanks. I'm going to need all the help I can get."

By the time Lily made it slowly down the stairs, JT had moved whatever it was into the kitchen. "Hey, is that for me? Are those flowers?"

JT turned to face her. He placed his finger up to his mouth and pointed at the pack and play and the sleeping Andrew.

JT foraged through the tropical flowers for any devices of an explosive nature. "Here's your card. It's just signed by the initial J." He handed her the opened white envelope.

"I can't even open my own card? Really? What are you afraid of? Some sort of poison on the glue? You've gone crazy on me, correction, crazier," Lily lashed out. "I can't take this much longer. Can you call Dev? I would like to complain."

JT completely ignored her tirade. Part of his training over the years consisted of hours of verbal abuse while water showered down on you, very cold water. Lily was no match for some of his instructors. He continued his search of each bloom and of the vase. He picked up the item and began to walk through the living room with it.

Lily stopped him midway. "Where are you going with that?"

JT lowered the flowers and with steely eyes soberly announced, "The garage."

"Why?"

"Unless you can tell me someone you know who has that initial, it stays in the garage until someone from the FBI can look it over."

Lily's eyes not only rolled they did somersaults. "Oh my Lord! Get a grip."

JT continued on his mission and texted a contact before he was in Lily's crosshairs again. "Look, you don't know anyone by an initial. It's not your birthday or your anniversary, and your husband is on an op. No family or friends sent these flowers. We have them looked over. Now, hand over the card. That needs to be fingerprinted. I shouldn't have given it to you."

Lily clenched her fist and shook them. "You idiot. Your name begins with a *J*."

JT smiled. "But I have a *T* too."

"What is your name?" Lily didn't smile. She was so tired of her prison guard.

"I come from a proud Navy family, Lily. My name is Jouette Tecumseh."

The disgruntled prisoner cocked her head to the side. "Navy, huh? I'll look them up later."

Lily plopped down on the couch. She pouted. She wanted a good cry, but then JT would think she was really losing it and probably call the doctor again. His call to them this morning was because she had been in the bathroom too long. *I was just hiding from you, Javert, the police inspector on my trail at all times! Ooh, Javert begins with a J. I'm already miserable.*

JT sat across from his friend. She wasn't pleased with him. He hated that. But Dev said to not allow her to go out at all. "Lily, I'm sorry. I just thought about something. My name does begin with a J."

His chuckling seemingly displeased her more. She was finding no humor in his joke. "Did you send them and just forget the T?"

"No." JT figured it was the better part of valor to not say anything more.

"What do you want for dinner?"

"I don't care. Anything that won't make you sick, Sweet Pea."

Lily sighed. "Let's make our own pizza. I would order it, but you probably won't trust the pizza delivery guy either." She emphasized her sarcasm with a stuck out tongue.

JT slapped his legs as he got up out of the chair. "I can live with you hating me as long as you are still healthy and alive, and that little sleeping boy over there gets to grow up." He pointed at Andrew who was napping peacefully on the floor surrounded by two stuffed animals and all his blocks. "I'll check out the refrigerator. We aren't having pizza."

Lily was surprised at his outburst, but she did deserve it. "I'm sorry," she called after him.

His silence made her feel bad so Lily joined him in the kitchen. "Look in the freezer. Is there anything in there?"

JT looked, but nothing sounded appealing. "Hey, how about breakfast for dinner? Andrew would like that. It's easy, and it is a little cool today. What about blueberry pancakes? There's frozen blueberries, oh, and turkey sausage links. That's even healthy."

"God forbid I eat something that's unhealthy," Lily murmured. As JT turned toward her for her approval, she finally smiled at him. "That sounds great. We can start in an hour after Andrew wakes up."

Lily felt some cramping and immediately sat down in one of the kitchen chairs. JT joined her. "Hey, hurting?"

Lily attempted to breathe through it. "A little. I'm sorry I'm cranky. I know you're only trying to keep me safe."

"I'm cramping your style."

"You're keeping me in this house."

JT truly didn't know what to say, but he knew he needed to say something, anything to his friend. "It's a great house."

"That's all you've got, SEAL? That's pathetic." Lily pointed at JT's phone. "Again, call Dev. I need to complain."

JT looked past her and smiled confidently. He knew something she didn't.

"And what do you want to complain to me about?" Dev's low voice brought a smile to his wife's face.

Dev leaned over his wife before she could get up. His arms softly wound around her. As she looked up, he kissed her. "Honey, I'm home."

"I'm so happy. Can I be paroled now?" Her question tugged at his heart.

"Not yet. Hey, does anyone have a large cup of coffee?"

JT acted quickly. "Caffeine or not?"

Dev sat down next to Lily. "Caffeine."

His wife ran her hand over his unshaven face, her fingers lingering on those full lips. She placed a kiss on them. Touching his arms, she looked for bruises but found none. She counted his fingers. He didn't even have a bandaid visible. "I missed you so much. You look like you're in one piece. Did you get the bad guys?"

"We are working on it." Dev looked up to hear the coffee brewing. He needed that caffeine in order to last a few hours at home. He used eye drops to rid the telltale red of insomnia, but he knew Lily was studying him and realizing he was fatigued.

JT looked at his phone. His text had been answered. "Dev, the FBI or Homeland is coming out to check over a delivery. It just came. I have it in the garage."

"Did you check it for the obvious?" JT nodded. "What was it?"

"Flowers," Lily answered. "The card was signed with the initial J."

Dev stood up, touching his wife's shoulder as he passed. "I'll be back. Let me check it out."

Lily leaned her head on her hand. "Great. Now I'm going to have two jailers all because of a flower delivery. What is with this house and flower deliveries? I'm not sure Shakespeare would find humor in that irony."

JT brought Dev's coffee to the table and snapped his fingers in front of Lily's face. "Hey, knock it off. This is serious stuff you got yourself into."

"You were okay last year with the mission to capture Khalid," Lily replied.

"That was different. All of us were there. We knew we could keep you safe. There was no doubt about it, but this time we don't know who or what we're dealing with, and apparently this is in Dev's wheelhouse. He's in charge, Lily, and if he says you stay, then you stay. If he tells me to block the door, I block the door. Now, shut it."

Lily's eyes widened. "Wow. Okay. I'm sorry. Can't a girl feel sorry for herself now and then?"

Before any answer could be said, Dev returned to join them at the kitchen table. He smelled the cup of coffee and took a long drink. "I needed this coffee. Thanks. I'm pretty sure the flowers are just flowers, and I know who sent them and why. A man I know wants me to understand he knows everything about me, and about you."

"That can't be good, can it?" Lily asked.

Dev cocked his head. "Well, he's assured me in his own way that he won't do anything. But he's warning me, or giving me a head's up about someone else. The flower delivery was a nice touch."

"Oh, you mean like Margot's flower deliveries?" Lily's face lit up for the first time in days.

Dev kissed her again. "Exactly, honey. There's a search warrant being delivered within the hour. This should all be over by tonight. Now, I could use some food. What are we having for dinner?"

"Breakfast," JT answered joyfully.

"That sounds great," Dev replied.

"I'm so happy for the both of you," Lily lamented. Beneath the table, she held her lower stomach area. The cramping was continuing. She'd been miserable because of JT's prison sentence, but her concern with this pregnancy was weighing heavily on her. She had a little over two months to go.

After a dinner of blueberry pancakes, eggs, turkey sausage, and melon, Dev and JT overstimulated Andrew while Lily took charge of her kitchen again. She found that cups had been moved, the coffee maker wasn't in the corner where it belonged, and her favorite dish towels weren't hanging on the oven door. She heard her son's giggles and softened. *He loves all the guys, but he misses his daddy. He changes his behavior so much. Hmm, I guess I do too. I'll need to apologize to JT.*

"JT attempted to kill your child," Lily mentioned as she joined them in the living room. With her warm cup of tea in her hand, she sat down in one of the chairs and propped her feet up on the ottoman.

"What did you do?" Dev continued to play peek-a-boo with his son.

"I threw him up in the air."

Dev laughed. "And he hit his head? My dad did the same thing to Jackson. Maybe that's the reason why my brother is the way he is?"

"Could be," JT answered in solidarity.

"You two are so funny," Lily complained. She balanced the cup on her belly. *This is one good thing about being pregnant, a built-in shelf.* Actually, as another area of her body enlarged, she had two more shelves if you count both of them.

Dev and JT exchanged glances. "Has she been like this the entire time?" Dev whispered.

"Something is bugging her."

"You both do know I can hear you, right?" Lily's tone was not lost on either man.

It was the perfect cue for JT to yawn. "You know, I'm pooped. I think I'm going to hit the sack, maybe watch whatever sport is on."

Dev lifted his son into his arms. "And you, little man, need to go to bed too."

"Night, night, J," Andrew called out as he waved.

Lily snorted. "See, you could've sent the flowers, J."

JT chalked a point in the air in honor of Lily's joke. "Goodnight." He headed over to the guest suite and shut the door.

Dev pulled up from the floor and crossed by Lily. He leaned down to kiss her. Andrew repeated his father's motion. "I'll put him to bed. You enjoy the peace and quiet."

Did they have some secret code? Alone, Lily's mind raced. Something was nagging her again, and it wasn't even her concern about the baby. *There's just too many moving parts to this mystery. It has to be simpler than all of this. Doesn't it?*

Eventually, Lily shuffled into the kitchen and filled up a glass with ice and water. She turned off all the downstairs lights except for one and headed slowly up the stairs. *When did these things get so tough to climb?*

She was on her way into the bedroom when she saw Dev departing Andrew's room.

As he joined her, his arm wrapped around her shoulders. They parted as Lily headed into the bathroom. By the time she exited, Dev was laying in bed supposedly watching the Caps play hockey. Both of his eyes were shut.

He looked drained. He was unshaven and so unlike the put together Devlin Pierce she had first met. He didn't look like he worked for the government. *He looks like a bad guy. I've always had a thing for bad boys.*

He stirred as she crawled under the covers and pushed her way over to her favorite pillow, his chest. "I've been thinking."

"That's not unusual for you," her husband mumbled.

"I know there's a lot to all of this Margot mystery, but maybe we are missing the smaller picture. I was thinking that maybe jealousy or revenge played a part--"

Lily continued to talk and talk. Dev heard every other word, and then nothing, until he woke from a playful slap on his chest. "What? I was listening?"

"You were not. I just said I was going to dress Andrew in a pink satin dress for Thanksgiving out at the vineyard."

Dev chuckled. "Well, I missed that part. I just heard Thanksgiving. Besides, I'm not sure if that's his color, honey."

"I'm sorry. You need your sleep, and I can't sleep."

Dev rubbed her back. "The baby?"

"No, Laurel."

Dev's body tensed. "Baby, just forget Laurel."

Lily scooted up excitedly so she could look into his eyes. "I knew it. So, here's what I think happened. The doctor did take the deal from Margot, and he thought they would rule the drug world side-by-side, and she enjoyed her job too much. She didn't want him controlling her, plus Margot had the other doc, the doctor of misery."

"Miserli."

"Same difference," Lily added quickly. "So, Margot had him on the hook, but she needed out of the whole wifey existence. The other doctor didn't participate so she got rid of him. Maybe he threatened to tell the police about their operation. I'm thinking that's what happened back in Kansas City, or she was instructed to do it to warn someone. Anywho, she took off, but not before she needed to get rid of the flower delivery guy. Maybe Laurel saw it? Maybe Laurel had a thing for the petal pusher? Maybe Laurel figured it all out? Maybe, Margot was just the worst mommy dearest. But I think Laurel became involved in all of this when she became an adult. She is a defense attorney. What better way to funnel messages and continue operations with other drug dealers on a national, if not global basis?"

Dev patted her head. "And all that is going on in that pretty brain? Don't you ever get tired?"

"All the time, but I know that I'm on the right track or you wouldn't be diverting my thoughts right now. Your attempt is very weak, by the way. You're off your game, Pierce."

Dev gathered all his energy and flipped his wife on her back. He looked down into a bright, hopeful face, and a woman who looked back at him with only love. "With you, I never play. I take you very seriously."

Lily's breath caught. She touched his face, outlining his jawline. "You do play with me."

"But I do it in a very serious way." The first kiss warned her that even though he needed sleep, he could push through fatigue. The second kiss on her neck was meant to push all of her thoughts out of her mind. He was successful by the time his lips lingered on the hollow of her throat.

"I guess we could talk about this in the morning." That was the only sentence Lily could muster.

"Yes, in the morning. Not, tonight." Now Dev knew why his wife had been so cranky. He would've been miserable too if he had figured it all out, and yet hadn't been allowed to participate in the operation. She was too smart for her own good, and very soft. In a manner of minutes, there were no thoughts and no inches between them.

"I guess I'm right," Lily murmured.

"About what?" He raised his head to look into her eyes.

"I must be right or you wouldn't be distracting me like this."

Dev continued to tenderly capture her lips. "Distraction can be a very, very good thing when done correctly."

Lily giggled. "And you always do the right thing."

"Yes, I do," Dev murmured as he nuzzled his lips against her neck.

"So, you'll tell me in the morning?"

"Yes, in the morning."

Lily played with his hair. "You are certain you'll--"

Dev lifted his body off her and sat up. "You won't be happy until you know everything, and I won't get a minute of sleep or anything else, will I?"

Lily smiled up at him. "Nope."

Dev slapped the bed with his hands. "Fine. I don't know all of the details, but Laurel and the delivery guy had something going, but I don't know if it was a love match or a drug deal. I don't know if Margot brought Laurel in so they could sell to the high school, or if Laurel brought herself in on it. Several people we interviewed described her as a spoiled brat."

"But Mrs. Parrot said she was a sweet girl," Lily commented.

"Mrs. Parrot says everyone is a sweet girl or boy. She's a lovely woman who taught for so many years that those kids were like her family." Dev laid next to his wife and grabbed her hand. "There's still holes, but the doc didn't look for Margot because I think he was part of it, almost from the beginning. Back to Laurel, I think she killed her best friend."

"Bridget, yes."

Dev rolled his eyes. "Yes, smarty. Bridget knew too much. Her mother has her diary and apparently she has some information written in there that the police at the time misunderstood as teenage angst."

"Those are the toughest years." Lily turned to face her husband. "Did she have Andrew and me almost killed on the interstate or did Margot?"

"Laurel. I know that for sure, and don't ask me how. I can't tell you even if I wanted to, which I don't. She has her own little company going with her own thugs. It's actually pretty impressive how she gained her way into the cartel networks, but she controlled some very valuable product. She also had access to a considerable amount of intel through the prison system and her defendants. Actually, it was pretty brilliant."

"If only people like that used their skills for good, wouldn't this be a better world?" Lily whispered.

Dev unlocked his hand and turned inches from his wife. "I wouldn't have a job then."

"We could run the vineyard. You could ride every morning. You could present the wine tastings and help me decorate wedding arbors."

Lily outlined his lips with her finger. Dev kissed it tenderly. "That sounds good. You know, I have a little experience with flowers, and I love to drink wine."

"Then it's settled. When you're done fighting the bad guys, we become winery owners."

Dev slowly nodded. "Sounds lovely, but right now, I don't want to think about wine, weddings, or bad guys and women. I just want you."

"I'm a given, honey. I always will be."

"And I'll always search for you. Always and forever." Dev removed Lily's finger, kissed it and placed her hand on his heart. He pulled her closer and began to kiss her senseless.

There wasn't one item or one list in her thoughts the rest of the night.

Chapter Thirty-Eight

"I can't believe this story didn't make the front page," Lily complained as she read the newspaper a week later. "It has everything that should make it readable--mystery, murder, seduction, money, and drugs."

Dev removed the last plate from the dishwasher. "There's no rock or roll. That may have sent it to the second page." He shook his head as he watched Andrew play with the pepper shaker. He was pretending it was a race car. He handed him a peeled banana.

"Thank you," Andrew responded.

Dev brushed his son's head with his hand. "You are so smart. Our son is the smartest child ever."

Finally, Lily looked up. "No, he isn't. This story isn't on the second page. It's on the sixth! The reporter really got this all wrong. He's writing that the justice department in collaboration with the FBI took Laurel into custody. Really? Her father knew her stepmother wasn't really missing. Well, they made some sort of bizarre agreement. There's no mention of the drugs, Margot's killing ways, the friend's overdose, my car chase, the DEA, nothing--"

"And no mention of you and your successful investigation?" Dev stood over her with arms folded.

Lily folded the paper up and placed it on the table for later. "I don't expect praise, but they could've gone into more detail. Really! This is incompetency at the highest level."

Dev began to laugh as he turned to pour another cup of coffee. "You are beginning to sound like Gretchen. It isn't incompetency. Honey, it's called a gag order. Reporters don't need to make all the details public while we still have more investigating to do on our end."

"But don't you think that the public has a right to know?"

Dev took a deep breath from his coffee mug and then took a drink. "No. Can you imagine how upset people would be if they knew everything we did? Just look at our neighborhood. Neighbors bothered Mrs. Parrot when they saw the FBI at our house months ago. They were upset when the police canvased our block asking questions. People just want us to do our jobs and keep them safe."

Lily pursed her lips. *Lord, we need to have a little talk about people. Well, it might be a lengthy discussion. How can you stand us?* "Fine." She looked over to the dying flowers on the counter. The huge tropical bouquet, sent by some-one Dev described delicately as a retired elderly man he knew who lived in the Caribbean, had run its course. *At least I enjoyed them for a few days after they were allowed out of garage imprisonment.*

"Honey, who exactly is the man who sent those flow-ers? Oh, and we need to throw them out."

In hopes of distracting his wife, Dev immediately reached for the vase and moved it toward the trash basket. "I'll do it later. Um, I have met him occasionally when I'm down there."

There is more to it! I knew it. The man was probably a drug dealer in his previous life. Dev is doing his agent thing again.

"Good morning everyone," JT announced as he entered the kitchen. He kissed Andrew on the head. "Hello little man. Where's the coffee?"

Dev handed him a full cup. "Black like you like it. I see your bag in there. Are you leaving us?"

"Yep." He turned to Lily. "I've already stripped the sheets off the bed and left the towels on the counter by the sink. Thanks for letting me crash."

"As I recall, I didn't have much choice," Lily said without emotion.

"And I love you too, Sweet Pea." JT winked at Dev. "What did you do to put her in a mood so early in the morning?"

Leaning against the counter, Dev sighed. "I think she's upset because I'm breathing."

JT nodded. "I get it. There are those days."

Lily stood up slowly, holding her stomach with one hand, while her other helped to lift her away from the table. "You two really are getting on my nerves, more than usual."

Dev and JT mocked her by repeating her insult.

She turned around. "You're making me miss Ari. I'm going to take a shower. Watch your son. JT, don't leave until I get back down here." She walked slowly away.

JT replaced her at the table. "Wow, what did you do?"

"Kept secrets. The newspaper article about the entire mess has been cleaned. Lily doesn't appreciate it."

JT rolled a grape in Andrew's direction, and the little boy laughed. "This country has more secrets than God."

Dev raised his mug in a mock toast. "All for the better good, son."

"Yes, that's what we're told. I got a call last night. I'm shipping out from Norfolk tonight. A car will be here in a couple of hours to drive me down."

Dev nodded. "Anything dangerous?"

"I can't tell you. It's a secret." JT laughed nervously.

"I know you. It sounds like it's more dangerous than you may like." Dev took a towel to Andrew's face while the toddler attempted to escape. "I'll whip you up some eggs, bacon, and toast." As soon as he finished the cleaning, Andrew ran into the living room. He began to play with the small elephant stuffed animal. "Look at that. He either plays with blocks that cost nothing or Ari's designer animals that cost in the hundreds."

"It's good to have simple and expensive tastes. Hey, is Lily going to be okay? She doesn't seem as healthy as she was when she was pregnant with the little man."

Dev began to move from the refrigerator to the stove. "I'm hoping she'll be okay. I'm praying she will be. I won't lie to you. She is having some health issues, and her constant need for excitement doesn't help."

JT thumped his fingers on the newspaper. "I get it. We all need that, don't we?"

Dev smiled. "When did you get so smart? Actually, I don't need it like I used to. Maybe I never did need that adrenaline rush? I enjoy my time being bored, being normal."

"Oh man," JT yelled. "You've gone domestic on us. Lily didn't do that to you. She likes the rush; she thrives in the rush, well except when she's pregnant and not feeling well."

"Exactly," Dev said as he turned with a plate in his hand. "It isn't good for her. I like being domestic, being here in my house with my family. I guess it's something I needed, but I didn't know it."

JT watched as his friend piled scrambled eggs and bacon onto the plate. "I get it. If I had the little guy, and if I had Lily, I'd want to be settled too. Sometimes, I do want that."

Dev placed the food in front of the SEAL and sat down to finish drinking his coffee. "You could've had that."

JT nodded as he placed a fork full of eggs into his mouth. He chewed and took a drink of coffee before he looked at his friend. "I know. I think about that almost every day."

"That's a good thing, JT...the thinking part. By the way, as your friend I need to inform you that my wife, the great investigator Lily Pierce, has come to learn that Ace and you are still married."

The fork dropped onto the table. "What? How?"

"She suspected there was something up, but then she overheard Dan and me."

JT leaned back on the chair. "You two are useless. How did you ever survive Afghanistan or Syria? He is the biggest gossip ever, and you, well, I expected better from you."

Dev chuckled at the desperate SEAL. "Lily isn't stupid. She already suspected that the two of you used to be together. She just didn't know how together you used to be."

"Does she know anything else?"

Two hands came upon his shoulders. Lily's head leaned over into JT's face. She was smiling. "What else don't I know?"

"Ah crap." JT was only happy he could add to her better disposition this early in the morning.

It was the longest two hours of JT's life before the black car pulled up into the driveway. He hugged Dev, and he gave Andrew a pat on the head. It was Lily who stood with outstretched arms to say goodbye. He was afraid.

JT stepped into her arms and lowered his head and body to return her embrace. "Take care of yourself and that baby, Sweet Pea."

"I will find out," Lily whispered.

"Lily, please don't. It only hurts. Goodbye." JT pulled up and looked into her face. "Please." He turned and walked slowly down the drive, only turning to offer a salute before he entered the car.

"Dev, is he going to be okay?" Lily's concern could be heard in her tone.

"Truthfully, I never know. Just pray for him." Dev placed his arm around her waist and steered her into the house for another day of mundane life. *Thank God.*

Mundane became boring for Lily as the holidays approached. But the baby would be here soon, and she'd be the mother of a walking little boy who put his head into every cabinet, and a newborn. *Did I really sign on for this?* She had a couple of early holiday parties to coordinate out at the vineyard, and then she would be unemployed at least until next spring. She could do some phone and online work, but venturing out of the house would be unheard of, again.

"Lily, honey, where are you?"

"In the garage." Mrs. Parrot would be welcome company in Lily's days of incarceration. She wasn't really in jail, but between the cold temperatures and the occasional snow burst today, she had no business taking the risk to step one foot out of her home.

"I used my key when I didn't hear you." Mrs. Parrot came upon a very pregnant woman who was covered in a heavy blanket and wearing oversized snow boots. "Dear, what on earth are you doing out here? What's in all of those boxes?"

Lily's eyes brightened when she saw the plate in her neighbor's hands. *I was just praying for cookies, or cake. I'm not picky.* "These are the boxes from that reporter Mr. Livingood. I know there's more in them."

Yvonne Parrot shook her head. "Lily, they're all in jail. Let it go."

"I know I should, but I have these nagging questions." Lily could smell sugar. "What did you bring?"

"Pecan snowball cookies. You need to limit yourself."

"I know. I know." Lily shuffled through another file. "I just know there's something else, and I think Mr. Livingood knew it, but he didn't have the pieces we do."

Mrs. Parrot didn't understand Lily. But she was with her now in thick and thin. "Well, we better find the missing pieces then." She began to place the plate on a nearby shelf when Lily stopped her.

"How about some hot tea and cookies first?" Lily's expression was that of a hopeful child.

"Sure. Let's get you warmed up too." Mrs. Parrot extended one arm out and welcomed Lily into her hold.

After an hour of nonsensical conversation, Lily and Mrs. Parrot were back in the garage searching for something.

"He has an entire file on Laurel in here. He did suspect her. I haven't seen this before," Lily commented.

Lily's neighbor stopped her own search to view the discovery. "That's the stack of files I found under his newspaper collection."

Lily scanned paper after paper until she found something of interest. "Here. Here is something. Laurel did date that flower delivery guy. Mr. Livingood has notes from the owner of the shop. Laurel used to come in to see him while he was working, and if he was out on deliveries, she tracked him down."

"What are you thinking?"

Lily brought the file over to Dev's worktable. "I'm not sure. Wait, here's an arrest report." Lily's finger trailed over the copy, until she hit the paper. "She was arrested for drug dealing, and her dad got her off. She was a minor. She was Margot's mule with that delivery boy."

"Does this matter in any way?"

Lily was stunned by her question. "No," she muttered. "Laurel is still in jail, and so is her father, and Margot. But, I have a feeling Laurel killed that guy because he cheated her, or Margot killed him because he was cheating with Laurel. We'll never know, will we?"

"No, and does it really matter, Lily?"

Why does it matter so much to me? Dev is right. Some things just need to be left alone. "Not to me anymore," Lily answered confidently. "We have so much to be thankful for, and I don't need to be worrying about all of this." Her hand swept over the boxes. *But it still makes me wonder if a reporter who handed over boxes of files to me really did have a heart attack or did someone help him into everlasting peace?*

"But it does make for a great mystery," Mrs. Parrot acknowledged. "Maybe you could write about it one day?"

It wasn't a light that went on over Lily's head. It was more like a nightlight. "Yes, someday. I could do that."

Two days later, Lily looked out the window to her back yard. "You know, I still don't have a magnolia anywhere in this yard."

Dev hung his head. "Really? You still want the blasted tree, bush, whatever?"

"Yes. It will be perfect for this yard, and there is nothing like the fragrance of a magnolia. It is summer to me."

"Right now, it's Thanksgiving. We need to get going if we're going to be on time at the vineyard. Dad will be here in just a few minutes."

Lily continued to focus on the back yard. "I think I want it right there." She pointed toward the back window of the guest suite. She'd given up on the sweet aroma in the air while she sat in the front porch swing. *What about a tulip tree out front? Maybe a crepe myrtle would look nice there?*

Dev pulled out the sweet potato casserole from the oven. The dish was their only contribution to the family dinner. That, and a cooler of beer. He figured the aunts were letting them off the hook this year because of Lily's pregnancy. "I'm going to dig the hole this time, and I'll have the area scanned before we really do find Jimmy Hoffa."

Lily turned sharply. "We didn't last time, smarty."

"Well, with your luck then, Amelia Earhart will magically appear." Dev continued to pack the casserole and a few items for Andrew just in case he suddenly became a picky eater. Luckily, Andrew ate just about everything, including calamari. They had told him they were onion rings. *How many times can you lie to your child before you go to eternal damnation?*

"Amelia was lost over the Pacific. That would be impossible."

Dev stopped in his tracks to face his wife. "Honey, again, with your luck, all the history books were wrong, and we'll find her. Besides, you never know what will be dug up when you're involved. Pun intended."

Lily smiled. "I thought I was the comic, and you were the straight man. When did that change?"

Dev came over and embraced her, kissing her on her head. "Things are always changing when I'm around you. You keep me unhinged in so many ways."

Lily didn't answer. She snuggled up against his chest. *It's good to keep you on your toes, Agent Pierce.*

"But I guess that's what I get when I live in Lily's world," Dev whispered.

Lily smiled and shut her eyes. *Note to self, get a plaque and hang it over the door. Lily's World. I like the sound of that.*

Epilogue

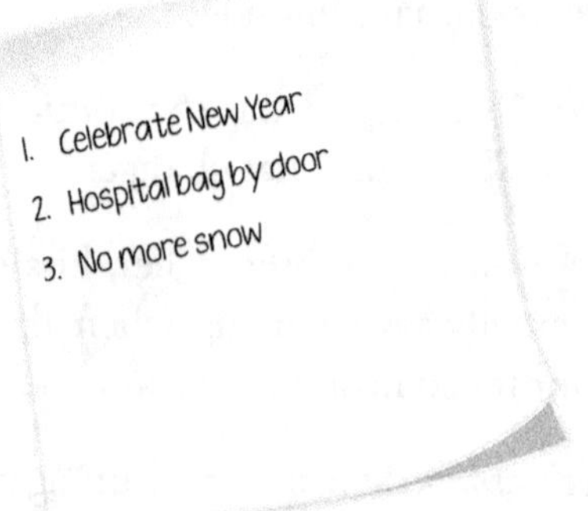

"The doctor said everything is great, Beth. We should be good with you coming here around the tenth of January." Lily rocked Andrew to sleep while she spoke to her sister on the phone. "What are you guys doing tonight for New Year's Eve?"

"The kids are going out, but we're staying in. Our party will consist of popcorn, hot chocolate, and a sappy movie. Hubby and I will be asleep by ten."

"I was thinking about partying like there's no tomorrow," Lily joked. "We have a kegger."

Elizabeth laughed. "Sure you do, in your dreams."

Lily sighed. "I would kill for a sip of beer, or even better a full glass of wine. Actually, liquor of any kind at this point. Oh, and foods that I haven't been able to eat. But you should see me. I'm bigger than I was with Andrew.

I didn't think that was possible, but yet here I am. I'm going to apply for statehood after the first of the year."

"Stop. I'm sure it isn't that bad."

"It is. The other day Dev suggested I sit in the back seat because there was more room back there."

"Your husband would never say that," Elizabeth answered.

"He did, and I wasn't even offended because it was easier to get out of the backseat. I just sort of slid out, but that was the last time I've been in the real world. I'm forbidden from driving in the snow and ice. Besides, I can't fit behind the wheel, and frankly, when I walk I might bounce if I fall."

"You need to hang in there. Happy New Year! I'll see you in just ten days."

"Thanks, sis. I'll talk to you in a couple of days. Tell the family hello from us." Lily and Elizabeth performed their own well-honed smooching noise and ended the call.

Lily looked up from the couch as the front door opened. The cold wind blew onto her feet. She threw her throw down to cover them. Two snowmen entered the foyer, one tiny and one remotely reminding her of her husband.

"It's snowing again," Dev announced as he stopped Andrew before he entered the living room. "Let's get your boots, mittens, and coat off, little man. You can warm up with mommy in just a second."

Andrew shook as Dev unzipped his jacket. "Cold, Mama."

"I need another log on the fire too," Lily called out. This New Year's Eve was certainly different than any she'd experienced before. Usually, she would go to church, and then...who was she kidding, except for not being able to go out for Mass, this was exactly the same night she'd had for many years. Except, she was sipping decaffeinated tea across from a roaring fire. And her handsome husband and very cute little boy were making pizza tonight in celebration of the New Year.

As soon as boots, mittens, and coat were removed, Andrew ran toward his mother and climbed onto her for warmth. "Mommy. Snow."

"Did you make a snowman?"

Andrew nodded then rested his head on Lily's chest. He patted her belly lovingly. He was waiting for his baby sister. He seemed delighted, but Lily knew once a girl was following him around that joy would diminish. Over the years, he would probably come to loathe her. *What have we done to you, little man?*

Dev continued to remove his snowy wardrobe. He finally walked through, grabbing a large piece of wood and adding it to the fire. He blew on his hands.

"There won't be much partying tonight. We already have eight inches, but the way it's coming down we could have a foot or more by morning. Dan canceled church for tonight, and for tomorrow."

Lily caressed her son's head. It would be good to have a quiet night. Soon, she'd be offering all her attention to the new baby, and Andrew might feel neglected. Who was she kidding? Of course he would feel as though his mother had forgotten him. *Please, little man, remember today.* She looked down and realized he was asleep. His hand continued to pat her.

"They're talking about fourteen inches," Lily told her husband. "What about the car, just in case?"

Dev blew on his hands. He rubbed his nose to warm it. "I'm going out every hour to shovel. The drive is clear now, and I have the SUV parked on the street so if we have to go, we'll be able to get out. Your bag is over there, along with the bag you packed for Andrew and me, just in case. The infant car seat is already in cargo."

"Elizabeth will be here on the tenth. During the last doctor's appointment, he said the baby could be early, or she'll come on the due date, the thirteenth. How's that for vague?"

"We could get a second opinion, but what's the point in that?" Dev backed up to the fire to warm himself. "The baby will come when she comes."

Lily nodded. That was inevitable. One way, a baby always came. She'd begged with Andrew to just let him stay inside her, but he came out anyway. That was life. It really was life. "Did I tell you Abby is providing flowers tonight for a large party that Gretchen planned? Auntie G invited Abby and Jeremy to stay for the party. The detective will be there too."

Dev's brows rose. "Really? They are getting tight. I like the man. I don't know how he tolerates her on a daily basis, but everyone has their own tastes. Oh, hey is that the party the Fullertons will be at too? It's at some swanky gallery, and the donations are for a veterans' group?"

"That's the one. Abby is sending photos in a few hours. They may Facetime us. That might be fun." Lily sighed. "Fun for them."

Dev looked into her empty tea cup. "Do you want a refill? Or what about some hot chocolate?"

"There's so many reasons why I love you, and the fact that you're a hot cocoa pusher is one of them. Yes, please."

Dev leaned over and kissed her, sweeping his hand over his son's head. "He's so angelic like this, and so are you."

"Yes, I'm the guardian angel of aircraft carriers and semis."

Dev grimaced. "Stop. Soon, you'll be just an angel." He headed into the kitchen. "Hey, I think I'm going to start the pizza early. That kiddo is going to be hungry when he wakes up."

"I can eat at any time. In fact, could you bring me a piece of toast with strawberry preserves on it, please?"

"Yes, my love."

Lily smiled. *Ooh, his love. I love that.*

After her cup of hot wonderfulness, Lily napped along with her son. Dev covered them with another afghan and settled back in his chair to read a book Lily had gifted him at Christmas. In an hour, Andrew stirred. He woke up, lifting his head and smiling at his father. Dev scooped him up in his arms, and they headed into the kitchen to begin dinner. Lily stumbled out after she heard the sizzling of Italian sausage.

"I'm actually loving this night," Lily announced as she finished her first piece of pizza. She winced.

"What? Normal cramping or--" Dev searched her eyes for the pain level.

"Usual, no worries. May I have another piece, chef?"

"Go for it. You might have to guzzle some pink stuff to settle your stomach later." Dev wiped off Andrew's tomato stained mouth before he decorated his sleeves. "He loves this."

"I made your favorite pie yesterday." Lily took another slice of pizza and added an ample amount of parmesan.

"I love you. I thought I smelled pecans. So, that's dessert?"

"Yes, sir." Lily winced again. "Wow, that was a cramp."

"You're sure it's just your usual cramping?"

Lily rolled her eyes. The pizza was so good she didn't want anything, not even a baby kicking or cramping to destroy the feeling in her mouth right now. "Yes. Stop worrying."

But Dev began to worry. Yes, Lily was having her second baby, but they weren't professionals at this. Possibly, they never would be. There was no protocol, or rule book for having a baby. *If there is, I'm picking one up if we have another. But, we're already blessed.*

It was almost eight when Dev joined Lily on the couch. Andrew was sound asleep, full of pizza and tired from playing in the snow. Lily's phone rang. It was the Kansas City crew.

"Happy New Year!" Dev and Lily waved back at the Fullertons, the newlyweds, Gretchen, and the man in her life. Gretchen turned the camera toward the ballroom.

"Here's Abby's gorgeous decorations." Lily clapped as she saw tall glass vases with silver and gold sticks bursting out of flower arrangements of assorted orchids and lilies.

"I did good, boss," Abby burst out. Lily nodded.

"Hey Dev," Jeremy yelled as he waved. He grabbed Abby and twirled her out onto the dance floor.

"Jeremy has single-handedly drained a bottle already. Can you tell?" Tom asked.

"Of course not," Dev answered. "Happy New Year."

Tom and his wife replied with their salutations and headed to the dance floor, leaving Gretchen and the detective filling the screen. "Look, dearie. Don't you love this?" Gretchen asked. The screen was filled with a huge amethyst ring and bracelet on Gretchen's left arm. "It matches my dress perfectly. Daniel gave it to me for Christmas."

"At least it isn't a print," Dev whispered into Lily's ear.

Lily grabbed her belly. "Yah. It's great. How are you, detective?"

"Great. It's a wonderful night. Happy New Year to you both."

"You too. You both look festive," Lily answered.

Gretchen whispered to her companion, and he waved goodbye. "Lily, that's all you have to say when I show you my jewelry from Daniel? It matches perfectly?"

Dev's right arm supported Lily's shoulders. "You okay?"

"No." *It's just indigestion from the tomato sauce. Or maybe it's from the mushrooms, or the peppers, or the sausage? What was I thinking about eating all of that stuff?*

Gretchen's pout could be seen from space. "What do you mean, no? It does match perfectly! You don't need to make that face, Lily."

"Yes, I do," Lily grunted slowly. "I need to go. I think I need to go."

Dev nodded and ran off to prepare.

"I can hold on while you go to the bathroom." Gretchen's voice irritated the laboring Lily.

"Gretchen, listen to me. I think I'm in labor. I have to go to the hospital now! Happy New Year, goodbye."

But before she pressed the button, Lily saw Gretchen begin to cry. She stopped and looked at her friend.

"Lily, be safe, and go get our little girl. I love you."

Lily's tears began to fall. "I love you too, you nut. Go party for me. I'll have Dev call you later."

"Have him call me first, well, maybe second after his dad. But he has to call me next. I've been an integral cog in this production."

And she's back. "He'll call you. Gotta go. Bye." *And I'm ignoring your part in any of this. Except for the pain. Gretchen can have full credit for the pain in my--*

"Ow." Another cramp hit her solidly. *These are early contractions. Oh no.*

Dev ran downstairs with a bundled, still sleeping Andrew. He laid him down beside Lily. "I'm loading the car, getting it warmed up, and then I'm back in for you and him." He stopped to touch her shoulder as he watched her breathe through another cramp or contraction. "You have this?"

"Yes. My water hasn't broken yet, so put something down in the car just in case. That is so gross when it gets all over."

The snow had covered the driveway again. Dev started the car, drove it up the drive, and brought it closer to the walkway. In the back, he lined the seat with plastic and with two towels. He made sure he had two blankets placed in between Andrew's car seat and where Lily would sit. He'd already filled the cargo area with water, a bag of snacks, a shovel, and kitty litter.

"I'll call the hospital and Dad as we're driving. Let me douse the fire and turn off a few lights, and we are ready to roll." Lily watched as he moved quickly and deliberately around the house. Her beautiful fire was nothing but a little smoke now, but there was more cramping beginning.

Lily lifted her phone. "I already called the doctor's emergency number, and he's actually at the hospital so he'll meet us in the emergency room. Now his nurse is saying the baby will be early. You think?" She began to rise up slowly. She grabbed her lower back. "Dev, I need help."

"Stop. I'll be right there." Dev cradled Andrew in one arm and reached his other arm around his wife. "Let's just put the afghan around you." He looked down at her slippers. "I have another plan." He laid his son back onto the couch. "Come on." He walked Lily over to the open front door. "I'm going to carry you."

Lily's eyes widened. "No, you can't do that. I mean, you really can't do that. You'll hurt your back, you'll hurt everything."

Dev pressed a finger against her lips. In one swift movement, he picked his wife up in his arms and stomped through the snow slowly to reach the car. Her feet never touched the ground. Lily watched as her husband ran into the house for Andrew.

"Lord, this isn't how we planned this. Is she really coming this early?" Lily felt a warm sensation flowing down her legs. "Ah, crap."

Dev belted Andrew in. The baby opened his eyes, looked at both of his parents and smiled. His eyes shut again. *Such a sweet little man. You have no idea how your world is going to change. I'm so sorry.*

"Dev, my water just broke." She pointed down at the floor of the car. "I am so sorry."

But Dev smiled. The man smiled. "We're having a baby. It's all good. Are you ready? I don't think I forgot anything." He snapped his fingers. He reached into the front seat and pulled a pillow back for her. "For your back."

"Always prepared. Thank you, honey." Instead of moving it to her back, Lily braced the pillow against her belly. Dev pulled out the driveway as the next contraction came. She screamed out, waking her son and receiving a look in the rearview mirror from her husband. She breathed in and out.

Lily looked out the window as a form of distraction, but it wasn't the best idea. The roads were treacherous, full of snow and a layer of freezing ice forming on top. It was like a winter wonderland on steroids. Her only consolation was that her husband had driving skills that could put any action movie stunt driver to shame. She grabbed onto Andrew's hand to settle him. As she leaned back her head, she shut her eyes. *Baby girl, you were supposed to be born almost two weeks from now, not now! Elizabeth is right. You're going to be trouble.*

The only time Devlin Pierce's car slid was the turn right before the hospital. At the same time, Lily was having another pain. He corrected the car smoothly and arrived at the emergency drive. It was completely clear under the covering. Lily's doctor came out to the car and transported her into a wheelchair.

Dev was directed to the parking area. With Andrew in one arm, and the two bags in the other, he wandered into the hospital to find his wife. A very kind nurse took mercy on him and took him to her. "We're just keeping her down here to make sure she's really in labor."

"Her water broke in the car."

"Oh, well that's another story. We're having a baby sometime now, aren't we?"

Dev nodded, but he was laughing on the inside. *Lily would tell you there's no we in this. She's having the baby!* The nurse took him into a small room where Lily was being hooked up to every machine possible. Dev sat down in the corner and dropped the bags. He brought out his phone.

"Danny, we're at the hospital. The baby is coming early. Yah, we're in the emergency area for now. A nice nurse took pity on us because of the snow and didn't kick us out yet, but Andrew can't be here. Could you do your thing and pick up Dad? I need him to take the little guy. You two can have the car seat in my vehicle to get him home or back to Dad's. I don't care at this point, but the roads are bad. Dad can't make it down here."

"We'll be there as soon as we can, Dev. No worries. I know that route to the hospital like the back of my hand. I'll text when we get there."

The next call was to his dad. "Danny is on the way over to you. We're at the hospital."

"He's calling me now. We'll see you, son. Tell Lily to hang in there. You too."

Lily continued to be checked by nurses as they attached line after line to the monitors. Andrew rubbed his eyes and asked for her, but Dev decided it was a good time to take a walk.

Nearly an hour later a nurse came down the hallway to tell him that his father had arrived. Andrew took one look, climbed out of Dev's arms, and ran toward his grandfather and Dan.

"You look like hell already," Dan said as he looked his friend over. "How is she doing?"

"Everything is a go. It'll be a few hours though. Thank you so much for driving him here." He hugged his friend and patted his father on the arm. "And you are a rockstar, Dad."

"I'll keep my grandson alive, but I'm not promising we won't eat pancakes every morning." Andrew played with Jack's coat collar and the toggle that hung from it.

"Deal," Dev answered quickly before his father could change his mind. "I'll meet you in the lobby. I'll go get his bag and then we can transfer the car seat."

Once they were reunited, they headed out into the cold night. Small ice particles were mixing with large snowflakes. Dan's car was illegally parked.

Dev ran to his car and removed Andrew's seat. "Hey, they'll tow you."

Dan opened the back door for Dev to secure the item. Dan surely didn't know how to do it. "Nope, priest."

Dev attached the car seat to the car, shoving it back and forth to make sure it was secure . "It's good. Dad, give him to me please." Dev placed Andrew into the car and secured him. "I love you, Andrew." His son was already wiping his eyes and yawning. He kissed him and turned to hug his father. "Without you, Dad, I'm not sure Lily and I could do all of this."

"You know you could. You can do anything." It was what Bernie and he always told both sons.

"We need to get going," Dan suggested. "It's getting bad. We're going to your house. If you need us, just call. We both have extra clothes so your Dad and I will be fine. You take care of Lily. Love you, brother." Dan hugged Dev quickly and got into the car.

Dev waved goodbye to his son and closed the car door. "Dad, I love you. Thanks again. There's homemade pizza in the fridge." He walked his Dad around to the passenger side and hugged him one more time. Then he turned and raced back into the hospital.

Within the hour, Lily was taken to the baby and mothers area. The baby was coming within hours. Dev held her hand. He had felt pain before, but this was special. He remembered it from Andrew's birth. Lily had the grip of a gorilla. She would pray through a contraction.

"Hail Mary, Mother of God, Oh Crap!"

"I'm not sure that's how it goes," Dev corrected.

"It does tonight. Don't be smiling either. This is not funny, mister."

"I understand." His smile vanished instantly. She wanted him to talk to her, to recite anything. He did. She wanted him to be quiet, and so he was. He wiped her forehead and rubbed her back. Nothing was enough. Lily had to do this all on her own. And so she did.

Dev heard a few popping noises outside. The room's clock was reading midnight. "Happy New Year."

"Well, happy freaking New Year to you too," Lily shouted. "She's coming."

The doctor yelled for one final push and a new Pierce entered the world on January first. Gretchen had her girl. Andrew had a little sister, Emilia Helen Bernadette. It was a large name for such a little girl, but somehow Dev and Lily thought she'd fill it out nicely.

Before noon, Lily was completely coherent, holding her baby, and waiting for lunch. The nurses promised her mashed potatoes and gravy, fried chicken, and cherry pie. They had promised her heaven.

"Where is Andrew?"

Dev laughed out loud that she was finally asking about her son. He looked at his very tired wife. Her question was totally understandable. She had been very busy at the time. "We had a hand off last night. Dan drove Dad, and they have Andrew at our house. I just called them, and they're all doing fine. Andrew even talked on the phone. I'm not sure what he said, but I think he was tattling on Dan about how many pancakes he ate this morning."

"I don't remember anything, except were you reciting the West Point Code of Honor and the Constitution?"

Dev channel surfed to find the Rose Bowl football game on the television. "Yes, I did. I also recited the Gettysburg Address."

"Did you call everyone?"

Dev looked toward her. "I called Dad and Dan last night. I called your sister and brother this morning. I texted the guys, and the Kansas City group. I took a photo of you sleeping with the baby, and Gretchen wrote that you looked awful, but then she called me. She was in tears saying you are amazing and that the baby is absolutely beautiful. She's already planning our daughter's wedding."

Of course she is! Lily looked down on the baby in her arms. *I'll never tell your daddy, but I have plans of my own. I'm thinking peonies?* "Dev, I heard an alarm earlier. Was there a problem in the hospital?"

Dev found the game and settled back in the chair. "There was a security breach on this floor. A hooded figure tried to grab a baby."

"Really?" Lily's face lit up like a Christmas tree. Dev did a double take as he watched color flush her cheeks. As soon as the words left his mouth he knew he was in trouble. Her eyes were sparkling.

"No, Lily."

"Oh, come on, Dev," Lily pleaded.

"No, honey."

The baby cried out. "See, she agrees with me. Let's find out more about it."

Dev sighed. In Lily's mind it was now two to one. He had never lived with two females. His mom had been the only woman in a household of men. Lily was a handful all on her own. Now there was double the trouble. He stood over the two beautiful girls in his life. When he reached down to touch Lily's hand, his daughter's hand grabbed his finger. He knew right there and then he was hooked.

"Fine. I'll check into it after lunch and bring you back the intel. Are you happy now?"

"Yes, perfectly." Everything was perfect in her life. *Now, if they have ice cream on that piece of pie, I'll be in heaven.* She looked up as Dev leaned down to kiss her and then their daughter's head. Their daughter made a noise similar to one of Lily's snorts when she laughed too much.

"And now I have two of you," Dev murmured.

Lily closed her eyes to pray. *Thanks, Lord. Everything is perfect in my world with or without the ice cream. But life is always better with ice cream.*

A New Lily List Mystery
is Coming in 2022

<u>A Lily A Day</u>

Hello everyone! Lily here. I am living a life I never thought I'd have. I have a beautiful home, a handsome husband, wonderful friends and family, an energetic son, and a happy daughter. What more do I need?

Houseguests? I know. You're thinking it's probably Ari or JT sleeping in our guest room after some dangerous mission. The super agent is in Paris and the SEAL is somewhere doing something. He can't tell us, and I really don't want to know this time. I already have my hands full with a toddler and a baby. And the houseguests.

Dev's past seems to be creeping into our present. You know I'm up for the mystery and the intrigue, but I'm having doubts on how you entertain...my houseguests! You'll have to wait until 2022 to discover who I'm up against, and what puzzle we are piecing together this time.

Let's just hope Gretchen doesn't show up for an impromptu visit. I'm running out of bedrooms, but there's no end to the trouble I can get into. I'll need a bigger package of post-its.

C.L. BAUER

C.L. Bauer grew up and lives in Kansas City, Missouri. Her first novel The Poppy Drop, A Lily List Mystery was well received by the top 100 Books of Independent Publishers when it launched in 2018.

The Lily List Mystery Series features the highly organized, post-it note, and list making florist Lily Schmidt. Readers have enjoyed the adventures of the mystery loving woman and the wedding stories that are highlighted in these novels. Ms. Bauer draws on true events from her family's wedding and event flower business. With over one hundred years of serving families on their special days, Clara's Flowers has received numerous awards in the wedding world, including "best of" and "legacy winner" for service and design.

C.L. Bauer's first love of writing provided an early career in journalism. During high school, she began as a sports reporter, became an editor in college, and continued professionally in every writing medium including advertising and creative direction.

The author enjoys her family, travel, a good book on a rainy day, bulk post-it notes, and meeting her readers. She can always be swayed to feast on Mexican food, watch a hockey game, and drink the occasional fruity libation. If you've read her novels, you already know she loves Kansas City during the holidays.

You can reach C.L. Bauer on all forms of social media including her author pages on Facebook, Instagram, Twitter, Amazon, and Goodreads. Please review this and any of C.L. Bauer's published works. They are widely available for purchase in print and e-book forms. She's available for book club discussions virtually or in-person.

As always, happy reading!

Sign up at www.clbauer.com for this author's newsletter, promotions, pre-order information, free chapters, and upcoming publications. Contact C.L. Bauer directly at clbauerkc@gmail.com.

Coming in 2022…A Lily List Mystery Exclusive! Can't get enough of your favorite characters? The Exclusive novels feature more adventures with Lily's friends. Mysteries, murders, and more romance are coming your way!